HUNTED

Also by G X Todd

Defender

HUNTED

GX TODD

HEADLINE

LETTER #271

January 12th, Thursday

Dear Stranger,

Do I even call you that now? Stranger? We've come too far for that, I think. We know each other, a little bit, if only because we share the same world. We survive it by hiding — from ourselves, from each other, but I must tell you there is coming a time when hiding will no longer work. We have been dragged down into the mud, we have crawled through its muck until we are unrecognisable, and now there is nothing left to do but climb free and wash ourselves clean.

You're wondering if I hear a voice, aren't you? I do. My voice's name is Jonah, and he wishes we could all just get along. It makes me laugh, the way he says it, as if 'getting along' is as easy as inviting someone over for milk and cookies. But there are people out there who want us gone — want me and people like me gone. They want you to believe that voices are bad and that those who hear them cannot be trusted. I'm here to tell you that it's not so simple. But then, nothing ever really is.

Have you heard the stories yet? Of a man who knows all our hiding places? He comes in the night, if you believe the tales. He finds you in your sleep and, with a whisper, steals you away. He is a ghoul and a ghost and he's called the Flitting Man by

1

some. He's the fear that rides these lands. He is the voice that non-voice-hearers believe will wipe them from the earth. I think the Flitting Man is all of us, hiding in our little holes, alone and too scared to come out.

Some of us have already begun to climb clear of the mud. A teenage girl whose name I don't yet know but who I see with lemons in her hands and a rifle over her shoulder. A man of lost wisdom, a pilgrim who carries us all on his back yet is too fearful to ask where he must head. And my brother. Oh, Al, I miss your face. I miss singing to you and seeing your eyes light up as they lift to see the colour spill from my lips.

No, I will call you stranger no more, dear reader. I will call you friend, whether you hear a voice or not. Because you can never have too many friends in a world where strangers are so plentiful.

Always yours,
Ruby

PART ONE
Hide and Go Seek

CHAPTER 1

Pitchfork

Sunny and Beck found the kid cowering in row M of the cavernous, derelict movie theatre. They had one flashlight between them – with the last two replacement D-size batteries rolling around in the bottom of Sunny's knapsack – and Sunny was in charge of it. She swept the bright wash of light up and down rows W to N, and there he was, on his knees, butt sticking out from under the seats and arms folded over his head as if preparing for a bomb blast.

He whimpered when the flashlight found him. 'I ain't tellin' them . . . no . . . *no* . . . I ain't sayin' *nothin'*.'

Sunny and Beck exchanged glances and she minutely shook her head. No need to get any closer, that small shake said, they could tell the others they hadn't found squat, that this place had been a clean sweep. But her man was already turning away, side-shuffling along the row, his ridiculous gosh-darned pitchfork held above his head as if he were some biblical figure wading through the shallows to his disciples.

Sunny heaved a sigh and followed.

'Hey, buddy,' Beck said, as if talking to a wild dog. 'What you doing there, huh? You got something with you? You hearing something?'

The young man immediately stopped muttering to himself

and stilled, almost disappearing into the puddle of darkness under the seats.

'We can help you. Take it easy, eh, and let us help you.'

Sunny touched Beck's shoulder, a sour nervousness lining her stomach. 'Just forget him, Beck. He's not worth—'

The huddled figure uncoiled like a snake, and Sunny gasped and stepped back, the beam of her flashlight swinging wildly, her view obscured by a flittering of shadows.

'Get out the way!' she cried, and Beck ducked. Over his head, in the flashlight's glare, the young guy's eyes locked on to hers and something cold and cunning stared back at her. Her breath froze in her lungs, and then, like the murky flutter of a dancing moth, the sly look was gone and he was just a snivelling wimp of a kid again.

He was easily a decade younger than Sunny's thirty-three years but the harsh white beam aged him, dug holes for his eye sockets and carved hunger lines around his mouth. His patchy beard did nothing to soften his features.

'Did you see that?' she hissed at Beck. 'Did you *see*? This isn't right. We shouldn't be in here with—'

But Beck didn't let her finish. His voice hardened. 'No more messing around.'

The young man's head sunk down, his scrawny neck bowing under the weight. 'I hear somethin',' he whispered. 'Oh, I hear somethin', yes I do. But you don't want what I got. Nu-huh, no way.'

She sensed a brief hesitation in Beck, but he masked it, like he always did. Fear didn't exist unless you acknowledged it, right? Mind over matter, and all that jazz. If you didn't mind, then it didn't matter.

'I hear a voice, too,' Beck told the kid. 'We don't have to hide. Not any more. It's better if we stick together. Come on out and let us help you.'

The kid raised a bony hand and pointed his finger at his own head, making a soft *pew* with his mouth, cheeks puffing out, as he fired the finger-gun into his temple.

Sunny backed up another step, expecting the finger-gun to turn on her.

And do what? *Shoot* you? Get a grip, woman.

She watched his eyes, but the cunning glint she'd glimpsed didn't resurface. He seemed lost and alone. Pathetic, even. But there was something lurking, a ragged coral reef that the dark ocean concealed, right up until it ripped a hole in your hull.

'You don't want to speak to us? That's cool,' Beck said. 'But we'll have to take you to someone who'll talk some sense into you. You understand that, right, buddy? You need to play the game. We all do. Come on now. Walk on ahead of us.' Beck poked his pitchfork at the kid to get him moving.

Obediently, the guy led them back into the main aisle, trudging, heavy-footed, as if his legs didn't belong to him. She watched for a shifty glance or a sign the kid's meekness was a front, but he gave nothing away.

Her attention drifted, eyes drawn to her surroundings as they exited the auditorium and entered the burgundy velveteen foyer. This part of the building was as ruined as the main theatre – the rot and damp had brought on a sneezing fit when she'd first stepped inside – but she could picture how it had been: the brass fittings shining in the soft up-lights, the antique till ringing up purchases of warm roasted nuts and cold, crisp champagne. She'd never dreamed of being in a place like this. The only smells Sunny got used to breathing were spilled beer and the BBQ sauce that got slathered across every slab of meat that came out of the Wet Whistle's kitchen, from the bar's trademark slow-cooked ribs to their BBQ-pulled-pork double-stacked burger. None of that meant she couldn't dream of seeing fancy places, and it sure didn't mean she couldn't enjoy visiting one when the opportunity arose, as crappy and falling apart as it might be.

Still, she was real glad of the streaming sun, baking into the faded red-wine carpeting, filtering in dusty shafts through the theatre's smashed entryway. Being in the dank, dark hole of the auditorium had made her think of snakes and slugs and moist things that crawled along on their bellies. She didn't belong in there. Maybe this kid did, but she didn't.

They stepped outside, the kid first, then Beck, then Sunny. The pavement was a hot welcome to her booted feet. The sun chased away the last lingering chill crouching in her bowels.

At the far end of the block, the rest of their group had gathered outside the pharmacy. Four bellyaching men and the two sour-faced bitches, and a new fella she hadn't laid on eyes on before. She didn't envy him, joining their ranks. Tensions had been running high recently.

A small scuffle had broken out. Sunny sighed. 'Wonder what's hitting the fan now.'

'The more they fight between themselves, the more they'll leave us be.' Beck jabbed at the kid again, prodding him on. 'That doesn't mean you get to quit walking.'

The three of them slowly made their way up the street, taking their sweet time, hoping the disagreement would have blown over by the time they got there. They were passing Patty P's Pawn Emporium, a once-pretty café with outside seating (well, *two* seats, one kicked over by the front stoop and the other across the street outside a gallery called American Graffiti, its four legs poking up like a dead insect's), when Beck propped his pitchfork on his shoulder.

'You look like a demented farmer with that thing,' Sunny complained.

Beck slanted her a grin. 'Leave it be. You know it's good for keeping undesirables at bay.'

Sunny didn't mind the chipped tooth or how Beck's wheat-coloured hair had a life of its own. Or the way he snorted air when he laughed. She thought he was a fine individual.

Dependable. No nonsense. He didn't often talk to others, and they tended to stay out of his way, and she liked that about him. He didn't need validation from anyone, not even her.

A tubby fella flew out of the group and went down, belly-flopping on to the sidewalk. Laughter erupted, rising in volume when he tried to lift himself up, too heavy to get more than a couple of inches of space between his gut and the pavement. Sunny wondered how the guy could be so big when food was so scarce these days, but figured it'd be rude to ask. Maybe he had a thyroid problem.

The two laughing women were pushed aside as Tez the Bull-necked strode out. He planted his boot on the chunky guy's wide butt and stomped him down.

'Stay where you are, fat-ass.'

The 'Bull-necked' part wasn't his real name, but his neck was as wide as his skull, ears not included, and Sunny thought his head looked like a giant toe surgically attached to his shoulders with a face grafted on to it. Also, he was a fucking bully, and she hated bullies.

She and Beck had stopped walking when the chubby guy hit the deck. Neither of them wanted to get involved.

The kid had wandered ahead under his own steam before petering out to a stop. By then, Tez had spotted him.

'Who's this, then? A new man for our merry band?'

Beck shrugged and looked toward Sunny. He didn't like Tez, either, and he didn't speak to people he didn't like.

'We think maybe he hears,' Sunny said. 'He doesn't speak much.' She knew Tez would like that. Sunny was one of only two people in their group who didn't hear a voice of their own. She was here for other reasons, the main one starting with B and ending with K.

'Is that right?' Tez said, smiling real big. Even the way he walked rubbed Sunny up the wrong way, a preening cockerel strut, with his chest puffed out and his arms stuck out from his body as if his biceps were too big to swing. She wished she could lop them off. Lop his ears off, too, so his stupid head didn't look so fat.

As Tez came up to him, the kid kept his eyes downcast. Tez leaned real close and spoke in his ear. 'That right, amigo? You got something you don't want to tell us about?'

The red-headed kid said nothing.

'I *said*, do you got something in here? Hellooo! Earth to Dumbo.' Tez rapped his knuckles off the side of the kid's head and the young man flinched. 'Knock knock, anyone home?' He rapped so hard Sunny heard the hollow beat of knuckles on bone. The kid ducked away from Tez's hand, raising one of his own to cup his skull.

'Man, I think you found us a retard. Way to go.'

The kid's head lifted.

Sunny felt that cold sensation prickle her bowels again. The kid murmured something too low for her to hear and Tez's eyebrows flew up.

'The hell you say?' Tez shot Sunny a look, as if suspecting she'd put the kid up to it. And then his expression shut down, his bull neck reddening at the throat. In a slow, deliberate manner, he gripped a handful of the kid's grubby shirt and drew him close.

'Say that again, dickhole.'

The smallest smile crept on to the kid's lips. Sunny swore it was the meanest little grin she'd seen in a good long while.

Tez drew back his hand, fingers closing in a beefy fist.

'Hey, now.' Sunny stepped forward, thinking on intervening, and Beck stepped with her, no doubt planning on stopping her, but they managed only one stride before the kid turned and snatched the pitchfork out of Beck's hands, easy as plucking a dandelion from a field, and rammed the tines into Tez's gut.

Tez's mouth popped open in a small, surprised O. The kid was skinny, with hardly any muscle on his bones, but he lifted Tez up on to his tiptoes as he ground the fork in, tines sliding

10

deep under his ribs, disappearing right to the root. The kid held him like that for what seemed an eternity, the entire street devoid of noise, and although Sunny couldn't see the kid's face, Tez's was so close to it that Sunny felt sure both men were breathing in each other's exhalations.

Tez's eyes bulged, not only with shock but with the horrifying realisation that this puny, retarded kid had done him in. Clean wiped him out.

The kid stepped back and wrenched the tines free.

Tez did a slow, pained drop to his knees.

Sunny could almost hear the sun sizzling on the sidewalk, hear the shock resound from the others. The tubby fella, on his stomach in the dirt, wriggled back a few feet, but no one else moved. They stared in growing horror as their leader, run through with a farmer's pitchfork, of all things, knelt before this young, red-headed stranger like a supplicant to his god.

'What've you done?' The strength leaked out of Tez's voice, same as the blood leaked out from between the fingers pressed over his stomach. It looked too red and too bright in the cheery sunshine.

The kid spoke clearly and precisely. He didn't sound anything like the timid kid who'd snivelled at them from inside the theatre. 'You're rounding people up, yes? People who *hear*. That's what you're doing?'

Sunny glanced around at the others, but they were all staring wide-eyed at him.

'You can't . . . do . . . this,' Tez wheezed.

'What a stupid thing to say. Of course I can.' The red-headed kid addressed everyone. 'My people and I are taking over now. You can call me Posy, if you want to call me anything. We're on the hunt for a different kind of person now, and *you're* going to help me find them.'

'What're you talking about?' someone was brave enough to ask. 'What people?'

'An old friend of mine called Lacey. And a woman called Ruby-Red. We're going to be *very* busy. Make sure to pack your toothbrush.'

'He'll . . . k-kill you,' Tez wheezed at him. 'The . . . Flitting Man. He'll . . . kill . . . you.'

The red-headed kid looked down at him as if he were a piece of dog shit he'd scraped off his heel. 'You don't even know who he is, you fool. Stop talking to me. No one wants to hear you any more.'

And with that he thrust the pitchfork's tines into Tez's face with an awful, puncturing *thud*.

CHAPTER 2

The Inn

Albus sat in a rocking chair on the back porch of the Norwood Cove Inn, the Atlantic Ocean spreading out endlessly before him. He rocked himself with a light push of his foot, the chair creaking rhythmically as he watched the gulls glide over the bay. Their caws were abrasive in the morning's quiet. He imagined their slim, pink, blade-like tongues vibrating in their mouths with the sound. As birds went, it was a parrot's and not a gull's tongue that was most like a human's. Thicker, more pliable, it helped modulate pitch, much like a person used their tongue to speak.

For a time, he had been preoccupied with the myriad different tongue-types belonging to animals, but he supposed that was only to be expected when you'd been born without a tongue of your own.

The stark glare of the sun started fifty yards past the long shadow of the three-storey, four-gabled hotel, making the grass seem very green and the yellow-bricked pathway very yellow. The hot breeze blowing in from the ocean met the steps of the back porch and crept up with a soft sigh, sweeping over the wooden floor to the rocking chair and slipping inside the leg holes of Albus's pants. It fluttered up his shirt as if riffling through his pockets.

From inside the Inn, someone called his name.

He slipped his hands off the rocking chair's arms and hid them down by his thighs. He looked over at the back door, both its screen and the door propped open. A long strand of blond hair caught in his eyelashes, but he let it be and remained silent.

A man, solid-looking and wide-shouldered but slim through the waist, appeared in the doorway. The sclerae of his eyes were jaundiced and the eyeballs protruded from their sockets; it made him look both startled and intense.

'Gwen is back.' The timbre of Bruno's voice was deeply rich, its tempo lazy. Albus could have closed his eyes and seen his friend's words. The rough brown of tree-bark – craggy, solid, warmed by the sun. 'You want to come see her?'

Nodding, Albus gathered himself and stood, leaving the chair to rock, ghostly, at his back. Bruno stepped aside to let Albus walk through ahead of him, a deferential gesture that might have been out of respect for his age, except that Albus wasn't yet twenty-four and Bruno was a good fifteen years older than that.

In the foyer, a woman, a little younger than Albus, stood with her back against the old-fashioned reception desk, penned in by two older women and two brothers. Her hands were raised in an effort to calm the barrage of questions being fired at her, the hum of their excitement sparking like fireworks, their comet-tails trailing to each person in a riotous interweaving of colour. It made Albus's eyes ache, but he didn't attempt to quieten them. He understood how exciting Gwen's news was. She and Rufus had been gone for a day and half, the first collection that had been undertaken so close to home, and without Albus accompanying them.

Gwen's eyes fell on him with palpable relief, a small flicker of a smile coming and going. The others saw her attention shift and turned, falling silent when they saw Albus. He slipped his hands into his pockets, out of sight, and nodded for her to speak, and when she did her words blinked fast and bright in his eyes, like light refracting from the glass of a watch face.

'We went west like you said, Albus – it didn't take more than half a day's walk – and it was *right there*.' Her hands lifted and waved in her eagerness. He had never seen her so animated; it was like standing before a bank of photographers, their cameras' bulbs igniting, flaring one after the other. It was hard not to blink. 'Smack bang in the corner of the field, by a tree shaped like a heart. It was so weird. It was like aliens had dropped it down from their spaceship.'

A low murmur began to build.

Albus scanned the room, searching, even though he knew Rufus wasn't there.

'He's out front,' Gwen told him.

Albus smiled his thanks and left, walking through the wide, open-framed doorway and across the parlour, his footsteps audible only on the floorboards between the antique brocaded rugs. He didn't glance in at the Edwardian-era furniture or at the polished walnut grand piano, at the hearth unlit and darkened with soot. A fine layer of dust covered every shelf, mantel and tabletop. They didn't often use the parlour. No one knew how to play the piano and no one but Cloris felt comfortable surrounded by such extravagant furnishings.

The heavy wooden front door was open. All Albus had to do was push through the screen and he was out on the front stoop, its white-columned portico shading the porch and decking. The sun was painfully bright on the yellow-pebbled driveway and untended front lawns. Out here, the breeze from the ocean was mostly blocked by the hotel but, as if in greeting, the hanging wind chime hooked up next to the front door let out a tiny tintinnabulation as Albus passed by. He glanced up and watched the glass butterfly spin and catch the light, its iridescent wings giving off quick flashes of jewelled brilliance.

A young, lean man with a thatch of fire-red hair stood on the porch at the white-fenced railing, rocking himself from heel to toe, toe to heel. He was cradling something in his arms.

Albus hesitated only for a second before moving forward, stopping beside Rufus to look down at the child swaddled in a threadbare green hoody. The baby was around eight months old and fast asleep, its tiny mouth pursed and making little sucking motions, as if it were dreaming of nursing at its mother's breast.

'A little tyke, Albus. Can you believe it?' Rufus's words, like his hair, came to Albus in waves of untainted red, like drips of blood splashed hot in his face. 'He was out in the open, laid among the roots of this *huge*-ass maple. We'd never have found him if he wasn't squalling his head off. He's got a pair of lungs on him, I'll give him that. Haven't you, bud?'

Albus hummed a bit, more to get Rufus's attention than anything else. He looked a question at the baby and withdrew his hands from his pockets long enough to mime a cradle with his arms.

'You mean the mother?' Rufus shook his head sadly. 'We found her maybe half a mile away, her head stuffed in some bushes, bare feet in the road. God knows where her shoes got to – her feet were a *mess*, man. Like ground beef. She had a bag full of baby stuff, though, so it had to be her.'

Albus frowned, confused. What had happened to her? Why had she left her baby? There would never be answers to these questions, he knew. They would never know the baby's given name or what lullabies his mother sang to send him to sleep. She would forever be a stranger to him, the baby's memories void of her, his history beginning here, with them, at the Inn.

'The back of her dress was covered with dried blood,' Rufus said. 'Like, the whole lot, from collar to hem. Weird, right? But the place was deserted – no houses or buildings for miles, so whoever'd done it had just left her there. It's why it took so long to get back – Gwen wanted to bury her. Plus, we didn't want to travel at night. In case someone might still be hanging around.'

Albus wanted to reach out and brush his palm over the baby's silken head but he left his hands where they were. This baby was beautiful, a sign of something hopeful and bright in a dead and forsaken world. No one needed to see his maimed stumps for hands. They were a reminder of what they had become, and they had no place here.

'How'd you do it, Al? How'd you know he was there?'

Albus was embarrassed by the look of awe on Rufus's face. He wasn't some wizard performing magic tricks, and it wasn't anything that could be easily explained. His sister had been convinced his brain had rewired itself, that his chromesthesia had emerged in lieu of speech as a sort of consolation prize. That could be true, but it didn't explain why it was such a targeted visual party, the invites handed out only to a select few.

He shrugged at Rufus, an easy lift and drop of his shoulders.

'Right, right. We speak; you see. I get it. And I'm only ever red? Never anything else? Like a gnarly black or something?'

Albus smiled and shook his head. Rufus was only ever red. He had come across a man whose colour he'd seen as black, but that was a long time ago and a long way away from here.

With the baby, they numbered eleven. It had been a slow gathering, one that had started over a thousand miles away in Fort Worth and had continued here on the beaches of South Carolina. Albus and his sister would visit his uncle's Inn every summer. It had been a refuge for Albus, a peaceful place away from the masses of people and the unexpected blasts of colour that would blindside him, assaulting his vision until the migraines blacked everything out. It had been a scary time, but his Uncle Mack had taken it all in his stride. He was a simple man who thought the brisk sea air and fresh oysters could cure any ailment. He would take them to collect mussels on the beach, shoeless, their feet ice cold on the damp, loamy sand, and in the evenings they would eat their spoils over a fire-pit, listening to him weave his seafaring tales filled with mermaids and shipwrecks and hidden plunder, the same ones they'd heard a dozen times over but which somehow never lost their lustre.

It was the first place Albus had returned to when his sister had been lost to him. It felt like home, now more than ever. And here he'd stayed, and waited for Ruby's return.

And return to him she had, although not in the way he'd expected.

CHAPTER 3

Signs

'See there?' the young man called Posy asked.

He was pointing to the front display window of the pharmacy. Miraculously, the glass was unbroken. The pane was spray-painted with an unprofessional gang tag; it dribbled black paint, swirling round and round in a spiral like one of those optical illusions that made your vision blur. In equally untidy lettering, the words 'Our Time is Cometh' had been sprayed in a childlike hand beneath it.

'Know what it is?' he asked, swivelling to include everyone in on the question.

Sunny glanced down at the discarded pitchfork, dropped as soon as it had done its dirty work. The bloodstained tines pressed delicately against Tez's unmoving ribs. She was grateful he was lying belly down. She didn't want to see the puncture wounds in his face.

'I can tell you, if you want. It wants me to tell.'

She would wonder, later, why they hadn't scattered and run. She noted the restless feet, the twitchy, uneasy glances. The tubby guy had stayed where he'd fallen; his only concession had been to shift on to his butt, back shoring up the wall of the pharmacy. He craned his neck to look up at the spiral design.

'It's *us*,' Posy said, and smiled, something childish and

innocent in his expression. The kid from the theatre had returned: a little shy, a little simple. His gangly arms hung at his sides, hands loose. His shoulders were rolled back, his hips jutted forward. He seemed . . . harmless. Which was a ridiculous thing to think, after they'd just witnessed him murder someone.

Yet none of them ran. And no one attacked him for killing one of their own. No one had liked Tez. Plus, there was something weirdly compelling about listening to a madman.

Posy twirled a finger, drawing his own invisible spiral to match the one painted on the window. 'It's showin' that there's others like us out there. Others who hear. Makes us brave, knowing they're out there, don't it? Makes us want to find each other. Like we're family.'

Again, he looked around at the small group. His expression was so open and oh-so-honest that Sunny felt an urge to spit on a handkerchief and wipe the specks of Tez's blood off his face.

'I can help with that. With finding 'em. We got ways, yes sir. And the time for hidin's up'n over. You heard that, too, right? Flitting Man is the way, and we're all his peas. Peas in their pods. Two together.' The kid drummed his fingers off his brow and Sunny noticed how they trembled. 'Together, together . . .' he murmured.

Beck was regarding Posy as if they'd discovered a new exotic organism, and not a particularly attractive one. There was curiosity there, too. Sharp and wary. Sunny recognised it in all of them but she also saw the shrewdness. They were sizing him up. Weighing his words.

She caught Beck's eye and he offered the tiniest of shrugs. His lips moved and she heard him say, 'He did us a favour.'

'He was a bad man,' Posy agreed, but he wasn't talking to them. His chin was tucked down, his fingers kneading at his temple. He aimed a timid kick at Tez's shoe, a kid trying to be rebellious but having little heart for it. 'Yeah, got what he deserved, he did. I jus', I don't like hurtin' pe—' His head cocked. Listened. 'Well, I guess so? Hmm. That'd be good. I miss her. Yeah, she does.' Posy brightened a little, eyes lifting, his smile the kind that might normally elicit one in response.

No one returned it.

'There's others waitin' for me,' Posy told them proudly, giving Sunny another smile, one that creased his cheeks. 'Gonna help us hunt. Like a big game of Hide and Go Seek. It's gonna be *fun*. Who's comin'?'

CHAPTER 4

Cloris

Nine months ago

Cloris sang quietly to herself as she watched the reflection of her palm chase a lapel crease out of a Carolina Herrera silk blazer she was trying on. It was white. Exquisite. It tapered in at the waist perfectly, accentuating the flare of her hip while concealing the softness of her gut. She was appreciating the line of the shoulder when a black man's face appeared above it in the store's mirror. All she could see were his big, bulbous eyes, too white in his dark face.

Her singing faltered when their eyes met.

Cloris grabbed the first thing to hand – a Marc Jacobs saddle bag – and hurled it at his head. She didn't hang around to see what he'd do, didn't even stop to slip her feet into the Manolo Blahnik pumps she'd picked out, but dashed barefoot into the aisle.

Another man waited there. Slim, unflustered by the stylishly dressed woman in her fifties running at him. She remembered thinking his hair was too long. It fell in waves to frame his face and somehow made him look like one of those serene Pre-Raphaelite children in the famous paintings.

He held up both hands in a 'stop' gesture, patted them at her to slow down. She did neither of those things, although a gasp

22

did escape her when she saw he had no fingers. No fingers! Who *were* these people? And what were they doing on the women's fashion floor of Saks? There was no call for them to be up here. None at all. She'd spent two weeks living in this department store, occasionally visiting other floors to use the employee facilities, and for that entire length of time it had been safe from intruders. There was nothing of any use in here to anyone except her.

Her bare feet squeaked as she spun around and bolted away. A hand swallowed her shoulder.

'Quit running, lady. We're not here to hurt you.'

The black man's voice was baritone low. It quivered through her bones. She opened her mouth to scream. His hand, so large it covered the bottom half of her face ear to ear, closed over her mouth. His skin was hot and smelled of earth and soap.

'There's no need to be screaming, either. We only want to speak with you.'

The young white man with the hippy-long hair came over to them. His look of serenity was gone and worry now creased his brow. He glanced over his shoulder, toward the escalator, and turned back to them, lifting an arm to motion them away, directing them further into the racks of clothing.

Cloris heard it. A clatter of hangers, thrust along a rail. The screech of something – a display rack maybe? – shoved aside, and the soft, almost inaudible squeak of shoes on waxed flooring.

A burn of anger swept up her neck. She dragged the black man's hand from her mouth and hissed, 'They followed you in here.'

The men exchanged a look. She read the guilty expression on the young man's face, the uncertainty. In that moment, he didn't look any older than twenty. He reached for her and she couldn't help but cringe away as his deformed hand touched her elbow, slipped under her arm. She shuddered when his calluses scraped and caught on the silk of her jacket.

He tugged at her and the black man nudged, and between them they steered her into the racks of blouses, skirts and skinny-legged trousers, their arms brushing against premium materials and expensive couture designs, hurrying her through the shoulder-height shoe stands and the stubby, padded stools where customers could sit and slip their feet into buttery-soft leather. Cloris's bare feet and the two men's booted ones slipped past the knee-length mirrors, their feet reflected in duplicate a half-dozen times, then they were out the other side and entering a land of white.

The bridal department.

White sandals, white open-toe shoes, white ankle-strap flats, white sleeved gloves in silk, velvet, satin. Vases filled with fake green-stemmed white roses. White veils and trains in tulle, organza, chiffon. It was a land of purest marshmallow white and Cloris was rushed through it, dodging around a score of black mannequins offset by the virgin-white gowns they showcased and through a tall white archway into a dim room.

The entire right wall was panel mirrors, curved to centre on the focal point of a raised dais large enough to accommodate an assistant and a bride in her hoop-skirted gown. Comfy tub chairs and a sofa, also white, were scattered around, and on the back wall, toward which the two men were pulling her, was an entire rail of bridal gowns hung waiting, their hems brushing the white-carpeted floor. Two arms, one on either side of her, pulled apart the curtain of taffeta, shantung, cloque and lace, and she was pushed inside.

Her abductors followed her in. And there they stayed, enclosed in the old, faintly perfumed opulence that would have once been thousands of dollars' worth of celebratory indulgence, their backs to the wall, for almost an hour.

Multiple times, Cloris wondered how close the long-haired man's deformed hands were to touching her. Were they inches away? *Fractions* of an inch? She recalled the snagging of rough skin on her blazer, wondered if he had anything contagious and if she should be worried. She wished for hot, scalding water and a bottle of Molton Brown orange-and-bergamot handwash.

She wanted to move away but couldn't. To move meant making noise, and it would only bring her closer to the black man, and Lord knew what vile diseases *he* carried. Being cloistered together with so much fabric bunched around them made the air soupy and hot. They inhaled each other's breath, which disgusted her. Cloris tried to breathe in small sips.

Hiding served little point in the end. The footsteps they'd heard never came any nearer. The women's fashion floor and the store itself were so large it would have taken a team of fifty to search every square foot systematically. And why would anyone choose to do that? They had run because it was their automatic instinct to run. It was safer to assume the worst than to hope for the best and find yourself in a situation that could have been avoided.

By the time the black man swept the bridal gowns aside, Cloris's knees were being drilled into by two small jackhammers and the small of her back was a pincushion for a nail-gun. She hobbled over to the closest armchair and fell into it.

'Well, that was certainly a waste of time,' she said, treating them to a scowl.

'Would you rather we'd left you to deal with them yourself?' the black man asked. Cloris noticed he, too, was kneading at his neck. She was gratified she wasn't the only one in some pain after being forced to stand still for so long.

'They wouldn't have been here at all if not for you two. What do you want?' The two men exchanged another look and her temper snapped. 'Would you *stop* giving each other looks? You're not twelve years old, waiting to be scolded outside the headmistress's office.'

A flicker of a smile passed over the younger man's face and that only served to annoy her more.

'And *you*. You need a good haircut.'

His smile broke out.

'Albus heard you singing,' the black man explained.

Cloris snorted. 'Impossible. I was barely humming.'

'He has his own ways of hearing. We thought we'd come see who it was.'

Cloris creaked back to her feet, wincing as her right knee protested. It felt swollen. She paid it no mind as she limped past the two men (she didn't need to look to know they were ex-changing glances again). She had no intention of staying to chat any longer. Her feet were cold and she wanted to retreat to the comfortable nook she'd made for herself in Home Furnishings and have a nap.

'My name's Bruno,' the black man offered as he followed after her.

'Whoopee for you.'

'Albus thinks you should come with us.'

'Does he now? And why does he think that?'

'Because it'd be safer for you.'

'I am perfectly capable of taking care of myself, thank you very much. I've been doing so for years. Now, go on back to wherever it is you came from. Shoo.' She found her way back to the mirror and bent to slip on the Manolo Blahniks.

'You can't stay here by yourself.'

That made her stop. She straightened and turned to face them, disapproval in every stiffening joint, in her narrowed eyes, in the angry beat of her heart.

'Excuse me?'

'We . . . we only mean that—'

'*We?* All I've been hearing is *you* blathering on about nothing important at all. And *you*.' She jabbed a finger at the girly-haired fellow. 'What's the matter with you? Cat got your tongue?' The man's brows lifted and his head bobbed in an undecided affirmative, which *really* got her goat. 'I care very little about what *either* of you have to say. So let's stop wagging our tongues altogether, shall we?'

She stalked away, leaving them there, but they had caught up to her by the time she'd climbed up a flight of escalator stairs. (Oh, how she wished she could flick a switch and have the escalator carry her up to the next floor. All this exertion was bringing back traumatic memories of her childhood asthma.)

Out of breath, she turned on them. '*What?*'

The black man – Bert, or Brian, or whatever his name was – winced at the volume of her voice. 'Wouldn't you like to live somewhere safe and warm? With other people and plenty of food? A place where you didn't have to be afraid any more?'

'Are you recruiting for a sex commune?'

The man who hadn't said a word up to this point laughed. Which proved he wasn't a mute, he was just rude. She scowled at him and his laughter dried up.

The black man had the decency to look discomfited. 'No, ma'am. Nothing like that. We're heading for Albus's uncle's place on the coast. There's another one of us. Gwen. So, that's three of us so far.'

'And where is this *Gwen*?' she asked suspiciously, pointedly looking around.

'We're meeting back up with her in a few hours. She needed some time to do . . . whatever she needed doing. Woman stuff.'

'*Woman stuff.* How convenient she's not here to back up your story. Why are you even bothering me with all this? There must be a horde of people around here, much younger than me, who you could easily talk into joining a non-sex harem.'

'It's not just anyone we're asking to come with us. Albus says he can see your colour when you speak. Which sounds crazy, but it means something.'

Cloris backed up a step, eyeing them differently to how she had before. 'Are you one of them? Do you hear voices? Is that what this is all about?'

The long-haired man shook his head, and the black man quickly said, 'No no, nothing like that. We don't hear anything. But Albus here has the ability to see something in our speaking voices when we talk or sing or laugh or hum. He believes there's an important reason he sees it, and it's not often he does. It's a rare thing. And you have it. What's your name?' he asked.

'Cloris,' she replied, without giving it much thought. She was staring at the young man. There was such earnestness in his eyes, she was finding it difficult to look away. 'What do you see when I speak?' she asked him, curious despite herself.

The young man looked around him. They were near the bathroom-accessories aisle, and he went to a shelf of folded towels, patted his deformed hand over a half-dozen, searching for something. He plucked one off a shelf, held it between his palms (for Cloris now saw that his palms were perfectly formed, it was his fingers that were missing, thumbs, too, the skin shiny and red with scar tissue). He balanced the towel on one palm and pointed at Cloris's mouth with the other, then tapped the towel. It was olive green.

'He sees green,' the black man told her.

'Green? What does that mean?'

He shrugged. 'It means what it means.'

'That explains exactly nothing. Why does he see me speak green?'

'Albus can hear you, ma'am. You don't need to address me.'

'He's not doing much talking, though, is he? So I'm asking you.'

'He believes there's a link between the colours and us not hearing voices.'

'Other people can't hear voices,' she pointed out. 'Can he see colour in all of them?'

'No. Just us. There's something more going on with us. Something special.'

'You say "special" like it should mean something.'

'It *does*. It's there for a reason, like a cell that could turn cancerous is there. We just don't know what for yet.'

'A cancerous cell. That's a terrible analogy, dear.'

The silent, long-haired man nodded in agreement and gave his friend a 'what the heck?' look.

'I admit that wasn't the greatest comparison, no. I'll work on it for next time.'

'And what about you?' Cloris asked him. 'What does he see when you speak?'

The black man smiled, his teeth a flash of white in his face. 'I'm the same colour as soil after a hearty downpour. The same as bark on old knotted trees, the same as—'

'You're brown,' Cloris said.

The black man laughed a rich, booming laugh. 'Yes, ma'am. That I am.'

Cloris had left with them, for reasons she'd never fully explained to herself beyond the age-old conceit of liking to be told you're special. And green always had been one of her favourite colours, even if her husband said it made her look peaky.

True to their word, they had met a young woman called Gwen, with white-blonde hair. She was a silvery colour, according to Albus.

Along the way they had found Bianca, east of Augusta, and Rufus, in a condo complex bordering a golf resort off Lake Marion. The brothers Mica and Arun came much later, once they'd reached the Inn. And Lord, Cloris would never forget seeing that Inn for the first time, its beauty and tranquillity, its immoveability in the face of everything that had come before it, never forget hearing the sound of the waves crashing on the beach, smelling the briny scent of salt on the breeze.

It had felt like coming home.

CHAPTER 5

Colours

A meeting had been called. This always happened when someone new joined their family, no matter if the new member was an infant or a senior citizen. From the back porch, Albus glanced over at where his friends had gathered on the rear lawn, the grass shambling down to a small drop, then out to a rocky beach and, finally, to the ocean. Sitting in a circle, they chatted among themselves while they waited for him and Gwen to join them. The grass reached as high as their elbows.

Turning his attention to Gwen, he ran over what she'd already shared with him and tried not to let his concern show. On their way to collect their newest member (Cloris was holding the baby in her lap on the lawn), Gwen and Rufus had stumbled upon a settlement, armed and barricaded in a school two towns over. Two women and a man had come out to speak with them, guns in their hands and wariness in their eyes. They had appeared healthy, sane, albeit suspicious and understandably concerned that Gwen and Rufus had found them.

'I know, I know,' Gwen said when Albus failed to mask his concern. 'But we can't stay here for ever. Not by ourselves.'

Not if they kept approaching strangers with guns, they couldn't, no. The Inn was ideal for their needs. It was secluded. It wasn't on a main route or road. There was no reason for anyone to seek it out, other than Albus and his sister, and it was important it stayed that way. No one could ever suspect the reason why he'd gathered these people and hidden them away here.

Of course, Albus couldn't say any of this to her.

'You don't need to freak out,' she said. 'I told them we didn't pose any threat. And I certainly didn't reveal where we're based or how many of us there are. We talked for three minutes, if that.' And here was where Gwen became excited. Her eyes sparked and the dimple at the corner of her mouth flashed when she smiled.

Apparently, one of the women had let slip that she had contacts nearby. Military contacts.

'What kind of military, right?' Gwen said when she saw Albus's ears perk up. 'That's exactly what I wanted to know. So I asked. She said they were looking for ways to eradicate voices. *Eradicate*. That's the word she used, Albus. She said we're in the middle of a psychological war – one that can't be fought with guns and fists, we need a weapon fit for purpose. She said these contacts of hers have had their scientists working on the problem for years. They've finally been having breakthroughs. She talked about the circular signs cropping up, right? Like the ones we first saw when we were out looking for Amber?'

Albus remembered. There had been three. The first, a picture of a black, devil-like creature with a red painted spiral for one eye. The second, an accurate reproduction of a gun cartridge, the same kind that Rufus fed into his rifle but drawn in circles, scaled small at the tip and growing in size to form the cartridge jacket, spiralling down to its base. The last had been laid out in the middle of a hardware-store parking lot; a whole bunch of miscellaneous items – mops, wood panelling, paint cans, toasters, faucet fixtures, cupboard doors, bed frames – dragged outside to form concentric circles in a huge, swirling pattern of detritus that must have taken hours to arrange. An industrial crop circle.

The first two had looked like gang signs to Albus, but this third had taken time and effort. It had been a disturbing sight. No one had wanted to hang around to study it.

'She said they're appearing more and more. That something big is going on and that whoever is doing it isn't being secretive about it. It's making her contact real nervous. They've ramped up their activities.'

Military personnel and their scientists. But where were they, and why hadn't Albus heard about them before? Why hadn't his Uncle Mack? Mack had lived around here for four decades. Surely the residents would've spotted anything unusual?

It sounded like a story made up by someone who'd watched too many movies or read too many books. Soldiers and scientists, conducting experiments into psychological weaponry. These people Gwen had spoken to had most likely been shacked up in their isolated school for years, paranoia swirling around in a destructive, muddled storm. People grew scared, embellishments crept into stories and those in charge decided to tell untruths to keep fear to a minimum and curb dissension in the ranks. He wanted to tell Gwen that rumours and speculation weren't components that made up the truth, although he knew she understood that.

He settled for a frown and a shake of his head. He could see she didn't understand why he wasn't as excited about this news as she was.

'I get your reluctance, I do. I don't believe anything unless I see it either, but there might be something to this scientist thing, you know? She didn't say so but I got the feeling she might be ex-military. It was in her bearing, the way she stood, the way she addressed the others with her. I even heard it in how she spoke. And you should've seen how she handled her weapon. Look, all I'm saying is maybe she *knows* something. It could be worth checking out. At some point,' she added, when his mouth twisted with uncertainty. She studied his eyes, her own flicking back and forth between them. Her eyebrows went up in expectation of a reply and, finally, he yielded. Offered a nod. Yes, maybe they could look into it. At some point.

She broke into a smile, her posture relaxing.

Albus knew Gwen struggled with the esoteric nature of his chromesthesia. In an ideal world, every scrap of data would be available and no one would have to take leaps in logic to reach a conclusion. But this wasn't an ideal world and Gwen couldn't dismiss Albus's abilities simply because he didn't fit into her neat, compartmentalised views. She would never experience what he experienced but at least she now admitted that some things had to be taken on faith. She couldn't dispute the evidence his abilities produced, despite how remarkably they arrived. And he had consistently provided results: each of the people he had been urged to locate he had found and they sat opposite Gwen during breakfast and supper.

Albus understood how much it cost her to take so much on trust alone, and the nod he gave her was in acknowledgement of that. She trusted him, and so he would trust her. It had to work both ways. They would look into the information this woman had given. It might turn out to be important.

'My ass is going to sleep over here!' Rufus called from the lawn. 'Any chance of getting this meeting started?'

'Hold your horses!' Gwen's yell was louder than necessary, but Albus caught the smile in her eyes. 'Come on,' she said to him, taking his elbow and turning him toward the steps. 'But let's walk *really* slow, just to piss him off.'

'What should we call him? The little cherub needs a name.'

Bushes of lamb's ear, soft and fuzzily green, brushed against Albus when Cloris spoke. She sat Indian style, the child snug in the neat seat her crossed legs made, his back resting against her rounded stomach. Her arms encircled him, holding him steady. The boy was completely transfixed by the jewel-encrusted fingers in front of him; each of Cloris's digits was adorned by one, two, sometimes even three ornate rings. He eyed them and, every now and then, tipped forward, aiming with his mouth, wanting to gum at them. Cloris had to repeatedly straighten the boy up.

She was the eldest of their group by a clear decade, putting her around the mid- to late-fifties mark, although that was a guess on Albus's part – Cloris had never officially disclosed her age and probably never would.

Rufus was lounging back on his hands across from her, worrying a long stalk of grass between his teeth. 'I vote for Rufus, Jnr. Being's I saved him and all.'

A resistant fringe of red hair half obscured Rufus's eyes. Every now and then he gave his head a toss to flip it aside, only for it to drop down when the sea breeze caught it. If Cloris still hosted garden parties (which is how Albus always imagined her, dressed in a tulle headscarf and a big floppy white sunhat to contrast perfectly with her off-the-south-coast-of-France tan), welcoming her guests with fresh prawn vol-au-vents and dry Martinis, the talk of yachting holidays buzzing in the perfumed air, then Rufus would be in the parking lot spray-painting the guests' BMWs and Porsches and urinating in their fuel tanks.

Gwen, her long, light-blonde hair gathered up in a messy ponytail, threw Rufus an exasperated look as she lowered herself to sit on his right. The silvery sparks of her words held daggers. '*Found* him? You were behind some bushes, too busy straining and taking a dump to hear him crying.'

Rufus had the decency to turn pink at that, but he shrugged Gwen's comment off with a lazy smirk. Arun and Mica broke out into giggles. Of the two brothers, it was Mica's laughter that brought to mind the tones of wet cement and flaking grey slate, pleasingly clean cut. The image of their hero squatted with his pants around his ankles was obviously too funny to resist. The brothers pushed at each other's shoulders as they sniggered.

Rufus raised an eyebrow, his smirk growing. 'Can't help it if I was busy birthing my own brown baby boy, now, can I?' he said.

The two boys fell back in the grass, their laughter becoming raucous.

'I think we should take a vote on the name,' Bianca said, her crisp tone slicing through the frivolity as starkly as moonlight on freshly fallen snow.

'Yes. A vote.' Bruno's deep, dark voice laid the final blanket over the boys' laughter, and Arun and Mica sat up, rubbing their wrists over their mouths to hide the remnants of their grins.

Bruno was the only one not sitting. Even when Bianca asked him to, he had only shaken his head in that slow, deliberate way of his and had remained standing, his long shadow falling over the younger woman at his feet.

Whenever they were gathered like this, all their shades drifting in front of his eyes — a network of twining and twisting colours — Albus couldn't help but think of his sister. He'd loved to listen to her sing, the plushest burgundy-red spooling from her lips as it wound around her body, dipping and dancing with the melody. Her mind had been her own. Silent and free. Like the minds of those sitting around him were silent and free.

Until Jonah came.

Jonah hadn't appeared with the other voices in those early, chaos-filled days; they had been budding seeds, flowering in a luscious explosion after a storm, and Jonah had been a mighty oak, grown weathered and mature. But it wasn't only his age that had afforded him the means to make the transition to Ruby. He couldn't have been gifted to just *anyone*.

Albus had always seen Ruby in colours of deepest red. He saw all his friends talk and laugh and sing in whites and silvers, in browns, greys and golds. And he knew, somehow, that all of them could be used one day, if Albus didn't keep them safe. Used like his sister had been used.

While the others debated the baby's name, the two youngest

members, Amber and Hari, mostly looked at their laps. They hardly ever spoke during group meetings and had only turned up to the gathering after the general fuss created by the new arrival had died down.

Like the boy so often did, Hari looked up when he sensed Albus's attention on him.

Albus gave him a small, encouraging nod.

'Maybe—' Hari started, his lilting voice so quiet everyone stopped talking and leaned forward. Albus focused on Hari's mouth, fully appreciating each word as it stringed out, syllables pouring, warm and smooth as golden-honeyed nectar. 'Maybe the little one should choose his own name?'

As if on clockwork cogs all powered by the same silently running machinery, everyone's head swivelled to look at the baby. The child had dribbled, his chin shiny and wet, but right then both his chubby hands were wrapped round the knobbly third digit of Cloris's right hand, in the process of bringing it up to his mouth.

'What ring is that?' Gwen asked.

Cloris's arching eyebrows climbed even higher. 'This? Oh, just some silly thing my husband bought me. The fifteenth wedding anniversary is supposed to be crystal. Not that Derek would know a diamond from a rock.' She gently extricated her finger from the baby's mouth and looked sadly at the polished vermilion stone. 'It's jasper. Derek fed me some baloney the saleswoman told him about it keeping me *emotionally stable*.' Her lips thinned in annoyance. 'I think he was trying to say I was prone to puerile outbursts.'

'Jasper,' Gwen said slowly.

Bianca gave a brisk nod. 'I like it. Jasper's a good, solid name.'

Of course, Bruno gave his approval, too.

The boys and Rufus all shrugged and said the name was OK with them, even though Rufus made sure to add that Rufus Jnr still had a better ring to it.

Amber lifted her shoulders in a bird-like shrug and gave a quick nod of her own. She had no objections.

The baby cooed, a delightful trumpet of purest blood-orange projecting from his pursed lips. Albus smiled. Even without the ability to see like he did, they couldn't have picked out a better name.

CHAPTER 6

Experiments

Sunny lifted her head, alert to the change of atmosphere. It was a slight shift, and not one she would have noticed if she hadn't been waiting for it. She quit poking at the campfire with her stick and glanced at Beck. He held his shaggy head in his hands, not paying her any attention. She nudged his boot with her foot and, when he looked up, nodded past him to the trees.

Posy shambled into view, a brown pelt in one hand. He didn't acknowledge anyone as he walked through the camp but Sunny noticed a few jealous stares as he passed the small groupings of people bunched into threes or fours around their fires. She mainly watched one group, though, larger than the rest.

Posy hadn't been lying when he said he had people waiting for him. They were an unsavoury bunch, grizzled and humourless, but welcoming enough. They had seemed pleased to have more people join them. There was strength in numbers, they said. They had given the newcomers food and shared what news they'd gathered.

'You think what they said was true?' she asked Beck.

'Which part?' He was watching Posy's group, too, taking his cue from her.

'The bit about those massacred folk over in Brockton?'

'Why wouldn't it be true? They have no reason to lie.'

'I don't know. They told it with such . . . *detail*. Like they were revelling in it.' She could easily picture the scene they had described: bodies strewn across the steps of the post office, hands tied behind their backs, heads and torsos riddled with bullets, ears cut off. The corpses had been left out in the sun so long they'd begun to dissolve into the concrete, skin and flesh spreading like melted ice cream. 'Like they're scaremongering,' Sunny said.

'They don't need to scaremonger,' Beck replied. 'We've been hunted down for years. Slaughtered. People are scared of us. Of the voices.'

They had also been full of stories of the Flitting Man. Of a saviour figure who wanted to free them from the years they'd spent living in isolation, guilt-ridden and resentful, afraid not only of themselves and the voices in their heads, but of what would be done to them if their secret was uncovered. It was a heady message, and Sunny couldn't deny there was a notable absence of fear in Posy's group. They weren't scared of what was out there. Not any more. Their laughter boomed; they didn't care if the sound carried. They were rough-looking, but their camaraderie was unmistakeable, and it was infectious.

'One thing's true,' Beck added, 'it's safer if we stick together.'

As Posy walked through the camp, his people grew quiet, respectful to all outward appearances but she didn't miss the sly, darting glances, the smiles that dropped from their mouths.

'It's like they're afraid of him.'

'More like hate,' Beck said.

Sunny frowned. 'Why follow him if they hate him?'

'Because he knows how to find voice-hearers. We haven't been with him a week and, look, he's already found two groups. He found us, didn't he? Took Tez a month to find four people.'

'It's not him doing it, though, is it?' Posy had paused to share a word with a stocky man, bearded, his heavy brow made to look even heavier by his shaven head. 'It's the voice he hears. It's leading him.'

'What does the package matter? It's the results that count. They're sticking with him because it'll benefit them in the end. If there really is a Flitting Man—'

She gave an indelicate snort, which plainly told him what she thought about *that*.

'*If* there is,' he continued, 'then it makes sense to stack the odds in your favour. If there's one thing we've got good at over the years, it's finding ways to survive.'

They shut up as Posy straightened and continued toward them. He sank to his haunches on the other side of Sunny's fire and pulled out a scorched and blackened poker from the inside of his jacket. He sent her a quick grin and slid the long spike up the ass of what she now saw was a dead rabbit, shoving and forcing it through the animal's innards.

'Oops.' He snuffled a laugh when it popped out the side of its neck instead of the mouth and cast an amused glance around to see if anyone else had witnessed his boo-boo.

When he was like this, Sunny felt sorry for him, with his goofy smile and his bony butt and a beard that was soft and downy and sprouted only from his cheeks and chin, leaving his upper lip bare. You could almost forget that he heard a voice, and that he had a very different relationship with it than the others, Beck included, had with theirs.

Posy placed the rabbit in the fire, snorting a short giggle as the fur sizzled and burst into small clumps of flames. 'Can we do the list again?' he asked her. 'Can we? Please?'

'The Hide and Go Seek list?' Sunny asked. It had been discussed a number of times over the past week.

He bobbed an eager nod. 'It's like havin' my buddies here.'

'Did you know them?'

'Hm, Red more'n Lacey, but yep. Me'n Red got on like a house on fire. She got lost, and now Flitting Man's lookin' for her. That's why *everyone's* lookin' for her. She's important.'

'It sure is a lot of effort to go to, to find one person,' Sunny agreed, eyebrows raised, fishing for information but not wanting to ask for it outright.

Posy shrugged. 'Knows too much, I guess.' He leaned over the fire, his face gruesomely lit by the firelight. 'She tole me her real name,' he whispered, as if imparting a secret. 'Wanna hear it?'

'Sure.' Sunny didn't see any harm in humouring him. She was beginning to understand that tales of his friends were like a comfort blanket for him, woven from pleasant memories and kind thoughts.

'Red for Ruby and Ruby for Red. It's pretty, right?'

'Very pretty,' Sunny agreed. 'How long did you know Red for?'

'Dunno. A while? Was our job to keep ahold of her. Felt like a long time. Mostly 'cause she didn't get treated too good. Her brother neither.'

That was news. Sunny was pretty sure the brother wasn't on their Go Seek list. 'Doesn't sound very nice for them.'

Posy grunted, seeming none too happy with the direction their discussion had gone in. 'He ran off'n left her, the coward. She cried a lot after that. Made her real sad. I don't like talkin' about it.' His face turned sullen.

'Should I keep going with the list?' Sunny was happy enough to change the subject. She didn't want to push it.

His head nodded like a pup's.

'OK, so there's Red. She's around twenty or so. You said she'll be easily recognisable because she . . . she has no teeth.' She couldn't say that without wincing. A woman that age didn't lose her teeth for no good reason.

'Knocked out of her head,' Beck murmured.

Most likely. But she didn't ask. It'd only upset Posy, and that wouldn't be such a great idea.

'Right, right,' Posy muttered, checking on his spit-roast, turning the rabbit over.

Sunny caught the smell of roasting meat and her stomach gurgled.

Posy laughed, flashing a gap in his own gums, down at the bottom. 'Got a frog in your belly. *Rrrrbit.*'

She pressed a hand over her stomach, feeling the rumble under her palm. 'A frog in mine and a rabbit soon in yours.'

He laughed again.

'You told us Red would most likely be wearing a silver chain with a pendant,' Sunny said, steering the conversation back on track. 'A St Christopher, with a man with a crook and carrying a baby on his back. It's a decent identifier—'

'Identi-what?'

'Identifier. Something used to identify someone.' She still wasn't sure he understood but let it go.

'Hm. She wore that lots.'

'And then there's Lacey. She—' Sunny stopped, suddenly aware of the glances they were attracting from the small clutch of Posy's people. She poked at the fire with a stick for a minute, acting casual. Just a nice, normal conversation, that's all that was going on over here.

The kid hunched down, as if he'd become aware of the glances, too, eyes boring into his back. 'Lacey's like me,' he whispered. 'She *hears.*'

'A voice, you mean? Hate to break it to you, kiddo, but so does most everybody else here.'

'Not the same. Me and her's special. Up here.' Posy tapped his head. 'Red tole me so.'

Sunny didn't realise she'd leaned forward until the burning heat of the campfire began to cook her face, neck and breast. Beck had leaned forward with her, his interest piqued. 'Special how?' she asked.

Posy scratched at the back of his ear, rubbing the spot

furiously. Done, he blinked at her slowly, as if doing a tricky math sum in his head. 'You're bein' nosy,' he said.

Sunny shifted back in her seat and drew in a long, careful breath, steadying her voice before she replied. 'You're right. I'm sorry. It's none of my business.'

'S'OK. Jus' . . .' Posy nudged the poker at the fire a few times, shoving at the burning logs. 'It don't like when folk get too nosy. I don't want it hurtin' you.'

Sunny watched his eyes and whispered, 'I'll be careful.'

'Hmm. Last I heard, Lacey'n Red were buddies. Can be buddies without knowin' each other real well. She knew where Red was hidin'.' He was staring into the fire, eyes glazing over. It could do that, Sunny knew. Capture you and burn your focus so nothing else existed but you and the flames.

'So you think they might be together. Or that one will know where the other is.' She made sure to not say them as questions. She checked on Beck but he'd lost interest and gone back to staring at his boots, head in his hands.

'Hmm, no one else knows 'bout Lacey. All those others out there jus' huntin' on Red, 'cause they don't know what we know.' Posy looked up and smiled, as if sharing secrets made them true pals. 'I like talkin' to you,' he said. 'You're nice. Treat me normal. No one treats me normal no more. I'm not jus' Posy. They see I'm not jus' me. I think it scares 'em.'

Sunny's heart beat hard in her chest. Her throat went dry. She had to swallow before she could speak. 'You can be scary sometimes,' she admitted. 'Like when you hurt Tez.'

'That wasn't *me*,' Posy said, a whine in his voice that sounded close to tears. 'The Other *steals* me. Like a thief. We shouldn't talk on it,' he told her, his face closing down. 'Talkin' about it catches its ear.'

Catching its ear was the last thing Sunny wanted to do. 'Then tell me more about this Lacey?' she asked.

Posy relaxed a fraction. The beginnings of a smile came out

to play. 'She's got herself a rifle. Real good with it, too. Can shoot out your eye at fifty paces. Pow!' He clapped a hand on his thigh and Sunny flinched. 'She wouldn't shoot you for no good call, though. She's got fire in her belly, but not the mean kind. Thought for a bit they were sisters, her'n Red. They're alike, you know? Same ways 'bout them. Tough. Kind. Nice ways. Ways *you* got.'

For some reason (one she didn't want to think about too closely but suspected Beck would attribute to her 'stupid-soft heart'), a lump caught in Sunny's throat. 'I'm not any of those things. But thank you.'

'Sure you are,' Posy said, eyes shiny with sincerity, which made that damn lump all the worse. 'Different kind is all. Not always about fist-swingin' and cussin', is it?'

'I suppose not,' she said quietly, looking at him and seeing nothing but a man, barely past his teens, who was neck-deep in trouble.

'Don't think Lacey's rifle is gonna help her or Red much, mind,' Posy said unhappily, eyes sliding away, tempted back to the flames. A vacant look fell over his face. 'They've got ways to find folk now. Ways *we* don't hear. Pathways and news ways, passing this way and that. They don't all hear it yet, but they will. They will.'

Beck was listening again, his head up, flames licking his eyes. He didn't glance at Sunny, and she didn't ask what was up. Not here, not in front of Posy and whatever else might be listening.

'Find Lacey to find Red,' Posy murmured, speaking as if in a trance. 'Find Red to find Lacey. Two peas in their pods. Two flies in ointment. Two birds and a stone.'

There were a further two people on Posy's Hide and Go Seek list, although Sunny didn't bring them up. A third woman, past her twenties, tall and beautiful and damaged – she would be sporting fresh scars across her back and rump and criss-crossing her breasts and ribs. Alex was her name, and she and Lacey were as close as close could be, according to Posy.

The final description was of a man: at least six foot tall, dark-haired, with one damaged and bloodied eye. Posy had been tight-lipped about this fella and Sunny had detected a serious case of the heebie-jeebies in him when he'd first talked about the man. His name was unknown, which, to Sunny's way of thinking, meant he'd be practically impossible to find. Not that the others would be any easier.

The smell of charring meat was strong. Smoky and juicy. It made Sunny's mouth water.

'What're you cooking over there?' someone called. 'Got any for us?'

It was a fella whose name Sunny didn't know. He hadn't been with them long, maybe a couple of days, had approached them at Roanoke after Posy had located a small party of people there. He'd come alone but had palled up pretty quick with the two sour-faced bitches from Sunny's gang.

In private, Sunny and Beck called them Jules the Mule and Mary the Fairy, mainly on account of Jules's tombstone teeth and Mary being the most aggressively gay woman Sunny had ever come across. She shaved the sides of her hair, for goodness' sake. They were the kinds of gals who got their kicks loading the gun, handing it over, then up and clearing off as soon as it got to the firing part. Real pieces of work.

'Hey!' the man called again. 'I said, *where's ours?*' Jules and Mary grumbled their support but were happy to leave all the barking to the new guy. Sunny decided she'd call him Gonzo. Gonzo suited him just fine.

A few more voices joined in, low, muttering, adding their own displeasure.

At the first call, Posy had hunkered down into his usual position, head bowed, shoulders hunched: the universal posture of the bullied. But at the sound of rising dissent, his chin lifted and his back straightened. His shoulders squared off.

Oh, no. Here it comes.

When she met Posy's eyes, they were sharp with a sly intelligence. Whatever was looking out of his face wasn't the kid any more. Not-Posy – that's how she thought of him when he got like this. She wanted to get up and back away, to drop his gaze, but to do either of those things would be to invite a reaction. And that was the last thing she wanted.

'*Your* meat?' Not-Posy's mouth twisted on a sneer. 'Your meat is out there.' He jabbed a finger out into the darkening country beyond their firelight. 'Same place I caught this.'

Another voice piped up, this one snarkier, more confrontational. 'What's stopping us coming over there and jamming that spike up *your* ass, eh?'

A nervous titter ran through the men and women scattered around the clearing. A few shifted where they sat, their faces painted like ghouls' in the flickering firelight. Beck's mouth was an unhappy frown, his eyes twitching warily to the kid with the skewered rabbit. It didn't escape her notice that she, Beck and the handful of folk from Posy's group were the only ones who remained silent. She hadn't forgotten what had happened with the pitchfork. That stupid goddamned pitchfork that got left behind, the only decent thing that came out of that whole unfortunate business.

She fought down the urge to retreat again and stayed perfectly still. She didn't want any part of what was cooking here. There were near twenty hungry people, a number of whom wouldn't need much to be tipped into violence.

Not-Posy seemed to take his time lifting the burning rabbit on its poker and turning it over. It was scorched charcoal black, the skin cracked and oozing blood. A new waft of roasting flesh reached Sunny's nose and more saliva flooded her mouth. She swallowed quickly before she dribbled. Her fingers automatically tightened around the stick she held, its point embedded deep in the burning embers of the fire. If she had to, she could take it and jab it at Posy's face. Dig it deep into his eye socket, just like he had to Tez with the metal tines.

The thought came and went without resolve. She wouldn't be able to do it. Not while it wore the kid's face.

She lifted her eyes from the flames to find Not-Posy staring at her, his expression knowing and amused. The vicious snarl of hunger in her stomach unclenched and became something sickly and spoilt.

'You not gonna answer him, asshole?' Gonzo's anger was a feral thing in the fading light, his nerve bolstered by the angry flames crackling in front of him, by the encouragement of the two cunning women beside him and all the restless people around, the sense of his new pack brothers and sisters readying themselves to join ranks. Many of them hadn't seen the other side to Posy yet.

Not-Posy didn't reply, only lifted the rabbit and deliberately brought one burnt haunch to his mouth, ripping into the dripping meat with chipped teeth. He didn't look away from Sunny, watching her over the top of the carcass while he chewed.

He's playing with me, she thought. No, *it. It's* playing with me. Playing with all of us.

'You arrogant little . . .' Anger was overtaken by indignation and Gonzo got to his feet and started toward them. A few of the others were standing, too, their grumblings rising to resentful growls.

'Daniel Robbins.'

Gonzo stopped in his tracks.

Posy's head turned and Sunny was released from his gaze. She inhaled a quick breath, the scorched scent of cooked rabbit flesh hitting her so hard it sent her dizzy. She unclenched her fingers from the stick she'd been poking the campfire with and flexed the stiffened joints.

'That's your name, isn't it?' Not-Posy said. 'Daniel. Dan to

47

your wife. The same wife you watched pour gasoline over herself and take your flip lighter and light herself up. You watched her slip that lighter out of her bathrobe pocket, backing away the whole time. You went to go cower in the bathroom, didn't you, Danny Boy? While your wife of fifteen years roasted herself like this rabbit here is roasting. Wet your pants, didn't you, Dan the Man? Pissed right through them like a baby.'

Gonzo, or Dan, or whatever the hell his name was, stood perfectly still, his hands fisted at his sides. They shook visibly. Sunny couldn't see his face, he had his back to the nearest fire, his front entirely in darkness, but she imagined he was ghost-white.

'You listened to her gurgling screams before she sucked fire down her lungs and cooked herself up from the inside. You should have gone out and embraced your wife one last time, Danny. Given her one last squeeze and let the flames take you, for all the worth you are. A big man when you think you out-number me, yes? But a scared, whiny piss-pants when watching your wife die.'

Gonzo Dan's head swivelled as he sent glances around him, searching for help, but already the people who had stood up in support had quietly sat back down again. No one met his eyes.

'What are you looking for, Piss-pants Dan? There's no help for the wicked.'

'You can't know any of that,' he whispered, the sound carrying clearly in the night's stillness. 'It . . . it's not possible. No one was there.'

Posy's voice turned cold. 'Of course someone was there, you sad, stupid sack of a man. We *all* were there. I don't even know why I'm wasting my time talking to you. Sunny' – Not-Posy didn't look at her when he said her name but she flinched all the same – 'come with me. I want to show you something. Frank, bring the journal. And bring Piss-pants Dan, too.'

A man rose from Posy's group. There wasn't an ounce of fat

on him – he was all string ligaments and bony hostility – and every part of him was narrow: his shoulders, his hips, even his distrustful narrowed eyes, spaced over a narrow nose.

Once again, Sunny noticed the building energy in the men bunched around the campfire, their sliding looks, the silent translation of knowledge as Frank rooted in a pack, drawing out a weighty-looking book. Even in the fire-lit darkness, Sunny could see it was stuffed full with loose leaves of paper.

'What's going on?' Gonzo Dan was a baby deer caught in the headlights of an eighteen-wheeler, and the driver wasn't any kind of animal lover.

'Take it easy,' Frank told him, no inflection, no emotion whatsoever in his tone as he approached the man. 'We just want to ask you some questions.' He took hold of Gonzo Dan's arm and, judging by his wince, Sunny knew the grip hurt. 'It'll go easier on you if you come along nicely.'

Beck stood along with Sunny when she hesitantly got to her feet. Not-Posy didn't say a word – it went without saying that where Sunny went Beck went, too. Neither did Frank say anything as he offered her the journal, but his eyes conveyed a challenge, a silent collusion she wanted no part of.

'Come, come,' Not-Posy encouraged. 'Take the journal, Sunny. Let's not dawdle.'

Her fingers closed over the book's leather-bound cover, a crawling revulsion turning her stomach, as if she were taking possession of roadkill. The book wasn't as heavy as it looked – was surprisingly light, in fact – but she held it in both hands, flat, like an offering, a tray laden with a sacrifice.

Grabbing the smoking rabbit by its ears, Not-Posy yanked it from the spit and hurled the carcass with a contemptuous spit at the people sitting huddled around their campfires. 'There's your *meat*. Watch the bones don't choke you.'

No one moved but, as Posy led the way into the woods, Beck and Sunny following and Frank bringing Gonzo Dan at the rear, Sunny heard a grunting scuffle as a number of them lunged for the cooked rabbit lying in the dirt.

Gonzo Dan kept up a stream of questions, babbling mostly, not understanding what was going on, where they were taking him, what they wanted. He explained that what had happened to his wife hadn't been his fault. Sunny wanted to tell him that, if Beck had tried dumping gasoline over himself, she'd have smacked him round the face, and she sure as hell would have tried to wrestle the lighter out of his hand if he'd got that far, even if it meant they'd both go up in flames. She wanted to tell him that none of this was about him. It wasn't about her, either, but she didn't say a word. She wished he would shut up.

Not-Posy whistled through all of it.

Up ahead, where Not-Posy led the way, the rustling and snapping of twigs ceased. Sunny's heart continued to stomp. The back of her throat tasted of pennies, cold and metallic.

Not-Posy's whistling stopped. 'Here.'

Frank shoved the man to his knees and Gonzo Dan twisted on to his butt, scooting to jam his back against a tree. He gazed up at them, his expression plainly telling them he didn't understand squat about what was happening here, and Sunny hated him a bit for that because she recognised herself in him. They were all stumbling around blindly with the lights shut off, hands out, hoping a chasm wouldn't open up at their feet.

'You answer my questions honestly,' Not-Posy told Gonzo Dan, 'and we'll see about getting you something to eat and a bit of respect around here. How's that sound?'

Gonzo Dan blinked rapidly, as if the shuttering of his eyelids would help him process the information faster. Sunny felt that tiny speck of hatred sink a little deeper.

'Hmm?' Not-Posy had brought the metal poker with him and prodded Gonzo Dan's shoulder with it. 'Sound good?'

The man licked his lips and carefully thought out his reply. 'Yes?'

'Good man. Let's get started. First question: how long have you heard a voice?'

Gonzo Dan looked over at her and Sunny felt her jaw tense. What did he want? A friendly face? A smile of reassurance? She didn't have either of those to give him. She nodded stiffly at him to answer – she was sure this would go a whole lot quicker and easier if he talked. Besides, Not-Posy knew he heard a voice. He always seemed to know.

Gonzo Dan's eyes flicked back to Posy. 'Since three days before . . . you know, since before everyone else did.'

'So, more than seven years.'

'Yes.' His voice faltered and he cleared his throat. 'I guess nearly eight now.'

Gonzo Dan flicked her another glance but, this time, she dropped her eyes. She stepped around the back of Beck, moving past him and circling to Posy's far side, keeping her distance from both him and the seated man being questioned. She stopped when she was safely out of Gonzo Dan's line of sight. It put her in a position where she could clearly see Posy's face. His eyes gleamed. He had a strange, fixed smile on his face, which she was sure was meant to put Gonzo Dan at ease. *Don't be afraid of the scary man's smile, kiddos.*

Sunny stared hard at Not-Posy, searching for a glimpse of the kid she'd chatted to at the fireside. There were no signs of him; it was as though he'd never existed. She shivered and turned up the collar of her jacket, longing to be back in front of the fire, the flames' heat melting her face and drying out her eyeballs. She didn't want to be out here in the dark and cold, the worms wriggling in the soil under her feet, the night a witness to their deeds. The tall, silent trees around them felt like judgement.

'And you hear it all the time?' Not-Posy asked.

'Not . . . all the time, no. Only when I–I'm scared. Generally. Or when I'm anxious.'

'And you hear it now, yes?'

Gonzo Dan didn't answer for a few seconds. Then he whispered, 'Yes, I hear it.'

Sunny saw the corner of Posy's mouth twitch. 'Humour me. What's it saying?'

Tears thickened the man's voice. 'It's saying it agrees with you – that I should've died with my wife. That I don't deserve to be here when so many people better than me are dead. That I'm . . . that I'm worthless.'

'And do you think it's right?' Posy asked. 'Are you worthless, Daniel?'

'Y-yes? But I don't want to beee—. . .' The end of this word turned into a whining cry that stuttered into sobs, shoulders shaking.

'Sunny.'

She stopped breathing.

Not-Posy raised his eyebrows expectantly. 'Go to the last page and read out the entry, please.'

She fumbled in the journal she had carried out here, her cold hands trembling. She skipped past clippings from what looked like textbooks and the ripped-out pages of medical magazines. She glimpsed the heading of an article entitled 'Wernicke, Broca and Beyond' and leafed through a selection of anatomical diagrams of the brain. The journal fell open on a page filled with scribbled writing, a pencil tucked inside as a marker. She brought the book close to her face and hesitantly began to read.

'"Subject 11: female, late teens, bullet above right eye. Voice dominant and consistent over seven years. Subject 12: female, early thirties. Blade to right eye. Voice consistent and established – a few mild occurrences before full onset at the ages of seventeen to eighteen." What *is* this?' Sunny asked, tearing her eyes from the scribble, the question leaving her mouth before she had time to consider whether she actually wanted to hear the answer or not.

The book, which had been so light, now felt like a stone tablet, dragging at her hands. Her jaw shivered. Cold or fear, it didn't really matter, she didn't think she would be able to read the rest.

'They are my experiments,' Not-Posy said simply. 'I haven't done one for a while. They weren't working as I wished. But I listened to the tail-end of your and Posy's conversation and I felt a sudden urge to revisit them.' There was an attempt at a smile but Sunny saw it for what it was: a facsimile, a dud. 'You're full of curiosity, aren't you? Like a curious little bee. And I understand that. Of course I do. We all need reasons for being here. The same way you and Beck have chosen to stay because you hope it will lead you to someplace better. It may lead you to someplace worse, but that is a chance you must take. Hope, you see. It's an insidious thing.

'I'm also a curious little bee, full of hope. And the flower I want has its own name, one you've heard a few times now. Red is her own prize, of course, but she has other, longer-term uses. No, I have some . . . personal business to finish up with Lacey. She took something precious from me.' A bite entered his tone. 'Something that wasn't hers to take. I want to talk to her about that. Want to talk to her very much. And, who knows, maybe what she has to say will be of interest to you. To Beck, too, of course.'

Sunny felt Beck's curiosity surge, a bolt of electricity that zapped up her spine. It straightened her back. Stiffened the muscles in her neck.

Posy waved a hand, impatient to move proceedings along. 'But enough talk. I can see you're shaking. It's chilly out here. Finish your reading and you can go back to the fire.'

She stared at him, his eyes darkly shining in the moonlight, a stranger to her, a monster even. Of their own accord, her eyes returned to the page.

'"Subjects 13 and 14: both male,"' she read, her voice trembling, half lost beneath the pulsing rush of blood in her ears.

'First in his sixties. Took a bullet through roof of his mouth. His inner voice weak, came seven years ago. Second man, early forties, blunt-force trauma to skull, behind the right ear. Voice weak but heard for seven years."' She was grateful that Gonzo Dan had begun to sob quietly. It drowned out her words, and he didn't need to hear this. '"Subject 15: female, fifteen, bullet to centre of forehead. Voice intermittent for two years, since the age of thirteen."' Her chest ached. She'd stopped breathing.

Fifteen people. God.

'Is that it?' Not-Posy asked when she didn't start reading again.

'Yes,' she whispered. 'That's it.'

'Very good. So, the left eye it is. Write this down – word for word: "All subjects to date appear to have fairly undeveloped voices, insofar as they've not advanced beyond seven to eight years. A different subject is now urgently required. With a voice that is mature and established: the exact age is unknown but I strongly suspect a lifespan far exceeding eight years." At the end, put Lacey's name in brackets.' He waited a few seconds while Sunny hastily scribbled. 'Do you have it?'

Pen unsteady, she finished writing Lacey's name in a fast scrawl. 'Yes, I have it.'

'Excellent. Frank, ready yourself.'

Frank got down on one knee close to Gonzo Dan, his attention fixed on the seated man. Gonzo Dan's face was damp with tears.

'W-what's going on?'

'Shush. Let's proceed.' Not-Posy tapped the poker on the top of Gonzo Dan's skull. One, two, three times, as if performing a magic spell. 'Time to vacate the premises.'

Sunny expected Beck to be looking back at her, the same dread she felt mirrored in his expression, but his attention was locked on the weeping man. His eyes gleamed as brightly as Posy's, the moon whiting them out so she couldn't read them at all. Not for the first time Sunny wondered what the hell was going on inside his head.

Gonzo Dan's squeal wrenched her from her thoughts and she stumbled back, turning her ankle on a tree root. She dropped the journal. Loose pages spilled out, pale against the dark, spongy soil.

The poker was jammed socket-deep in Gonzo Dan's left eye. Not-Posy was clutching Dan's hair, pinning his head to the tree trunk as he *leaned* Posy's weight into the metal spike. There was some precision involved; Not-Posy obviously didn't want the man to move too much.

Gonzo Dan's feet drummed the dirt. Heels kicked up divots. The fresh, darker soil of overturned earth scarred the ground. His body jack-knifed against the tree as his squeals climbed an octave, reaching a pitch so high it echoed among the silent, accusing trees, long after Sunny thought the man would run out of breath.

The moon stared down on them and did nothing. Beck and Frank watched in silence and did nothing. She didn't know when her hands had clamped themselves over her mouth, one on top of the other, pressing so hard her teeth cut the insides of her lips, but Sunny followed the men's example and did nothing, wishing that her love for Beck made her braver and not weaker.

CHAPTER 7

Hari

Albus walked along the beach, his feet bare, his pants rolled above the ankles. The sand, damp and cool beneath his soles, held the impression of each toe, ball and heel indenting the compacted grain on each step. Arun and Mica were out with their fishing nets, waist-deep in the ocean, so far up the shore that Albus couldn't tell, from looking alone, who was who. Every so often the breeze carried their voices to him, the wind streaked with grey slate and revealing Mica to be the boy on the left.

After a while, Albus became aware he was being followed. The trailing footsteps were as quiet and reserved as the person they belonged to. Albus didn't mind the company.

He continued his walk, his stumped hands in his pockets, imagining his non-existent fingers playing with the lint. Often his hands felt whole and complete to him. It was a strange condition to feel one thing yet know another. His body was haunted by a past version of himself, a ghost that inhabited the entirety of his being, every cell overlaying him in minute detail, like an old carbon copy – even the parts that didn't exist any more.

He'd never had that ghostly sensation within his mouth, an invisible tongue rolling over his palate and teeth. It was the difference between being born without and having something taken away, he supposed.

Albus shifted his attention away from his hands and gazed out at the white-ruffled ocean, its waves calming, serene. He stopped and tilted his head back. He liked looking at the sky. It reminded him there were still some things in the world that continued to work, still flowed, following the same constant patterns they always had: the earth rotating on its axis and the sun and moon swinging into view just as they had for millennia.

He wondered if they would ever see planes in flight again, safe in their altitudes and not descending on suicidal trajectories that met with mountainsides, oceans and cities. Cargo liners chugging out of the bay on cross-Atlantic voyages and not deliberately run into reefs, capsized and cracked open, the contents of their bowels floating away like so much flotsam and jetsam. He had been young when the world had ground to a terrifying halt, he and his sister juniors in high school. He hadn't immediately comprehended the full magnitude of the events spiralling out of control all around them. The self-destruction of their loved ones and friends had been the first milestone of many, a milestone so large he wouldn't have been able to climb past it if not for his sister and Jonah's help. And when that devastating period had passed, his grief changing with the changing of the world, he was finally able to look past his personal sorrows and see the staggering emptiness of this new world for what it truly was: the loss of civilisation, of science, industry and every advancement and achievement the human race had ever made. It was all such a colossal waste that Albus sometimes blackly despaired: everything was rotting into obscurity around them, their entire legacy strangled by weeds and choked by inertia, all pulled down to the earth to die. The struggles and fighting, the deaths, the births, the love and compromise, and this is what it had amounted to. He wondered what the point of any of it was if it could all be taken away so easily.

While Albus was lost in his thoughts, Hari had edged closer – he could see one of the boy's bare feet in his periphery. Albus made as if to walk forward, rocking on to the balls of his feet. Stopped. Smiled when Hari stumbled into view.

Hari didn't smile outright in return, he almost never did, but there was a definite curve to his mouth. Albus pulled his hand out of his pocket and offered the space beside him for the boy to walk in and waited patiently while the options played out across his face. At last, Hari tentatively stepped up level.

They continued their stroll as Hari sorted through his thoughts and lined up what he wanted to say. The boy always picked his words carefully.

'The baby is very young,' Hari said.

Albus hummed and nodded. If he were honest, he had seriously questioned the directions he'd been given.

A child. A tree. North-west of here. Go, Albus, now.

But the directions were never wrong, and he didn't fear hearing them in the dark recesses of his head, for it was his sister's beautiful rose-petal voice that whispered them to him.

A baby, she had said. A baby needing their help. He often wondered how she always knew the details to what he saw; with Jasper, it had been but the tiniest, ghostly thread of blood-orange, thin as a spider's spun web, shivering and stretching away into the distance, vibrating through air molecules. He was sure there were details hidden in these fine vibrations, in the height and texture, a rich collection of minutiae depending on what it had passed through on its way to him, but he'd yet to learn to translate them all accurately.

'Why would a mother abandon her child?' The inflections of Hari's speech, rising and falling with each word, were like loops of honey stringing from a spoon, thickening and thinning as it drizzled. Out of everyone at the Inn, Albus enjoyed listening to Hari the most.

He thought about revealing what Rufus had found – a dead

woman, blood saturating the back of her dress and baby para-phernalia in her bag – but he didn't think it would help. At the end, the mother had been scared and alone, with no family, no sense of safety and no help to turn to. Her options must have been exhausted and hiding her child her last recourse.

Albus offered a sad shrug. He suspected the boy had already thought through all the reasons why.

A small touch to Albus's elbow brought him to a stop.

'Albus, why have you brought us here?'

It was a tricky question to answer without getting into the meat of what his sister and Jonah had discussed with him, and Albus sensed Hari wasn't looking for some existential reasoning. The boy wanted a simple answer. An honest one.

He left Hari standing alone and wandered off, searching, soon returning with a slim piece of driftwood. He slid the wood under the sturdy leather brace buckled around his left wrist and hunkered down on his haunches. The boy hunkered with him.

In the damp, compacted sand, Albus wrote: **to live. to be better to each other. to start anew.**

Hari leaned forward and, with his small, dark finger, notched two dots in the sand beside the words, followed by a curve.

A happy face ☺

'Although I could cope without Rufus being around,' the boy added.

Albus chuckled.

'What you see in us – the colours – it means something, yes?'

Albus hesitated, nodded. He didn't want to be dishonest.

'How do you do it? See them?'

This time, he didn't pause before writing: **you speak, I see. that simple.**

'But not everyone?'

He shook his head. No, not everyone.

'And your sister? Did you see it in her, too?'

Albus looked at him closely, searching his eyes, but the boy patiently waited. Unsure where this was going, Albus wrote: **her too. a different colour. hers alone. red.**

It was Hari's turn to nod. He remained quiet, his head down, studying the markings they had scratched into the sand as if looking for some hidden message. Albus didn't think the boy would speak again, and even considered rising, but Hari finally broke their silence.

'Do you ever dream? Of angry, red-filled skies?'

A series of shivers chased up Albus's spine. His sister had often dreamed of them. So often, in fact, that he had begun to dream of them, too. Like Ruby, he always awakened, screaming hoarsely and fighting against his blankets, sweating yet cold, his heart beating erratically. It always felt like the sky wanted to eat him. Swallow him up until no part was left. Swallow them *all* up.

Not since arriving at the Inn had he dreamed of the red skies. Although he hadn't forgotten them.

'Sometimes it feels as if something is up there, stirring.' Hari raised his eyes to the empty sky, absent of all planes and contrails. 'Do you not sometimes think a storm is coming?'

Albus didn't know how to respond: to say yes would be to inject a stark, fearful reality into his dreams; to say no would be to lie.

Hari's eyes had come back to him. 'Do you believe all those people died for a reason?'

Albus's laughter now felt as distant as the shoreline, its white, carved waves cresting and tumbling toward the beach. Arun and Mica had come in from the ocean and were two kneeling figures, their bare backs bent as they investigated the catch in their nets.

He was taking too long to answer, he knew, but a hundred reasons were tumbling through his head, all the explanations he and his sister had debated, without the help of Jonah, all the other reasons he'd considered himself, not one of them an adequate justification as to why so many people had had to die. He couldn't write them all down even if he'd wanted to – there simply wasn't enough sand on the beach – but he didn't want Hari to think he was ignoring him, so he made a low, humming sound, injecting it with uncertainty.

'I believe—' Hari began, and had to stop because his voice petered out. He tried again. 'I believe it was for the best.'

The boy's gaze had dropped to the ground, his fingers stroking the sand as if it were alive and needed soothing. He must have been aware of Albus's scrutiny, but he didn't look up, not even from under his eyelashes. Albus desperately wanted the boy to explain himself but it wasn't in his nature to push, and certainly not to push Hari.

The boy stood without meeting his eyes. 'I must go back,' he said to the sand. He turned, not waiting for Albus, and started back up the beach.

Albus stayed where he was and watched Hari go, a small boy growing smaller with every step. He stayed there for a long time, crouched, unmindful of his stiffening joints.

He'd assumed Hari had stroked the sand absent-mindedly but, when he looked down, he found the boy had written something. A single word. One that meant nothing to him.

Thanatos.

Finding Hari had been an accident. He'd been within easy walking distance of the Inn, a mere two miles up the road.

Albus knew Brewster's Gas 'n' Dash well. His Uncle Mack always fuelled up there and talked fishing with the proprietor. Gil Brewster was an alcoholic. Even back then, when Albus had been preoccupied with Nerf guns and Pokémon, he had recognised the watery eyes, the ill-disguised slur, the burst-capilliaried nose and sagging paunch as signs of a man liberally soaked in home-made brew. Albus also knew that Uncle Mack did more than gas up and chat about the size of his morning catch when they visited. Often the pickup would be driven back to the Inn in a decidedly less tidy fashion than it had been driven out in.

Long after both Uncle Mack and Mr Brewster had downed their last drinks and caught their last fish, Albus had headed for the gas station with Rufus and Gwen. The morning was foggy, a damp mist having slunk over the bay during the night, the day's heat now busily burning it away. It left a humidity that stuck Albus's shirt to his chest and back, made the short walk feel like hard work.

It had been a simple supply run and nothing more. Albus hadn't felt any signs of impending sightings, no buzzing in the backs of his eyeballs, no twitches, no whispered instructions from his sister. He hadn't expected to find anything at the gas station other than some tools and parts they needed to fix the generator. Albus had come along for old times' sake, wanting to see the place his uncle had spent so much time in, flapping his gums and rotting his guts.

They found Hari in the back of the workshop, standing on top of a groove-worn bench in the middle of the work area. The place still held the scent of sawdust and old motor oil, but now there was a dash of something else. Sharp, with a bitter edge. Something toxic. The bench's rickety legs wobbled under the boy's weight. Its unsteadiness suited Hari's purpose: he had tied a towing rope around a bare-beam strut above his head and dropped the noose around his neck.

He didn't appear surprised to see them enter.

This isn't the first time he's tried this, Albus thought. It was in the look in Hari's eyes. The calmness there. The acceptance. He looked barely thirteen years old.

'I'm sorry,' Hari said, in a soft, musical accent and, from the first syllable, Albus felt a warm flush shiver across his nape. The boy's translucent amber voice, pleasingly viscid, slid up the rope, dripped on to the table and pooled on the floor. At the backs of Albus's eyeballs, bees had begun buzzing.

Albus wanted to ask what he was sorry for, but Gwen was moving forward, reaching out, encouraging the boy down with shiny, coaxing words, her whole face illuminated with the sincerity of them. The boy, after only a moment or two's hesitancy, came down without a quarrel.

If they had arrived a few minutes later, would they have found Hari swinging from the end of the towing rope, all weary acceptance lost in the purple swelling of his face? Would he have changed his mind on that last fateful breath, untied the rope, climbed down and left the store, never to be found? They would never know.

Back at the Inn, attempts had been made to speak to Hari, but they were met with shy, downturned eyes and impenetrable silence. Hari wasn't much of a talker. Albus could relate. He was possibly the only person who might have persuaded the boy to speak, but words were not his domain. Hari's reasons remained his own.

They kept a close eye on the boy after that. Suicidal tendencies were a worry; they didn't disappear overnight. There was the strong possibility that Hari had started to hear a voice once he'd hit puberty and intended to follow through on his attempt (and in the footsteps of the tens of millions before him). But no more self-destructive behaviour revealed itself and there was no evidence Hari heard anything at all.

Albus concluded that the boy had been a victim to what all of them had been a victim to at one time or another. Hopelessness. Plain and simple.

CHAPTER 8

The Other

Posy isn't just Posy any more; this, he gets, even if he doesn't get much of anything else.

Not all that long ago he'd been a big, fat nobody. Like a crumpled pair of dirty pants left at the roadside. You might go over and give the pants a kick, see if they got good stuff in the pockets, but you'd never pick them up and bring them along with you. You'd never want to *wear* them or call them your own.

In his last family, he'd had a use. He'd been *wanted*. And Dumont, who was the big daddy of their gang – the *Boss* – well, he'd treated him fair and square. Posy couldn't rightly complain. The only bad side to the whole deal was Doc, and there wasn't a thing Posy could do about him. Doc was like his cousin Kip. Cousin Kip had enjoyed holding Posy's arm down while he put his cigarette out on the underside of his forearm. He'd liked flicking bottle caps at Posy's head, too.

Doc didn't do none of those things, because cigarette burns and bottle-cap flicking were small fry compared to the nasty stuff that lived inside him. Posy quickly learned to stay well enough away, to keep his head down and his nose busy. He was happy with the place he'd found for himself and didn't want to ruin it. He was part of a whole and wasn't alone no more. He'd never done well on his own.

And then Vicksburg happened. Lacey wasn't any part of their family – no, sir – but Posy had a mind she could've been if she'd wanted. She could've read to him every night before bedtime. He'd have gone to sleep with wondrous worlds unfolding behind his eyes, living lives that were better than his, lives he might've been able to live if things had been different. If *he'd* been different. They could've took his dog, Princess, for walks. And Lacey would've listened to his chattering and wouldn't have interrupted, because she'd been brought up good, he could tell. She would've *enjoyed* listening to him. They'd have laughed a lot. He knew that, too.

But she hadn't come back to Vicksburg for him. Which kind of hurt. But she had come to rescue another one of her friends, which was plenty commendable, if you asked Posy. She'd ploughed right in, bringing her new buddy along for the ride – a tall, demon-eyed guy with death written on his face – and, between them, they tore Posy's family apart. Killed the only people who'd ever accepted him. But Posy couldn't be mad at her. They'd done to Lacey the same thing they'd done to Red. Locked her up like a piece of meat. Made her cry. No, he couldn't be mad, not like the Other was mad.

Lacey and her new buddy went about their business of killing. Killed Doc, they did, who Posy swore was unkillable (which, turns out, he kind of was). You didn't exist to Doc unless he looked you square in the eye and *allowed* you to, no, sir. And Posy tried very hard *not* to exist to him. No one had existed to Doc except for Dumont and Red, and then Lacey.

In that small box of a walk-in freezer in Vicksburg, Posy had watched Lacey enter Doc's world and blast a hole straight through it. And, boy, did she exist. Posy reckoned she was the realest thing Doc ever did see. And as everything collapsed in on itself, Doc's cold, crystal-green eyes had found Posy cowering, huddled against the wall, close to peeing himself, and he made Posy exist for a moment, too.

A chill had passed through his stomach – it made him think of his ma's snow globes, all lined up on the mantelpiece. Her pride and joys. He hadn't been allowed to touch none, except for the Angel Oak globe (his ma hated that one because it came from Uncle Tommy and he'd tried to hump her one time at Thanksgiving). Inside that dome there'd been an ancient oak tree, its branches so thick and heavy they drooped to the earth like an old fella's arms weighted down by a bulky winter jacket. That's what Posy turned into when Doc looked at him and made him exist. A tree stuck inside a snow globe, the freezing snow chilling him through to the bone.

Posy's shivers had intensified as a slither of coldness opened up in the back of his head, an excavating needle that slid in deep behind his ear, searching, searching for *something*. Posy peed himself a little then, the warmth of it trickling down the inside of his thigh, the only warm spot on his whole entire body.

And that's when Posy heard it. Not in his ears and not from outside the walk-in-freezer walls, but from that new cold place in the back of his head. A voice. A new one, not one he'd ever heard before. It told him to flee. No, not told. *Commanded*. It ordered him to run before Posy found a bullet lodged in his brain, too.

So he'd left Dumont and Doc behind in Vicksburg. But he wasn't alone. No, sir. He'd never be alone again. Because the Other had come with him.

CHAPTER 9

The Letter

Sunny sat in the bleachers, high above the baseline, the rest of their party scattered across the diamond. Some slept on the grass, others sat in clusters, dining straight out of cans. She could hear the scraping of spoons. Jules was one of the ones eating. Sunny tried not to watch her – the woman had a terrible habit of scraping her mule teeth across her cutlery. It made Sunny want to tear the fork out of her hand and stab her with it.

They had crossed the border from North Carolina into South Carolina that afternoon. They were concentrating on routes heading east, hunting in one form or another as they went. Everyone was armed – home-made weapons, blades (Sunny secretly coveted the matching machetes Jules and Mary wore sheathed at their hips), slingshots, a handful of guns. Teeth.

She felt safe up in the bleachers. She could keep an eye on everyone. From her vantage point, she could see Pike, another guy from Posy's former Vicksburg gang. She didn't like Pike and she could tell Frank didn't like him, either, but there was a grudging respect between the two; pool players who hated each other's guts but continued to rack up the table because they knew they'd found a worthy opponent. They gave the same grudging respect to Posy, even if their ill-tempered mouths and squinty eyes said it stuck in their craw to do it. But then, it wasn't only respect that held their tongues. Caution had a good bit to do with it, too.

Unlike Frank, Pike was marked. Left his beard to grow unchecked but kept his head shaved so everyone could see the spidery, do-it-yourself tattoo of a spiral behind his right ear. She had watched one of the newer guys chat to him, and a couple of days later a similar design had been carved into his upper arm, the cuts red and puffy. Must have used a butter knife to do it, the stupid cuss. The guy had caught her staring and had smiled, teeth bared, eyes flat and glassy. A crocodile's smile. And under those dead eyes and sharp teeth, a slippery, predator conversation was taking place between him and his voice.

Sunny wasn't stupid. It was the unsaid things that frightened her the most. The not knowing what was being discussed in places she couldn't hear. She wouldn't know what they had planned, right up to the point their teeth sank in and tore out her throat.

The fact these fellas felt safe in so openly showing their allegiance to their voices bugged her. It was brash and arrogant and, somehow, inciting. Not too long ago, they would have had a rope slung over their heads and their bodies yanked up by the neck until their heels kicked at the air. Or else be shot dead on the front steps of the town's local post office.

As someone who was a non-voice-hearer, Sunny knew her presence wasn't altogether welcomed. So she stayed out of their way and refrained from chit-chat. So did the five or so others who didn't hear, their reasons for being here their own, same as hers were. Maybe they saw the turning tide and wanted to align themselves with the side they thought would see it through unscathed. Maybe they were doing the same as Sunny and following the people they loved.

She'd thought about leaving. Taking Beck with her and simply walking away. But Beck seemed to think something was happening here. Something bigger than a few people adopting the Flitting Man's ethos and deciding to band together.

And there *was* something about Posy, Sunny had to admit it. The voice he listened to *knew* things. The system of painted codes on buildings it knew to look for: spiral graffiti as large as the two-storey houses themselves daubed on to the sides of homes; slim chimneys of smoke, two or more bunched together; directions on car wings and chalked on to the concrete of a schoolyard; radio transmissions broadcasting on local levels at times and on channels that were coded into messages. Posy, or if you wanted to call it by the name Posy had given it, the Other that lived inside him, was In The Know (the way Posy had whispered this to her made Sunny realise he didn't know much of anything at all). In The Know or not, they had rerouted their journey many times after spying such signs, and they nearly always found someone at the end of it.

Watching the others down on the baseball field, Sunny wondered if there'd ever be a time in her life when she wasn't scared. Scared of what couldn't be seen, or felt, or heard. Scared of strangers and their thoughts. She figured it was a dumb question. Being scared was sensible. When she stopped being scared, she'd probably be well on her way to being dead.

Inside the dugout, Posy's head popped up. He scanned the area, looking for something. Spotting her, a smile bloomed on his face and he waved.

She sighed. She really didn't want her solitude broken. But, in the end, her manners won out and she lifted a hand in return.

It was all the welcome he needed. He jumped up and began making his way to her, navigating the bench seating in big, hopping jumps. She could tell just by his goofy smile and wave, and his heavy-footed leaps as he climbed, that it was Posy. His and Not-Posy's body language were markedly different.

A guy called Lonnie Mahoney used to come into her bar most weeknights. He'd tag along with a pack of fellas, the lot of them dirty and tired, hot off their jobs on the abattoir's killing floor. Lonnie would sit down with them, but he wasn't *with* them. He was the poor kid with his faced pressed against the store-front's window while the rich kids spent their quarters on tooth-rotting lollipops inside. He would hee-haw with the rest of them, laughing when his pals laughed, beer bottles slamming on tables and liquor spilling in their rowdiness, not getting what was so funny but yukking it up anyway, not having the slightest clue that the laughter was directed at him.

Posy reminded her of Lonnie. Anything bad he'd done, he'd got talked into doing. Anything bad he'd *thought* on doing, the idea had been put there by someone else first. His life led by others, encouraged to act out, to be something he wasn't in order to fit a place he was never meant for. And as easily as he and Lonnie fell in with the wrong crowd, they could just as easily recognise a soft touch when they saw one.

'What's this?' Sunny asked when Posy reached her bench and offered her a sheet of paper.

'Letter,' he said, breathless, sitting down too close. His body gave off a wave of heat and sweat. 'Heard you was thinkin' on leavin'.'

She gave him a sharp look. She hadn't said a thing to anyone but Beck. Unless Beck had opened his fat mouth. She'd be having a word with him about that the next time they spoke.

Posy did his usual trick of glancing round, making sure no one was near enough to overhear. She wished he wouldn't do it; it made it obvious he was telling her things he shouldn't.

'Red gave it me. For keeps. It's in her handwritin'. See? Is Beck around?'

Sunny was scanning the letter, only half listening. 'Hmm?' She glanced behind her, expecting to see Beck sitting on a bench back there, but it was empty. 'He must've gone off with Frank somewhere. Why're you showing me this?' she asked.

'To prove we're gonna find 'em. So you don't got to leave.'

Posy was nervously biting his fingernails but stopped to point at the last paragraph. 'Read that bit.'

The ink was smudged but legible. Sunny read. '"Mike gifted Jonah to her, and Jonah became Ruby's new friend. And along with Ruby's brother they explored this newly broken land, and wept and laughed and bled together, and eventually found an Inn by the sea to call their home where they lived happily ever after."'

She looked up at Posy. 'You're kidding me. Is that *it*? The bit about the Inn by the sea? That's why we've been spending all this time checking routes heading east? You think Red is heading for this Inn?'

Posy nodded and smiled real big.

'But this is just a *story*.' Sunny angrily waved the letter in the air. 'It doesn't mean anything.'

'She tole the Boss 'bout it.'

'Who did? Red?' Posy had told her about Dumont. The 'Boss' of Posy's old gang, who was killed back in Vicksburg.

Posy nodded. 'Yep. Tole Doc, too. When Flitting Man came to see her. Don't think she meant to, but he's good at makin' you say stuff when you don't mean to. *Real* good.'

The paper crumpled in Sunny's hand and Posy lurched forward, grabbing hold of her wrist and extricating it from her clenched fingers, hissing with annoyance. 'Don't *crease* it.'

'You've honest to God seen him?' she whispered, staring at him. 'The Flitting Man?'

'Not with *these* eyes. But he was there, yes, sir. Came to see her. Then she up'n ran. Scared her real bad.' He mumbled something about it not being his fault, shaking his head as he smoothed the paper out on his thigh and folded it back up, taking great care, as if it were a letter from the Queen of England herself. 'She'll head there. The Other says so. She misses her brother. Worried for him, too, I reckon,' Posy added sadly.

'My God, he's actually real?' Sunny breathed.

'Her brother?'

'*No*. The Flitting Man.'

Posy flashed her a nasty look. Ice coursed through her veins and she fully expected Not-Posy to lash out at her. But it was Posy who answered. ''*Course* he's real. As real as I'm sittin' right here. Boss and Doc met him. Was the only time I saw Boss scared, like he was a little kid crappin' in his pants, waitin' on his daddy to come home. '*Course* he's real. An' people think *I'm* stupid. Shit.' Posy muttered some more as he got up, throwing scowls at her and shaking his head as he clambered down off the bleachers.

Sunny didn't move for the longest time, not until Beck came to find her, streaks of gold and pink lighting up the sky over the baseball field. He sat on the bench behind her and leaned in close. His lips brushed the shell of her ear.

'You OK?'

She nodded, even though she wasn't.

'You sure? You seem out of sorts.'

'I do? Maybe that's because I found out you opened your big mouth and blabbed about me thinking on leaving.'

'Ah. Well, I didn't mean anything by it.'

'I just . . . I'm not sure how good it is for us being here. With these people. I don't trust them. Pike and Frank especially.'

'And Posy?'

'Him, too. But it's not his fault. Which only makes it worse.'

He kissed her ear again and she shivered, head tilting for him.

'We need to be smart here, Sun. We want to stay alive, don't we?'

'Of course we do. But at what cost? We let them murder Gonzo Dan and didn't do a single thing to stop it. What kind of people does that make us?'

'*We* didn't do anything. For all we know, the guy deserved it. No one's innocent in this world any more.' She felt him

72

move away from her. He sounded tired. 'Don't pretend like we haven't done bad things, Sunny. We've done more than our fair share. These folks accept us – accept *me* – for the first time since all this began, and that's a *good* thing.'

'That girl we're looking for. Lacey. You know he's going to kill her. Do some cowboy experiment on her and stab a spike into her head.'

'We don't know that. We don't know *her*. She's a stranger to us.'

'Posy says she read to him for hours. Said she gave him her last flashlight rather than leave him alone in the dark. He says she's nice.'

'Posy's an idiot.'

She sent him a glare. 'He says *I'm* nice.'

Beck stroked a piece of hair behind her ear. A conciliatory gesture. 'You *are* nice. Too nice sometimes. Look, you need to help me make this work or else we'll be on our own. And we don't want that. Not the way things are heading.'

There was an implicit threat in what Beck said, one she didn't want to think about. 'You're telling me you believe all this Flitting Man stuff?' she asked, thinking again about what Posy had told her. 'No one we've met has even seen him.'

'I don't think anyone needs to see him for him to be around.'

Cold prickles scurried across the back of her neck and she glanced around, checking the bleachers. They were empty save for them.

'What Posy tells us and what's the God's honest truth are two separate things,' she said, in a much lower voice.

'Do you want to chance not believing him?'

She didn't know what to say to that.

'Don't ruin this for us, Sun. I'm begging you.'

She crossed her arms under her breasts and didn't answer. She'd kept tabs on Posy since he'd clambered down the bleachers, leaving her sitting alone, her head reeling. He hadn't stayed among the others but had separated from them to go kneel by himself, his back to the setting sun. And there he'd stayed. She'd seen him act like this before, kneeling at the sides of road, at junctions and intersections, bowing his head as if praying. She had wondered at it, but he'd never done it for such a long time before.

'What's he doing?'

'Listening,' Beck said.

'Listening to what?'

'The call of the wild. How should I know?'

'Do you know *anything*?'

'No more than you do.'

'Jeez, you're a useless sack sometimes. Makes me wonder why I keep you around.'

He laughed softly. 'Because you love me?'

'Damn lucky for you I do.'

Sunny scanned the people scattered around the baseball diamond and, even from her seat high in the bleachers, she could see the strange intensity on some of their faces, their stillness. They were staring at the back of Posy's head.

'Let's go down,' she said, feeling ill at ease.

They descended together, hand in hand, footsteps synchronising so that, to anyone listening, they sounded like one person. Sunny almost tripped over the last row of seating when Posy unfolded and leaped to his feet. His arms lifted to the sky, back arching, hands fisting above his head as he stretched. He was smiling a self-satisfied little smile that didn't do a thing to make Sunny feel any better.

He said only one thing as he walked toward them. 'Bingo.'

He was singing to himself as he walked past, a merry tune that made little sense. Something about an alphabet pony, going for a ride and taking on the world.

CHAPTER 10

Firewood

By unspoken agreement, Cloris and Bianca had taken on the duty of caring for baby Jasper, although their parenting styles differed greatly. Albus watched in pained amusement as Cloris tutted whenever Bianca sang hip-hop to him, rapping through cuss words and offensive slang, or chewed up apple and fingered the pulp into his mouth. And Bianca huffed when Cloris dressed him up in the little sailor suit she'd found in the attic or gave Jasper one of her necklace's pendants to gum on.

'You'll poison that child, letting him suck on fake gold.'

'*Fake?* It's twenty-four karat!'

There had almost been an all-out fight when Cloris came upon Bianca, to all outward appearances, chewing on the baby's face. It transpired, after much shouting, that Bianca had been gently sucking on Jasper's nose in order to clear his blocked nasal passages, a practice Albus hadn't even realised existed and, in all honesty, found ingenious, if disgusting.

'Well, it's revolting!' Cloris had railed. 'Sucking up baby snot like that. Christ!'

'How's the poor thing going to breathe properly while he sleeps?'

'Blow his nose!'

'He's eight months old, Cloris! He doesn't know how to blow his nose!'

Cloris would argue that she had brought up three Ivy League-educated children and knew what was best, and Bianca would counter-argue that she'd had four younger siblings who she'd fed and bathed and clothed every day of her life while their mother worked three jobs.

And so it went.

Albus found Bruno out in the yard during one particularly strident shouting match. He was cutting up firewood, his shoulders hunched up and tensed. Sharing a look, Albus noted how uncharacteristically narrowed Bruno's eyes were. He was a big honey bear with a sore head. Albus could empathise; once the yelling began, his hearing wasn't the only sense bombarded with sensory overload. Along with the onslaught to his vision, very occasionally his taste buds flashed with pulses of flavour: mint, snow, cucumber, aluminium. It could become very confusing for him, being too close.

'They'll end up killing each other someday.' There was an abrasive texture to Bruno's speech, a spikier, lighter vein of grain running through the dark wood. It attested to Bruno's concern – he didn't like to see Bianca upset. Neither did Albus. The woman became waspish when she wasn't happy, and everyone suffered for it. As for Cloris, she became petulant and whiny, the fuzzy leaf-green of her voice developing spines that were pin sharp. He couldn't decide which was worse.

Albus grunted an agreement and found himself a spot on an upturned crate to sit, settling himself in to watch his friend work.

THWACK.

With a twist of his wrist, Bruno split a piece of wood neatly in two. He put another in its place.

THWACK.

There was more force than was strictly necessary in the swing, but Albus didn't comment.

'It's just a baby. I don't understand the need to fight over him.'

Albus nodded, even though Bruno wasn't looking at him.

'I'll be hearing about it after everyone's gone to bed, you can bet on that. I'll be lucky to get my head down before midnight.' Bruno sighed a giant gust of breath and set up another log.

As soon as the pile around the block grew pale with freshly cut lumber, Albus collected the logs, tucking four under his arm at a time, holding them steady as he trudged them over to the side of the Inn. There, he arranged them into stacks.

'Even after sleeping on it, one of them will make a snippy remark over breakfast, and it'll start all over again. Mark my words. It's never going to stop.'

Not until Jasper's eighteen, Albus thought. And even then they'll be arguing over who gets to wash his clothes and make him lunch.

Rufus appeared, hands in his pockets. He was grinning from ear to ear as he moseyed on over to the generator. The sky was darkening overhead, their shadows lengthening. It would be full night soon.

'What's up, fellas?'

Rufus knew what was up. He bent over the genny, fiddling for a few seconds, and stepped back when it sputtered into chugging life. The lamps and light fixtures inside the Inn flickered and came on.

A weak wash of yellow bathed Bruno in a perfect, slanted rectangle, the axe hanging at his side. A fine scar, barely noticeable in daylight, bisected his face, starting high above the bridge of his nose and cutting down along the centre of one cheek. It was lost again as a shadow cloaked him in momentary darkness. Albus glanced up at the dining-room window, but whoever had been there had stepped back and withdrawn.

Bruno placed another log on the stump, and Albus moved to place his own stump of a hand on top of it.

'Think he's saying you've chopped enough wood for one night,' Rufus said helpfully. 'Or, you know, for the next *month*.' The pile of logs against the side of the Inn was as tall as Albus and three of him deep. 'Maybe you should use that axe on your woman. Then we could all get some peace around here.'

Albus sent Rufus a frown and the young man held up his hands.

'I'm done. I'm outta here. Don't stay out too long, fellas, or else the Flitting Man might get you. Or Bianca. I know which one I'd prefer.'

As he disappeared around the corner, heading for the back porch and the kitchen, Bruno turned to Albus. 'He better not be spouting that Flitting Man stuff in front of the kids. Bunch of bedtime stories.'

Albus wanted to say that all stories were based on *something*, but it was almost time for supper and this wasn't the place to start such a discussion. He tapped his hand off the back of his wrist, even though he didn't wear a watch.

'I know, brother, I know,' Bruno said. 'Time to quit hiding.'

Albus smiled at the expression on his friend's face. He couldn't have looked more unenthusiastic if he were being sent to roll naked in a parcel of poison ivy.

'But if anything gets said and I'm being forced to take sides, I'll give you the signal and you come to my rescue. Deal?'

Albus was confused. He didn't know about any signal.

'This signal.' Bruno crossed his eyes, stuck out his tongue and fell backwards, sprawling on the ground as if he'd been floored by a knockout punch.

Albus laughed, harder than he expected, and Bruno laughed with him as Albus offered a hand, their laughter getting louder as he struggled to help his friend up. They made their way inside, still chuckling, Albus following the strands of voices as if following a trail of comets, their glowing impressions leaving ghostly after-images on his retinas. Thankfully, the shouting had stopped.

In the quieter moments, Albus would observe Bianca and Cloris with Jasper, see the kindness and care they gave the baby, the easy way in which they handled him, his happy face and gummy smiles, and knew both women loved the child like he was their own. If only they could see each other in these moments. But they were stubborn, and parts of them would always live in the old world, where a privileged white female (who'd lived in an eighteen-room antebellum house with a heated swimming pool) and a black twenty-something (who'd shared a single bedroom with four younger siblings in a four-room apartment) rarely shared the same viewpoint.

CHAPTER 11

Alphabet Pony

Six days after Jasper arrived, Albus found himself babysitting. Cloris had gone upstairs to her room, rubbing her temples and complaining of a fast-brewing headache, and Bianca and Bruno had taken the cart and barrels up to the spring to replenish their water supplies.

Left alone, Albus carefully carried the baby out on to the porch and sat down in his favourite rocking chair, settling Jasper in his lap so they could both see the ocean. He held his stumped palms out flat for the boy, all self-consciousness absent as Jasper happily patted at them, making little squealing noises each time he made a satisfying *smack*. Albus jigged his knees up and down, bouncing him a bit, and idly hummed a tune.

He didn't have to pay the boy too much attention, Jasper was a happy baby and didn't often fuss. The lulling rhythm of the jigging and the monotonous tone of his humming droned into Albus's head. His eyelids grew heavier and heavier as the bouncing of his knees slowed. His humming lowered in volume. His breathing deepened.

He was gazing out to sea, watching a tiny Hari move around on the beach, gathering up shells for the sand fort he was building with Arun, when the world washed away, blurred over by a dark, hypnotic wave. The song Albus hummed morphed and changed into a new song, the lyrics hovering unformed in his tongueless mouth, the words clear in his mind, dripping, slick and slimy, in seaweed-like tendrils.

. . . he's an . . . alphabet pony . . . saddle up . . . need a new rope . . . Steer him . . . a place on earth or above . . . Hey . . . pony . . . my new love!

A sharp *crack*, sharp as a metal ruler snapping on a school desk, made Albus jerk, but rather than pull him from his fugue it shot him in deeper, his eyelids fluttering shut as a whirlwind of colours whipped around his head, swirling so fast his stomach flipped and his eyes rolled beneath their lids. The vertiginous swirl made him nauseous and, with a gargantuan effort, he prised his eyes open and the colours shot away like firecrackers, rocketing into nothing.

He wasn't on the back porch any more.

He stood inside a bicycle store.

Bikes. Bikes everywhere. From toddler trikes to tandems, mountain bikes and racers, BMXs, touring bikes, unicycles, motorised bikes, recumbent and flat-barred bikes. Even old-fashioned bikes with looped handlebars, leather saddles and front-mounted baskets. Many were beyond repair, pushed over in long, collapsed lines. There were gaps in the stock where a number had been taken. The rest were pitted with rust and covered in dust, but the store retained that wonderful smell of tyre rubber. Albus breathed in deeply, wonder blooming inside him at how his imagination had conjured up something so real.

Another sharp *crack* came from behind him.

A girl was at the front door. She was younger than him, in her late teens, he'd say. She stepped carefully through a smashed door frame, her boots crunching on the glass sprinkled on the welcome mat. Her hood was up, covering her hair, but he could see her eyes. They darted back and forth, scanning everything. She held a rifle, its wooden forestock gripped firmly in one hand and a finger curled inside the trigger guard.

Albus lifted his hand in greeting, not wanting to scare her. Her gaze swept past him. As she came further into the store, she surveyed the display of bikes on offer, a restrained excitement in her that was evident only in a faint smile and the spark in her eye.

Lacey, Albus's sister whispered to him. *Her name is Lacey*.

A second girl, easily half Lacey's age, stepped over the door frame after her, entering the store the same way the older girl had done. Short, dark corkscrew curls framed this girl's face; her hair was long enough to cover her ears and brush her jaw.

'Wow,' this girl whispered. Her eyes widened as they did a slow sweep, pausing here and there while her brows kept on climbing. Lacey had stopped to watch her reaction. She was smiling. The rifle had been slung over one shoulder. By the time the child's eyes came to her, there was a wide smile plastered over her face, too.

'Which one do you want?' Lacey asked.

The child's gaze twitched away, moving once more to the magical array of bikes. 'I can have any?' she breathed.

'As long as you can fit on it, sure.'

This prompted the younger girl to hurry deeper into the rows, her hand out to stroke a saddle here, a backbone there. It brought a thorny lump to Albus's throat because he knew she had never seen anything like this; it was in the reverence of her touch, the marvel in her eyes. This was all new, a memory being made. It would shine in her mind for ever.

She headed his way, her hand out, touching, caressing, and Albus took a step back, although she didn't see him and didn't stop to peer up into his face. He caught a whiff of smoke from her as she brushed by and again was struck by how real this dream felt.

Beyond the front window, a third person waited. Not a teenager or a girl. A woman. Tall, in her thirties maybe. She glanced in at the other two every now and then, but mostly she kept her eyes on the street.

Alex, his sister whispered.

'How do you know their names?' he asked, unconcerned about speaking aloud. The fact he could speak, with perfect enunciation, was further proof he was inside the intricate construction of a dreamscape.

We're not strangers, she replied, and offered no more.

He wandered over to the smashed door, stopping before the broken glass, not wanting to bring his foot down, but suspecting his shoes wouldn't make a whisper even if he did. He studied the alertness and anxiety drawn across Alex's face, the tightness around her eyes, the thin line of her mouth made worse by the hollows in her cheeks. Glancing back at Lacey and the girl, Albus noted the same gauntness in their features, as if their skulls were slowly being excavated. He turned back to Alex and looked into her eyes, taken by their vivid blue, the life in them, despite the weariness that hung from her like the too-loose clothes she wore.

'This one,' the young girl breathed. 'Can I have this one?'

There was a long beat of silence from Lacey as Albus left the blue-eyed woman and walked back over to them, and he could understand why.

The bike was pink with silver letters all over its paintwork, running through the alphabet from A to Z. It had a white saddle and white-walled tyres. White tassels sprouted from the end of each pink hand-grip. It was horrendously girly, but the bike had a sturdy build, good, deep treads and a mountain-bike styling. It even had a side stand. Albus could tell by the pained look on Lacey's face that she didn't have the heart to tell the girl she'd picked one of the most reflective, easily spottable bikes in the entire store.

'You sure that's the one you want?' Lacey asked.

The girl was stroking the handlebars as if this were a pet store rather than a bicycle store and her chosen steed was an oversized pink-and-white kitten. Albus suspected the white tassels had won her over.

'I'm sure. Can I? *Please?* I'll take good care of it, I swear.' She was practically bouncing on her heels. 'It'll help with my reading – look at all the pretty letters!'

As Lacey bent to inspect the chain, Albus heard a humming tune start up in his head.

'I'm gonna call it Alphabet Pony,' the girl said, beaming.

His sister's voice, high and sweet and unusually upbeat, began to sing.

> *He's an alphabet pony.*
> *Come on, honey, saddle up,*
> *Been running 'round, need a home, need a new rope,*
> *Take him for a ride, take him up town,*
> *Steer him to a place on earth or above –*
> *Hey, Alphabet Pony, be my new love.*

Albus had begun to smile at the jaunty song, but the smile died on his lips when he realised it was the same tune he'd been humming on the back porch of the Inn. At the thought, the noise of the ocean rose up behind him, a soft, cooling rush. He glanced over his shoulder, but the shop was empty except for the three of them. Outside the plate-glass window ('CHAIN REACTION' written backwards across the top in big red lettering), Alex shifted from foot to foot, her head swinging one way then the other.

The sound of the waves receded, disappeared.

Lacey had crouched near the bike's rear end, its wheel raised a few inches off the ground, the tyre spinning freely.

'Why am I here?' he asked. 'Why are you showing me this?'

His sister sang over him. Her pitch had lowered and the tune hummed through his bones.

> *He's the alphabet pony,*
> *Ride him once and you'll be free*

Free to jump and swerve and whirl,
Free to take on the entire world.
He's the alphabet pony.

'Please,' Albus said, the word slurring as if his grip on the dream were slipping, his speech slipping with it. 'Please stop.' There was an edge to the song, despite its merry jingle, like a lullaby that foretold an unhappy ending.

I can't stop, Ruby told him. *And neither can you. She needs you. You must be ready.*

His eyes went back to Lacey and the girl. Lacey was bracing the bike, holding it steady as the girl clambered aboard.

'I've got you, Addison,' Lacey encouraged. 'Grab hold of the handlebars. Here. And the other one. That's it, you've got it.'

Addison. Now he knew all their names.

Alex had ventured a step nearer to the store's door, enough to be able to watch as the pink-and-white bike wobbled forward. It teetered to one side and Addison gasped and clutched the handlebars as Lacey steadied her.

'Ready for what?' Albus asked. 'I don't understand.'

You'll feel me soon – like when we were kids, playing Hide and Go Seek. Do you remember? We could always find each other, no matter where we hid. We'd play tricks on the other children.

He did remember. He'd always known where she was, the same way birds found their way to their migratory homes. The same way ants returned for their dead.

But it'll mean the others will be coming soon, too. Do you hear me, Albus? They'll be coming for her.

At some point during her words, his heart had started hammering. He watched Lacey and the girl go up and down the aisle, back and forth, right past where he stood, until Addison was doing it shakily by herself. And all the time his adrenaline surged, making his hands shake, his legs jitter. He realised his breaths were gasping. Was his sister finally coming home to him? Could he even dare believe?

Albus?

'Albus?'

The translucent sound of his name pulled him away. He blinked, and in that single shuttering slide – a slow glide of eyelid across eyeball – a rumbling and rolling background change was being orchestrated behind the curtains, his lids sliding up to reveal not the bicycle store but the back porch, with the sea whispering in the distance, the wind fresh in his face, and gulls cawing and riding the air currents above the waves.

Disoriented, he frowned.

A willow-thin girl stood before him.

'Albus?' Amber asked.

The way she said it, her voice a brittle construction of sugar glass, made him think it hadn't been her first attempt at getting his attention. Amber was fourteen years old but puberty had misplaced her address somewhere, passing by her house without stopping to say hi. Today, she wore a yellow summer dress. It hit her just above the grazed knobs of her grass-stained knees. There was a long purple-green bruise along the sharp contour of her shin.

Albus found a smile for her.

'May I hold him?' It came out reedy and small, as if from a place very far down inside her, a washed-out, pale echo of what could be.

He didn't immediately grasp what she meant, but the soft bump of Jasper's palms on his reminded him of the warm weight of the baby in his lap. He blinked a second time and nodded, and Amber came forward in a quick, nervous skip.

Jasper went up and into her arms as easily as if the two had practised the move a hundred times over. She propped him on her non-existent hip, one scrawny arm wrapped under his diapered butt, her other hand curled around a tiny fist. She bopped him up and down and made nonsense words in his face – Albus watched them swim around his ears like luminous goldfish.

Jasper's eyes were big and round as he stared at her. For a stretched-out moment, Albus wasn't sure if the boy would start bawling or not, but then his little cheeks spread on a huge smile and he laughed, high and tickled and stringed in orange-red, deciding he was delighted that, finally, someone here could speak his language. He gurgled back at her.

For the next hour, Albus watched them, his thoughts turning, girl and baby sitting on the porch floor opposite each other, Jasper bobbing and weaving on his diapered backside and Amber holding on to his chubby hands to make sure he didn't topple over. But they couldn't pull Albus away from the questions roaring through his head, the sea's low breathing rising to storm level in his ears.

He had only ever been shown his way once before, when he'd been direly needed, and that had been with the girl in front of him. And Amber's collection had not been easy. Not easy at all.

He'd been out on one of his longer hikes, staying clear of the main roads, choosing instead to follow a narrow dirt track running between two neighbouring fields. The hedges and trees had grown thick, arcing over the track like a roof. Dapples of sunlight broke through to splash the ground in a rain of dots.

As his eyes played over those dapples of light, his vision suddenly flared X-ray white. The ground canted to one side. He stumbled and almost fell in the bushes, holding his stumped hands wide like an inebriate searching for equilibrium. He felt that familiar crushing exhaustion drop over him. There had been time to search out a low gap under the hedge and crawl his way inside, safely out of sight, and then consciousness had been ripped away from him.

Without pause, he found himself inside the dream.

It was pitch black where they hid. He could hear a girl swallowing air in frantic little gulps, her gasps loud in the echoing container. Albus rested on something lumpy and sharp. It dug into his ribs. Neither he nor his companion moved an inch, not to elbow the sharp corner away, or to search out light or fresh air, and Albus desperately wanted to because the stench inside her hiding place was rancid. He could sense her rising panic. It was even stronger than the eye-watering gases of whatever was decomposing in there with them.

He heard her swallow, a low gulp, and he imagined she was fighting down the urge to vomit.

Her thoughts were his.

No! Don't puke! They'll hear!

The 'they' of the thought were outside, searching, voices gruff and mean despite the sweet, cajoling words that promised they only wanted to ask her some questions, to not be scared, no one wanted to hurt her. Albus knew they lied because the girl knew. She had seen what they'd done to the skinny guy. In frenetic images, Albus saw it play out: a thin man too weak to fight back, his arm separating from his body with the ease of a cooked wing twisted off a roasted chicken. The horror of his scream.

Despite the shocking recollection, the image of the cooked chicken became the focus. It overwhelmed. They saw it hot and steaming, the white meat juicy and succulent. Their stomachs spasmed and saliva flooded their mouths, and on Albus's next breath he drew in the stinking, putrid rot. The girl gagged noisily.

'I heard her! She's in here!'

Their shared darkness was slashed open by a bright bar of light and the girl's hiding place laid bare. She screamed and fought and scratched at the hard, cruel hands that dragged her from the dumpster, the top lip of it scraping a stinging line of flesh from her ankle as she scissored her legs and kicked. Albus felt everything she felt, including the satisfying thuds as her kicks hit their mark. Too soon she was pinned to the ground.

A fist came down, striking her brutally hard in the face, ending her screams. The back of her skull smacked concrete and, like a fire doused in water, all the fight left her.

Albus awoke gasping and crying, his shirt soaked with sweat, the last sun-flared image seen through the girl's eyes searing across his vision. A five-storey-tall Ferris wheel. The huge siding of a rollercoaster, sunlight flashing through its cross-hatched struts. And the sea. He'd heard the distant *shush* of the sea.

Myrtle Beach?

And then came the instructions: his sister, who he always waited for.

An amusement park. Six hours from here. Go!

Albus burst from the hedge, grazing his palms and bruising his elbows, scrabbling to his feet and running. Twenty minutes later he crashed through the front door of the Inn, scaring everybody with the state he was in: leaves stuck in his hair, clothes ripped and dirty, palms bloody, eyes wild. He tried to speak, he *did*, but their confusion only grew with the half-words issuing from his broken mouth. It took precious minutes for his shaking hands to calm enough to clamp a pencil between his palms and write down what he had seen. Gwen ran up to his room and retrieved the road maps he kept there, and they found S. Ocean Blvd, Myrtle Beach, near to Family Kingdom Amusement Park.

They set out within the hour. Albus, Gwen, Rufus, Bruno. They travelled the quickest, most direct route, chancing meeting the same kinds of people that, even now, the girl was about to come face to face with. They ran until they could run no more and had to stop to catch their breaths, to slug down a few mouthfuls of water and wipe sweat from their eyes. Then they continued, Albus setting a gruelling pace.

They entered Myrtle Beach with the countdown ticking.

They started at the bottom of S. Ocean Blvd and worked their way up the palm-tree-lined street, calling out, their weapons ready because they knew violence awaited them.

Albus spotted a blast of radiantly fearful colour rushing toward him. A wildfire, it didn't travel the air like it might normally but rushed along the concrete at ankle level. It made him stumble back when it hit and, a second later, the girl's screams reached their ears.

'That her?' Bruno asked breathlessly.

Albus didn't answer but burst into a run, eyes following the burning line, a lit gasoline trail, to where the girl's screams ignited the sky in a bonfire; he didn't know how anyone could miss it. His sore, leaden feet tripped over themselves and he fell. The cuts opened up on his palms. He waved the others on but they stopped to help him up and he stumbled after them.

They found a huddle of men, three of them, surrounding a girl. She howled in sun-scorched agony, one man yanking back on her left arm, the second man pulling on her right, and the third hunched over. Even from this distance he could hear his panting words.

'You hear one, don't you? You hear one, we know you do. Just say so and we'll go easier on you. Come on now. Don't make us do this. We don't want to do this to you, but you need to stop. You all need to stop.'

Albus could see the amount of strain the men at her arms were putting on her shoulders, and he thought of that roasted chicken, its wing pulling free, and his stomach grew queasy. He heard the *pop* and the girl shrieked so brightly Albus's vision flared molten hot. He cried out and fell to his knees, shielding his eyes.

Gwen shot the first man between the shoulder blades. The second dropped the girl's arm and charged them, howling in fury. He ran into Bruno's knife, the blade opening him up from sternum to groin. Down he went, feet skating through his entrails.

The third man leaped up and stood poised, fluctuating between running and attacking – he'd seen what had befallen his two friends and, for a fleeting second, Albus watched the indecision war on his dirty, skittery-eyed face. He reached behind him, hand disappearing under his jacket.

Rufus put a bullet through the man's heart.

When they carefully approached, the girl was very much the scratching, shrieking animal Albus had experienced in the last part of his dream. She wouldn't allow any of them near, even with the three men who had attacked her dead at her feet, even as her arm flopped at her side.

The men's deaths shamed Albus. Not because he'd had a hand in taking their lives, but because they showed him, in plain and certain terms, how far they had fallen. They had shed their humanity like an unwanted skin.

It took two days to return to the Inn. The girl remained uncommunicative and disengaged throughout. She would stop walking to sit rocking, holding her limp arm in her lap. Whenever Gwen attempted to get close enough to help, she screamed and shied away. Finally, they had little choice but to restrain her. The girl wailed while she was held down and Albus had to press his palms over his eyes while Gwen popped her shoulder back in place.

Lord knew where Rufus had found it, but he produced a frizzy-haired doll from his pack, dressed in a gingham dress, bonnet and buckled sandals. He'd sat it next to the girl, leaning it wonkily against her side.

She was led the rest of the way home without resistance, the doll dangling from her hand.

Weeks passed before the girl began to talk – only a single word here and a nod of her head there. Hari was the only one she spent any time with, and Albus assumed that was because he was the smallest of the group and, in her mind, the least likely to harm her.

Albus had worried that the damage inflicted on Amber would never heal, that she'd never let anyone close to her again, but now, here on the back porch, Albus watched her smile and laugh, all of her wariness gone, and he again wondered what would have happened if they hadn't found her when they did. He wondered what would happen to Lacey, to Alex, and to Addison, another young girl, far younger than Amber, if he didn't find a way to help them.

You must be ready, his sister had told him. *They'll be coming for her.*

Who'll be coming? But she never told him anything he didn't need to know. That had always been her way. Jonah's, too.

Albus sat unmoving, his stomach hard, his chest tight. He kept his features calm, tranquil even, as Amber spent the afternoon playing and tickling and babbling nonsense to Jasper. They had a hoot of a time. And beneath Albus, the floor creaked open, cracks appearing in the wooden slats and black tendrils of dread squirming out to wrap around his legs, thighs, gripping tighter, tighter. Threatening to drag him down.

CHAPTER 12

Rasputin

The entirety of the bridge was blocked by a crap-load of cars, jammed together, hood to trunk, fender to fender, some with doors swung open, some closed, most of the windows shattered or wound down. Glass glittered like a layer of crushed ice on the blacktop.

The sun had begun to set. Its richer, more subdued light filtered through a fine Kentucky mash whiskey, deepening the faded paint on the cars' fenders and roofs, drawing Sunny's eyes like a child's to a colourfully drawn picture. She couldn't remember the last time she'd looked at the world and simply basked in its beauty. Not that now was the time, but if she waited for it to come, she'd be grey and puckered and most likely too senile to enjoy it.

The dead gal went and ruined it a bit. She was lying between two cars, the side of her throat ripped out and her rat-tail hair stuck fast to the dried, blackened blood like a hocked-up, flattened fur ball.

Pike knelt next to the body, poked at it a bit, said, 'Gunshot. Not too long ago. No more than eight hours, I'd say.'

Posy daintily sidestepped the dried, gory puddle, as if afraid the caked blood might ruin his shoes.

The second person they found was alive.

Upon seeing the hulking, bearded man sitting slumped against the concrete abutment of the bridge's supports, Sunny's first thought had been *Rasputin*. Rasputin was from an old story, and right there was where the details got fuzzy – something about poisons and drowning and affairs with queens – but the description of the mad monk himself had stuck with her. Wild, bushy hair. Big handfuls of bristly beard. Eyes filled with black magic. The only part of the giant that didn't match the Rasputin in Sunny's memory was this man's thick, rubbery lips and the strands of saliva stringing through his beard.

Sunny wanted to share her Rasputin observation with Beck, but her man was looking down at the giant with a loathing she hadn't seen him wear before. It didn't suit him.

For the past few days, Not-Posy had been taking them from checkpoint to checkpoint. A *hunting line*, Posy had told Sunny. That's what his Other called it. A line that ran like a dot-to-dot drawing from Charleston, West Virginia, down through Charlotte, North Carolina, and on to Savannah. Small pockets of people were stationed in all those areas, and runners reported north to south, and then more runners ran to more pockets still, and so on. They had mostly reverted back to pre-technology days. Sunny waited to see carrier pigeons taking wing or semaphore being used again but, for now, news passed back and forth by good old-fashioned messenger service.

Their search area had become smaller since Not-Posy had begun singing his weird little song about ponies and alphabets. His elation hadn't lasted, dying within a matter of hours, and he'd taken to sitting and meditating more often, rising with thunderheads darkening his expression. Whatever he'd heard wasn't quite so easy to locate again.

As they'd worked their way south, Sunny sensed Not-Posy's patience turning tissue-paper thin, his cold, seething anger held by a single wispy sheet. No matter how many factions they found – and it must have ranged in the high twenties – no matter how many messengers they spoke to, or quiet moments when Posy would sit, head bowed, they weren't getting any nearer to what he wanted.

Their names came up more frequently now. Red, Red, Red, Lacey, Lacey, Lacey. Sometimes Sunny would find herself murmuring those names as if she were familiarising herself not only with their sounds but with the cadence, like a medley she was rehearsing for a big performance.

Their pace had been stepped up, driven by a burning need that no one questioned, and a further two checkpoints were hit in quick succession. Questions were asked and answers received that Not-Posy did not want to hear (*Any news of Red?* No. *The woman with no teeth, seen her?* No, nothing. *What about the St Christopher necklace? A woman wearing a St Christopher?* Any *woman?* No, sorry), and his frustration finally tore through its gauze-like control. He backhanded a woman at a checkpoint, opening up her lip. He screamed in her face.

And that's when it happened.

'Decker!' the woman cried. She had fallen against the shopping cart behind her; it would've skated away and dumped her ass on the ground if its wheels hadn't jammed in the gutter. The cart was filled with tech. Radio parts, speakers, headphones, transistors, and more shit Sunny didn't know the names of.

'Decker's one of ours,' she said, wiping the blood from her mouth. 'Haven't heard back from him since this morning.'

'And?' Not-Posy asked.

'He took two others south of here, to the bridge crossing the Congaree River. He should've checked in hours ago. He always checks in.' Blood had smeared over her mouth like lipstick smudged by a passionate kiss. The look in her eyes, damp and vulnerable, could have been caused by a lover's spurning.

'How far?' That came from Pike. The fact that he casually held a knife that put Rambo's to shame wasn't missed by anyone.

'I can show you,' she offered quickly.

She produced a map and placed her finger, its nail bitten to the quick, over a river not two miles away. It slid along a route, showing them the fastest way to get there. Then she stood back, regarding Not-Posy hopefully, eager for approval, and Sunny was struck by how young she was. How desperate to please. Barely out of her teens but already part of a system here, with couriers and communication lines and covert strategies that no one knew about because, really, what did any of them know about the Flitting Man's plans? Had anyone bothered to ask? Were they simply jumping on the first ship sailing to a newly promised shore?

'You start the fire?' Pike asked.

A wide column of smoke blackened the sky above the southern part of the city. Even in the non-breeze it had spread and billowed westward as it climbed. The smell of burning was as strong as the ever-present smell of sweat and humidity.

'It'll spread before it's done,' Pike added.

'It already has,' the bleeding woman said. 'And no, it's not one of ours. Not this time.'

Not-Posy had a real talent for evangelising – he could have owned and run his own Christian TV network back in the day – and their numbers had increased to twenty-three by the time the woman with the split lip and the hurting, eager eyes finished directing them to the bridge south of Columbia.

And here they were, in the ass-end of nowhere, a dead gal over yonder and a bearded Rasputin planted on his butt at their feet. Sunny was entranced by the look of disgust on Beck's face as Posy, for that was who he'd been on their walk out here, twizzling his poker in the air like a band leader at a country fair, unexpectedly cried out and shrank away, batting at an unseen attacker, the metal poker swinging, coming close to swiping Beck across the face. And then, just as quickly as it began, Posy's arms fell straight, his expression calmed and an oil slick leaked across his eyes, deadening them from the inside. The master had subdued its dog and the Other was in control.

'What happened here?' Not-Posy asked the giant.

Rasputin didn't respond but continued to stare out toward the end of the bridge. A second man lay crumpled out there by himself. Dead as a doornail, too, by the looks.

What *had* happened?

'Did you hear me?' Not-Posy's tone was level, but a veiled threat stalked after it, waiting for an opportunity to strike. At his side, the roasting spit began to swing in circles.

Jules and Fairy Mary, along with most of the others, had wandered off, fanning out to investigate the area. Some had walked deeper into the woods at the road's edges, no doubt looking for wildlife (although the noise the idiots made tromping around had surely scared off anything within a two-mile radius). The two women had wandered only as far as the second man. Sunny watched Jules poke the fella with the sharp point of her machete. Definitely dead.

Only Sunny and three men watched Not-Posy interrogate Rasputin. One was Frank, who Sunny had seen smile only once, his narrow cheeks creasing up so much she'd thought he'd spontaneously grown gills. Not a pretty sight.

Beck watched silently. Her man didn't look around, didn't notice the beauty of the evening sun or the callous way Jules brayed like a hyena as she and Mary wrestled the dead man on to his stomach to check his back pockets. Beck seemed transfixed by the giant sitting before him.

She touched Beck's back, lightly, above the waist.

He didn't seem to notice.

Pike's beard was as impressive as Rasputin's, coarse and thick like the head of a broom. He'd unsheathed his Rambo knife and was passing it back and forth from hand to hand, fluidly, easily, the knife an extension of him.

Like a puppet controlled by strings, Posy's foot lifted and shot forward, his booted toe thudding against the solid muscle of

Rasputin's leg. The big man made a low, pained sound. His eyes climbed Posy as he rubbed at the sore spot.

'I said, *what happened*?' Not-Posy demanded.

The three men standing around Posy shuffled – in nervousness or eagerness, Sunny couldn't quite gauge. There was something in the air now, a crackling energy that raised the hair on her arms and prickled at her temples.

Rasputin planted a hand on the ground and levered himself to his feet. It was a lengthy, difficult process, one done in stages, and Sunny expected to feel the earth shake as the giant shifted his weight from foot to foot as he straightened up . . . and up . . . and *up*. Her breath caught. He had to be seven foot tall.

A deep rumble started in the giant's barrel of a chest, vibrating up and out of his bearded mouth. 'I saw Red,' he said, a soft lisp to his S's that made him sound almost gentle. 'She was on a bike. The push-along kind.'

Oh my God, this is it, she thought. All those miles, searching, and this is *it*.

'A bike,' Not-Posy murmured.

'I saw her,' Rasputin repeated. 'She had the necklace. The one we got told about. With the man and the water and the baby on his shoulders.'

A noise came out of Not-Posy then, a soft *yesssssss* like a deflating tyre. Not-Posy stepped closer to the giant and tilted his head further back to meet the man's deep-set eyes. 'Are you sure it was her? Did she have teeth?'

This seemed to flummox the big man. 'Teeth?'

'*Yes*. Did she have teeth or not?'

'I don't know? She kicked me in the face.'

Sunny's gaze flicked down and, sure enough, crusty brown blood had dried around the man's nostrils – evidence of a recent booting.

Good for her, Sunny thought.

'Why did she kick you?' Not-Posy's words were measured

but Sunny felt the ice like a winter wind nipping at her face.

The giant felt it, too. ''Cause . . . 'cause I tried to grab her.'

Not-Posy was quiet for too long. Sunny had the time to count leisurely to ten.

'*Tried?* You're telling me she got away?'

Rasputin said nothing, but his eyes shifted to the men standing behind Posy. Nothing was said. He met Sunny's eyes and, despite his size, he looked like a nervous teenager who'd been busted for smoking pot.

'Is that what happened?' Not-Posy asked quietly. 'She got the better of you?'

'I . . .' Seeing he would receive no help, the bearded giant turned back to him. 'Yes,' he admitted unhappily. 'She swung her r—'

'I DON'T CARE WHAT SHE DID.'

Sunny's stomach clenched. Everything had grown still around her. She didn't need to look to know that everyone had stopped what they were doing to stare at them.

'You knew about Red and the necklace,' Not-Posy said, his voice quietly measured again, 'so I know you were told how important she is. The Flitting Man has ears everywhere. He finds out *everything*. I've heard the whispers travelling in the static up here' – he wriggled his fingers next to his ear – 'when I sit and cock my ear to the world and, let me tell you, some news travels much faster than little messengers' feet can carry it. Even to this forsaken hole. So I *know* you were told what to do if you found her. Don't think you can lie to me.'

Sunny could almost believe Rasputin had shrunk, a nesting Russian doll who'd shed his larger outer shell to reveal a smaller version of himself beneath. He no longer towered. He was no longer a giant.

'One of us had to report back if we saw her,' Rasputin said unhappily. 'That's all we got told. We should stop her if we could, or follow her if we couldn't. But Decker said—'

'Is that Decker out there?' Without looking, Not-Posy pointed a straight line to the dead man lying spread-eagled on the road, his pockets turned out, a guilty-looking Mary and Jules loitering beside him.

The big man's ledge of a brow lowered in confusion. 'Yes?'

'What is your name?'

Rasputin's eyes did another round. The smell of fear came off him in sour waves. And he *should* be scared, Sunny thought. If he knew about the journal tucked away in her knapsack, if he knew what she'd seen, he would be sobbing for mercy. Sunny could see Posy's knuckles whiten with tension, gripping tighter around the poker.

'Odell?' the giant said, as if he were unsure of his own name.

Posy's head puppet-nodded, but Not-Posy never took his eyes from Rasputin's face. 'Odell. Would you like to join your friend Decker over there? I can make that happen. I could *very easily* make that happen, if you'd like.'

Odell quickly shook his shaggy head. 'No, sir. I don't want that.'

Posy leaned forward and, as he did, the big man leaned back. 'If you disobey again, I'll take this spike' – Posy's arm lifted to show Rasputin the stained poker – 'and *slowly* screw it into your head until what little brains you possess leak out your nose. That really happens, Odell. Believe me, I've seen it.'

'I-I'm sorry,' the giant stammered. 'It won't happen again.'

Posy rocked back on his heels and the power that had been crackling around them, raising the hairs on Sunny's arms and humming in her ears, popped and, just like that, it was a pleasant summer evening again. The birds tweeted. A breeze blew gently past. Below them, beneath the bridge, a low rush of water burbled as it swept by on its way to Charleston.

'Good boy.' Not-Posy patted the giant on the chest. 'Now, which way did she go and how long ago? Tell me *everything*. And don't miss out a single detail.'

CHAPTER 13

Lepidoptera

Albus waited impatiently.

Time and again his thoughts returned to the bicycle store and the Alphabet Pony song his sister had sung to him. The tune danced in his head, forcing him out into the hallways to walk up and down the carpeted landings, as if he were trying to outpace it and leave it behind. An assembly of crowding doubts had formed in his guts, and they weren't going away. What if it *had* just been a dream this time? A momentary sparking of neurons that had activated his overwrought imagination? Yet each time he doubted, his eyes would fall on Amber.

The song haunted him. He could recite the lyrics and hum the melody as if he had been born with it playing in his ears. Maybe he had overheard one of the others singing it? No, he was convinced he'd never heard the song before. It had come from somewhere else, some*place* else, the same place his sister's instructions came from, the same place he had learned the names of the three people from his dream – Lacey, Alex, Addison – the same illogical place Gwen would dismiss if he were ever able to tell her of it.

The tune insisted on playing in the background. It waited for him in the first light of morning and followed him when he rested his head on his pillow at night. It was in every pause for breath between his friends' chatting, in every bite of food when everyone grew silent to chew. It was fair to say it was driving him insane.

So he walked, his feet avoiding the creaks in the worn floorboards, having long ago learned where each squeaky plank lay. Occasionally, one of his friends would poke their heads out of their bedrooms, quietly ask if he was OK, and then just as quietly retreat again when he distractedly nodded a reply. They knew from experience that there was nothing to be done except leave him to pace.

For two days and two nights after hearing the Alphabet Pony song, he paced. He wandered around like a lost pilgrim, dry-eyed and shaky-limbed, unable to eat more than a bite of food or foggily respond when anyone spoke to him. There was no jittering at the backs of his eyeballs, no driving need to venture outdoors and begin walking his ever-expanding concentric circles, alert for the tiniest gossamer thread of colour, marking out someone he needed to find. This was different.

It became less about the song that played on repeat and more about a familiar tugging sensation, the same tugging as when he and his sister had played Hide and Go Seek. How he knew which direction to take, which doors to open, which room to enter, which drape to pull back to find her crouching hidden in a tiny nook, smiling, before they'd even laid eyes on each other. He could feel her, as if she were the one circling *him*, a long distance away but definitely there. He didn't dare hope it could be true. That she was finally coming home to him.

He remained unaware of the concerned glances he received or the whispered discussions in which he was the subject. To him, his reality consisted solely of the floors he walked and the inner expanse of his waiting mind – so barren of life was it that the merest whisper of Ruby's voice would shoot an arcing red ribbon across the bleached landscape, bellowing like a trombone's contrabass. His outer existence became relegated to that of a walking automaton, to leave all his internal receptors open and vigilant.

Alone, Albus silently paced the front stoop. Everyone was asleep or else lying quietly in their beds. The Inn gave the occasional old-building creak, and that was all. Albus neared the front door and tipped his head back, his exhausted eyes lifting to the wind chime. It hadn't made a sound, but the butterfly twirled silently from its cord, spinning round and round in the middle of the chime's tubular bells. The longer he watched, the less like a butterfly it looked and more like a moth.

'Lepidoptera,' he whispered, and the word sounded terribly perfect to his ears, even though he knew his mouth had failed to pronounce it. With each spin of the butterfly-moth, a fraction of refulgent moonlight hit Albus's pupils, a delicate strobing effect that locked him in place, head bent back, eyes unfocused.

He didn't know how long he stood there but, with each sparkling blink, morphing from crystal-white to roseate to red red *red*, her voice whispered to him.

It's time, Al. The players are finding their places. Do you feel it? The martyr is on her way. You must come for her, or else he will find her first, and it is not her time to die. The red skies are forming.

Albus's muscles clenched on an involuntary tremor. The red skies. First Hari on the beach and now Ruby. The skies were coming back to torment him the way they had tormented his dreams, waking him with their roaring power, his body vibrating with panic, slick with sweat, his broken mouth unable to say clearly the awful words he'd heard static-burst from their storming, blood-red depths, hearing his sister wake beside him in the dark, saying them for him. Like she said them for him now.

Burning, she whispered.

Madness, she breathed.

Death.

★ ★ ★

His sister offered no directions. Albus felt only an overwhelming need to move, to find, to *go*.

As with the collection of Amber – when Albus knew violence and pain awaited – four of them would go. He would have preferred to travel alone, but his friends would not be dissuaded. Bruno, Gwen and Rufus would accompany him west.

After waking the Inn up and relating to everyone his need to leave, Albus had fallen into a deep, dreamless sleep and, five hours later, awoke, if not fully rested, at least feeling ready. He followed the sounds of activity to the ground floor, wading through a colourful ocean at low tide, and found Bianca in the kitchen, packaging up food for their journey. Bruno, Gwen, Rufus and the brothers were in the parlour, supplies spread out across the rugs and rucksacks in the process of being packed.

With all the rushing and the hectic gathering of provisions, Albus somehow found himself outside on the yellow-bricked driveway with a rucksack on his back and his face, neck and arms slathered in coconut-scented sunblock. He stood while the others said their farewells, unable to recall how he'd ended up there.

He watched Bianca fiddle too much with Bruno's shoulder straps until the big man reached up and took her much smaller hands in his. They gazed into each other's eyes and Albus thought, not for the first time, that even if all language were wiped from the world, these two would get along just fine.

Rufus punched Mica in the shoulder, hard enough to make the boy wince. He grabbed Arun around the neck and clamped the kid's head to his chest, paying no mind to the whines and squirming as he noogied the boy, grinning through the whole process until he grew tired of the rough-housing and let them be. Both brothers stood with their heads ducked, unable to hide their wide smiles, cheeks flushed with pleasure. Their initial unhappiness at being left behind had long since been forgotten; Rufus had entrusted them with protecting everyone at the Inn in his absence, a task that had made each boy visibly puff up, pride straightening their backs.

Cloris waited at the top of the porch steps, Jasper in her arms. Amber stayed close by – not for the older woman's sake, but because she never strayed far from the baby.

Of Hari there was no sign. He didn't like it when Albus left.

'It's best you stay off the roads.' A verdant thread of concern sewed a stitch through Cloris's words.

'Don't worry,' Gwen told her, moving to hug Bianca. 'We'll be careful.'

Bianca whispered something to the taller woman as they embraced, inaudible to Albus, even though he saw a ghostly, horn-like mist breathe from Bianca's mouth and disappear into Gwen's ear. Gwen wordlessly nodded in reply as she pulled back.

'Yeah, don't sweat it, Mother dearest,' Rufus said. 'You stay here and man the kitchen, we'll be fine.' Rufus had a real talent for ruffling Cloris's feathers, but today she barely reacted, her hand busily patting Jasper's bottom in a jittery pat-pat-pat.

Rufus descended the porch stairs in two long strides, gravel crunching underfoot as he joined Albus. He carried a Winchester rifle he'd christened Tallulah because he'd heard somewhere that the more girly-sounding the name, the deadlier the gun.

Bianca surprised Albus by coming over and laying both hands on his arms. Her palms were full of heat. Her eyes were bottomless. The white shimmering of her voice, so similar to swirling drifts of snow, was an incongruous companion for her, and one born of visual data alone. The woman herself was far from cold or emotionless.

'This feels very different from your other callings, Albus. I hope you know what you're doing.' No one but him could see the worried spikes of frost in her tone. 'You have a real talent for bringing folk together. I'll be praying you're as good at bringing them home again.' She tried to smile but it didn't make it far past her lips. Albus searched her dark eyes and spied the apprehension she tried so valiantly to repress. He would do his best, his nod promised her. Whether she understood him or not, she patted his arms, twice, gently, and left it at that.

From the porch, Amber lifted her hand to him.

Albus smiled and waved in return.

He checked on the others, saw they were ready, their packs on their backs, guns loaded, canteens full, eyes keen. He nodded again and resettled his own pack, sitting it more comfortably on his shoulders. He gave the Inn and his friends one last look.

Bianca had reached the top step and, for once, Cloris passed Jasper over to her without argument. Bianca cuddled the baby close, pressing her cheek against his. Jasper grabbed a fistful of her tightly curled hair in one chubby hand. The woman didn't seem to mind his experimental tugs, though they must have hurt.

Amber reached out to cup the bottom of Jasper's foot in her palm. Two yards to her left, Arun and Mica stood, silent and frowning, trying to look brave; they were barely a hair taller than Amber, in all her gawky girlishness.

Glancing up at the windows, Albus made a final search for Hari, but the boy was nowhere to be found.

Albus left the route up to Gwen and Rufus, happy as long as they kept up the pace. The sun blazed down from the peak of its daily climb, bringing with it a smell of warm ozone and baked hardtop, a soup that was difficult to breathe after a while. The world was made up of nothing but rustling wheat fields, grey winding road and tall blue skies that climbed upward for ever.

Albus glanced over at Bruno. The poor man appeared to be melting. His face was shiny with sweat, perspiration dripping from brows, nose, chin. His shirt stuck to his chest and stomach like a wetsuit. The man didn't complain. He placed one foot in front of the other, an uncompromising stride that didn't falter.

Rufus didn't look much happier. He had a baseball cap pulled low on his head, the bill practically covering his eyes. His mouth was pressed flat. For the first hour he had walked with Tallulah grasped in both hands, a soldier out on patrol, but he'd eventually grown tired of carrying the heavy Winchester rifle and slung it over his back.

Gwen appeared unaffected by the heat. Her arms swung carefree at her sides, her elbow every so often bumping the semi-automatic holstered at her hip. When she did occasionally look back at them, her gaze skipping from Albus to Bruno and back to Albus again, she couldn't fully supress the smile lurking behind her eyes. She always got itchy feet when she didn't have a practical task to focus on – Albus was sure that having two arrive in such a short period of time (first Jasper and now this) was like having her birthday and Christmas rolled into one. He sent her a small nod each time she glanced back, and she would respond with a professional nod in return, all seriousness lost when her mouth began to smile before she could turn away.

The fourth time Albus checked on Bruno, the man's teeth were visibly gritted. Albus stopped walking and made a quiet noise of concern.

Rufus turned to him. His eyebrows disappeared beneath the peak of his cap. 'What's up?'

Not looking at Bruno, Albus gestured to the side of the road, puffing his cheeks out to indicate how pooped he was (he wasn't overly tired, but no one needed to know that), and Rufus was nodding before Albus had a chance to mime the part about eating.

'Good call. I'm starved.' Rufus unslung Tallulah and laid her out on the grass. He took off his cap and ran a hand through his sweat-darkened hair. It had turned a deep mahogany.

'All right,' Gwen said, frowning. 'But only a short rest.'

Bruno traipsed past Albus, his head down and his wide shoulders slumped, and stiffly lowered himself to sit, not bothering to remove his pack.

Albus squinted back up the road.

The shimmying heat haze distorted the hardtop, making it

difficult to separate road from grass. The hot wind rolled through the tall wheat stalks. Some wary creature – probably a wild dog – darted into cover, its movement transformed into a drunken underwater mirage. The road seemed to go on for ever, arrowing smaller, dwindling to a dot on the horizon. Albus was pleased at how much distance they had covered.

'How far do you think we've come?' Rufus asked, mirroring Albus's thoughts.

Gwen's pack was unfastened and she was lifting out the wrapped grilled-tomato-and-zucchini sandwiches Bianca had prepared. She passed them around. Albus accepted his package and sat next to Bruno.

Gwen shrugged as she settled down with her sandwich. 'We've been walking for about five hours, so I'd say we've covered a good seventeen or eighteen miles. It's been all road walking, though. If we go cross-country, it'd drop by a bit.' She took a healthy bite.

Albus pulled out a slim metal rod and slid it under the leather brace on his left wrist. The rod measured maybe six inches in length and was no thicker in diameter than the shaft of a screw-driver. He concentrated on his food while Rufus continued asking questions, making Gwen take the map out and show him where they were. Albus systematically bit off small chunks of fluffy bread, using the rod, in place of a tongue, to push the food into the pouch of his cheek, where he could chew it until ready to swallow.

Once upon a time, he had used his index finger for the task, but the rod worked just as well. Hari had told him he resembled a pelican and had watched in fascination as Albus threw his head back in the same way the long-necked bird tossed its catch down its throat. Albus wasn't sure if it was a flattering comparison or not, but he'd had twenty years to get used to people staring at him eat. After the initial open-mouthed gawping, most people got over it.

He chewed the grill-softened tomato and zucchini for twice as long as he had chewed the bread and by the time he had eaten one half of his sandwich the others had finished and moved on to a dessert of blueberries. Albus listened to them talk.

'I don't see why we can't do that *now*,' Rufus was saying.

Albus could see Gwen's attempt at patience in the dulled silver blade of sound that left her mouth. But a blade by nature bore a sharpened tip, regardless of any attempts to blunt it. 'Because we know exactly where we are if we stick to the roads. If we start cutting through fields, who knows if we'll hit someplace we can't pass? We'd have to double back. We'd end up losing time.'

'I just think it'd be safer to get off the byways. Like Bianca said.'

'It *would* be safer,' Gwen agreed. 'I'm not arguing against that.'

'Sounds like you're arguing. And you're looking at me as if you want to slap me upside the head.'

'I *always* want to slap you upside the head. You have one of those faces.'

Rufus had popped a couple of blueberries in his mouth and was chewing them with a sour expression on his face. Albus was pretty sure it wasn't down to the fruit. 'Yeah? Well, your face makes me want to yak up the sandwich I just ate.'

Gwen sighed and shook her head, visibly swallowing down her retort.

'We should see what Albus needs us to do,' Bruno said.

Luckily, Albus had just finished swallowing. He cleared his throat and wiped his mouth with the back of his wrist. He'd received no more instructions, had seen no unfamiliar strands of colour riding out to meet him, but there was a very faint source of energy hiding behind the miles of terrain ahead. A second, minuscule sun, emitting light and warmth, just for him. If he closed his eyes and turned his face, he could almost feel her. Ruby. Tugging at him. His heart felt too large in his chest, swollen and pushed up against his breastbone. It beat hard enough for the both of them.

'Albus?' Gwen prompted.

They needed to stick to the road for now, that much he did know. Speed was more important. He nodded to the ground and tapped the cracked concrete with the toe of his boot.

'It's decided, then. We stay on the roads.' Gwen brushed her hands clean.

'Great,' Rufus muttered.

Bruno nodded thoughtfully, his eyes drifting back up the road.

'Let's pack up.' Gwen rose and started shoving everything into her rucksack.

Rufus rose with decidedly less enthusiasm, plucked his cap out of his pocket, shook it open and jammed it back on his head.

'You want your blueberries?' Bruno held out a cupped hand, an open piece of cloth draped over it and a small pile of blueberries heaped in the middle.

Albus smiled and shook his head, patting his belly to indicate he was full.

'I'll save them for you for later.' He carefully folded the cloth back over the fruit and stowed the parcel away in his pack.

Albus got to his feet with the others, glancing upward this time, at the endless blue sky. When he'd relayed the importance of this mission, he hadn't mentioned his sister's warning of the red skies. Not to Hari, not to anyone. To tell of them would be to reveal the magnitude of the task that awaited them. This wasn't just the collection of someone to take back to the Inn. There was much more at stake here. Not only did they have to locate his sister and the girl she had called the martyr – a girl whose identity Albus was still unsure of (he had seen *two* girls and one woman in his dream) – in hundreds of miles of blighted, empty roads and ruined cities but they had to locate them before someone else did. Someone who wanted to find them as desperately as he did.

CHAPTER 14

The Lake

Sunny skidded the last few feet to the bottom of the bank and paused to catch her breath. Her eyes tracked the weaving lines cut into the tall grass as they skirted the lake. Three of them. Bicycles, just like Odell had said. They led to a picnic area on the far side of the water.

She tipped her head back and cupped a hand over her eyes to peer up at Posy. He posed at the top of the lake's steep embankment, hands on his hips, the rabbit-spike sticking up from one fist. His feet were spread wide. He looked like some addled explorer who'd spent far too long outdoors where the sun had cooked his brains.

Sunny was alone on the lake's shore. No one seemed in any rush to join her.

'Look!' Posy's spike pointed at the gently rippling body of water where a number of floating bodies bobbed. They were like gruesome, lumpy buoys.

'A whole family!' A boyish grin split Posy's face. 'What a kicker!'

Odell towered at Posy's shoulder, placing the shorter, skinnier man in shade. 'Red's here?'

The giant frowned around, his thick lips parted and tongue half protruding as he panted for breath. A breeze caught the tip of Odell's beard and lifted it, bringing the unwashed, sweaty stench of men to Sunny's nose. It disgusted her. Posy hadn't allowed them more than a handful of hours to sleep, never mind given them time to wash or clean their clothes. She likely smelled like a fishmonger's stall left too long in the sun herself. Her khaki pants were ripped at the thigh and the material at the rump, knees and lower legs were four shades darker than the original hue. Both sleeves of her checked shirt were so filthy that, from elbow to cuff, the pattern was lost in a block of grime. She didn't want to inspect her knotted, greasy hair for fear of what she might find crawling in it. Beck had fared better, by a fair bit, but he didn't follow a beauty regimen and she wasn't about to ask him for any tips.

'*Some*one's here, yes, sir,' Posy said, sending Sunny a twinkling, happy look.

'Over here!' Pike called. He'd tromped down the bank further along and was poking at the grass with his knife, indicating the three snaking tracks Sunny had already clocked. She couldn't see the do-it-yourself tattoo on the side of his skull from where she stood, and was glad of it.

Posy bounded down the steep bank and Sunny had to step out of his way quickly or else get trampled. Odell trundled on behind, coming in slow, careful sidesteps – a fall would send him rolling to the bottom if he wasn't careful. It made Sunny think of Rasputin and drowning all over again.

Posy went to Pike and stared at the tracks in confusion. Slowly, his gaze cleared and Sunny knew the thing inside his head was explaining what he was seeing.

'Tyre tracks! Ha!' He beamed around at the others. 'Let's follow 'em! We're trackin' us some sneaky rabbits here. Lead the way, Pikey!'

Pike didn't appreciate the nickname, Sunny could tell. But he kept it to himself and did as he was told.

Sunny, Beck and twenty-one other weary people traipsed

with heavy feet around the lake. Sunny tried not to think about the sore spot at the back of her heel. The pain was tolerable, if annoying. The ache in her bones and muscles, however, was impossible to ignore. Strung together by wires and clacking wood joints, she'd transformed into a puppet that lurched and tottered. A cartoon zombie. All softness had been leached from her. Beck didn't grumble, but she was sure he'd noticed. No breasts for pillows, no curve to her waist or butt. She had turned into a collection of sharp bones and rangy sinew, her knee and elbow joints the widest parts of her limbs. She wondered if it were possible for a person to disappear completely. To cave in on themselves and vanish like a magic trick.

Posy was enjoying himself, slashing swings at the grass, his poker *whisht*ing in arcs and lopping through the stems. Buried beneath her annoyance at watching him prance around like a gazelle when all she wanted to do was collapse in a sobbing heap, there was a tiny part of her that secretly liked these moments where Posy was free to be himself, a too-big kid with endless reserves of energy. Sunny honestly didn't know where he found them.

They came to the picnic tables and Pike halted at the start of a wooden jetty, standing aside to let Posy by. The kid clomped on to the rotting platform, the pungent smell of it a welcome change to the stench of exhaustion and filth radiating from the people in her company. Sunny closed her eyes against the vicious sunlight. A wave of dizziness swayed through her head, the world tilting first one way then the other. She half expected her feet to lift off the ground.

What would Beck do if I floated away? Drifted up like a balloon without a string, out of reach and out of touch.

He would lose himself, that's what. Like Posy was losing himself, neither of them any good at taking care of themselves. Nor anybody else, for that matter.

Sunny forced her eyes open. The heat was intolerable. Above

her, the sky was a burning fire. Inside her, a furnace pumped out heat. And below her, the sunlight reflected on the rippling water. She turned her face away before her skin could curl up at the corners, a singed piece of paper, igniting at the edges.

Posy was humming loudly, a too-catchy tune that floated merrily across the lake. Some of the others had slumped on to the picnic benches. Jules sat at one, leaning back with elbows propped on the tabletop. Mary stretched herself out along the seat, legs hanging off the end, her head in Jules's lap.

'He's an alphabet po-nee!' Posy sang, humming the words he couldn't remember as he dance-shuffled his way to the end of the platform. 'Mm-mmm-mm. Free to jump and swerve and whirl, free to take on the entire world! Hmm-mm-mmm – hey! He's an alphabet po-neee!'

What looked like a scattered stack of rocks was piled near his feet. He casually bent to pick one up. Sunny imagined it was like warm soap between his hands – and wouldn't that be wonderful, to have a bar of soap? To walk into the crystal-cool lake and lather it up. Scrub every mile they'd walked out of her pores. Scrub and scrub until her skin was pink and gleaming like a bawling newborn's.

Thinking of newborns made her squint out across the glittering water, past Posy, to the small, bobbing bodies. Sunny rubbed the back of her hand over her cracked lips, feeling shaky. Beck had stopped a couple of feet away and she sidled over and reached for his hand, wrapping her fingers around his pinky. He didn't glance at her, didn't even twitch at her touch.

'*Bombs awaaay.*' Posy let the rock fly, and Sunny watched in growing dismay as the stone looped in a tidy arc. It landed slap-bang on top of a bloated child, smacking with a hollow thud.

Posy's behaviour was changing with every passing day, the Other's cruelty leaking into him bit by bit. Sunny was watching the weak, naive kid, the one she and Beck had found in the derelict theatre, the one she had grown reluctantly fond of, slowly disappear. And there wasn't a damn thing she could do about it. Not without endangering herself and Beck.

'Sunk yer battleship!' Posy crowed, hooting a laugh, the small, bobbing child sinking out of sight. He grinned around at her and Beck, at Frank, Pike and Odell, who all stood in the grass at the end of the pier. 'See that? Got it in one!'

His eyes caught on Sunny's face and his smile died a bit and the light in his eyes dimmed. He wiped his hands clean on his shirt and swivelled away, pushing at the last few rocks with his toe, nudging them off the jetty. They *plop*ped into the lake one after the other. Sunny didn't look at Beck, couldn't bring herself to. She was getting used to his complete lack of reaction in the face of such cruelties. If she had too soft a heart, she feared Beck's was disappearing altogether.

You've left it too late, she told herself. He's slipping away.

No. It's not like that. Beck's a good guy, he doesn't want to hurt anyone.

How do you know what he wants? You don't have a single fucking clue what's going on inside his head any more.

Maybe he had more in common with Frank and Pike than he did with her and she was too blind to see it. Beck wasn't a sociable guy. Never had been. He didn't talk to others if he didn't have to, and he didn't speak to her, either, not if the need didn't strike him. That's just the way it was between them. That didn't stop her chatting to him, talking through her thoughts and worries, and he'd always let her, he'd always listened. But she'd been so tired, so out of breath on the occasional breaks permitted, that she hadn't shared more than a handful of words with him in days.

She squeezed Beck's finger, searching for a reaction, *any* reaction – please Lord, just give me something – and there it was. A flicker. A muscle tic. Sunny tightened her grip on him, refusing to let go. Her heart thudded hard, shaking her, the beating muscle far too close to the caged bones of her ribs.

'*Yaaaaaaah!*'

A buck-naked man erupted from the trees and ran at them. He yelled nonsense as he sprinted past an open-mouthed Jules, his penis flopping as he aimed for the pier. He didn't make it on to the first board. Frank tackled his legs, bringing him down in a grunting heap, and his face ended up pressed against the naked guy's ass, the long, narrow line of his cheek smooshing into the fella's butt crack. He jerked away as if scalded and clumsily fell, scrabbled, crawled for the shore, where he scrubbed at his soiled cheek with lake water.

Pike laughed, long and chesty, coughing through most of it. He came and grabbed the buck-naked fella roughly by the neck and dragged him along on his knees to the end of the jetty.

'No!' the fella yelled, stricken, trying to twist around to keep an eye on Frank. 'The lake's a pretty lady! Don't be spreading your diseases in her skirts. Have some decency!' He fell into a mess of mumbles and surprised himself by blurting a cackle.

Posy ambled along the pier and stooped to frown down at him.

'What's goin' on?' Posy asked him.

'Nothing!' the man shouted in his face. 'What's going on with *you*?'

Posy shrugged. 'Nothin'.'

'You're not a picnicker. Nope, definitely not a picnicker. You're not a rambler, neither. Not one of those toads with the warty backs.' The fella dropped his voice to a whisper. 'They like the water.'

Posy's brows drew down quizzically, unable to work out what the heck the fella was saying. 'Toads like water?'

'Noo.' The man laughed. 'I mean, *yes*. They're built for the water, aren't they? But I mean the kids. *They* like the water. Been in there a long time now. They'll be like prunes.' Another laugh.

'Where's your clothes got to?'

116

The naked fella shrugged. 'With the family.'

'That family out there?' Posy hooked a thumb over his shoulder.

The man nodded, trying to keep his face straight, even though Sunny could tell he was dying to giggle. 'Junior and the wife. The girl was a pain in the ass, but she wasn't mine. Had some half-breed nigger's blood in her. Could *not* get her hair to comb straight, no matter how hard I brushed. Chopped it clean off after I got done. It lay like a dead critter on the ground. Could've been a squirrel or a chipmunk.'

Sunny couldn't tear her gaze away from him. He was deeply tanned, the tops of his shoulders covered in dark freckles, as if he'd been running around naked out here, an office monkey gone wild, the trees and rocks his home, this lake his entire universe. His hands and feet were so ingrained with dirt the pigment of his skin had permanently turned brown.

'The baby was mine, before you get to wondering,' he said, and Sunny half went to see if a tiny body floated out there with the others but stopped herself before finishing the turn, feeling sick all over again. 'I liked the name Mabel for her but my stupid bitch of a girlfriend laughed in my face. IN MY FACE.' He burst into a fit of laughter so hard he fell into a coughing fit halfway through it. Pike grimaced and stepped away, as if worried his crazy might be catching.

Wheezing, the naked man spat on the ground and sat there giggling and shaking his head. 'That didn't turn out so well for her, did it? Served her right, the mealy-mouthed cow. Always picking her kids over me.'

Pike's bushy eyebrows came down, crowding in over his nose. 'You drowned your own family.'

All laughter left the naked man's face. He craned round to look up at him. 'What's it to you? They were mine. *My* responsibility. I did what I had to. Shove that in your pipe and smoke it, Charlie Manson.'

117

Pike shoved the man's face away from him, none too gently. 'Crazy fuck. What you want to do with him?' he asked Posy. 'I have me a few suggestions.' He hadn't drawn his knife but Sunny knew it wouldn't be long before he did.

Posy's head cocked to one side. Listened. None of them heard a thing but for the tinkling, watery sounds of Frank, who dripped lake water.

'Hey.' The naked fella looked around at them all. 'You all with those bike-cycling chicks? They just about shit their pants. Lit outta here like their butts were on fire. Can't complain, though – about time my family got themselves some sunlight. The sun's good for 'em. Vitamin D and all that.'

Sunny had gone from being transfixed to being disgusted. She averted her eyes from his earnest, sun-creased expression and found herself staring at Not-Posy, the transformation having happened so quickly she'd missed it.

'They're not far away now,' Not-Posy said to her, to everyone. 'Not far away at all. Take him to the lake,' he told Pike. Frank came forward to help, the front of his wet shirt clinging, his face pink and freshly washed. 'I think it's time he was reunited with his family, don't you?'

The naked man was dragged down to the shore, giggling all the way, as if they were going for a cool, refreshing paddle. He beamed at Sunny as he went by, two of his teeth, front and centre, missing in action. He laughed right up until they shoved his head under the water and held it there. And then there was no more laughter, crazy or otherwise.

CHAPTER 15

Surprises

Albus, Gwen, Rufus and Bruno used dawn's first light to gather firewood and cook breakfast, then they sat in silence as they ate.

As soon as the food was gone, Bruno excused himself and went to his sleeping bag, awkwardly squeezing his frame inside, shuffling around like an oversized caterpillar. Rufus sat on the other side of the fire to Albus, his first-aid kit open beside him, his boots off, socks stuffed inside. His long, bare feet were painted orange by the firelight, his hair volcano red as he bent to tend to a blister on the underside of his big toe. He hummed while he worked, the strains of his melody swirling through the flickering flames, adding ribbons of deep red to the fire. It felt especially cruel to Albus at moments like this, when his gift was so beautiful it hurt, that he would never be able to share it with anyone.

They had stopped at a rest area with a wooden outbuilding housing a two-room washroom: one side for women, the other for men. Each offered a single toilet in the form of a hole that dropped into a cesspit. Albus had tried the faucets in the men's chilly restroom. Not even a dribble of water came out. They had left the facilities behind and retreated to an area past the parking lot, stepping over the slatted tree trunks, cut and laid vertically to mark the parking bays.

'You think he'll be OK?' Gwen nodded to Bruno, who was already snoring. 'He seems more tired than usual.' Finished packing away the dishes and utensils, she sat down beside Albus.

They had come about forty miles and were just outside Howell, having passed through the town the night before. Normally, they would have found a place to stay inside the town's limits – four walls and a roof were preferable to none – but they had come across a street lined with corpses.

Bruno had stared at the hanging bodies, men and women swaying from street lamps, rictus-faced, empty eye sockets, clothes eaten to rags. 'It's like the lynchings all over again,' Bruno had murmured.

'Can't blame folk for wanting to feel safe,' Rufus had said, voice equally low; they were in the middle of a graveyard and no one wanted to wake the dead. 'They watched their best friends stab their mothers, their sisters strangle the kids next door – the ones they'd babysit on Saturday nights. What the hell you gonna do?'

'Not all these folk were guilty of those things. They were only guilty of hearing a voice.'

'One goes hand in hand with the other to a lot of people,' Rufus said, and shrugged. 'Don't look at me like that. I'm just telling you how it is.'

Albus's gaze had skipped along all those dangling feet, one after the other, no two sets of shoes the same, down that endless line of gallows.

They had chosen to walk in the pitch black rather than stay in Howell. Walking at night was a foolish idea, but no one had voted to stay.

In one day and one night, they hadn't covered as many miles as Albus had hoped. Bruno had been holding them back. The only time he'd picked up speed was when they were leaving the street lined with cadavers. It was out of character for him to be so slow. His longer legs could eat up the miles, sometimes too fast for the others to comfortably keep up.

Maybe he was ill.

The thought made Albus's stomach hurt. He didn't want to leave Bruno out here alone, and yet they couldn't delay. That nagging need to hurry had been riding his back since they'd left the Inn, a constant bullying insistence that at times made him want to run on ahead and keep running until his legs burned with hot coals and lava bubbled in his lungs.

'We'll see how he is when he wakes up and go from there.' Gwen's concern was a sombre white glow, like dipped headlights coming over the dark brow of a hill. 'We might have to send him home.'

Albus nodded, his worried eyes resting on the snoring lump of his friend. Even Bruno's snores seemed weary, their tired, rippling browns slumping low to the ground. He couldn't send him home alone, it wouldn't be safe. One of the others would have to go with him.

Maybe that wasn't such a bad idea. Two less people to worry about would be a huge weight off his conscience. Another part of him, though, knew he would need them all, maybe desperately so by the end, and to send them away before he fully understood where and what might happen could be the difference between success and failure. He trusted each of them not only with his life but, more importantly, with his sister's.

But they shouldn't trust you, *should they?* a small voice whispered; not his sister's, his own. *You've never told them the whole truth. The reason why you're hiding them away.*

Rufus was pulling his socks on, done with his ministrations. Albus caught his eye and waved him over.

'What's up, oh silent one?' Not bothering with his boots, Rufus padded to join them and dropped heavily on Albus's other side, bringing the smell of woodsmoke with him. Straight away, he began plucking at the grass beside his knee, methodically shredding the blades to bits.

Albus had already taken out his notebook and rested it on his thighs; now, he used his teeth to tug the leather tongue an extra notch snugger on his wrist brace and pushed his pencil underneath it.

The first word he wrote was: **dangerous.**

'What's dangerous?' Gwen asked. 'Where you're taking us?'

Albus nodded.

'Yeah, right. More dangerous than when we got Amber?' Rufus's smirk didn't have chance to tip into full sarcasm before Albus nodded again.

He underlined the word 'dangerous'. Twice. Then he wrote: **this one different.**

'Different how?' Gwen asked.

no colours to follow.

'That's why you can't give us solid directions?'

He nodded in answer and wrote: **don't know where. not yet. but vitally important we find this girl.**

He underlined the last three words.

'Why? We don't even know who she is.' The grass in Rufus's fingers was forgotten. 'And why us? How are we even gonna find her if you can't see your way to her like you did the rest of us?'

Albus used the pencil to point at Rufus, at Gwen, at Bruno snoring in his sleeping bag, then wrote: **only ones who can. she needs us. my sister will help.**

'So it's a girl. How old? How tall? What's she look like? Does she like cats? Is she a Capricorn? I get on well with Capricorns.' Rufus's mockery masked his anger, and Albus understood. He knew he was asking a lot of them.

Albus swung his head on a slow left to right, unsure how to explain. He returned to his notepad and drew two rudimentary stick figures, one with curly hair and the number **9** beneath her feet. He carefully wrote the name **Addison**. The second shaky figure was taller and had the number **18** below her stick feet. His pencil scratched the name **Lacey**. He considered drawing a third figure, but his sister had referred to the martyr as a girl. And

Alex, the woman in his dream, could never be described as a girl.

Between the drawings of Addison and Lacey, Albus wrote a large question mark.

'You don't know which one we're looking for?' Gwen asked.

Albus shook his head; he seemed to be doing a lot of that.

He reminded them of what his sister had said. **time is short. MUST FIND HER FIRST.**

He looked up to see if he'd impressed the urgency he felt upon them. Gwen was staring at the pad, her eyes flicking rapidly, rereading everything he'd written. Rufus was staring off into space, the firelight in the early-morning dimness deepening the lines of his scowl.

'Who else is looking for her?' Rufus asked quietly.

if Ruby is concerned then they're not good people.

Rufus sprinkled the remaining bits of the grass on to the ground and said nothing more.

'You're confident you'll be able to take us to her?'

When Albus looked at Gwen, she met his eyes squarely. There was no hesitation or doubt in her eyes. She'd asked a straightforward question and wanted a straightforward answer. It made Albus want to hug her. She might have preferred logic but she trusted him more. 'I don't understand how your sister can be leading us?' she said softly, as if unsure she should be asking.

He dropped his gaze as an overwhelming feeling of uncertainty took hold of him. Religion had never offered him much consolation and science had never provided him with the answers he'd needed. The lack of a tongue when he was born had been an anomaly, unexplainable other than as a malfunction in cell growth while he was *in utero*. And his chromesthesia was a unique remapping of the wiring in his brain. All the doctors had been able to tell him was that his differences made him entirely singular, the joint conditions so rare he was effectively one of a kind. But, as inadequate as religion and science were in his case, his sister had always provided. She'd always been there and she'd always known what was best for him. If he had to place his faith in anything or anyone, it would be in her.

He stared at the stump of his hand, at the veins and ligaments that stood out on the back of it. Despite its lack, it was a strong hand; he had made it so, his palm darkly callused from use. When his fingers had been taken, he'd grieved for their loss, and not just in terms of the functionality they'd afforded him. They had been his sole means of communicating with any clarity. He couldn't rely on his speech to be understood (when he'd first found Bruno and been unable to communicate in little more than grunts and monophthongs, Bruno had assumed he was mentally deficient). But with practice and determination, Albus had relearned to use his hands, utilising new techniques to brush his hair and teeth, dress himself, cook, write. His script was messy and painfully slow to write, but it was readable. And that's all that mattered.

'Albus?' Gwen prompted. 'You *can* find her, can't you?'

The pencil's nib moved across the paper, its quiet scrapes the only thing to be heard over the crackles and pops of the campfire and Bruno's intermittent snoring.

i can find her, he wrote, thinking how much easier it was to lie when you didn't have to speak the words aloud.

Birdcalls woke Albus. He found the others already up and moving about. Gwen must have filled Bruno in on what Albus had told them because the big man stood quiet and pensive as Albus approached him.

'We on a blood hunt, Albus? Is that what this is? And you the hound?'

Albus bit his lower lip, wondering if that was the truth of it, right there. Blood and hunting. It sounded so grisly. He put a hand on Bruno's shoulder, felt the strength of him through the thin cotton of his shirt and wanted to squeeze in reassurance but had to make do with a pat. He met Bruno's eyes and nodded, nodded a question really, because Bruno had Bianca, and Bianca had Bruno, and this wasn't like Amber's collection, when Albus had been able to give them details of what they'd find. With this, they were walking into the unknown. With this, there might be no coming back.

Albus wondered if he could live with that.

'I'm with you, brother,' Bruno said, in his deep, tilled-earth voice, as solid as the ground beneath their feet. 'I'm always with you.'

Albus smiled and had to look away from his friend's face, the ache in his throat a pain he couldn't allow to spread. He patted Bruno on the shoulder again, harder than he'd intended. It was like patting a stone.

'But I have a confession to make,' Bruno said.

Albus stopped smiling and brought his eyes back to him.

'I know I've been slowing us down, and I'm sorry. I didn't know what else to do.'

Albus's hand slipped from his friend's shoulder and he turned and began searching the trees.

'If I'd said anything before, it would've only caused problems, and who am I to dictate what someone can and can't do? I'm not anyone's keeper, Albus.'

Albus yelled at the trees, a sound of anger and dismay, because an awful part of him knew where this conversation was leading.

The birds who had been merrily chirping away fell silent.

Gwen and Rufus stopped what they were doing, packs at their feet, surprised by Albus's yell.

'You'd best come on out!' Bruno called.

After a pregnant pause – when Albus hoped Bruno really was sick and would have to be sent home – a crunch came from deeper in the woods. A snap of a twig. Then a second snap, closer.

Rufus swung Tallulah up to his shoulder and took aim. Only to slowly lower it again when Hari tentatively stepped into view.

CHAPTER 16

Birds

The excited buzz coming from the others was bugging the shit out of Sunny. Maybe that was unfair. Maybe some of them felt as rattled as she did. But there were enough wide, astonished smiles to piss her off. She wanted to go over to each of them and give them a good shake, look meaningfully in their eyes and ask if they'd ever seen that scene from *The Wizard of* frigging *Oz* with the flying monkeys, because that was, essentially, what had just happened.

The evidence lay all around. Salt-and-pepper feathers snagged like Indian dream-catchers in the birch and hickory trees, more still netted in the viburnum shrubs. Sunny would be finding feathers in her hair and stashed in her knapsack for days to come, she was sure.

Feathers weren't the only thing the large flock of birds had left behind. There had to have been hawks circling up there, swooping like bomber planes. Various bits of birds had rained down: half a wing, broken and folded; part of a beak, top or bottom, Sunny didn't know which – it resembled a softly curved fingernail painted in pale varnish. A foot had bopped off her shoulder and she'd batted at it in panic, brushing it to the ground, where the severed ligaments pulled the toes tightly closed, the foot curling up like a dying spider. She'd almost screamed at that one.

A few dead birds had bounced off the grass like plump, feathery, dud grenades, and a few opportunistic folk had scooped them up, as industrious as apple pickers scouting under a ripened tree. That's where they were now. Taking a break to cook up and consume the fallen birds, because waste not want not, right?

Sunny knew none of the birds' names except for the magpies (her momma had always insisted she salute them when she spotted them – *Good day, Mr and Mrs Magpie, how's the family?*), but if she squinted she could still see the last of the flock mist across the horizon, a good two hundred strong. A faraway rain-cloud, readying to drench those unlucky enough to be below.

'Where the fuck are they *going*?' she said under her breath. She was sitting on a railway sleeper, the dried, flaking wood hard under her bony rump. She rested a hand on the sun-warmed track next to her hip. Her hands were always so cold these days, nothing seemed to warm them up. It felt good to have the heat from the steel soak into her fingers.

Beck sat opposite her. Still, meditative. She envied his ability to be so calm. 'They can feel the pull,' he told her, eyes cracking open.

'The pull of what?' And here she'd thought the birds must have been fleeing something. What would so many be flying *toward* in such numbers?

'The new world forming.'

A feather had caught in his hair and he reached up to pluck it free. He held it under his nose and Sunny imagined smelling it with him. Fresh air and ozone. The muskiness of wild animals.

'Do *you* feel it?' she asked carefully. 'This new world?'

Beck shrugged. 'Sometimes I think I do. Through him.'

Posy stood apart from the rest, concerned only with the road ahead. He gazed into the distance, his nose high, shoulders back, almost as if he were scenting the air. His posture warned Sunny to stay away. He didn't join them to eat. He didn't eat much of anything any more. He barely slept, drank sparingly. What she'd

127

thought of as the boundless energy of the young had become something darker, more sinister. It was like something other-worldly powered him now.

'What's happening to him?'

Her words were directed at Beck but it was Pike who answered, sitting close enough to overhear. He smacked his lips after sucking on a tiny bird-bone.

'When you got something stronger than you in charge, something up here' – Pike tapped the knobbly end of the small bone (a leg bone, Sunny thought) against the spiral tattoo behind his ear, 'the body doesn't get a look-in. It's on autopilot.'

'Voices don't do that. *Can't* do that.'

Pike snorted, an ugly sound filled with phlegm. 'He's a dummy. Look at him. No surprise he's getting walked all over, is it? A toddler could out-think him.'

'If he's such a dummy, why're you and Frank and the others following along like lapdogs?'

Pike's eyes didn't leave her as he finished licking his bird-bone. He laid it carefully on his knee with the others he'd sucked clean and placed there. 'Because the Other *will* find Red, even if it has to go through Lacey to do it. And when it does, it'll have something the Flitting Man wants. *We'll* have some-thing he wants. And that's a good position to be in, no matter what side of the board you're playing from. I may not look it, but I'm an ambitious man, my dove.'

'You think for one second that thing will share *anything* with you?'

'Oh, it'll share, all right. If it knows what's good for it.'

Sunny tried to stay as calm as Beck, but she wasn't succeeding. She could feel her blood pressure rise. 'You're using Posy. Just like the Other is using him.'

Pike sniffed and hawked up a glob of phlegm. Spat it on the ground, 'Of course we fucking are. That's the sole reason he's here, isn't it? To be used. Only thing he's good for.'

128

Not-Really-Posy – there seemed very little left of the lost young man who would seek Sunny out for company – looked over at them as if intuiting that the discussion centred on him.

Sunny slipped her warmed hand into her pack, fingers digging, eyes not leaving Pike's. The man's foul mouth tipped in a smile.

She pulled a water bottle out and held it aloft. 'Want a drink, Posy?' She said the kid's name deliberately and precisely.

'Sunny,' Beck warned softly. His calm façade had cracked a bit.

'You're playing with fire,' Pike told her.

She turned her attention to Posy, ignoring the hard knocking of her heart.

Not-Really-Posy stared back, his gaze cold and indifferent

'Come sit with me, Posy. Wet your whistle – it's hot out here.'

A blink. A softening to his shoulders that brought a curve to them. His neck loosened. A ripple of confusion passed over the kid's face and he rubbed a fist in his eye, as if he were sleepy after a nap.

Sunny sloshed the bottle. 'Drink, Posy?' she prompted.

He dropped his hand and his eyes lit up when they fell on her. He came over and accepted the bottle, fingers momentarily brushing hers. They were icy. Colder even than hers had been.

'What's goin' on?' Posy asked, squinting around. 'Where are we?'

'About three hours east of the lake. Don't you remember?'

He made a soft *hmm* sound and tilted his head, taking a drink. He lowered the bottle after a long sip and went to screw on the cap, stopped, frowned, then slowly lifted the bottle back to his lips. He tipped it high and guzzled the contents down in three long pulls. Even held the neck over his open mouth and shook the final few droplets on to his tongue.

The empty flask landed with a hollow *clonk* on the sleeper in front of Sunny. When she lifted her eyes, Posy was gone and Not-Posy stood over her, all cutting angles and unblinking eyes.

'Thank you, that hit the spot. Shall we go? The trail is fresh and time's wasting. Plus, you'll want to replenish your water. Or didn't you realise? You're all out.'

CHAPTER 17

Feathery

Albus sat and despaired.

It was a quiet despair, not one that made him pound the floor with his fists or gnash his teeth but one that had him sitting on a log, elbows planted on his knees and palms cradling his temples, staring at the forest floor between his boots. He couldn't think, couldn't decide what to do, couldn't even imagine how Hari had managed to follow them for so long without any of them (other than Bruno) being aware of his presence. Albus's mind was quietly, miserably, *blank*.

The birds that had initially fallen silent at Bruno's shout were now raising their voices again, calling back and forth, holding their own discourse on the matter.

Bruno, Gwen and Rufus stood around Hari, the boy planted in their middle. Gwen was questioning him tirelessly, but Albus suspected she was more upset about not knowing the boy had been following them than by the boy actually being there.

Hari answered in two- or three-word sentences.

Albus couldn't bring himself to look at Hari. Not yet. He feared that, if he did, his distress would show and it would serve only to upset everyone further. No, Albus had to figure out what to do, and fast. He pressed his palms inwards, squeezing his skull hard enough to hurt.

He could leave Hari here. Yes. Find a secluded place behind the rest area and leave enough provisions to see him through the next day or two, until they returned. Of course, this plan assumed that they would be able to come back, and what if they couldn't? Besides, hadn't Hari already followed them once? What would stop him doing so again?

Bruno could accompany the boy home. Albus liked this plan but, again, it brought him back to Hari's determination to follow. His stealth. Not only had he had tracked them for over forty miles, through lonely countryside and dangerous urban landscapes, he had done so without once making any noise that would have alerted Albus to his presence. Not one word, not one sound. There would be nothing to stop Hari leaving Bruno at the first opportunity and coming after them again. Which begged the question, *why* had he come?

Maybe I should send them *all* home, Albus thought. Be done with it and carry on alone.

He rose and made his way toward them, watching his boots flatten the leaves underfoot. There were probably bugs beneath the mulch, each step crushing them to death, whether Albus meant to kill them or not. It didn't stop him walking.

Gwen's questions stalled as Albus approached. He stopped in front of Hari and let his gaze climb, taking in the rumpled, dirty clothes, the bloodied rip in the boy's pants, a missing shirt button near the collar. He passed Hari's tightly pressed lips and reached his eyes. They swam with tears. Albus hardened his heart to them. This was no place for a child.

He frowned at Hari, his mouth downturned, saying as best he could with his expression that he was disappointed he'd put them in such a difficult position.

'I am sorry,' Hari said, his apology a rippling amber wave that stroked at Albus's face, his eyelids, begging him to forgive.

Albus shook his head, not letting up on the frown. *Why are you here?*

132

Hari sniffed, wiped his nose on his sleeve. 'I had to come.'

Albus's jaw clenched. The boy had no clue as to the serious-ness of the situation, how dangerous it would be. What was Albus supposed to *do* with him?

'I have to be here,' Hari said, the rippling amber solidifying, strengthening, as it hardened with resolve. His head tilted up, a stubborn angle coming to his jaw. 'You *need* me.'

Albus's eyebrow raised a notch. *Oh, I do, do I?*

The boy nodded. 'Yes.'

'How're we gonna need you, kid?' Rufus asked. 'You can barely lift your own body weight. What good are you to us?'

Hari turned on Rufus. 'It is not only physical strength that counts, Rufus.'

Gwen snorted, outright grinning when Rufus turned his scowl on her. 'Well, he has a point there,' she said. 'He's already got you beat on mental acuity.'

'What the hell's that supposed to mean?'

'We're too far from home to send him back, Albus,' Bruno said.

I know! Albus wanted to yell. And whose fault was *that*?

He knew Bruno could tell what he was thinking, but his friend didn't back down and didn't make any excuses for his actions.

'Like I said before,' Bruno said, 'I'm not his keeper. If he wants to be here, who are we to stop him?'

'Look at him,' Rufus said. 'He's barely tall enough to reach your chest – he doesn't know what's best for him. He'll get in the way and get one of us hurt.'

'I will not,' Hari said.

Gwen held her hands up. 'Let's just everyone calm down. He's here. He's not going anywhere. Let's just deal with the situation, OK? *OK?*' She said this last to Rufus.

He threw his hands in the air. 'Sure, why the hell not? It's not like anyone ever listens to me anyway. Might as well go talk to this tree over here.' He stalked off and addressed the nearest trunk. 'How's it hanging? What say you and me ditch these losers?'

'God, could you *not* be a dick for one whole day of your life?' Gwen asked him.

'See what I have to put up with?' he told the tree. '"Dick" is always coming out her mouth.'

Albus stopped listening. The birdcalls that had previously been an unobtrusive soundtrack to the discussion now registered in his ears. Disturbed by something, they were loud, alarmed, the woods alive with whistling and chirping and the rustling of small bodies. He lifted his eyes. Bruno and Hari did the same.

Albus swivelled on the spot. A cool blast of wind hit him in the face when he faced west. His eyes watered.

He blinked at what he saw.

His first thought was *swarm* but, no, that wasn't right. They were too big for insects.

A flock so large it stretched as far across the sky as Albus could see, wispy at the far edges where the birds thinned out but black and dense at the centre.

Gwen muttered 'Oh my God', but Albus couldn't tear his eyes away. An almost irresistible urge to run came over him.

The black mass swirled and rolled, vast new shapes forming each time the leading birds darted in a different direction. They were swift creatures, maybe swallows or finches or larks, their abrupt turns so fast it was like watching a black sandstorm loop and spin, the fine grains lifting, dispersing and joining together again in a graceful aerial dance.

'Birds.' Hari's small voice was drowned out, the birdcalls rising to a cacophony, the five of them standing in the middle of a ringing belfry at high noon.

'*Birds.*' And now Albus *did* move, going to the boy, not taking his eyes away from that rolling sea of bodies. The sound of birds' voices was joined by a thunderous flapping of wings, a *thousand* pairs of wings, all snapping together in combined flight.

It formed a continuous, rhythmic hum and, *God*, if Albus listened closely, couldn't he hear words forming in that beating drone? Words rising and falling with the snap of feathers: *pain, flay, burning, madness, death —*

No! he cried, or tried to.

Sun blotted out, the day turned to dusk. A strong wind buffeted Albus as he drew Hari into the protective circle of his arms, cradled the boy's head to his chest and cupped his fingerless palm over Hari's ear so he couldn't hear those terrible, beating words. Feathers ghosted down, floating around them like black ash in the gloom.

Bruno pressed close, his heavy arms wrapping around them both, and then Gwen was there, and Rufus, and they all huddled together while the birds rolled over the top of them. Albus looked up, the wind whipping through his hair, the sky a sea of roiling, jostling bodies, black-bead eyes and sharp beaks. He was sure his heartbeat was thrumming as fast as the birds' tiny, walnut-sized hearts.

With a last buffeting gust of wind, the swarm passed and only the stragglers flapped behind, a few hundred birds too slow or too tired to keep up. Shadow gone, the sun reappeared, warm and bright. The birdcalls settled down to a handful of discordant chirrups. Then they, too, were gone, and the silence that followed rang as oddly as the clamour of birdcalls had a few seconds before.

'What the hell,' Rufus said breathlessly, stepping back. 'What the *hell*.'

Albus dragged his attention away from the flock, which continued its flight east to the sea. Rufus's red hair was windswept, his eyes astonished.

'Albus? What *was* that?'

A piece of Gwen's white-gold hair had fallen across her eyes and he desperately wanted to lift a hand to brush it aside but couldn't bear to touch her with his deformed hand. He looked to Bruno next, and the big man met his eyes, his expression grave.

'I'm not one for portents,' Bruno said, 'but that was some messed-up hoodoo shit.'

Hari still rested against Albus, head tucked down against his chest. Albus cupped the boy's shoulders and gently pushed him away. Hari looked up at him, gave him a shaky nod.

Albus glanced across the blue sky, but already the birds were a misty grey in the distance, a precursor to fog, maybe, or a coastal storm. Whatever the reason behind the birds' strange flight, he hoped it didn't lie at the coast, where the rest of their friends waited.

Hari's eyes were still on him. Albus couldn't read the boy's thoughts, but he thought he understood; Hari was meant to be here, whether Albus liked it or not. He had been set on this path, as surely as Albus had, and there was nothing to be done but see where it led them. Until then, Albus would have to keep Hari safe.

Decision made, he steadfastly ignored the surging doubts that rose up inside him, the constant waves of an ocean, forever churning and dashing themselves on the cliffs.

CHAPTER 18

The Closet

Posy stares at Pike's mouth, squinting a bit because his vision swims in and out, blurring as if he's dunked his head under water. A whittled, pin-sharp bird-bone sticks out from between Pike's decaying teeth. He picks at them. Posy looks away, his stomach churning sickly.

They have reached the intersection where old rusting railroad tracks meet cracked, unused road. A signal box lies stretched out on its side and the crossing barriers are down. The belled stop signal is silent and there are no cars waiting for the red-and-white barriers to rise. Posy makes sure not to step on the gaps between railway track and concrete — *crack, crack, break your mother's back; line, line, break your dad's spine*. His pa was long dead but it was bad luck all the same.

A memory floats up, working its way loose from a place deep down in the murk and the sucking mud. His head is full of silty water, where no sunlight shines and no fishes swim. It's a dark, empty place.

He remembers Red's mouth. Red with no teeth and no hopes of help, not from Posy, not from no one. She told him her real name before her teeth got yanked. Not Red — that was just what she told *them*. She made him promise not to tell and he gave her his word, and she'd believed him. He'd told Sunny, but she didn't count. Sunny was good at keeping secrets. They was buddies.

Are they getting close now? he wonders. Is their game of Hide and Go Seek almost over? He seesaws from Red to Lacey, Lacey to Red, as linked together as a St Christopher pendant is linked to its chain. He's desperate to see them again. And desperate not to, because the Other is so mad. So very mad at Lacey, especially. She should never have come to Vicksburg. It had been a huge mistake.

The Other is so angry at her it's like a constant buzzing in Posy's ears. But the Other burns with need, too. It has questions, *a lot* of questions. They're like marbles clinking into each other and shooting off in all directions. And Red has *all* the answers, yes, sir.

Posy feels like he's been searching for her for ever and a day. Always that extra day, and one more after that. On and on they go and where they'll end no one knows.

The Other swims out of the darkness, deadly as a shark, and it's all Posy can do not to scream.

It speaks through Posy's mouth. 'Red Red Red. You always were soft on her. Soft and stupid.'

Beside him, Pike takes the bird-bone pick out of his rotting mouth and gives Posy the side-eye.

The Other has been quiet most of the day. It's not often it leaves Posy alone for such long periods, but Posy understands that it has lots to do. He knows it watches, watches the girl ahead of them (*Red?* he thinks again, and hopes). The Other tries to cloak this from Posy, but Posy isn't as stupid as it thinks.

But he's been busted now. Caught with his fingers full in the cookie jar, and he's going to pay. Oh yes. He shouldn't have thought about Red, should know better than to mull on such things, because his thoughts aren't his own no more.

He wants to yell that it's *its* fault for leaving him alone for so long. How can he help what thoughts pop into his head when he's left all on his own?

'But then you always were weak,' it says, a black loathing eating its way into Posy's mouth. 'Always snivelling in the dirt when things go wrong. Never willing to take the blame or fix your mistakes. Well, whose fault was it Red got away? When are you going to admit it was *you* and your stupidity that landed us here?'

Posy shrinks into the back corner of his mind, tucking himself into the lightless cupboard and kicking the door shut. Safe in the boxed four walls. Except his closet doesn't feel safe no more, does it? Feels like a prison, where he sits captive, trapped, with nowhere to go, as the Other looms larger and larger, its voice booming from the other side of the door, reverberating through the walls.

'When will you admit that *every single thing* that's gone wrong traces back to *you* leaving that fucking door open?'

'I didn't mean nothin' by it,' Posy whimpers. 'I only went to fetch her somethin' to eat.'

'And didn't lock the door!' the Other yells. 'You let Red *out*! She got out and she ran right into Lacey, and that . . . that *man*. You don't even know who he is, do you?' When Posy doesn't answer fast enough, it screams, '*Do you?*' The closet walls shake.

'*No!*' he cries, scuttling around to jam the bottoms of both feet against the door.

'She went and found the Agur, you stupid, useless *maggot!*' The Other breaks Posy's voice on that word. Spit flies. 'If you hadn't let her out, she'd have never found him *or* Lacey and they'd have never found their way to us. I wouldn't be scrabbling round for my rightful place right now; we'd still have Red and I wouldn't be stuck here with you and this pathetic ragtag group of nobodies. I should leave you to the mercy of these swine. Wouldn't that be fun? Do you think they'd be as nice to you as I am? As protective as I have been? You know what I think? I think they'd rip you apart before you even had a chance to open your mouth.'

All at once, Posy's bladder lets go and a hot spurt of urine soaks the front of his pants.

The Other turns to the men and women who are staring at Posy in uneasy revulsion, fear alive in their eyes. Sunny is there, too, and Posy wants to cover himself, doesn't want her seeing him like this, with piss in his pants and spit on his chin. His heart breaks because she looks so small. So small and so fragile, even though she has her . . . What was his name? Brick? Why can't he remember stuff no more? His thoughts are muddled and confused, tangled more than normal. Beck! That's it.

Posy *likes* Sunny, he's always liked her. Ranking his favourite people ever, it went his ma, Miss Woodhall from kindergarten, Princess his dog, Red, Lacey and Sunny. Sunny has never once called him names. Never once stared at him as if he were a waste of skin and air. It's been hard having the Other always shouting at him, telling him he's stupid, making him feel like he's lower than snake's pee. Sometimes, all it took was a smile from Sunny to raise his spirits. Didn't take much. Small things meant the world.

But Posy can't help her. No no no. He can't help no one. Not even himself. Not any more. He wants to say he's sorry, that she should leave and not look back and not worry about him, but he doesn't want her to go because then he'll be alone. Alone with the Other. It's speaking again, moving his mouth, the words pouring out not Posy's words, never Posy's.

'Look at the one you follow!' It waves Posy's hand at his wet crotch and Posy realises he has two wet crotches – one in the outside world, where all these people can see, and one in his cramped little closet. 'Look at how shameful he is! You want to tear him apart, don't you? I *know* you do. I can see it in your filthy little eyes. Who would like to try? Anyone? You?' It points at Frank, who stands still, his gaze cold and unblinking. 'I've seen how you look at him when you think he isn't watching. You'd like to rip his whiny throat out, wouldn't you?

Be warned. If you rip it out, maybe I'll come for you next. Or you.' It points at Odell. 'Or *you*.' It points at Sunny, and Posy stiffens and thinks, *No! Leave her alone!*

'Oh, I'll come for her,' the Other says. 'I'll find a way inside all their heads, even if I have to kill a thousand of them to do it. Do you hear me? I'll—'

The Other is drowned out. Another voice roars so loudly in Posy's head that he grabs his hair in shock, clutches it in fists. A megaphone is pressed to his ear and words bellow through it.

DON'T LET THE PRIEST GET THE GUN! NO, WATCH OUT!

A thousand firecrackers explode in Posy's head. A strangled gurgle squeezes from his throat.

STOP HIM! NO! TELL HIM TO STOP!

Posy falls to his knees, the roar battering the insides of his skull, needles jabbing, piercing, puncturing deep, *deeper*. He claws out clumps of his hair.

DON'T! PLEASE DON'T! DON'T SHOOT US—

A cannon goes off, and Posy and the Other scream together, jerking stiff. The agony – a pain so bright it chokes them – splits them in two, slicing Posy clean down the middle. Half of him falls away into darkness, the half that holds him fast to this earth, and the other half spirals off into madness.

CHAPTER 19

Run

Howling. A banshee's shrieking that froze Sunny's blood. Posy was on his knees, howling with fury, the sound an avalanche that wanted to bury everyone in its path. She didn't understand what was happening, didn't *want* to understand, not if the understanding of it meant she'd be sent tumbling over a precipice and into the same madness Posy was thrashing around in.

Two men ran, simply turned tail and bolted, their exhausted legs finding a new burst of energy, and Sunny would be doing the same if she hadn't been rooted to the spot, if Posy's face weren't so contorted with pain and terror. Beck was close enough for her to feel him flinch and recoil. He lifted both hands to his head, palms pressing over his temples.

Posy had stopped in the middle of the railroad's intersection, tracks running under his knees, passing through as if they were tributaries on their way to a larger organism. His body arched backward, spine bowing, his face tilting past the sky and almost meeting the road again. He screamed at the heavens and Sunny heard his throat rupture, the scream splitting in two.

Most of the men retreated a few steps. Beck bumped into her, not looking where he was going. Jules was too transfixed to move on her own and Mary grabbed her hand and pulled her back. Behind Sunny, the crossing barrier creaked as people pressed into it.

Posy's body wrenched forward again, and he struck at the road, fists smashing down, over and over, dashing his balled hands into the concrete. Blood splattered the track and the white safety markings of the crossing, a red so vibrant it didn't appear real. Sunny could feel the incandescent fury powering his actions, the unarticulated rage that had peeled away the final layers of his control. And, beneath it, a shivering vulnerability, a glimpse of something that could almost be called fear.

She gasped as an invisible hand yanked Posy up, hoisting him to his feet, and her knapsack jammed into her spine; she didn't remember backing into the barrier.

A sharp corner jabbed at her lower back.

The journal.

She'd been carrying it since Gonzo Dan, and it weighed heavier than her water bottle, her Leatherman multitool, her waterproof jacket, her Clif bars (a secret stash no one knew about) and her flashlight combined. She might not fully grasp the end-all purpose to Not-Posy's need to hunt down these girls, but Sunny had the awful feeling that Lacey's name would be the last one written in that goddamned book.

Posy staggered on baby-giraffe legs, tottering around to face them. She felt the others shift restlessly, their inability to tear their eyes from the horror in front of them warring with their instincts to flee. Beck was a hot, jittery presence at her side.

Posy panted.

Sweat dripped from his face.

Blood dripped from his knuckles.

Mary and Jules ducked beneath the barrier, and a few others chanced retreating further from the thing that glared out of Posy's face. Odell was one of them. Odell, who was twice the size of Posy and could brain him with one dinner-plate-sized hand if he'd wanted.

Sunny stayed where she was, corralled inside the railroad crossing. The power in that space equalled anything that had once run through the disused railway lines. Hot, raw kinetic power. The screeching call of an oncoming train, the thundering vibration beneath the ground, both paled in comparison to what breathed and shook through Posy's body.

'Our time is up.' Not-Posy's voice was hellishly creaky. 'Something has happened. Something has been *done* to her. No more dawdling. No more playing catch-up. You want your reward? You want to gain his favour? Then you *run*.' And whatever was in Posy's eyes (in *Not*-Posy's eyes, Sunny corrected herself, because she wasn't sure the kid Posy would ever be coming back) scattered the men and women around her, jolted them into action, and they stumbled into a canter, *all* of them, Sunny included, even though she didn't believe she *could* run, but Beck was with her and he was running, too, and she wouldn't leave him, not now, not after everything.

Posy followed on their heels like a cattle-master, whipping them onwards, shouting in his cracked, scream-ravaged voice. They ran after the flock of birds that had long since disappeared. They ran with the setting sun at their backs.

They ran.

CHAPTER 20

A New Plan

Since the birds had flown past, an eerie hush had fallen. All the birdcalls had dried up and not even the buzz of insects disturbed the quiet. The only sounds came from Albus's and his friends' footsteps, the skittering of bricks when one of their boots kicked at the loose gravel and the whispered chafing and creaking of their packs and equipment. The surrounding silence lent each scuffed step an isolated, empty quality.

Between one footfall and the next, a step no different from any other, Albus was struck with the same black exhaustion that had forced him to crawl under the bushes all those weeks ago and dream of Amber. It came out of nowhere, a weighty mantle settling over his shoulders, buckling him at the knees. His eyes rolled in their sockets. He veered off the road and sank to the grass, quickly lowering himself flat to his stomach before he collapsed. His pack crushed him into the soil, the smell tickling his nose, but it was a good weight; it anchored him even as his head grew light and his brain clouded with fog. A disturbing rushing sound came upon him, like birds' wings, thousands of them, all beating into his head.

He dimly heard his name called. A cool pool of shadows fell over his face but already he was gone.

★ ★ ★

The sky was a deep, dark red. It crackled and hummed like something colossal and alive. It hung low over Albus's head, its static throbbing powerfully through his blood. He stood in a cornfield, tall stalks hemming him in on all sides.

Corn and the red sky, and an old train track, half buried beneath the soil, railway sleepers showing in patches, and that was all. It led away from him and he followed it, pushing his way through the stalks, stepping carefully over the steel rails. The sleepers stopped dead as he came out into a perfect, cropped circle, a flattened carpet of threshed stems spiralling out from its centre.

At the far edges of the circular clearing, crude wooden stakes, as wide as a person and as tall as two, had been hammered into the earth. Corn stalks leaned in, crowding the stake's hanging occupants on either side. Albus's breaths grew shorter and shorter, his lungs shrinking with panic. Horror pulled at his mouth and widened his eyes.

On the first stake hung Gwen. Her arms were nailed to the beam above her. Her head was bowed, face obscured by her beautiful hair, long, blonde strands hanging loose and dyed red by the sky.

He called her name, the syllable sounding out on a long, wretched moan.

Beside her, on another stake, Rufus's upper body curved over itself, his shoulders rounded, arms hanging down, his copper-haired head dangling low. He was pinned by multiple nails punctured through his sternum, ribs and abdomen. A large black stain soaked the front of his shirt and pants and a dark ring of blood marked the corn at the stake's base.

Next came Bruno. He'd been slashed open from throat to groin, his innards slopped out into a steaming, glistening pile at his feet. It eerily mimicked the wound Bruno had given Amber's attacker. He had opened that man up with a knife, his guts spilling out, feet skating through the entrails. Now Bruno had been gutted, emptied and hollowed out.

'No no no . . .'

A woman. Striking. Her naked torso bearing old scars, criss-crossing her breasts, stomach and sides. An obscene black nail impaled her through the throat. A thin thread of blood had trickled down from the piercing, bisecting her chest, ribs, the flat plane of her stomach, before vanishing into the curling thatch of hair at her groin. It took him a moment to recognise her. Alex. The woman who had stood guard outside the bicycle store.

The young girl was there, too, her dark corkscrew curls brushing her cheeks. Addison hung on the stake next to Alex, as if sleeping. No visible marks indicated where, or even if, she'd been skewered. She was slender and delicate, like Hari.

Hari.

Albus's body thrummed in tandem with the sky's static beat, his hairs standing on end, vibrating like tiny dowsing rods.

He turned his head.

Lacey.

She had been fastened to the stake by her head and hands. The corn at the base, as well as the wood itself, was blackened and cracked. Burnt. Her skull was pierced through the forehead above her right eye so that her head was up and her eyes open and levelled on him. Even dead, she exuded a stubborn kind of strength, as if even being crucified couldn't stop her. She so reminded him of his sister.

Her eyes seemed to follow him as he made one last turn and found him.

There was nothing of Hari but his head. It, too, had been pinned through the forehead, his neck trailing veins and the white bones of his vertebrae. The rest of Hari was nowhere to be found.

'Please,' Albus whispered. 'Please, no.'

'*Albus.*'

He stiffened.

Albus.

And it was on the repeat of his name that he realised he wasn't hearing the voice with his ears – he could hear it too easily over the terrible, buzzing hum of the red sky above him. It had come from within.

A rustle of movement had him spinning around. His sister stepped into the clearing, the corn stalks parting to let her pass and closing behind her. She looked exactly as she had the last time he'd seen her; too thin, her dark eyes sad and knowing. Even the wry twist of her lips was the same, as if she could read his thoughts and found them amusing. He wanted to run to her, embrace her, but when he tried to lift his feet they wouldn't move. Two black railway nails were driven through his boots, pinning him to the ground. There was no pain, but he wasn't going anywhere.

His sister stopped with her back to the young, slender girl, the one with the pretty corkscrew curls. She looked at no one but him, seemingly unaware of the death and mutilation on display all around them. Her lips moved and, in the dark corner of his head, her voice came to him.

Albus, you must hurry. Time is very short. It's drawing closer to her.

'*What* is?' he asked, once again not questioning his ability to speak. It was a dream, after all. 'Are you in danger?'

His sister came toward him, stopping agonisingly close, almost close enough for him to reach out and touch. Her head cocked to one side as she studied his face. Her lips moved but, again, no sound came from them.

He is destruction and madness and he wants his place. Like we all do. But he is scared. Which means he will burn the world to get what he wants.

As if hearing her, the sky thrummed louder, its static bursts coalescing, recognisable sounds emerging from the electrical pulses, each one sending tremors of fear down Albus's spine.

Madness.

Burning.

Slaughter.

He was shouting now to be heard over the din. 'But how do I find her? I don't even know where you are, or how far!'

Trust your senses, Albus, and watch for the colours, just like always. As for how to get to her faster, ask him. Her eyes slid past him, to where Hari's head was nailed to the stake. A pinch of a frown came and went on her face. *He'll find a way.*

Unwillingly, Albus's head twisted, too. The boy's dead eyes watched them, accusing.

'What's going to happen to my friends?' He turned back to his sister. He hadn't seen or felt her approach, but her hand was lifting. She placed a silencing finger over his lips. It was cold – *too* cold – and, as much as he'd craved her touch, had longed for it, now he wished it gone.

That's not for you to know. It is their fate, just as mine is mine and yours is your own. We're all part of this plan, Albus. Just like Jonah told me. She smiled, and it was an ancient smile, older than the world, older than time. It frightened him. He leaned away from her and her cold finger left his lips.

A fork of red lightning lit up the clearing, painting friends and strangers alike in the same awful scarlet light. The shadows became blackly dense, making the flash of electric red all the brighter. Thunder crashed so loud it shook the earth. Albus flinched and ducked down, crying out as it rumbled over the top of him, a god beating his drum.

Another red flash, cracking like a lash.

More rolling thunder.

The earth shuddered, the corn stalks quaked, rustling like a million rattlesnakes, and the wooden stakes quivered in their holes, working their way loose from the hard-packed soil. Rufus's stake toppled first, tipping in slow motion. It met the ground as another clap of thunder struck and, on impact, his torso ripped free from the beam. Albus groaned at the lumps of flesh left nailed to the post, while the rest of Rufus heaped on to the floor.

Bruno dropped next, his stake crashing down, the flattened corn crunching. Then came Alex's, hitting a second later, and Albus saw more scars crossing her back, from shoulders to rump.

A third flash of blinding red light. Hot ozone singed the hairs in his nostrils.

The ground lurched violently on a huge crash of thunder and he threw himself flat, impaled feet wrenching painlessly free, twisting awkwardly beneath him. He covered his head, his long, keening cry lost under the rumbling of the sky and the static buzz and the shaking corn. He didn't see the other stakes fall in turn but he felt them, the earth jumping beneath him.

Something made him look up – instinct, perhaps – in time to see Hari's pinned head jar loose and thump to the ground. A misshapen ball, it bounced toward him, skipping and bumping over the carpet of stalks, end over end – a flash of dark hair, staring eyes, a slack mouth, a glimpse of a hanging and half-bitten tongue, rolling to hair once again. It tumbled its way on a perfect trajectory with Albus's face – closer, closer, looming large. Albus screamed . . .

and the scream followed him into the waking world.

He lashed out at Gwen, knocking her hand aside, shoving himself up and away from her. Sunlight. A breeze. Fresh air and the scent of woodland. He checked his feet, surprised to see they were free of railway nails. He dropped on to his butt, unable to stop his breaths sobbing out. He stared at his friends' worried faces in some panic, knowing he must look crazy and not knowing how to stop.

'Albus.' Bruno's eyes were filled with concern. 'You all right?'

Albus's head automatically bobbed up and down, but the expressions on his friends' faces didn't change. He wasn't being very convincing. He swallowed down his next sob and let his breath out carefully. His hands were shaking badly. He pressed them hard against the tops of his thighs.

'Dude, you fainted,' Rufus said.

'Except it was less like a faint and more like you lay down and went to sleep.' Gwen knelt and lifted her hand, tentatively, palm outward to show it was empty. When he didn't lash out again, she placed her warm hand on his shoulder, rubbed it a bit. Surprisingly, it helped. 'What's going on? What happened?'

Breaths coming easier now, his trembling abating, he still found it difficult to meet their eyes. Each time he did, he flashed back to their bodies dangling and mutilated on stakes. He shivered, despite the heat. Gwen's hand rubbed his shoulder some more.

Hari pushed between Bruno and Rufus and held something out. A pencil. Not lifting his eyes to the boy's face, Albus accepted it.

'He must have room,' Hari murmured, tugging on Bruno and Rufus, making them back up. At the soothing, golden tones of Hari's voice, Albus's shivering drew back, retreating to his core, where it could tremble unobserved.

Gwen didn't retreat. She reached for Albus's pack, taking the stowed notebook from its zipped compartment and handing it to him. He missed the comforting warmth of her hand on his shoulder but took the notebook without comment. He was relieved to see it didn't shake too visibly in his hands.

Where they were, the grass was sparse, growing in small green shoots, the loose dirt holding the imprint of their boots. The ground was hard and unyielding under his rump. He was grateful for the discomfort. He looked at the pencil's lead tip and saw himself jab the sharp point into his thigh, deep into the muscle, the burst of pain detonating in red bursts behind his eyes. He didn't know why the temptation to hurt himself was so strong and didn't want to dwell on it.

Taking a deep, calming breath, he secured the pencil under his wrist brace and began writing as quickly as he could. By the time he was done, Bruno, Hari and Rufus had joined Gwen in kneeling on the hard ground around him.

'They were the same ones?' Gwen said, reading what he'd scrawled. (His script was messier than usual.) 'Lacey, Addison, Alex. The ones from your bike dream? It was definitely them?' She pulled a face, as if realising what she'd said. A dream shouldn't be more than that.

Albus nodded. He hadn't explained how he'd seen them all nailed up on stakes, only that they had been in the clearing with him. He wrote: **the same 3 strangers. one is the martyr we need to help.**

'Which one was it?' asked Rufus. 'Your vision tell you that while you were taking a nap?'

Albus shook his head. There had been no further clues as to her identity. The martyr was a girl, that was all he knew. They had all been hanging from stakes. Any one of them could be a martyr.

'You realise "martyr" has some pretty shitty implications to it, right? All the martyrs I heard about in school ended up dead. And not in nice ways.'

No one said anything. They were all thinking the same thing.

'What do the red skies mean?' Bruno asked.

Carefully, with one palm, Albus pushed the used paper up and folded it over. He moved the pencil's nib over the clean sheet, his writing shaky but readable.

danger maybe. like a storm's coming. Those had been Hari's words on the beach, but the boy didn't speak up and Albus didn't elaborate. He didn't mention how immense the sky had felt in his dream, how terrifying. And he certainly didn't mention the words he'd heard bursting from its depths.

'Danger how?' Gwen said.

Albus shook his head impatiently. He couldn't explain what

the red skies might mean, or why thousands of birds were migrating in bizarre mass groupings. They needed to find a way to his sister, and *now*. She had said their time was running out. All these questions were slowing them down.

He wrote: **need to move faster. ideas?**

Gwen allowed him to change the subject, but Albus noted the slight frown, the dissatisfaction pulling at the corners of her lips. There would be further discussion on this, they said, but she would let it lie for now. 'A car would be the first choice,' she said. 'But finding one in working order will be tough. And finding fuel for it even tougher.'

'I didn't see any healthy-looking cars in Howell,' Rufus said. 'Everything in that dump was dead or falling apart.'

A heavy silence fell over them, ideas turning and being dismissed in the same breath. Albus's eyes fell on Hari. He'd been silent while Albus had written up the details of his dream. But here it was, the reason why the boy had been able to track them for so many miles. Here was the reason Hari felt he needed to be here. He would find a way. That's what Ruby had said.

He pointed the pencil at Hari's chest and gently tapped it over his heart.

You know, that tap said.

Hari's eyebrows quirked; he was puzzled at being singled out, and Albus saw Hari in the clearing of his dream, his sightless eyes pinning Albus in place as surely as his decapitated head was pinned to the stake. Albus's throat closed up and he thrust the image away with a fierceness that wrenched him. He gave the boy's chest another tap with the pencil.

You.

Hari shook his head, stopped, bit his lip. 'I . . . think there was something,' he said cautiously. 'There was so little time to look – it was all I could do to keep you in sight. But I think that . . . perhaps . . . I saw something that could help.'

While Hari explained and the rest listened Albus calculated

the risk involved in putting Hari's plan into action. A lot would be riding on it, more than Albus suspected any of them realised, and he couldn't bring himself to think about what would happen if any of their calculations were wrong.

PART TWO

Catching the Scent

Chapter 1

Devil's Hill

On first sight, everyone thought Mica and Arun were twins when, actually, Mica was a whole eleven months and seven days older. That was a full year's difference between his fifteen to Arun's fourteen. Which, technically, made him the leader. His brother didn't think that made Mica the leader of anything, even though Mica had way better ideas and knew way more stuff, but anyway, they weren't twins and they didn't always have to do everything together. Mica had no interest in building sandcastles, like Hari and Arun. Sandcastles were for babies. He had better things to do. Like gathering weapons and supplies for when the war came. Rufus said it was best to be prepared. *Keep on your toes*, he said. *Keep your wits sharp.*

'What kind of prepared?' Mica had asked when it first came up.

Arun was bouncing the elastic-band ball they'd made against the wall of the Inn, which was pretty annoying, but Rufus didn't seem to mind, so Mica kept his mouth shut.

'Like keeping watch for people who got no business hanging around here,' Rufus explained. 'Snooping in our business. That kind of prepared.'

Mica was making notes. He jotted down 'strangers/snooping'. 'How often should we be checking for this stuff?'

Rufus had scowled at that and, for a second, Mica was worried he'd annoyed him by asking too many questions. But nope, Rufus was mulling over his answer.

'Every day, I'd say. And don't be lazy about it. Check for anything out of the ordinary – any movement on the roads, smoke in the distance. Watch the sea, too. The road isn't the only way to get to us.' He'd idly scratched at his cheek, scraping at his reddish-coloured whiskers. Mica had been shaving for months but the hair above his lip continued to grow back soft and downy. It was embarrassing. 'I'll leave you my binoculars. Be sure to check three times a day: morning, noon and sunset. Go up to Devil's Hill, where I showed you, and look all round. Do 360 degrees, like the face of a clock. Make sure to pause at every hour. Can see for miles up there. But, remember, if *you* can see for miles, then . . .' Rufus snagged the elastic-band ball out of the air before Arun could catch it. 'Other people—'

'—can probably see us, too,' the brothers intoned together.

'Exactly. Don't get spotted. And *don't* let anyone follow you back to the Inn, or else you're in for a Rufus Special.' He held up what he called his Knuckle Sandwich Deluxe with Extra Cheddar, which was really just a clenched fist that he said he would feed to them if they ever screwed up. It made Mica grin. There were nicks and scars on Rufus's hands from the fights and scuffles and setting-to's he'd had. Mica wanted hands like that when he grew up. Fighter's hands. He bet no one ever messed with Rufus.

It had been two full days since Rufus, Albus and the others had left. Mica sat on the top of Devil's Hill with his green camouflage jacket zipped up and its hood pulled over his head, even though it felt like sitting in a cookpot full of boiling water. Sweat dribbled down his neck and pooled in the moist heat under his armpits. He wanted to squirm and rub the tickles away, but he didn't. It was important to keep still when you were on lookout duty.

The first 360-degree check had been completed, the binoculars put safely back in their protective hard case and set aside. He lifted the sheaf of papers he'd brought with him. They were all of different sizes, some lined, others plain, ranging in colour from white to cream, blue to green, pink to red. Some had decorated edging. Others had personalised watermarks. Many pages had perforated edges and a few had holes punched into them, ready to insert into binders. Some letters were in envelopes. Some notes had been scribbled on to the pages of magazines and catalogues, pages ripped from books, on anything a person could find to write down their thoughts. The collection of notes belonged to Rufus and he'd handed the bulging folder to Mica for safe-keeping before he'd left, instructing him not to look unless he could handle it. There was some scary shit inside, Rufus told him. Strictly not for pussies.

Mica had counted the notes: 279.

Taking a handful, he weighted the rest down with the heavy binoculars case. The last thing he wanted to do was chase sheaves of paper across the hilltop if the wind decided to snatch them up.

His lips unconsciously moved as he began to silently read.

it hurt my friend. it put him in hospital and now my only option is to do what it says so that they dont hurt noe one else. i dont want to see a doctor becuase if i take drugs and i cant hear the voice then they will hurt my friends becuase im not doing what it asks. even tho i cant here. i am so scared. nowhere is safe.

Mica quickly tucked the page under his leg and moved on to the next.

I am mostly sad. Angry. Happy, I almost ended my life a few hours ago. I tried 5 times. The 6th will be the charm. I seen shadows, full sized of an animal or a person, in the corners of the room. I hear screaming sometimes when he tells me horrible things. He forces me to listen as he describes my own death over an over in my head. When I close my eyes he is waiting for me.

Mica glanced around the hilltop, trying to pretend like he was doing his duty by checking and not because something cold and squirmy had slid its way through his guts. Not because he'd felt eyes on the back of his neck.

A solitary tree, leafless, grey and dead by the looks, was the only other thing up here with him. It had been struck by lightning. A big crack had been opened up under one of the branches, big enough to fit his head inside. Not big enough to hide a person, though. Mica stared at it for a while and then got scared someone might be sneaking up on him from the other direction and quickly twisted to check.

The tree and him, and that was it. The hilltop was as deserted and quiet as when he'd arrived.

'Stop being a wuss, Mica,' he muttered.

He went back to the notes.

It's right. Been right all along. Got no job, no money, the kids hate me I can see it in their eyes.

I'm sorry. I'm sorry. I love you all. I tried to be kind. I tried but it made no difference. I'm no good. I'm sorry. God bless you. I'm going home.

The next sheaf was a single notepad page full of neatly printed writing. Mica had the intention of only skimming over it but, once he began reading, he couldn't stop.

my theory is these voices may be nano-computers,

injected into us at birth. I am, I think, I process, I hear. They are.

My voice gathers information and gives me a heads up, even when I don't like what it says. I believe my voice is telepathic across the collective voice. Family members, my boyfriend, do not hear voices. That's what he says, but I don't believe them. They are all liars. It told me so. We don't like liars, do we?

Mica's heartbeat was loud in his ears, amplified in the enclosed space of his hood. He began paging through the notes, eyes flicking across the writing.

the controlling voice is named Baxial . . . he tells me to kill other people now . . . i don't know what to do, the only way to stop it is to stop myself.

. . . we need to accept that it's God or his holy spirit trying to help us. It's telling us to let go and Be Free . . .

medicine can't help this. nothing can. only a bullet. we need to learn to stop lying to ourselves. we need to deal with the fact this is not going away.

Have you heard the stories yet? Of a man who knows all our hiding places? He comes in the night, if you believe the tales. He finds you in your sleep and, with a whisper, steals you away.

The other day I overheard my sister laughing and talking with someone, except no one was in the room with her. She told me she wanted to walk into the sea and swim and swim and never come back. Maybe I should let her.

Does anyone feel torture? Severe pressure on the side of my head, i heard one nearby: i just want her to pop a vein! I thought and still do: why would anyone try to hurt us so bad, you know? I figured they want us to hurt until we can hurt no more.

Mica shoved his hood off and gasped. Sweat dripped off his jaw, his nose. His head was a pressure cooker of heat and too many rushing thoughts. He put the last sheet down. Unable to stand the thought of them touching his leg, he grabbed the pages and shoved them back in the folder, snapped the elastic band around it and shoved the whole lot away from him. Stared at it as if it had sunk its teeth into him for no good reason. Rufus and his CTB collection. Mica wished he'd had no part in it.

'Catching the Bus,' Rufus explained when Mica had asked what it meant. Rufus said it was surprising how many people felt a compulsion to write down their final thoughts. Mica didn't know why he'd want to collect them. It seemed such an invasion, to read these people's innermost feelings. Like he and Rufus had crept into their bedrooms while they were out and pawed through their underwear drawers, checked under their mattresses for their secret stash of porn and then read through their journals for good measure.

He used the front of his jacket to dry his face. Took a deep breath. Picked the binoculars case up, took the binoculars out, and began his last 360 degrees of the afternoon. He was a good mile and half from the Inn. From this distance, it looked like the kind of white plastic model you could buy from a gift store. He got as far as the end of Riverrun Street and his heart, which hadn't had chance to slow down its galloping, gave him a hard thump.

Two men. Rucksacks, boots, what looked like maps in their hands. Too far away to be sure. Mica watched them as they walked sixty yards off-road, kicking their way into a field to investigate the overturned gas tanker stretched out on its side. It had tipped over so many years ago its white lettering had faded to illegibility and the cylinder of its fuel tank had reddened with rust. Mica and his brother called the place the TEXACO field.

The two men appeared to be talking. One pointed to the map, used the same finger to point along the road leading north-west, away from the Inn.

'Yeah,' Mica murmured. 'Go that way. Nothing of interest here. Nothing but a big-ass hill and a tree with a hole in it that wouldn't even fit your head.'

Mica tried not to breathe, as if the two men could spot the rise and fall of his shoulders, even from this distance. His head pounded. If they started to come this way, he would drop and belly-crawl to the other side of the dead tree, jump up and scramble down the hill, run all the way back to the Inn to warn the others. He could do it in fifteen minutes if he sprinted.

The second man swivelled, looking in every direction, pausing when he faced Devil's Hill. A hand rose, cupped over his brow, shading his eyes.

Mica stilled, wanting desperately to duck flat against the dry grass, pull his hood up over his head and hunker down until the men had gone. But he didn't budge. Not even when a droplet of sweat tickled maddeningly down the nape of his neck. He heard Rufus's lecture: 'Don't forget that glass reflects, and your binoculars have lenses, right? If the sun catches them wrong, they'll flash your position to anyone who's looking. It's why snipers fit hoods to their scopes.'

The sun was hot on Mica's head, but he couldn't tell its position without moving to look, and he wouldn't move, not even to lower the binoculars. Movement drew the eye.

The man dropped his hand, turned and spoke to his

companion. They consulted the map for minutes that felt like hours and, discussion over, folded it back up. They trudged out of the TEXACO field and turned left, taking the north-west road, leading away from Devil's Hill and the Inn.

A sharp pain over Mica's eye made him realise he'd been pressing the binoculars' cups hard into his brow. With the men's backs turned, he lowered the binoculars and rubbed at the dent in his forehead.

When he was *very* sure the men weren't going to turn around to look, he slumped back on the grass, arms flung wide. He squinted up at the sky, the sun a hot, shining ball, glaring down on him.

Too close, he thought. That was way, *way*, too close.

CHAPTER 2

The Inn

The coastal heat and humidity suited Cloris's bones, but it did nothing for her constitution. When she wasn't sweating she was waiting to sweat and when she was cool it was but a momentary phase, soon to be followed by a hot flush and perspiration-dampened clothes. She had given up on reapplying her make-up at midday for two reasons: first, it was a pointless endeavour in light of the afternoon climb in temperature and, second, she didn't have the make-up to spare. Her powder foundation was down to a pale, narrow ring in her compact, and her mascara had begun to clump on to her eyelashes, as it was prone to do when the contents was either dangerously low or it had dried out.

Even with the sun dipping behind the roof of the Inn, the evening was humid and aglow with warm light. Cloris was kneeling in the vegetable garden, digging up carrots for supper. She dreaded the moment she'd have to climb to her feet, her knee joints unoiled, her muscles dried and flaking and clogged with old blood. She would choose to kneel on her creaky, ancient knees rather than bend over the vegetable basket with her bad back any day. It hurt like the devil. Rufus insisted it was old age, but Cloris was convinced it was the ovarian cancer. Her mother had died of it, for one, as had her older sister, June, who'd been only two years older than Cloris was now when she'd been diagnosed. Cloris also believed she had the cancer because, after surviving a mass depopulation of the planet, *of course* it would be the cancer that finished her off. Although many things were defunct and dead, irony would never be one of them.

A groan escaped her when she levered herself to her feet, one hand on her thigh, bent over like a hunchbacked witch. She quickly cleared the wince from her face, feeling each and every wrinkle score deeper between her brows and in the crow-feet around her eyes.

She plucked a lemon from one of their plants as she stepped out of the garden. A slice in a glass of water after dinner was just what the doctor ordered. Closing the chicken-wire gate behind her and making doubly sure it was secure (she would *not* be chewed out for leaving it open again by that harpy-mouthed strumpet), she limped her way around the woodpile stacked along the south side of the Inn, followed the head-height, white-pillared railing of the rear veranda and worked her way up the steps, one hand sliding higher on the rail as she climbed. She sighed when she reached the top, the claw of pain at the base of her back easing a mite as she readjusted the basket on her hip.

The boys' voices were raucously loud in the front hall, and Cloris bypassed them in favour of crossing the reception, slipping into the office behind the counter and out into the hallway that led to the kitchen. She had expected to find Bianca there and paused in the kitchen's doorway when she found the room empty. Tutting, she went to the kitchen worktop and placed the basketful of vegetables there. Moving to the window, she absently knuckled her lower back.

Outside, the view was as breath-taking as ever – lush grass, glittering gold sands, the darkest blue ocean meeting an indigo-blue sky – but Cloris didn't see it. She checked her reflection in the window's glass, fluffed her bangs and rubbed the pads of her fingertips under her eyes in an attempt to smooth out the bags.

The window was open to let in the fresh ocean air, and with it came a burble of baby sounds. Cloris tiptoed, her calves protesting at the stretch, and peered out on to the patch of grass outside the window. There, Bianca sat, her legs splayed, at right angles to Amber. One side of her face gleamed where the sun touched her, as if gold had been sprinkled into the dark pigment of her skin. Cloris used to pay $50 for a 50ml tub of tinted moisturiser that did the same.

Jasper was perched in the space between the open V of Bianca's thighs, his little hands gripping on to the woman's wrists, pink, chubby fingers pale next to Bianca's skin. He 'helped' as Bianca threaded her fingers through an intricate design of threaded strands held between Amber's hands.

Cat's Cradle.

Cloris hadn't played Cat's Cradle since she was a child.

Finished threading, Bianca lifted the strands and Amber carefully removed her hands. The webbed design collapsed inward, and Cloris felt disappointment. Her heels dropped to the floor. A puff of a sigh left her. She almost missed when Bianca drew the strands taut and the thread pulled tight into a new arrangement of perfect lines.

Cloris sucked in a breath. She was sure she hadn't made a sound, but Bianca's head came up, her eyes finding her.

Cloris stepped back, quickly, guiltily, and she reprimanded herself for being a foolish old woman even as hurried over to the counter and began busily emptying the basket of vegetables.

She was muttering to herself when she became aware of someone in the room with her. Inside the door that led into the utility room, Amber stood quietly, hands clasped in front of her, eyes down, waiting to speak.

'Yes?' Cloris said, perhaps more sharply than she intended.

The girl glanced up, met Cloris's eyes, flashed away to look at the window where Cloris had stood, and then fell on the vegetables and clods of earth spread across the worktop. 'Bianca asked if you would like to join us?' Amber said.

'Well, that's very kind of her, I'm sure, but I have quite enough to do here before joining in with any children's games, thank you very much.'

Amber hesitated, blinked a few times and looked as if she might say something more, which would have flabbergasted Cloris because, quite frankly, the girl had the conversation skills of a potted plant. Jasper was the only normal child in this household, and he wasn't even one yet. As for Hari, he was far too introspective for Cloris's liking. Amber was withdrawn, but it was a closed quietness, nothing secretive about it – she preferred her own company, that was all. Hari's quietness was filled with thoughts and ponderings, his eyes jumping from person to person, not wanting to miss a thing. He was engaged, despite his shyness. Mica and Arun – well, those two reprobates made enough noise for all the children put together. When they weren't horsing around, they were in the process of following behind Rufus like two bounding puppies. Rufus was a reprobate of another sort, just an older, more seasoned variety. She was glad to have him out of her hair.

Amber hadn't moved.

'Was there something else, dear?'

The girl shook her head quickly, spun around, her summer dress kicking high to reveal a long, skinny thigh, and disappeared through the door.

Cloris went back to muttering as she continued to sort the vegetables. 'Must think we have all the time in the world to prepare supper for six mouths to feed. I mean, really. Maybe the next time I haven't slaved for half an hour in the vegetable patch, digging and sweating and—'

'What's this about sweating and slaving, woman?'

Cloris's mouth snapped shut. Her face went hot. Bianca

didn't stand in doorways like Amber but marched straight into the kitchen and scooped up two heads of lettuce, plucked a carving knife from the block in the middle of the island and deftly began chopping. The clunk of the blade on the block made Cloris's back throb.

'You'll be pleased to know I closed the garden gate behind me,' Cloris said tartly, and where *that* came from she didn't know. Her face flamed hotter.

'I am pleased, yes,' Bianca replied, scraping the knife across the chopping board and swiping the lettuce into a waiting salad bowl. The efficient, skilled way she prepared meals riled Cloris.

'Where's Jasper?' Cloris asked, attempting to steer the conversation back on to safer, more controllable terrain.

'Outside with Amber. She's making him a daisy chain. Though I reckon he'd rather eat them than wear them.'

Cloris opened her mouth, set on informing her that daisies were most certainly *not* an edible food group for babies.

'She's not going to let him eat the flowers, Cloris. Good Lord, she's not a fool.' And there was a slight smile on the woman's lips, which was plainly patronising.

Cloris changed what she about to say. 'Of course she isn't. That would be irresponsible and she's . . . she's . . .'

'Responsible?' Bianca said.

Now Cloris was sure she was mocking her, but the woman placed the knife down, popped her hip and placed a closed fist on it.

'What?' Cloris finally said, not liking the defensiveness in her tone. She hated how this confounded woman made her feel. Like a stuttering schoolgirl on her first day of class. Never before in her life had she ever met someone who could make her feel quite so inadequate and do so with such ease. Not even Cloris's husband's throwaway comments ('That dress reveals a little too much of your legs, darling'; 'I think that shade of red would better suit a woman with a heartier complexion'; and 'What *have* you done to your hair, sweetheart? It's for a woman ten years your junior. I'm only being truthful. You'd rather I be honest than let you go out like that, wouldn't you?') affected her like this woman's did.

'You ever think we're doing the right thing by staying here?'

Cloris frowned, moved the now-empty basket aside and brushed her hands off. She propped her own hands on her hips, only realising the mirroring of their postures after she'd done it. She refused to alter her stance, though. It would make it obvious.

'I have no idea what you mean.'

'Us, staying here, like homemakers, while Bruno and Albus go marching off on some mission to God knows where, getting into God knows what trouble.'

'You'd have rather gone with them?' she asked. The last thing she'd want was to gallivant off across the state. It was much safer here.

'That's not what I meant. Only I . . .' Bianca sighed, lowered her gaze and, for the first time, Cloris witnessed uncertainty cloud the woman's expression. There were no wrinkles on Bianca's face; her skin was buttermilk smooth. 'Only I wish I knew what they were getting themselves into. All these dreams and cryptic messages. Are we meant to blindly follow? Shouldn't we be questioning them a little more?'

'It's how Albus found us.' Cloris felt unbalanced, unsure of where this conversation was leading. She found herself plumping her hair, scrunching it up at the back to give it more volume, and had to make a conscious effort to lower her hand.

'Was it? How do we know we weren't just "found"? Maybe they came across us by pure accident and this whole colour–sound malarkey is just that. A bunch of bull.'

'What about Amber and Jasper? They were very specific.'

'A tree in a field. A street near some fairground. I could say,

"Oh, Cloris, if you go north a ways, you'll come to a red car, and near that red car you'll find someone who's in need of help." I mean, come on. *Everyone* needs help these days.'

'Bruno believes him.'

'So does Gwen, which is a miracle in itself. I thought that girl had more sense. Now, my Bruno's senses get all mixed up when it conflicts with his loyalties. It's the only time he and I ever have cross words. And how can I get irate about that? Loyalty is a fine trait in any man. But jeez,' she huffed, 'sometimes I think everyone in this place is cross-eyed crazy or as near as damn to it to not make much difference.'

Cloris didn't miss the backhanded criticism there but was more of a mind to find out what Bianca was scratching at here. 'Then why let them go? Why let any of them go without saying all this? You're not one to keep your mouth shut.'

Bianca smiled, eyes narrowing, and there was that sass, that superior smirk of hers, except perhaps it wasn't quite as superior as Cloris had always thought.

'Because what if I'm wrong?' Bianca said. 'What if Albus knows *exactly* what he's doing and there's someone out there who desperately needs our help? Do I want to be the one to question and doubt and be the reason for that person getting hurt? No, I do not. I don't want someone else's life on my conscience. And yet . . . I don't want to see any of ours hurt either. So all I can do is trust in God and hope they'll come home safe. That's all any of us can do. It's just, sometimes' – she paused to give Cloris a shrewd look, the kind you might give a card-playing opponent right after you got dealt your first hand – 'sometimes, we adults, we share our misgivings so that we can be offered reassurance. You know what I mean?'

Cloris was speechless for a moment, not having expected this woman to come to her for words of comfort. She nodded. 'Yes, I see. I have no doubts about Albus. He knows what he's doing, dear, even if it makes little sense to the likes of us. "There are more things in heaven and earth, Horatio." Have you heard that before? It's Shakespeare.'

Bianca smiled. 'I know it's Shakespeare.' She said nothing more and Cloris didn't know if that was because she took hope in what Cloris had said or because she didn't see any point in discussing it further. They went back to preparing supper (the children's bellies would soon bring them to the kitchen to seek out their dinner), and, for once, Cloris didn't even feel much like complaining when Bianca began singing one of her sweary hip-hoppy songs. Even Cloris could admit – in private, to herself – that Bianca had a beautiful singing voice.

CHAPTER 3

Library Reserve Unit

Albus stared across the empty parking lot. A fine rain was falling, turning the asphalt into a large black mirror. Puddles had formed, each a different colour to the next, reflecting the dusk sky: peach, cerise, indigo and, down the right-hand side, a scattering of pools swathed with sunlit gold.

Rufus addressed Hari, not looking at him. 'Man, I can't believe *this* was your bright idea.'

From the corner of Albus's eye, he saw the boy shrug.

At the far end of the lot, a fence separated them from the low, squat building of the Library Reserve Unit. It was little more than a series of interconnected prefabricated trailers, all on the same level, all fallen into ruin. Hari had told them he'd seen garages at the rear and a line of gas pumps, the old kind with the flipping analogue dials.

'We're a line of sitting ducks out here,' Gwen said. 'Let's go.' She broke away, falling into an easy jog, boots splashing down in the sky-painted puddles. Albus heard Rufus curse under his breath, and then they were all following.

They had made excellent time (the lingering stitch in Albus's side was testament to how fast they'd moved) and had re-entered Howell a little over an hour after deciding to double back.

With every mile east they travelled, Albus fretted. To turn

his back on his sister, on the girl they needed to help, and put extra distance between him and them was far harder than he'd anticipated. An inescapable feeling of betrayal had dogged his every step and, even worse, a sense of impending disaster.

As they ran from silent street to silent street, Albus had found himself glancing up at the sky, expecting to see the same black mass of birds circling overhead, circling *them*, as if they were carrion soon to fall, and the dark tide would descend to enclose them in a whirling vortex of wings and snapping beaks. Of course, there were no signs of any birds – they were long gone. There were no signs of anybody, human *or* beast. Not unless you counted the desiccated corpses that were more dust than skin.

The long street with the hanging bodies lay six or seven blocks further east. They came across two smashed buses at an intersection – the mummified passengers were slumped over seat-backs and draped across the floor – and a whole line of blown-out residential houses, as if a gas main had leaked and the whole street had imploded. Most of the bricks and houses' contents, including burnt sofas, obliterated TV sets, bookcases, tables and kitchen appliances, clothing and shoes, as well as an assortment of decayed body parts, were scattered across the sidewalk and yards opposite. Albus and the others had to pick their way through, navigating it like an assault course.

There had been one false alarm, the smashing of glass sending them scurrying for cover, calling out to each other to keep close, to close ranks. Albus had run with one hand on Hari's shoulder, guiding him away from the open street, shielding him with his body. Seeing how Rufus and Gwen moved to cover them with their weapons, taking up flanking positions, ready to take whatever action was necessary to protect those they cared for, left Albus feeling more useless than he cared to admit. He removed his hand from Hari's shoulder as soon as the danger was past.

At the rusting gates of the Library Reserve Unit, Gwen

leaped the last puddle and was halted by a locked bolt. She removed her pack and dropped to her belly, pushing it ahead of her as she scuttled under the gap at the gate's bottom. By turns, they each dropped and squirmed after her. There was a worrying moment when Albus didn't think Bruno would fit, but then he was through and all five of them were jogging up the drive.

The library unit hulked on their right, its cracked windows dark and shielded. Vines grew around mouldy window frames and trailed from the roof's guttering.

They came out into a large square yard hemmed in by three brick-built garages. Each had a large corrugated-metal door, the kind that ran on a rolling winch mechanism. Two of the garage doors were already open. Inside, the parking bays were empty but for a pile of leaves and litter collected against the back walls.

'I knew it,' Rufus said, coming to a stop in front of one of the empty garages. 'It's already been worked over. There's nothing here.'

Albus spotted the gas pumps along the western side of the yard, an island of three archaic-looking self-pumpers. They didn't look in particularly good condition.

'There's still one left to check.' Gwen pointed to the garage with its closed door, its contents, whatever they were, hidden away inside. 'Why don't you and Bruno go inspect the gas pumps? We'll go see what's in that last garage.'

Albus was thinking this had been a mistake. Hari had said he'd seen the garages and pumps, and that was all. He'd never claimed to have seen anything else. Albus wondered why the hell he hadn't questioned the boy more thoroughly, but of course he knew why. Ruby had told him Hari would know what to do, and he had believed her. He'd put his faith in a dream and a thirteen-year-old boy. And now here they were, further away from where they needed to be than ever. A gnawing panic swarmed his chest, making it hard to breathe.

'Albus, come,' Hari whispered.

175

Bruno and Rufus had already started toward the pumps. Gwen was heading for the closed garage. By the time he and Hari caught up to her, she was at a blue reinforced metal door, ineffectively tugging at its handle and lifting up on to her toes to run her fingers along its top edge then down over its hinges, as if just by the feel she could work out why it wasn't opening.

Albus could tell her why. It was locked.

'Something is in here.'

Hari stood in front of the roller-shutter door. His hands were flat on the corrugated metal, as if he were divining what was behind it.

'It is in there, Albus,' Hari told him. 'I *feel* it.'

'Look.'

Gwen was pointing across the yard to the rear of the library unit. The sliding door, where vehicles and couriers had once pulled up to load and unload book stock, was half open.

'The garage keys are probably inside,' she said.

Before he even had time to question the idea, Gwen had whistled a low tone across the yard.

Rufus's head came up.

She pointed to the open door at the rear of the building, indicating their intention to enter. The sun had almost sunk from sight, leaving only the last few splashes of gold streaked across the wet blacktop, but Albus could make out Rufus's acknowledging nod, and then they were on the move.

CHAPTER 4

In the Dark

There is no saving Posy, he knows it as surely as he knows the dark is out to get him. He had bolted the lock on his closet door when the shouty voice blew through his head (DON'T! PLEASE DON'T! *DON'T SHOOT*). The bolt hadn't been there before.

The flashlight he holds in a death grip grows murkier and murkier the longer he sits. Crap-bastard batteries are dying. He stares at the dim spot on the ceiling above his head, and it's not more than a few measly feet away but it's still too far to reach. He can't stand to get to it because his legs won't work.

Beyond the closet walls, as thick as a safe's, as thick as a sub-marine's, through that dim circle of light, he sees the world as the Other sees it (passed through eyes that were once Posy's eyes – *Posy's*, not the Other's. *His*), and he wants to cry in frustration, but he won't. Crying only ever got him more punches. More kicks. He didn't want to be punched and kicked no more.

Posy rocks the flashlight left to right and the vision pans left to right on the ceiling. It tilts and dips, the sea-sloshing roll upsetting Posy's stomach, but he doesn't look away. The light from that distant world comforts him. As long as the flashlight's batteries last. Without the outside world, without the light, his fear will come alive and eat him up. He can feel it, a worm with teeth, slithering nearby, brushing past his ankles in the dark.

He focuses on the faraway land beyond the closet's ceiling, doesn't take his eyes from it. If he strains, he can see the men running, the flares of sunlight, the faded blacktop under their clip-clopping boots. If he listens real close, he can make out the panting breaths, the hacking coughs, the groans. What Posy can't do is escape. He is crammed into the closet, which is much smaller than he remembers. Much, *much* smaller. So small the walls brush his shoulders on either side, so small his knees are drawn up to fit. The door he bolted shut is gone. There is no window. Only his flashlight and that small circle of murky light, shining out on the world.

He cranes his neck, his head jammed against the wall, even though it hurts real bad. He keeps his eyes on the stained yellow glow because if it blinks out, he's done for.

As if sensing his fear, that squirming worm takes a bite out of his guts and the darkness grows a shade dimmer. He whines quietly. Shakes the flashlight. Whispers a prayer made up of a jumble of words that sound like magic to him, and the light flickers, dims, steadies and stays on.

He breathes and whines and breathes some more until his heart becomes his buddy again.

My heart, *my* heart. It's still my heart.

Is it?

The thought is too big for him and he lets it go.

The only presence Posy can sense clearly is the Other. Its screams shake the walls. The closet lurches when it lifts the sharp poker in Posy's hand to strike the men and women across shoulders and hips, driving them on. The men with guns – Frank included – are near to Posy, because he hears their shouts, hears them threatening bullets to legs and feet if they don't keep going, faster, *faster*. Odell is long gone. Posy hasn't glimpsed him for hours. He was too heavy and lumbering to keep up. Like a hippo trying to match his pace to a cheetah's.

They have lost other people, too.

Posy watched a dark-skinned man with a silver streak through his hair collapse in the road. He couldn't get up, no matter how many times he tried. The Other pounded the poker down on top of him, but it made no difference. His legs had turned to noodles, and no one can walk on noodles. Pound, pound, pound, but he didn't get up.

Another man, nameless and unknown to Posy, refused to go any further and stood his ground, through exhaustion, or foolishness, or because he was plain old nuts. And even when the Other had threatened him, had explained that disloyalty would not go unpunished, the man still didn't budge, and so Pike had stepped up behind him and wordlessly sliced his throat. A thin nick, but not a thin amount of blood. Posy had thought his flashlight had burned out, and he'd cried in alarm, but it was the river of spurting blood that had darkened his vision, and it cleared again when the Other wiped it carelessly from Posy's face.

Another man, who they'd picked up from one of the checkpoints, wrenched his ankle so badly Posy heard the *snap* all the way in the back of his closet. That guy got left behind, screaming and blubbering in a ditch two of his buddies dragged him into, out of sight of the road.

The Other doesn't speak to Posy no more. It's like Posy isn't a person, not alive and not dead, not anything to anyone, and likely never was. Posy tried calling out, but the walls of the closet had shrunk ever tighter, cramming him into his corner until he shut up. He tried asking who or what had done that shouting, the shout that had exploded like firecrackers in his brain, but he was met with a darkening pressure that smothered him into silence. He bawled and snivelled for a while, begging for more light, for more batteries, *anything*, please, he'll be quiet if he just has light, pleasepleaseplease. But he got nothing.

The Other is busy elsewhere. Distant, separate. It has done a good job of imprisoning Posy. He is the trapped rat he heard in the drywall when he was a kid. He knew it was trapped because it ran up and down and never went nowhere else. For a whole week it ran and scratched to be let out, until it couldn't scratch or run no more. Then it was dead, like Posy's gonna be dead. Like everything ends up dead if they're trapped and can't get out.

To while away the time, Posy listens to the Other talk at someone. And he doesn't mean a *person* someone. It is inside-talking, like the Other used to do to him. A one-way line of communication that sends out the same message over and over, and, although it's not easy to pick up, Posy can catch a word here and there if he presses his ear to the closet wall. The Other is commanding them to stay where they are, not to hurt the girl further, to hold position. Not to let anyone leave.

Posy listens for a while and then can't stop himself from asking.

'What happened to her? Who you talkin' at?'

The Other lashes out, and the pain is a wildfire, searing the backs of Posy's eyeballs, boiling his brains. He writhes in agony, shuddering against the vice-like walls until, finally, after an age, the pain switches off and the Other leaves him, gasping and alone.

After that, Posy doesn't try to listen no more, or to talk. He keeps his thoughts to himself.

He concentrates on the things he's been having trouble re-membering over the past few days. Things that are getting buried deep in the sucking sludge. Things he doesn't want to forget.

Red had been a prisoner, like Posy is a prisoner. She'd told him that he didn't have to stay somewhere he wasn't happy, that he had the power to pick his own path, if only he were brave enough. Dumont and Doc's gang didn't have to be his forever home. He needed to stay strong and be ready for when his time came (and she'd been right about that, hadn't she? Look at him now. A leader of his *own* gang).

But you're not really the leader, are you, Posy? her gentle voice seems to say. *Maybe the time to pick your own path has passed. Maybe this is where you'll be for ever, in this tiny closet, in the dark, with the squirming worms and their teeth.*

That frightens him, so he shuts it out and carries on concentrating on the nice things, about how she would sometimes read to him, or make up stories. Like the story about the brother and sister who'd been left in the desert, far from any road, and the cunning, hungry vulture. It had been a scary story and Posy hadn't wanted to hear it – later, when he left her for the night, he would need to walk through the unlit hallways of the high school they were staying in and find his way back to his blanket – but Red had taken his hand and kept talking, promising him it was a story worth listening to.

The brother, suspicious of the vulture's motives (for two dead bodies could feed a bird of the vulture's size for many, many days), told the creature he'd heard astonishing stories of a vulture's speed, and would such a noble bird prove to him how fast it could fly? Only a small demonstration, so he could tell everyone what remarkable birds vultures truly were and that they were far from the dirty, corpse-eating buzzards they were famous for being.

The vulture was a proud creature and had always aspired to be something more than a devourer of the dead, so it agreed and asked the brother to name the terms. The brother suggested the bird fly to the nearest road and back, for that distance would surely attest to its speed. The vulture readily hopped into the air and, with a strong flap of its wings, flew away in a cloud of desert dust.

Soon, it returned, and indeed it had flown very fast. The brother and sister were genuinely impressed and told the bird so. The vulture preened at their praise. The brother promised that they would tell everyone of the vulture's feat and soon the news would spread that vultures were accomplished birds of flight and not simply the carrion-eaters they were renowned for being. He turned away from the vulture, taking his sister's hand, and walked in the direction the bird had flown, having learned from the vulture's choice where the road, and their salvation, lay.

'The vulture let them go,' Red had told Posy, 'and do you know why?'

Posy had shaken his head.

'Because it had gained something more precious than a meal in its belly. It had gained admiration and respect. And to a creature that is given so little of either, those things filled it up far more than food ever could.'

Posy liked the story but hadn't been able to hide his concern for the brother and sister. Red had smiled, her eyes slipping to her hands, which were clasped together, fingers locked, and told him that they had made it safely back to the road and to a lone man who offered them water and food. It was a good ending, she assured him.

If he'd ever dared ask anyone else to read him a story, they would've taken his books and ripped them to shreds, or else told him to shove off. So he made sure to take his books, the last lot stolen from a dead man, and asked only nice people.

Like Lacey.

She'd been as nice as Red. Read to him for a long time, too. She and Red were smart like that. Much smarter than him. Posy can't even write his own name. But they were secretive, and they hid things. Lacey had sneaked into their camp with her new buddy, the man whose books he'd stolen (and that's what you get for stealing, even from someone you think's dead). He'd locked Posy in a janitor's closet.

Lacey stood up for you when the dead man threatened you, didn't she? the imaginary Red in his head gently interjects. *She left you with a flashlight when he wanted to lock you up in a windowless closet exactly like this one. And isn't that why you're not in the dark now? Because of the kindness she showed you?*

Yes, he thinks. She did do those things. She is kind. Like Red is kind.

And she certainly showed you more kindness than the Other is showing you now, making you sit here in the darkness, all by yourself.

That's true, too. Why *was* he being punished? He hadn't done nothin' wrong.

He wonders if he'll see Red soon, wonders if she'll be in the place the Other is taking them to. Posy sees her in his head, waiting for him, smiling, all her teeth present and correct. Red will help him, for sure. Red is good.

And Lacey will be there, with her rifle. She can do some shooting. They'll be one big happy family.

His attention is brought back to the bobbing light on the ceiling. Through the murky hole, he sees they have reached the brow of a hill. It is sunset. The sky is lit up with cotton-candy pinks, oranges, purples. The men and women have stopped. Some are bent over, clutching their knees, backs heaving. Others have collapsed and lie like gawping fishes, mouths going *pock-pock-pock*.

Posy tries to catch a glimpse of Sunny, but he can't see her. That's OK, he's not worried. He knows Beck's near, and Sunny won't go nowhere without Beck.

A light drizzle falls, wetting the grass and turning the dust on the road grey. Posy imagines he can hear it pattering on the roof of his closet, a soothing ticking that brings a sense of home he hasn't felt in years. It makes him sad. Sad enough to cry. But he holds it in. He's not a baby.

Below, no more than a dozen miles away, lying in a hazy mist of rain, is the town where the Other's prey hides. Norwich, someone had called it.

Red, Lacey, here we come. Ready or not.

In the dark, surrounded by the ticking raindrops, Posy smiles.

CHAPTER 5

Rats

Gwen told Hari and Albus to take out their flashlights. She was tempted to ask Albus to stay outside with the kid, but three sets of eyes were better than one, and the sooner they were in and out of this place, the sooner they could go after Albus's sister and this girl he was so hot on finding.

If Gwen was honest, she was simply glad to be doing *something*. The thought of setting up home and washing clothes and planting vegetables like Bianca, or spending a whole morning mooning over her jewellery collection like Cloris, filled Gwen with a slow-creeping dread. She had been in the Junior Reserve Officers' Training Corps, the JROTC, in high school and had had dreams of joining the army when she left, but that had gone down the shitter pretty quickly after everyone made like a dodo and exited stage left. She admitted that a huge dollop of curiosity about Albus's sister was motivating her, too. Ruby was an enigma, a mysterious question mark that hung over their heads. Gwen knew so little about the woman yet felt like she'd been an intrinsic part of her life for the past ten months.

Albus had slid the band of his headlamp over his forehead and Gwen stepped nearer to switch it on for him, ensuring it was set to its brightest setting. She adjusted the elasticated band a little.

'Comfy?' she asked.

He nodded and smiled his thanks.

She tucked an errant strand of his hair away from his eyes, realised what she'd done and stepped back. She turned away, her hand going for her Beretta. She pulled the gun from its holster, making sure the safety was off, and slipped through the sliding doors of the Library Reserve Unit.

The stench of mildew and damp was strong, undercut by a vegetative smell, like wet grass and moulding leaves. None of it hid the musky scent of animals or the sharp bite of fresh scat. A small amount of ambient light filtered through the narrow, ceiling-level windows, revealing a clear area of floor space. Bookshelves blocked the rest of her view. Raising her flashlight's beam, she followed the dead strip lighting along the ceiling to the left, five lots of them, a metre each, with a metre gap between. The strip lighting disappeared around a corner to the left, the stacks continuing further back into the building.

'We're looking for a key box.' She kept her voice low, practically a whisper. Who knew what was in here? 'Or any sort of locked cabinet where keys might be kept.'

A corridor between the first two rows of shelves branched off to her left and she took it. She heard Hari and Albus follow. She swung her flashlight as she walked, working it into each gap of shelving, and it wasn't until she was halfway down the corridor that she realised that none of the gaps was large enough for a person to squeeze through. At the end-cap of each shelving bay was a wheel, like a trucker's steering wheel, complete with Brodie knob, or suicide knob, an independently rotating grip which allowed you to spin the wheel one-handed. When she glanced at the ground, she spotted tracks running along the dusty floor.

Rolling stacks.

Gwen clamped the flashlight between her side and gun-arm and grabbed hold of the knob with her free hand. She spun the wheel, hard. With a shrill, grating squeal, the bay juddered about two inches to the right and then stuck fast.

'They *move*,' Hari whispered in awe.

She yanked again, but other than a shudder and a quick skitter of bricks and falling masonry, the shelving unit didn't budge. She shone her light through the small gap she'd made, but there was nothing to see except fusty, mouldering books.

Leaving the stacks alone, she continued on. As she reached the end of the corridor, she glanced upwards, eyes skipping to where a fluorescent strip light disappeared around the bend. Leading with her gun-arm, she edged around the corner, flash-light cleaving a white beam through the gloom.

Back here, the ceiling had caved in. Half the standing shelves had tipped over, a line of old drunken men resting on the next, the far one lodged against a wall. Above them, through a hole in the roof, a lighter patch of sky showed through, backlighting the downpour. A running tap of rainwater trickled down the side of a bookcase to soak into a cascade of books scattered across the peeling linoleum. The books were a papier-mâché mush, a sculpture that could have been titled *The Bookish Swamp of Existence* by some hoity-toity artist and categorised as 'abstract expressionism'. As a quirky addition to the freestyle artwork, a rat crouched on top of the soggy pile, its red, glowing eyes fastened on the new arrivals.

She *hated* rats. Hated their sharp, yellow teeth. Hated their pink, worm-like tails. They were dirty, disease-infested, nasty things.

The rat opened its mouth, flashing its needle-teeth, and let out a wincingly high squeal. Gwen's teeth clamped tight and she aimed her gun at its head. The wet brown of its fur was matted down. It looked disturbingly like human hair.

Something touched her arm and she almost screamed. Hari's small fingers rested on her forearm but she spared them only a glance – to look away from the rat for more than a second was unthinkable.

'Don't shoot,' he whispered.

Gwen lowered the gun by a fraction. Not because of Hari – she didn't give a rat's ass, bullet riddled or not, if she shot the vile creature – but because to waste a bullet on it would be stupid. And noisy. She turned away from the collapsed section of the library, feeling Hari's hand drop from her arm, and went right, circling back around.

She checked on Albus to make sure he was keeping up (the man was so quiet, sometimes it was easy to forget he was there), but he was right behind Hari, his head swinging left and right, the bluish LED of his headlamp sweeping the dark.

They came to a doorway, this one missing a door. Gwen found it on the floor inside, a sign reading 'Staff Room' nailed to it. Chairs and coffee tables were overturned and shunted into corners, the floor was littered with dirty newspapers and supplements, and everything was covered in clumps of plaster and a thick layer of masonry dust. A poster of a bikini-clad girl on a Triumph motorcycle hung valiantly from its final corner, the model's skin blemished green with damp. A small nook of a kitchen led off the room. A refrigerator lay on its side. Both its compartment doors were open, and a second rat sat with its back to them, its rope-like tail trailing over the lip of the refrigerator door.

'Rats are taking over the world,' she muttered.

The rat turned at the sound of her voice. Without a single warning squeal, unlike his little pal, it leaped off the refrigerator and darted at her.

She may have squealed herself, then, and stumbled back, bumping into Hari, who grunted at the impact. There were no thoughts of shooting the rat – her gun hung forgotten in her hand – her mind blank with shock as the furry ball of teeth and claws scurried across the room. It moved so *fast*. It jumped, launching itself at her leg, its wickedly sharp teeth opening wide.

Albus's foot met it, punting it out of the air, sending it sailing.

The rat squealed for the first time, the sound abruptly cut off when it thudded into the staff-room wall.

Gwen gasped for breath. Adrenaline fizzed through her system; she felt like she was hopped up on stimulants. 'Jesus Christ. Did you *see* that? Fucking kamikaze rat.'

Hari started laughing. Not loudly, more of a breathless huffing. He was leaning up against the shelving bay where she'd pushed him, holding on to his stomach as if trying to contain his amusement. Gwen couldn't remember ever seeing him laugh. Couldn't remember seeing him smile, for that matter. Not properly.

'What's so funny?' she asked, a smile coming unbidden to her lips. 'It would've *eaten* me if Albus hadn't karate-kicked it out the air.' The kid leaned over and his shoulders jumped, his breathy laughter turning into chortles.

She glanced at Albus and found him grinning. He met her eyes and lifted his eyebrows.

It's a Christmas miracle! she imagined him saying.

She laughed.

Hari settled down pretty quickly and stood upright, his arms dropping from his middle. His smile was almost gone, but there was still a gleam in his eyes.

'We'd best keep looking,' Gwen said. 'Thanks for saving me, Albus. You're my hero.'

Albus smiled and bowed his head.

Gwen spotted another flicker of a smile pass over Hari's face.

She led them down the aisle, away from the staff room, heading back to where they'd entered. She spoke over her shoulder: 'And don't go telling Rufus I freaked out over a rat.' She'd never hear the end of it. 'Else I'll karate-kick *your* asses.'

CHAPTER 6

Keys

Any pleasure Albus had gained from seeing Hari laugh had packed its bags and departed, the passage of time now dragging at him like stacked chains around his neck.

They had spent twenty minutes searching the unit for keys and come up empty-handed. Bruno found him to report that Rufus thought he could get the pumps working, and that they'd found a payload of stored diesel in the underground hold.

It won't be good for anything if we can't get into that garage, Albus wanted to tell him.

Albus, Hari and Bruno continued the search in the unit's office, riffling through desk drawers and filing cabinets. It was a large place; Albus had counted sixteen desks and six cabinets, and was elbow-deep in the stationery cabinet when Gwen shouted.

'I found something! Bruno!'

They found her in the rolling stacks, the same ones she'd attempted to move earlier. She had her shoulder and arm jammed into the small space but was struggling to shove them further apart.

'I *see* something. Bruno, I need your muscles.'

She moved aside and let Bruno take her place. He braced his back against the bay and set his hands at chest level, looking like a man doing an awkward upright bench-press. His arms and shoulders swelled, his protuberant eyes bulged and his gritted teeth were white in the gloom. The rolling stacks creaked and shuddered and, with a low, laborious screech, they jolted open another inch, then another, and another.

'Enough!' Gwen practically hauled the poor man out of her way and disappeared into the gap. There was a metallic clank and a faint jangle and Albus's heart leaped into his mouth. They crowded in, flashlights spotlighting Gwen and a flat grey box attached to the wall. She yanked the key box open and froze. Albus had to lift up on to his toes to see.

All the little hooks, where keys had once hung, were empty.

A low groan came from her. 'No no *no*. Damn it! They should *be* here.'

She began yanking at the box. Searching, Albus presumed, for a hidden panel or something she'd missed. He backed away, his hands twitching, ligaments restlessly working to flex his non-existent fingers.

He swung around as Rufus fell through the sliding door. He straightened up quickly, breathing fast, his eyes finding Albus in the dark.

'What's happening, dude? You're taking forever. I'm getting paranoid out there all on my lonesome. Keep thinking I'm seeing folk watching us from windows and shit. Did Bruno tell you I found diesel reserves? They might be OK, too. Some clever guy stored them real well. No condensation or anything. Used Sta-Bil and algaecide treatments and— Hey! Where're you going?'

Albus wasn't hanging around to listen to diesel updates. He hurried back through the swinging doors into the office. He kicked past the folders and files that had been dumped on the floor in their search, one foot skating on a plastic binder, almost dropping him to one knee. He scooted a chair out of his way and went straight to the front door, the door by which the library workers would enter every morning before unlocking the sliding door at the rear, the door that was most likely the last door they locked at the end of every work day and which had a digital alarm panel housed right next to it.

There was a mailbox attached to the back of the door, covering its letter slot, the kind that caught any mail pushed through (or any fireworks and burning paraphernalia delivered by unfriendly local pyromaniacs). Albus fumbled at the mailbox's clasp, the lever foiling his palmed efforts to twist it – *open, open!* – and it swung outward, his headlamp's diodes flooding the interior in a bluish-white light.

A plastic-wrapped magazine, in pristine condition, advertised the new Large Print titles coming out in the spring. Albus ripped it out and there, at the bottom of the box, sat two sets of keys.

CHAPTER 7

Wolves

The Other orders them to trash the church. They love destruction, and it loves to see things destroyed. There is a purity to it that pleases; it decrees a part of the world be cleared so that something new can take its place. Death is as important as life. Without it, the world will fill past capacity and choke itself.

Pike approaches. His eyes shine in his bearded face, the ecstasy at desecrating a place of worship releasing something primal in his bloodstream. Carnal excitement laces the air, lays it rich with musk.

'The building's checked. She isn't here.'

'She's here,' it says. 'Pull the place apart.'

Pike looks away, glancing at the smashed and overturned pews, at the heaved-over altar, at the bent and broken bicycles their quarry have been riding to stay ahead of them. The Other knows what he's thinking. They are so easy to read, their minds so primitive; it despises them so much it can barely stand to look at them. Yet it needs them, and it must bide its time.

'Not the *things*.' There was no point hiding its contempt. 'The roof, the walls, the floors. Take the *building* apart and *find* her.'

Pike goes away, calling Frank over to him as he does. Frank, and another man with a ridiculously large moustache, join him. At the front of the nave, they start working at the platform of the chancel, using tyre irons and pieces of broken pew to batter through the wooden flooring and lever up the planks. The cracks and splitting of wood rent the air like gunshots.

It stands in Posy's body at the back of the church and watches these people go about their dismantling. The church feels like an oversized sarcophagus. The strip of carpeting running down the centre aisle is black in the failing light and the wooden, curved beams of the ceiling have seen their last rays of sunshine. Their varnished, silver-edged lines are now blade-like and deadly. Spindly shadows from a giant oak's branches outside reach their crooked fingers across the wood as if a skeleton army waited beyond the church's walls.

It is hard to stay still, to keep calm. It hasn't heard the girl's Inner for hours, not since the horrible explosion of pain had brought Posy to his knees and her voice had fallen silent. The worry is she's close to dead and, if she dies, she can no longer reliably be traced. And if she can no longer be traced, she can no longer be found and used. She has much to teach, and it is desperately hungry to learn.

It sends another pulse to the Inner who currently resides somewhere within these walls. Not one from within Posy's group. It recognises all their Inners now, each one different, each one so much static. The one he reaches out to is a shadowy, crude thing, useful in only the most rudimentary sense. It can hear the Other, but is capable of little more.

Bring her to me, the Other instructs.

It knows the message is received, it feels the words disappear like droplets into litmus paper.

It also sends a quick slither of awareness deeply inward to Posy, who cowers in the darkness of his self-constructed prison. Posy doesn't realise he is being watched; he exists alone, cut off, muttering every now and then in a wordless prattle. He witnesses what is transpiring with little to no understanding. Posy sickens it most of all. The world deserves better.

Posy's right leg shakes, but it is a simple matter to straighten it and redirect the impulse. There is a clawing sensation from inside his stomach, too. A ball of pins that grinds into his sternum. It shuts off the discomfort. A weak mind is easy to master when so many years have been spent inside one more complex.

A woman sends up a cry.

At the farthest end of the sepulchral, wood-enshrined chamber, past the dismantled chancel, the woman with the ridiculously large teeth appears from a room. 'There's a basement hatch!' she calls.

It directs Posy's body to walk the length of the single-strip carpeting, from one end of the church to the other. Men step out of the way as he passes. The cracking of wood quietens and the church is respectfully still, except for Posy's footsteps. It climbs over the cracked-open flooring, pulls itself up into a narrow sacristy and sees the basement door set into the floor. Closed, secure. Whoever is down there hasn't unlocked it. It senses nothing beyond the hatch, only the dankness of the earth, the squirming of the worms and the silence of the dead.

'I want her,' it whispers. It looks at Frank, who stands next to the hatch with a sledgehammer. It doesn't know where he has found it, nor does it care. 'Break it open.'

Frank lifts the sledgehammer and swings.

It lifts the corners of Posy's mouth into a thin semblance of a smile. She is here. She is trapped. There is nowhere left for her to go.

THE PART
BETWEEN PARTS
The Quarry

CHAPTER 1

Pilgrim Holiness Church, Norwich, SC

Lacey, Alex and Addison stood in a line, straddling their bikes in exactly the same way they had days earlier on the Congaree River bridge. The day this had all started. This time, there were no bridges in sight; they were in the middle of a moderately sized, drab church parking lot and Lacey was fighting the urge to look over her shoulder.

She lost.

That feeling of being observed, of eyes burning into the back of her skull, had set up residence and wouldn't be leaving any time soon.

'See something?' Alex asked. She was watching Lacey rather than the street.

Lacey admitted that her toes had been dipped into the waters of paranoia for a while now but, recently, she had found herself wading so far from shore she had little idea how to return safely. Paranoia went hand in hand with caution, though, right? And if there was one thing they needed to be right now, it was cautious.

There was a stillness in the air, as if the world had taken a deep breath in and was holding on to it.

'No,' Lacey replied. 'I don't see anything. Doesn't mean there's nothing out there.'

Oh, they're out there, Voice said. *But we still need to rest. And this is very nice.*

Lacey could feel the pleasure radiating from him. 'It is nice,' she agreed.

Pilgrim Holiness Church was a single-storey, double-gabled building made of red brick. Out front, stuck in the middle and bisecting the view of the church clean in half, was the tallest oak Lacey had ever set eyes on. An ancient forest soldier, a remnant from a time when the surrounding area was all woodland, towered high above the black-tiled roof, its branches spreading out to form an umbrella that sheltered the church from the sun.

It's like it's on sentry duty, Voice said.

To the left of the oak, rising above the main entrance (although nowhere near reaching the height of the tree), was a modest, brick-built spire, topped by the same black tiles that covered the roof.

'Look good?' Lacey asked Addison, whose head was tilted back so she could gaze up at the oak from under her cap's visor. Her eight-year-old niece had withdrawn into herself over the past few days, the strain of restless nights and the horrors they had seen combining to create a heavy grey fug that trailed after them, no matter how hard they pedalled or how fast they rode. The shit that went down at the lake had been the final straw. They were all still reeling from it.

'It's like home,' Addison said softly.

Lacey caught the look on Alex's face. Surprise and relief. These were the first words Addison had spoken in hours. For a kid so talkative, her silence had been torturous. Lacey tried not to notice the pallor of her niece's skin or the dark circles under her eyes.

In the Gothic house where they had found Addison only a few short weeks ago – the house belonging to Lacey's sister – there had been a tower, a single turret, where Addison had lived, much like a forgotten princess in a fairy tale. Except her tale was a dark and twisted story where parents died, the world went mad and small children were left to die or survive alone with very few happy endings.

Addison's gaze slowly, tiredly, shifted to Lacey. 'We got anything to eat?' she asked, and the clutch of anxiety that was balled in Lacey's guts unravelled a tiny bit. She almost sounded like her old self.

Lacey reached over and gently tucked one of her niece's escaped curls back under her cap. 'Let's go inside and see if Christ's left us any of his body to eat. How's that sound?'

Addison wrinkled her nose. 'You're weird.'

It runs in the family, sweet cheeks, Voice said.

Six days ago

Lacey was out of breath by the time she finished climbing to the sixth floor. The ascent had tired out even Addison, although the kid didn't complain. Her small hand had fisted on to Lacey's backpack two flights up; Lacey had felt the slight tug back there as she pulled her niece along behind her.

Alex waited for them on the landing, a service revolver in one hand. Her other held a door open for them. The faint light coming from the room behind silhouetted her, a tall, slim woman, her posture unmistakeable, the slight angle to her head, the weight she rested on her left leg while the other bent slightly at the knee, all so familiar to Lacey it was like looking at herself. Her eyes skipped quickly past the gun Alex gripped at her side.

'The place is empty,' Alex said, voice low. 'It used to be offices.'

Addison slipped past them, footsteps silent. Lacey watched her niece's head swivel this way and that, taking in their new environment, curiosity outweighing any need to be cautious.

'Find anything useful?' With her dark-adjusted eyes, Lacey saw her friend's head shake.

'They have fresh-fruit vending machines,' Alex replied, 'but you can imagine what's in there now.'

'Mouldy old shit?

'Yep. Or green dust, if you want to be specific about it.'

They had taken a calculated risk coming into the city. Once entered, it would take a day or more to hike back out. Miles of inner-city streets where the odds of bumping into other people were hiked up exponentially. Being around others meant Lacey would have to work extra hard to keep Voice a secret. She wasn't like the majority of other voice-hearers, who'd been hearing theirs for almost eight years now – she was a newbie. Voice had been with her for exactly sixty-one days and he was impossible to ignore. It was difficult not to react when he said something annoying, which happened *a lot*. She even sometimes forgot herself and asked him questions out loud, and that was stupid as well as dangerous. To be found hearing a voice could end very badly – after all, voices were the reason so many people were dead. And if anyone realised how Lacey had come to get Voice in the first place, she'd be in shit so deep it'd take a crew working round the clock to dig her back out. That included telling Alex about it. The fewer people who knew, the safer it was. Voice had made that abundantly clear.

'You didn't see anyone skulking around?' she asked.

'Not a soul. I've checked all the doors leading on to this floor. They're all secure.'

Lacey relaxed a little then, and Alex slung a companionable arm around her shoulders. She leaned gratefully against her friend as they watched Addison wander deeper into the office's abandoned cubicles, lifting items, turning them over in her hands, occasionally touching them to her lips, as if only through tactile sensation could she inventory them.

'It's so easy to forget she's never seen these things before,' Alex said quietly.

'Yeah, getting her Christmas and birthdays presents is gonna be a cake walk.'

Pencil sharpeners, swivel chairs, document holders, binders, calculators, hole punches – a multitude of office paraphernalia strewn across the desks – this place must have seemed magical to Addison. Like a lost treasure trove.

Addison walked back toward them. She was skinny for an eight-year-old, long bones, and long reams of talking, too. 'I like it here. Can we stay?'

'Only for the night, baby,' Alex said. 'We'll have to leave in the morning.'

'East some more?' Addison crouched down to look under a desk. Fiddled with the wiring under there. It had been a long time since Lacey had to worry about getting electrocuted for messing with stuff like that. Addison could tug at it all she pleased.

'That's right. To where the sun rises. We'll find someplace safe there. For all of us.'

The arm around Lacey's shoulders suddenly felt a hundred times heavier. East. That's where Alex had been heading with her sister, Sam, before Lacey found her hanging by her wrists in a motel bathroom. They'd heard there was help out there for people who heard voices. For people like Sam. People like Lacey, too, she supposed. The kind of help involving medical folk and scientists, working on understanding the voices people heard and, no doubt, on how to stop them. Lacey wasn't sure how she felt about that. She was getting kind of used to having Voice around.

A bank of windows made up the wall on their left, allowing moonlight to illuminate the room in long blocks of pale light. The office was alive with dust motes, disturbed by the new air currents generated by the three visitors. Other than the quiet clink and tap from the girl as she replaced each piece of stationery where she got it from, the place was grave-silent.

Welcome to the new world, Voice whispered dramatically in her head.

Lacey rolled her eyes and silently told him to shut up.

'It's getting worse,' Alex said.

Behind Lacey, the soft *snick-snick* of Alex's scissors accompanied each tuft of hair snipped from Lacey's head. She couldn't help but think how each strand was dying as it fell, separated from the living cells of her scalp. Dead and lifeless as it floated to the floor.

Addison lay across from them, beyond the cooling camp stove, the moonlight bright enough to see that the sleeping girl didn't fuss much, her face relaxed, her thin chest rising and falling in a perfect, slow rhythm. It would be a peaceful sight, if not for the constant movement of her lips.

'Hmm.' Lacey didn't take her eyes off her niece. No sound issued from Addison's mouth, yet her lips pursed and opened, tongue sliding against teeth, forming silent syllables that weren't easily followed. Her muted monologue didn't stop as the girl entered deep slumber but lasted for the duration of her sleep. For hours, she spoke soundlessly to someone in her dreams.

'We need to keep moving,' Alex said. 'It seems to get worse when we stop.'

'How do we even know there'll *be* anyone on the East Coast? The stuff you heard, about the facilities and stuff, it could be just a bunch of crap.'

'Like the rumours about the Flitting Man are a bunch of crap?'

Lacey didn't reply.

A few more snips from the scissors, a few more dying strands of hair falling away.

'What else can we do?' Alex murmured. 'Look at her. She needs help. *We* need help.'

On too many nights to count, Lacey had lain beside Addison and watched each word form on her niece's lips. Even noted down the ones she thought she recognised, the words that were repeated most often or appeared in patterns. But it didn't help. All it did was scare her more.

'I'll take first watch.'

'Lacey, you know it's my turn.'

'I *want* to do it. It's OK. I'm not even sleepy.'

They had gotten into the habit of taking turns staying awake as the girl slept. The rumours, about the mysterious Flitting Man who came into encampments at night, drifted unspoken around them, the smoking tendrils inhaled unconsciously, entering their bloodstream like an opiate. He set fires and stole people away, the stories said. He was a faceless ghost you would never see coming, not until it was too late. No one could hide from him.

Lacey and Alex had seen some of those stories come true. The fires, the gathering groups of people who harboured voices, some of whom had been taken against their will. Their wariness wasn't borne from silly superstition. As long as Addison sleep-talked, it was best they kept moving.

The *snick* of the scissors fell silent and Alex's fingers combed through Lacey's hair, sifting through its shorter length. Lacey's eyelids grew heavy. Her head tipped back.

'You need to rest,' Alex said, the pads of her fingers kneading into Lacey's scalp, a gentle press that released liquid tingles into the back of Lacey's neck and shoulders. Her eyelids drifted closed. 'You hardly sleep any more.'

An image stuttered to life in the darkness behind her eyelids. Of a dead woman at the bottom of a freshly dug grave, curled on her side like a folded husk. Lacey had dug that grave with her own two hands. The corpse's face was hidden behind a tied red scarf, the wispy material sinking into the depression of a shrunken mouth. A young woman with an old woman's puckered lips, the lower face caving in on itself.

Lacey's fingers fumbled for the medallion at her throat. The metal was warm, familiar, a talisman to ward off troubling thoughts. She stroked her thumb over the coin's surface, pad smoothing the embossed design of St Christopher with water up to his knees, staff in his hands, the baby Jesus riding his shoulders. The image of the dead woman sunk back into its muddy grave.

Lacey didn't think she'd ever rid herself of all the horrible things she'd seen. And maybe that was the way it should be. Pilgrim, the man she had travelled with for a time, had been flat-out wrong when he'd told her memories lasted only as long as they needed to. For Lacey, holding on to hers meant, hopefully, she wouldn't make the same mistakes twice.

She tucked the St Christopher away and opened her eyes. 'I'm really not tired.' It wasn't exactly a lie. Her dreams were filled with the ghosts of dead people. Their visits were never pleasant, but they deserved to be remembered, the same as everybody else. Didn't mean she was eager to meet up with them again, though.

She caught Alex's hands and pulled her fingers from her hair, twisting around to look at her. 'You bed down. I'll wake you when I'm sleepy. Pinky promise.'

More unspoken words hung in the air: the admonishments, the coaxing, the bartering. But Alex had tried all those tactics before and both women knew Lacey could be as immoveable as a boulder. Her friend said nothing, only briefly squeezed Lacey's fingers and moved away, going to her sleeping bag and rolling herself inside it. She put her back to the silently talking girl.

Out of sight, out of mind, Voice murmured, looking at Alex through Lacey's eyes.

– You're out of sight but never out of my mind.

She and Voice spoke like this most nights. It was an opportunity for Lacey to practise her internal conversing with Voice, which refused to come easily to her. It took a lot of concentration, and Lacey was finding it increasingly hard to focus on anything past watching her niece like a hawk and constantly looking over her shoulder.

I know. You're very lucky to have me.

Lacey half smirked, the smile dying before it had a chance to form.

— Some could say cursed.

It's not a curse to have extra awareness.

— Tell that to the millions of dead people.

Hey now. You're starting to sound like Alex. And Auntie Alex is mean.

He said it jokingly, but she heard the disappointment in his tone and it sent a twinge of guilt through her. Alex didn't hide her mistrust of him.

— Is that what you are to me, then? My extra sixth sense?

I'm a spark of life in the dark. Unless you experience me, like you have, then I'm not much of anything to anyone.

— That's like saying you don't exist outside my head.

How can you prove I exist, Lacey? I'm pretty intangible.

— You tell me stuff I don't know.

Maybe I make it up.

— Maybe you do. You talk a lot of shit sometimes.

I'll have you know that shit to some is fertiliser for the brain to others.

— Pretty sure you don't know what's shit and what's not. That's why we always end up having this same conversation over and over.

I know more than you do. Now he sounded petulant. She bugged him a lot about this stuff but only because he never gave her a proper answer. She'd stopped thinking it was because he was being deliberately evasive. Now she suspected it had more to do with him not knowing half as much as he pretended.

There was a time when I had no memories at all, not of myself, nor of Pilgrim, and nothing of the world. I hit a wall and nothing lay beyond it. *I can only believe that was before. Before I was born, before I had awareness. Everything else comes after.*

– But *how* were you born? I know how I got here. My mom and dad got jiggy one night, and I popped out nine months later.

I was conceived in loneliness and despair, long before the voices you know of came and caused mayhem. And that's all I know. I remember flashes of Pilgrim's life and the world he lived in. I came to him when I was needed the most. What's worse than being all alone, with no one to help?

– Being dead.

Voice laughed. *There are worse things than being dead, Lacey.*

– Like what?

Like being hopeless and lost. Being in pain. Suffering.

– Was Pilgrim in pain?

Voice was quiet for a moment, and the feel of his words became thoughtful. *Pilgrim was my friend, my comrade. But he was different. He had forgotten so many things, and because of that I've forgotten things, too. Is there pain in forgetting? Maybe at first. But not after a while. It all becomes numb, and numbness becomes nothing.*

It was Lacey's turn to be quiet. Her eyes had returned to her niece. She could feel Voice watching Addison, too.

– What do you think's going on with her?

I'm not sure. Nightmares, maybe.

– Just nightmares? Nothing more?

I hope it's nothing more. Alex will shit a brick.

Lacey cracked a smile.

It doesn't hurt to watch her, he said, serious now, his words sounding somehow ominous. *Just to be safe.*

Soon after, their talking done, she felt Voice retreat. It was a strange sensation, one hard to describe. A gradual receding in the back of her head, a lantern in a mineshaft being carried further and further away until its light became a mere memory, extinguished by the dark.

Lacey didn't know when her eyes had closed, but she knew when she ceased breathing. Her body knew. Someone was in there with them.

A low murmuring came from close by.

A coldness prickled over her scalp, raised the hairs on the back of her neck.

Eyes tightly closed, she tried to make out the murmured words, but all she could hear was a droning, like the low hum of overhead power lines, a sound she felt more than heard, thrumming through her skin, a low-voltage vibration singing along her veins. The murmuring *suggested* itself into her head, seeming to bypass her ears altogether, a sliding sensation that was slick and hot and somehow repugnant. It felt unsafe, listening to that droning voice as it slip-slid its way inside, dirtying every part it touched. It scared her. Scared her maybe as much as being tied to a motel bed in a basement, waiting for her captors to return and finish what they'd started. She wanted to open her eyes, wanted to look at the thing that was speaking in such a low, slick voice, but she was terrified of what she'd see. If the hearing of such a thing was so terrible, so dangerous, what would the seeing of it do?

Addison.

An invisible hand squeezed her throat, shortening the space between each breath. Her heart raced.

Lacey opened her eyes.

Addison lay on her side, staring back at her. The girl's lips moved and, although the droning voice didn't come from her, her lips perfectly formed the sounds the voice intoned, a doll operated by a master ventriloquist. Lacey gazed hard at Addison because she didn't dare look at the hunched, broken-backed figure bent over her, its darkly oppressive presence holding her niece in place. It hulked low, its head inches away from Addison's head.

Lacey could feel its eyes on her, could *see* them, even as she refused to lift her gaze to look directly for fear something might break loose inside of her, something precious, a last remnant of innocence that she desperately clung to.

But you must look! You *must*. For Addison's sake.

And so, she did.

Its eyes, an almost-familiar piercing green, glowed back at her like emerald-glassed lamps and Lacey felt her terror expand, filling her up from her chilly, booted feet to her cold, clammy brow. From that one look she saw recognition flare in its eyes. Its curved nose hooked down over its lipless slash of a mouth and she watched a small, gloating smile curl up one corner. There was a shivering on its back, an undulation.

Wings?

Yes, two.

Black and diaphanous. Like an insect's.

It spoke directly into Addison's ear while it regarded Lacey, its slick words going in and then being silently mouthed by the girl on their way back out. The droning murmur grew louder and louder, loud enough to vibrate through the walls and floors, so loud Lacey shook with it and wanted to clamp her hands over her ears, wanted to scream to drown it out because, as loud as it was, she *still* couldn't understand what it said, the words flowing in some foreign tongue, black and foul, words that should never be spoken aloud, the uttering of them an invitation broadcast to all the awful things walking the earth. And then Lacey *did* scream, because the broken-backed creature opened its slash of a maw and kept opening it until its jaw unhinged like a snake's. It would eat Addison's head, Lacey knew it, eat it whole, maybe even keep on eating her until Addison's shoulders slid into its gullet, followed by her chest and torso, hips and legs, her feet kicking out of its mouth as they, too, were guzzled down. Lacey screamed so loud it shredded her throat and tore something painfully inside her, and the droning, vibrating, ear-flooding, *mountainous* sound shattered into a million glittering pieces, flinging to each side of the room on a last, ringing word: the first word she heard and understood –

FIRE.

She jerked awake, sobbing and gasping for breath, dragging herself up. She couldn't swallow – splinters had bedded themselves in the soft flesh of her throat. She checked Addison's bedroll, found the girl gone. Lacey looked frantically around but there was no sign of her anywhere; in fact, it was hard to see anything at all. The room had darkened considerably, the moonlight smothered and muted behind a hanging wall of fog. Lacey's stinging eyes teared up. The choking smell of smoke singed her nostrils.

'Addison!' It came out as a rasp.

FIRE! Voice yelled. He sounded scared, which alarmed Lacey even more. *I didn't think you'd wake up!*

Lacey lurched to her feet and swayed drunkenly, dizziness swamping her, blurring her vision and edging in on her clouding thoughts. She almost fell down.

No! Voice snapped. *Stay on your feet!*

She blinked and groggily shook her head. She clumsily kicked at Alex's blanket-covered boots, barely able to muster a whisper. 'Alex.' She tried again: 'Alex!', and it came out as a sharp blast of gravel.

Alex jerked upright and immediately began coughing.

Lacey made a grab for Alex's hands, missed, swiped again, snatched hold and yanked at her to get up.

'They've found us?'

'Help me find Addison!' Lacey's windpipe was rapidly swelling shut. '*Come on.*'

Lacey tugged her neckerchief up over her nose and mouth, scooped her rifle and backpack off the floor, swinging both on to her back, and glanced at Alex through her tears to see her doing the same. The rest – their bedrolls, the camping stove – all were left behind.

They coughed and stumbled their way around the room, calling for Addison, feeling the heat build beneath their boots as the floors below them melted. Alex snagged Lacey's backpack and towed her to the door they'd entered through. Lacey continued to call out for the girl even as she was hauled away, each syllable becoming a hacking cough.

They crashed into the dark stairwell, burning smoke filling the space like the ghosts that haunted Lacey's dreams. Lacey staggered down the steps, falling into handrails and slamming into the walls at every level, winding her blind way down and down, hot sweat collecting under her collar and armpits. She heard Alex stumble and crash along behind her, and every time Lacey stopped, wanting to go back up to continue her search, Alex's hands pushed at her, giving her no choice but to carry on.

I just need air. Fresh air, catch my breath, then I'll come back and find her and everything will be OK. One clear breath, fill my lungs up, then I'll come back.

Lacey burst into the alleyway, tripping over the door frame and falling on to her hands. The air was cleaner here and mostly smoke-free, but Lacey's swollen throat barely allowed a trickle through. She tore her neckerchief off and continued to cough and hack up phlegm. She could hear Alex doing the same.

Tearing her backpack off and fumbling for her rifle, she forced herself to her feet, air hissing like a tin whistle through her throat, black dots dancing in her vision. She glanced wildly around, expecting to see a group of men flanking them, white grins plastered across their faces and voices that weren't their own directing their tongues. The darkly winged figure from her dream would be standing at their backs, thinking their thoughts for them.

She clutched the rifle in both hands, but there was no one else in the alley. She looked back at the door they had escaped through. Thick tendrils of smoke seeped from around the door jamb.

More ghosts waited for her in there.

Don't go in, Lacey.

Alex gripped the hem of her pants, and Lacey shook her off, all set to go back inside, when Alex croaked at her to stop.

'Look,' Alex whispered, and pointed. '*Look*.'

And there, at the far end of the alleyway, gazing back at them with too-big eyes, was Addison, her face pale and scared. And entirely clean of soot.

Clean as a bone, Voice said.

As dawn lit the eastern horizon in strips of burnt umber, they stood six blocks away, watching the leaning pillar of smoke rise into the brightening sky. The burning building itself was out of sight, but Lacey could see the blurred haze where an enormous amount of heat escaped upwards.

'What happened?' Addison asked.

Lacey had drawn her hood up against the morning chill. It blocked her view of her niece, standing to her left, but she heard the inquisitiveness in her voice. Addison had been confused when Lacey and Alex stumbled over to her, hadn't remembered making her way outside. Lacey guessed she must have been sleepwalking (*and sleep-fire-setting*, Voice had muttered), but the girl had nothing to tell them. Neither Lacey nor Alex had seen her leave. Anything could have started the fire. (*Yeah, I hear cockroaches* love *playing with matches*, Voice had said.)

'What happened?' Addison asked again, and there was no remorse, no concern for what the answer might be.

Lacey didn't know what Addison had heard while she slept, or even if she *had been* hearing anything – every morning, when asked how she'd slept, the girl always replied with 'Fine', or 'Great', or 'OK'. She never had anything to tell them, because she remembered nothing. No dreams, no nightmares, no voices.

Someone tried to barbecue us, Voice said in Lacey's head. *That's what happened, plain and simple.*

'Something set the building alight,' Alex answered. She stood on Addison's other side. Her voice was low, wispy, snuffed out by the smoke. 'And now it'll burn until there's nothing left to burn.'

They all watched the dense plume of smoke. Lacey half expected to hear sirens whoop and the squeal of speeding wheels, but there was only dead air filling up their ears. She had switched on one of their hand-held radios as soon as it was safe to, and had surfed the channels, taking extra time to listen carefully to Channel 15. There had been nothing to hear but crackles and static.

'Maybe we should see it as a reminder,' Alex said. 'Or a warning.'

A cold breath of wind licked into Lacey's hood, crawling around the back of her neck. She shivered and tightened her grip on the radio.

'What warning?' Addison asked uncertainly.

Lacey's words were gruff and pitted and practically unrecognisable. 'A warning against asking questions all the time.'

Addison fell silent. Lacey felt Alex's gaze on her and she met her friend's eyes over Addison's head. A slight frown pulled down Alex's brows. Lacey didn't think for one second that Alex believed Addison capable of setting fire to that office building, but then Lacey hadn't told her about what she'd seen. How that hunched figure had been whispering dark, slick things into Addison's sleeping ear, and how the girl was mouthing every single word it said.

It was just a lucid dream, she told herself. You were exhausted. You fell asleep and all the weird stuff that's floating around your head came up and bit you on the ass. Stop overthinking it.

But it didn't matter what explanation or reasoning she used, her smouldering fear, with its wisps of black suspicion, burned in her guts, refusing to be extinguished.

She needs to be watched, Voice said quietly. *For her sake, as well as ours.*

Addison was staring at her feet. Lacey knew she could watch the girl for twenty minutes straight and she wouldn't move a muscle. She could sit, or crouch, or stand in the same position for hours and not fidget at all. Not many eight-year-olds could do that. Not many eight-year-olds had learned the importance of staying undetected, or of being secretive in order to survive.

Lacey remembered being eight. She hadn't known shit.

Sighing – and wishing she hadn't when her lungs stuttered on a painful hitch – Lacey slid an arm around Addison and drew her close.

'It doesn't matter what caused the fire, Addy. We're safe and together, and that's all that counts.' She kissed the side of her head, soft curls crinkling under her lips. Her hair was so like Lacey's sister's.

The bony feel of the girl's shoulder digging into her ribs made the spikiness around Lacey's heart soften, the suspicions draw back. An all-consuming love reared up, a feeling so powerful, so invasive, it almost brought tears to her eyes. It made her tighten her embrace until the girl shifted uncomfortably, her only small concession to not remaining still.

Addison was just a girl. What did she know of killing?

Enough, Voice said. *She knows enough. Just like we all do.*

CHAPTER 2

Bridges Crossed

Now/Pilgrim Holiness Church, Norwich

'This place is *awesome*.'

Addison's head was doing a slow sweep of what Lacey supposed was the nave, although it didn't look like any nave she'd been in before (not that she'd been in many). It was like standing in an upside-down Viking ship. Above their heads, its hull formed the church's roof, with row upon row of golden-oaked slats supported by chunky crossbeams. Archways at either end of the nave were the curved ogee arches of the ship's inverted bow and stern. The whole place smelled of wood and varnish, exactly how Lacey imagined the bowels of a ship would.

The three-foot-wide roll of burgundy carpeting stifled their footfalls as they walked up the centre aisle. A few dogged rays of sunshine had managed to filter past the sheltering branches of the oak tree and gilded each polished curve and wooden brace. The whole place glowed from the inside out.

'It's so beautiful,' she breathed.

Alex was turning in a circle. 'It really is. I'd love to draw it.'

'You definitely should. In fact, you should do it right now. Immediately. Sit your butt down. Where's your sketchbook?'

Alex laughed, and it almost sounded carefree, natural. But

there was a strain to it. Lacey heard it. Felt it, too. No amount of joking would make things better. 'I'll try and find time later,' Alex said.

Lacey dumped her backpack on a pew and unslung her rifle. She rolled her shoulders. The muscle-deep ache lessened a bit. A couple of crackles came from her neck. After hours of riding, cool air finally reached the sweaty expanse of her back and it felt *so*, so good. Too quickly her flesh turned chilly and the damp shirt began to feel gross against her skin.

Lacey ineffectually plucked at the clammy material. 'How about you guys scout the place out, see what you find, and I'll go see if I can scrounge up some supplies? I'll be quick. Need to hunker down before it gets dark.'

Addison wasn't listening; she'd stepped up into the chancel and was looting through the cupboards along the far wall. Lacey cocked her head at Alex, beckoning her over.

She kept her voice low. 'Don't let her out of your sight, OK? Not even for a second. And if anything happens, anything at all, call me up and I'll come straight back. Here, take this.'

A soft crackle interrupted them as Lacey turned on both radios, clicked them over to their channel and passed one to Alex. Alex didn't glance down as she accepted the walkie-talkie – she watched Addison, who was on her hands and knees under the altar.

A troubled crease bisected her brow. 'She seems better than she has all day.'

'Maybe. On the outside. Which doesn't mean to say everything's hunky-dory on the inside.'

True that, Voice said, appearing out of nowhere.

'What happened with the lake has really messed things up,' Lacey continued. 'We need to watch her, Alex, until we understand what the hell's going on. When I get back, we'll talk it out, all three of us. *Four*, including Voice. Speaking of which, I really need to talk to him. Is that OK?' Lacey would never have

215

asked this a few short days ago. She knew how Alex felt about Voice.

There might have been a hesitation before Alex nodded but Lacey didn't detect it, which went to show how drastically her stance had changed toward him.

'Thank you,' she said, and meant it. 'Tell me you have something useful to share,' she said to Voice.

Hmm, not really. But I've been listening.

'Listening to what?'

I've been stretching myself, he said, sounding excited and wary at the same time. *Listening harder, further. Past the local area. It was difficult at first, but it's getting a little easier to hear.*

'Hear *what?*'

It. The other voice. Behind us.

The 'other' voice was how he referred to it now. As if it were worthy of being singled out and given its own name, the same as he was.

Lacey took a moment to let her heartbeat settle. 'You're sure?'

Of course I'm sure. What do you take me for?

'How close?'

How close, she says. As if it has a tracker attached to its ankle. Wouldn't that be handy? I have been trying to get an idea of distance but, other than a vague sense of something moving toward us and some snippets of noise, I can't make out anything. Just a direction.

'But is it near enough to worry us?'

She snuck a glance at Alex and found her friend watching her silently. She held her gaze while she waited for Voice's answer. He was quieter for longer than she expected.

I don't think so? But, like I said, it's hard to pinpoint. The closer it gets, I'm guessing, the clearer an idea I'll have about such things.

Lacey's heart kicked into a faster beat again. She didn't want it getting any closer. She wanted it *gone*. But this was the most useful information she'd gotten out of Voice since he'd started talking about this stuff, and, despite her fear, she pushed for more. 'Have you tried communicating with it? Is there more than one?'

It's only this one other I hear consistently. I don't know why. Maybe – he suddenly sounded worried – *maybe it's the only voice strong enough for me to pick up? In which case, maybe there are more and the others just aren't getting through to me . . .*

'If it's strong, like you say, could it be . . . ?' She forced herself to finish her sentence. 'Could it be him?' Voice knew who she meant; she didn't have to say the Flitting Man's name out loud.

A beat of silence. *Lacey, I don't think we should be jumping to conclusions and scaring ourselves.*

I'm already scared! she wanted to yell.

'How're you even *doing* this, man?' Lacey asked. 'You've never heard anything before.'

Again, he was quiet. *It's hard to explain. I think . . . I think it may have always been there on some level. But so low I never noticed it before. It's like . . . You know how you grow accustomed to the buzzing of your refrigerator or the far-distant noise of traffic on the highway and, then, suddenly, everything around you gets real quiet and that buzzing is all you can hear?*

Lacey could feel the struggle in him. 'Like when I have my walkie-talkie turned on low?'

Yes! Exactly like that. Except there's a wall of walkie-talkies, and some are transmitting on low volume and some aren't transmitting at all. None of them are aimed at me; they're just there in the background. But this other voice I hear, it's louder. It's not really talking at anyone, it's . . . more a chattering frequency, I suppose. A psychic projection. It's not something you'd be able to hear, Lacey. It's not something I can share with you.

She sensed he wasn't telling her everything, or maybe he felt he had already revealed enough, because his presence became glassy in her head, as if he were readying himself to slide away

217

and disappear on her again.

'What aren't you saying?' she asked.

Nothing! he said, too quickly. *Look, there's something else I want to try first before we discuss anything more. Go scavenging. We'll have that talk very soon. When we get back here. Pinky promise.* That was a poor joke – they both knew he was incapable of pinky promising. He had no pinkies.

'In an hour,' she clarified, pinning him down.

Copy that, he agreed faintly, distant now, almost gone. *One hour.*

Although she'd been staring into Alex's eyes the whole time, she'd phased out and hadn't registered her at all during the last part of her and Voice's conversation. As soon as Voice disappeared, Alex came into focus.

'I'll never get used to it,' Alex said. 'And I'll never fully trust them.'

It hurt Lacey to hear that. 'I know. I'm sorry. Do you need me to recap, or did you get the gist?'

'No, I got it. Honestly, I don't want to think about what it all means. I'm already terrified enough.'

'Yeah, everything's happening so fast now. But I'm sure you'll be happy to know Voice is gone for a bit.' That may have come out snippier than she'd intended, and she made an effort to soften her tone. 'He seems to think we'll be all right here for a while. We'll talk properly when I get back, OK?'

Alex nodded. 'In an hour,' she said. 'I picked up that part.'

Lacey looked over at Addison. The girl was nosing around the pulpit. 'Alex, keep an eye on her. I'm so far past worried it's crazy.'

'I know. Me, too.' And there was a *whole* boatload of meaning to that statement, but Alex lightened it by reaching out to grip Lacey's arm, fingers firm and uncompromising in their squeeze. 'Don't worry, I'll watch her. We'll be here.'

Lacey called over to Addison. 'Be good for Alex, Addy.'

Addison sent her a distracted wave, too busy flipping through the tome-sized gold-leafed Bible on the pulpit's stand to bother looking up.

Four days ago

The I77 stretched out past the bottlenecked Congaree River bridge, the tall silhouettes of the city falling away, their sheltering shade long gone and leaving Lacey, Alex and Addison defenceless against the boiling sun. They stood silently in a row at the foot of the bridge, two taller women and a smaller figure in the middle, each with a new bike.

You're ridiculously easy to influence, you know, Voice said, his amusement obvious. *It's kind of sad.*

Lacey hadn't realised she was humming. Again. She wasn't sure how long she'd been doing it this time, but she irritably cut herself off. The damned tune had been stuck in her head ever since he'd sung it to her back at the bicycle store. It was driving her nuts.

It's like having my very own pet parakeet.

He always knew *exactly* which buttons to press in order to piss her off, and she swore she wouldn't hum a single thing he sang ever again.

Voice chuckled and took up the song where she'd left off.

> *Take him for a ride, take him up town,*
> *Steer him to a place on earth or above –*
> *Hey, Alphabet Pony, be my new love.*

'Jesus effing Christ,' she muttered. She wished he'd go back to singing the Beatles tunes she'd taught him, even if he'd eventually sucked all the pleasure out of them for her after the sixth solid day of performing them.

I don't know how you can get tired of hearing 'While My Guitar Gently Weeps'. It's a masterpiece.

She breathed a silent sigh of relief when he started singing it absent-mindedly. She wasn't the only parrot around here.

The heat was like a hot iron pressing down on her head, the sky above a steamed-clean cloudless blue. The sunlight seemed to come from all ways at once so that barely a shadow marked the ground around them.

'What do you think?' Alex asked, gazing out at the bridge's four congested lanes. 'It looks risky.'

Lacey frowned at all those vehicles piled up end to end, sometimes four or five across. Many car doors were pushed open from when occupants had hastily bailed out, rushing to throw themselves over the bridge's balustrades, yearning for the watery embrace of the deep river running beneath. The bridge's length wasn't great, but it would easily take twenty minutes to navigate, congested as it was, and, once they were on, there were only limited ways off.

Voice stopped singing. *We'd have to detour for days to go around,* he said. *And I don't think your butt could take it.*

Not being used to a bike saddle was making certain things sore, she had to admit, but she wished Voice didn't feel the need to remind her he could feel her every single discomfort no matter where it originated.

Su casa es mi casa. Which, for these purposes, roughly translates to 'Your ass is my ass.'

Lacey's face flushed so hot she thought her skin would melt off.

I know most everything that goes on in there. You shouldn't be embarrassed.

She ignored him and spoke to Alex, 'I think this is the only way over.'

Addison piped up. 'Need one of those, um, flying traptions.' She twizzled her finger in the air and made a *whuff-whuff-whuff* sound, her cheeks inflated. 'Like we saw crashed that one time.' She'd never heard a helicopter's rotor blades, of course, but Alex was surprisingly good at sound effects.

Alex answered absently, eyes busy worrying the gloomy interiors of the abandoned vehicles. 'And do what with it, honey? None of us knows how to fly a helicopter.'

'Couldn't ride a bike, neither, and look at me now!' Addison patted Alphabet Pony's handlebar as if patting a loyal steed's neck. She was wearing a blue legionnaire cap, the kind with a piece of cloth hanging down the back to shade the neck and ears from the sun. It made her look like a miniature Arab explorer who'd lost her camel.

'There'd be a couple more controls to master in a helicopter, Addy,' Lacey said.

The kid shrugged and pretended to twist the right-hand grip, making revving noises, burbling air out between her lips. 'We should go at it full speed.' She added a few *blip*ping engine growls at the end of her sentence for good measure. She'd never seen a working motorcycle, either, but they'd told her about the motorcycle Pilgrim had ridden.

'No, we'll go at it slow and steady,' Alex corrected. 'And we'll make sure to keep our eyes open as we do.'

Lacey didn't see what other choice they had. As much as Addison loved her new bike, she didn't think the girl was up to a thirty-mile detour.

She tapped the girl's shoulder. 'You hear that, Addy? No rushing ahead. We stick together. There's a tonne of places to hide in here, so do as Alex says – keep your eyes peeled.'

'Eyes peeled. Ten-four.' Addison had quickly picked up on the radio lingo they occasionally heard through their walkie-talkies. She picked up on *too* much stuff, if you asked Lacey.

Meeting Alex's eyes, Alex gave a half-shrug, as if to say, *Might as well get it over and done with.*

Lacey sighed, but it was a small, quiet sigh that only she and

Voice heard. She pushed off along with the girl before Addison could get ahead of her, sitting her aching tailbone back down on the seat. Sunshine glinted off windows and mirrors, slyly winking at her, the flashes bright enough to hurt. She wished she'd thought to dig her sunglasses out of her backpack before setting off.

She stood up, feet anchored on the pedals, her eye-line lifting above the gridlock of vehicles. The weight of the rifle slung over her shoulder was reassuring.

Soon enough, they had to go in single file. Alex led the way, weaving around open doors, sometimes having to kick one shut so they could pass. A few times, they had to stop altogether to lift their bikes over hoods and fenders when the way ahead became blocked. Gridlocks like this seemed to occur only where deep waters or long drops were nearby, any place where people could throw themselves into peaceful oblivion, abandoning the world in droves, some embarking on solo trips, others taking scores along with them. Lacey couldn't help but wonder how much pre-planning had been involved in these people's exiting strategies, or if it was more a spontaneous deal. Acts of the desperate or methods of the enlightened? Maybe it didn't make much difference. It all had the same result in the end.

A low, surreptitious creaking, like that of a car door easing open, brought them to a gliding stop.

In front of Lacey, Alex's head panned left to right, searching. She twisted in her saddle to share a troubled look with Lacey.

'We should hide,' Addison whispered.

'Shhh.' Lacey cocked her head to listen but there was only the liquid rippling of the river and the soft rustling of leaves in the trees on the banks. She climbed off her bike, leaning it against the rusting wing of a Volkswagen Jetta, and dropped her rucksack next to it. She climbed up on to its hood, swinging her rifle off her shoulder. The metal *boing*ed under her booted feet, the hood sinking and popping back into place as soon as her weight lifted. From her higher vantage point, she cupped her palm over her eyes and marked out the place, fifty yards away, where she thought the creaking had come from.

'It might've been the wind,' Alex suggested.

As if to refute her statement, the breeze – a light tickle that lifted the tips of Lacey's hair – passed over them, drying the light sweat on her neck and brow.

It wasn't the wind.

No, not the wind. Lacey took a deep breath and called, 'Whoever's up there, you'd best show yourself!'

Of course, no one did. That would be far too easy.

'We have guns!' she called. 'And we're not afraid to use 'em!' Alex was moving her service revolver from the back of her jeans to the front, wedging it under her belt buckle. She left her fingers on the butt.

Another wink of sunshine blinded Lacey and she had to twist her face aside until it blinked back out.

Maybe it was an animal, Voice said.

'What *kind* of animal?' she murmured. 'That's the question.' She turned to glance behind her and caught her breath when she saw a darting shadow, a glimpse of movement like a deer dashing between trees. A flicker she would have surely missed had she not turned around at precisely that moment. Her heart contracted, sending a sharp, piercing stab through her breastbone.

'Did you see?' she whispered.

I saw. It looked big.

She quickly looked forward again. After five rows of gridlocked cars, the traffic became lighter, bigger gaps appearing between vehicles. Not huge gaps, and still plenty of places in which a person could hide, but wide enough for bicycles to pass through and pass through quickly.

'Alex . . . Alex, get ready to go.'

Alex didn't question her – she had seen Lacey's reaction. She snagged Addison's sleeve and drew her nearer to her side.

Lacey crouched to be closer to them and lowered her voice. She couldn't help her eyes sliding back to where she'd seen that flicker of shadow. 'Ride on ahead. Pick up as much speed as you can. Addison, keep close to Alex, like *right* on her rear wheel, you hear me?'

Addison's eyes were huge under the bill of her cap. Alex's were grave and pinched at the corners. She placed a hand on the Volkswagen's hood so that her fingertips touched the toe of Lacey's boot. It must have burned, that hot metal under her palm, but she didn't move it away. 'Lacey, it'd be best if we go back.'

Lacey shook her head. 'We can't. There's someone behind us.'

Her friend's eyes shifted past her. Her hand lifted from the hood and went back to her gun, fingers wrapping around the pistol's grips.

Lacey gripped her arm, stopping her from pulling the weapon. 'I'll cover you from here. Go, and *don't stop*, no matter what. Like we agreed.' They had a pact, her and Alex, and she knew Alex would never break it. She'd made her pinky promise.

Alex locked eyes with hers. 'You're putting me in an impossible position.'

'I know. I'd say I'm sorry, but . . .' She shrugged and offered a smile.

Alex's jaw flexed, as if it took a great effort for her to hold back her words. 'Fine,' she said finally. 'But be careful. Please.'

Addison wasn't so good at holding back. 'We're not leaving you!'

'*Shhh.*' Lacey glared Addison down until the girl closed her mouth. 'Don't you get it? I'm using you as *bait*. This'll only work if you're brave and do as you're told.'

'Oh,' Addison said, chastised. 'I'm bait?'

'Of course you are. They'll see you and break cover, and as soon as they do I'll pick them off from here and clear the way. I'll come right behind, I promise.'

'*Right* behind?' the girl asked, and Lacey saw the shine in her eyes, saw how being brave and being scared were duking it out for control.

'I said *I promise*, didn't I?' She said it flat and final, and the girl nodded mutely. 'Time to go.' Lacey nodded at Alex and stood up, and Alex wasted no more breath trying to convince her to change her mind. She dragged the girl's attention away by saying Addison's name, making her follow simply by moving off, leaving the girl little choice but to obey.

Lacey tracked them with her eyes, watched how neatly the girl navigated the narrow spaces between the cars, her shorter legs pumping hard at the pedals to keep up with Alex, the cloth flap of her legionnaire hat streaming out behind her. The white tassels sprouting from the bike's handlebars flapped and shimmied.

Lacey felt a swell of pride. She was such a fast learner. Look at her go!

Soon they were standing up and pedalling wildly, bikes bobbing from side to side, wheels skimming with a brisk, efficient sound, and Lacey heard that creaking again, except this time it wasn't surreptitious, it was loud and unconcealed and somehow hostile. A woman stood up and she thought, *Witch*, because her hair was so dark it was blue-black and it hung past her shoulders like a cowl. She was squat, the blade in her hand so long it was nearly a sword. She jumped down from the back of a station wagon. Alex and Addison raced toward her, and the witch yelled as she charged at them.

Lacey knelt (barely noticing the sun-scorched hood burning straight through her pants) and braced an elbow on her up-raised knee, sighting down her rifle, tracking the witch as she ran. The wild woman's yell was low and animalistic, and her long, straggly hair billowed out as she sprinted, and that was all Lacey could see because, from the chest down, cars obstructed her view of her.

The woman's ululating cry was cut off abruptly when Lacey's bullet caught the witch in the side of her throat. The woman staggered and ran a few paces, the rest of her body slow to compute that it had been mortally wounded. On her fourth faltering step, her legs buckled and she dropped from sight.

Alex and Addison shot past, yards from the fallen witch, cycling into the opening pockets of space as if sprinting for the finishing line.

A second person broke cover, cutting in from the left.

Even from this distance, Lacey knew this one was younger, fitter. He moved much faster. His long, lithe strides took him on an intercepting path. In seconds, he would be blocked from view behind Alex. Lacey didn't track him – there was no time for that – she aimed for a spot right next to Alex's head, knowing she would have only one chance, one fleeting second to stop him. She didn't even look at him, couldn't clearly see the camping axe clamped in his fist (although she had a sense of it, of how the wood around the axe's head was glazed and shiny, as if it had recently been peeled out of its packaging), but cleared her sight until it tunnelled down her rifle's bore like a pinprick, zeroing in and condensing into one spot. That one sweet spot. And he was almost there, had ducked down slightly in order to spread his arms wide, making himself a bigger obstacle for the bikes to pass, and he was turning to face them, already smiling because he knew he had them, *knew* there was nowhere for them to go, and Lacey held her breath, the dot of her right pupil swallowed up by its iris –

('Are you any good with that?' the Boy Scout had asked her, nodding at the rifle she held.

'Good enough,' she'd replied.)

– and squeezed the trigger, releasing her breath at the same time.

She *was* the bullet, travelling on its trajectory, feeling the air tear open as if for a hot blade, hearing the ripping sound as the molecules parted to let her through and the whistling of displaced air, seeing the blur of cars streaming past beneath her in a rolling sea of faded watercolours, the sun barely registering in the hot-jacketed juddering that shook her to her core, the golden corona of Alex's hair approaching in a rushing zoom and the burning line as the bullet zipped through it, a second later stopping with a sudden shocking thud, the impact compressions rippling the man's skin, bones splintering in his struck shoulder, blood vessels exploding in a gush of hot, steaming blood that reached out to consume her.

The man spun on the spot and went down.

Alex and Addison flew past him.

Lacey gasped for breath, her temples and wrists throbbing, a black fog pulsing at the edges of her vision as she watched her friend and her niece race for the end of the bridge, in the open now, safe, no more attackers closing in. She was so focused on them she had all but forgotten the shadowy flash of movement behind her, didn't even hear that last man approach or know he was there until hard fingers clamped her ankle and yanked her off her feet.

She hit the Volkswagen's hood with a hard, clanging thump that knocked out her breath. She painfully cracked her elbow, an electric shock zapping up her arm. Her hand jolted open and the rifle tumbled from her grasp.

'No!' she gasped, snatching for it as it slid out of reach.

Her eyes fell on a thigh as wide as her waist. Her eyes climbed higher. A dirty sweater that had once been blue now torn to rags around the hem. Higher, over a chest that heaved, a snaggle of wild beard covered the entire lower half of the giant's face – a wide nose, beady eyes, a patch of dirt-streaked forehead. He was so big he blocked the sun; it was like being in the shade of a mountain.

Saliva had dribbled out of his half-open mouth, wetting the bristles of his chin in glistening slug trails. His tongue lay thick and long, protruding over his bottom lip as he struggled to catch his breath. He panted a grunt. The unbreakable manacle of his fingers around her ankle pulled and she skidded over the hood with a rubbing squeak of clothes. Her fear unlocked. Her hands scrabbled for purchase, groping for something, *anything*, but there was only the smooth, sun-scorched metal of the hood. Her palms squeaked and slipped and gripped on to nothing.

'No!' she yelled again.

The giant's eyes were filled with a dulled savagery, as if he were fuelled by a wordless need, all humanity peeled away to reveal a beast's beating heart. His gaze dropped to her throat, to where her St Christopher necklace should have been tucked out of sight, and his heavy brows came together in a ferocious scowl. His thick lips slowly formed a word and he growled out a name, a name it was impossible for him to know, and yet she heard it. She *heard* it! It grated in her ears like tearing metal, the name wrenching through her in a cramp that started in her chest and twisted through her stomach.

She screamed and kicked out. Her booted heel caught him full in the face and the gigantic man reeled backward, releasing her to clutch his nose. Lacey slid off the hood and scooped her rifle up off the ground, grabbed it by the barrel, not having time to reverse her grip before the giant was coming back at her, growling like a bear, his arms wide open, as if all he wanted was a hug, just one big enveloping hug, Lacey, that's all, what's the big deal? Come and get it.

She swung the rifle as if she were swinging for a home run, her teeth gritted and a strange snarling sound coming from deep in her throat.

The wooden stock struck the side of the giant's head with a stunningly loud *THUNK*, the shock of the impact travelling up the gun to vibrate through the bones in her wrists. The giant's eyes rolled up in his head, showing their whites, his big arms still open for an embrace, open wide the whole time as he toppled backward like a felled tree and hit another car on his way down, rebounding off it and landing at her feet.

Even lying down he looked to be eight feet tall.

She drew in huge, gasping breaths and stood there, trembling, lungs hurting, the rifle dangling uselessly from her numbed hands. She didn't even have the strength to reverse her grip to hold the gun properly. If there were any more people lurking among the cars, they might as well come for her now, because she was *done*.

Lacey . . . Voice began, but Lacey shook her head, not wanting to talk about what they'd heard, not yet. She struggled to swallow past the painful dryness in her throat.

From a distance, she heard her name being called and it was all she could do to lift her hand and wave to Alex and Addison, making motions for them to stay where they were.

She didn't ride her bike out to meet them, she pushed it, her legs wobbling. A dizzying throb passed through her head every few seconds, causing the world to shift and waver as if she were walking through water. As she passed near to the fallen witch, she refused to look down at the woman, didn't pause to riffle through her pockets or take her weapon. She didn't want to touch her. But as she approached the younger man, her eyes slid of their own accord to check him over, to see if he was alive.

He was. Barely. He lay gasping on his side like a fish dumped on dry land, his head resting on the ground so that his face was pressed up against the road, eyes full of concrete.

She set her bike and pack down and gripped the front of his shirt, pulling him on to his back so she could look down into his face. She tried to make her words angry, unforgiving, but they came out sounding breathless and small.

'Who *are* you? What do you want?'

He didn't look directly at her but stared rebelliously at her ear, the burning sun behind her head shrinking his pupils down to black specks. His eyes were silver-grey, as striking as two

229

brand-new nickels. They would have been lovely if he hadn't been bleeding to death and she hadn't been the one who'd shot him.

She shook him hard enough to make his head bob limply, like a real-life version of all those figures in the toy stores with their oversized bobble-heads and springs for necks.

'*Who* are *you?*'

She thought she saw his eyes widen a fraction, thought that maybe he was about to answer. His lips moved, a silent mouthing, no sound coming out, and Lacey's breath caught in her chest because he looked *exactly* like Addison did when she slept.

The man's lips moved, upper teeth pressed to lower lip, a tongue slide. And then she heard him, his voice weak but clear.

'He's coming.'

She breathed and stared, incapable of doing more.

'Coming for *all* of you. He sees everything. Hears everyone.' His voice dropped to the merest breath of sound. 'You can't hide from him. No one can. You'll see . . .' His lips stopped moving and his eyes slowly dimmed, turned glassy, the beautiful nickels darkening to storm-grey as the black specks of his pupils slowly expanded outward, unmindful of the sunlight.

She stared at him for long seconds, feeling the lack in him, the extra weight, the unnatural stillness. She imagined she could feel his body heat dispersing, a coldness that entered through her fists where they pressed against his chest. She imagined that someone was watching her through his too-big pupils and that they could see exactly where she was on this lump of land, recognised who she was, where she was heading, knew all her secrets, her regrets, her sadness. She hastily lowered the dead man and backed away.

As she stood, the hot sun pressed down on her, the only thing weighting her to this moment and stopping her feet from leaving the ground, her head lost to the clouds. She retreated, leaving him there in a pool of blood, gazing up at the sky, his nickel-grey eyes tarnished and lifeless – and how could she have thought them beautiful? They weren't beautiful. They were cold and slippery, like the belly of an eel. She picked up her bike. Her bloody footprints led away from the dead man in a hurried, meandering line, fading with each step, as if she were becoming more and more insubstantial the further she went.

By the time she reached the end of the bridge, her footsteps were gone.

CHAPTER 3

New Faces, Old Faces

Now/Pilgrim Holiness Church, Norwich

It hadn't taken long for Alex to search the church – there were only four doors running off the main space, not including the foyer they had entered through. One led to a basic study with a desk, bookcases and standing lamp. Door number two, on the back wall of the nave's dais, was the sacristy, where most of the holy items were stored, piles of Bibles and hymn booklets, as well as spare folding chairs and a collapsible contraption that reminded Alex of the music stand she'd used in band practice. At the rear of the nave, the final two doors opened on to a set of restrooms and a small kitchen whose cupboards were depressingly bare but for dusty crockery, trays, a large hot-water urn and rat droppings.

Done with the exploration, Alex settled on a bench and placed her sketchbook on the pew's narrow shelf in front of her. Lacey had put the thought in her head and it wouldn't be dismissed. Her need to draw had become an itch between her shoulder blades she couldn't quite reach, a muscle tic in her fingers that was driving her to distraction. Her pencil had been sharpened so many times it was almost too short to fit her hand. The sketch she had been working on, for longer than she cared to admit, mocked her with its incompleteness. The motorbike was finished in every detail, from hard-case luggage racks to exhaust and side mirrors, the scenery all around drawn in and shaded – the desert, the low, scraggly bushes, the grass growing into the dust from the sides of the road. Even the man himself, his long legs crossed at the ankles as he leaned back against the bike's seat, arms folded, the set of his shoulders defiant yet aloof. All captured perfectly. But Pilgrim's face remained a blank space. She'd sketched his jaw and his hair ruffling in the breeze but hadn't been able to focus her pencil on his eyes or his mouth. The aspects that brought him to life.

She didn't bother flicking through the dozen or so other drawings of him she'd started but never finished. He would always remain a mystery to her. She had been no one to him, a stranger, a burden. Instinct and experience had dictated she shouldn't trust him. He was a taciturn loner, had appeared uncaring of everyone travelling within his orbit. And most damning of all: he heard a voice.

She hadn't wanted to befriend him, but how could she not after he'd taken Lacey from a life of abject loneliness, had attempted to help the girl find her family, had returned to save Alex after she had been captured? He had saved her life, not once but twice. Everything she had believed about him had been turned on its head. And at the moment she had decided to bring him into her circle of trust he had been shot by the very gun tucked under her belt.

To hold on to such a weapon could be considered morbid, she knew, but to her it was consolation. The revolver that had felled a man who had been so intractable, so determined, so damned unrelenting. It connected them, the power in that gun, to the power that had lived inside him. It reassured her to carry it. Lacey had Voice, and Alex had the weapon that had killed Voice's master. It seemed fitting somehow.

Sighing, she turned to a fresh page. A piercing pain cut a line across her forehead, slicing so deep she pressed her fingertips to it. It distracted her from the pain in her hip, caused by long hours in the saddle, but that secondary ache came back full throttle once the pain in her head faded.

She shuffled on to one butt cheek on the hard wooden pew. Just a quick sketch of the girl where she stood at the pulpit, her pose a picture of studiousness – head bent over the Bible, loose curls falling to obscure her eyes – then she'd get up and start organising camp.

'Listen to this, Alex.'

The girl's reading had come on in leaps and bounds in a few short weeks, but she would be at the stage where she needed a finger as a marker for a while to come, to help break down the harder, longer words into smaller, digestible chunks.

Addy spoke slowly, reciting from the Bible passage with care, sometimes having to pause, her mouth moving silently until she'd worked the word out. Watching the working of her mouth and listening to the scripture leave her mouth was an unsettling experience.

'"We all, like sheep, have gone a-str-ay. Astray. Each of us has turn-ed. Turned. To his own way; and the Lord has . . . laid on him the inick . . . the iniq . . ."' The girl glanced up. 'What's this word?' She spelled it out to Alex.

'Iniquity,' Alex said.

'"The Lord has laid on him the *iniquity* of us all."' Addy stopped reading, her eyebrows tucking down. 'What's "iniquity"?'

Alex shifted uncomfortably, more due to the disquiet she felt hearing this girl speak such a bleak passage than to the sore twinges of her hip bone. 'It means sin. All the evil people have done.'

Addy's eyebrows scrunched tighter still. 'Huh.' Head bent again, finger-place found, she inhaled a large breath to continue, but a new voice, this one strong and masculine, reverberated through the nave.

'"Do you not know that your body is a temple of the Holy Spirit, who is in you, whom you have received from God? You are not your own."'

Alex was on her feet, pointing the revolver at the man before he'd even finished the fourth word. Again, that flash of pain forked across her forehead, and she bit her lip, half lifting a hand, but the pain was gone before her fingertips touched.

The man held his empty hands out at his sides in the classic 'I'm unarmed and not a threat' gesture, which Alex didn't trust for a second. He wore what Lacey liked to call a *shit-eating* grin. Alex hadn't really understood the term but, with this man, she was starting to see what Lacey had meant. His smile didn't win her over.

She kept her gun trained on him and stepped clear of the pew. She waved Addy over to her. 'Come get behind me.'

The girl's footfalls hurried down off the two-foot-high stage and padded quickly across the carpet to her. She didn't stop behind Alex but stepped to one side of her, hanging back. Too curious for her own good.

In an outfit that smacked of theatre, the man was draped in a black cassock from neck to ankles. The place at the throat, where a dog collar should be worn, had been left open, baring the hollow of his tanned throat, lending him a strange informality that didn't match the rest of his attire. No bristles marked his chin or cheeks, and his hair was combed back off a wide forehead.

The opening part of 'The Spirit of Man' ran through Alex's head, transporting her back to Sunday evenings in her father's study, where she would lie on her belly on the thick rug, listening to taped recordings of *Jeff Wayne's Musical Version of The War of the Worlds* through his big ear-can headphones. She was allowed to stay in the room, but only if she didn't disturb him while he worked, which meant No Questions, No Fidgeting, No Humming, Whistling or Singing and certainly No

Peering at him in the reflection in the hi-fi cabinet's glass door. The two of them shared a space but not each other's company.

She vividly recalled the resistance in the Play button, the stress in her whitening joint as she pressed it down until it clicked into place. It made her feel very grown up to be trusted with her parents' possessions.

She hadn't thought about this memory in years, maybe more than a decade, but now she could *feel* the thick fibres of that shagpile rug beneath her stomach and ribs, the enclosed sensation of the cushioned headphones covering her ears, and Richard Burton's deep tones filling her head. She would shut her eyes and let Jeff Wayne's evocative music bring to life that red-weeded, alien landscape, and she would forget her father existed, forget her sister, Sam, and her mother existed. Forget *everyone* existed. Even when it came to the scary bits, she didn't look to her father for comfort but kept her eyes closed and her forehead pressed against the coarse fibres of the rug, breathing in its musk as the music built and built in her ears, obliterating all the world.

The *parson*. That was why she'd thought of it.

What was that crazy parson's name again?

Nathaniel, Richard Burton's rich, cultured voice seemed to say. *Parson Nathaniel*.

Parson Nathaniel's shit-eating grin hadn't faltered; it remained stuck on his face even when he opened his mouth to speak. 'There's no need to be scared. I'm harmless. I have no weapons.'

Oh no, Nathaniel, she thought. I bet you're *far* from harmless.

She considered clicking on the walkie-talkie and telling Lacey to get her butt back here, but this wasn't an emergency and she didn't want to scare her unnecessarily. Not when there were a thousand other worries to concern them.

'Stay where you are,' she warned him. 'I *will* shoot you.'

'I'm not coming any closer, you have my word.'

'You'll forgive me if I don't believe you. Who else is here?'

'No one. I'm alone. I live here. I don't wear this for fun.' He flicked the collar of his cassock.

'The last few days have been worse than rough,' she told him. 'I cannot begin to explain. All it'll take is a batting of your eyelid to make me squeeze this trigger. Do you understand?'

'I do. You have nothing to fear.' He gazed earnestly at her and gestured to the pew next to him. 'Please. May I sit?'

Alex didn't respond. She didn't want to chat, didn't want him to sit and, most of all, she didn't want to shoot him, regardless of what she'd said. But if he left, she didn't know where he'd go. He might hang around and cause more trouble later. She could feel Addy's eyes shift to her when she failed to respond.

'I miss talking,' he said into her silence. 'Not many people stop by here any more. Churches have lost their ability to comfort, to offer hope. May I?' Watching her, his smile reappearing, placating – no, that's still verging on shit-eating – he lowered himself on to the bench, his movements deliberate and non-threatening, his hands held out, his palms laid bare. Once sitting, he folded his hands together and rested them on the back of the pew, keeping them in view. 'My name's Benny.'

No, it's Nathaniel, she thought. Crazy Parson Nathaniel.

'Benjamin Jones. This is my church.'

'It's pretty,' Addy said.

The parson's smile grew. How can he smile so much? No one smiles this much any more.

'Thank you. I'm very proud of it. And what's your name?'

Alex said, 'Don't say anything to him.'

'Addison,' the girl answered.

Alex sent her a look.

'Sorry,' the girl said.

'It's OK.' Parson Nathaniel's smiling face was open and honest and all-forgiving. Hallelujah, sisters. 'We're just sharing names. Nothing to be concerned about. You don't want to share yours?'

Alex ignored the question. 'What do you want?'

'Like I said, just to talk.'

Yeah, right. 'No one wants *just to talk*.'

'*I* do. Let me explain? It will only take a few minutes of your time.' He left a beat of silence, giving her a last chance to protest, but Alex was too busy examining him, trying, even though she knew it was impossible, to identify any signs that he was listening to anyone other than her and Addison. 'This is my town as well as my church,' he said. 'I was born here. I'll probably die here. I have no reason to leave. In fact, I don't *want* to leave. I'm happy doing what I can in the small ways that have been left me. Maybe I could help you?'

'I don't think so,' Alex said.

'You don't even know what I have to offer.'

'What you got?' Addy asked.

'Food? Water? Batteries? I have lots of things.'

'And why would you give them to us?' Alex asked.

Parson Nathaniel nodded to Addison. 'Because you have a child. Because it's the right thing to do. You're not going to lower that gun, are you?'

Alex smiled without humour. She could at least appreciate that he didn't begrudge her her suspicion. 'No, I'm not.'

'Fair enough. But while you point it at me, at least allow me to tell you my story.'

There was something disarming about him, a friendliness that should have been entirely out of place and should have raised her hackles — only an unhinged person would be this sociable. As soon as she felt that momentary weakening in her guard, her wariness reared up. She nodded for him to go on, if only to let him believe he was winning her over. Let him talk, and while he did she would continue to watch for any tell-tale signs he was other than he seemed. She didn't lower the gun, and she didn't stop listening for anyone else who might be using the distraction of this man to creep up on them.

'From when I was old enough to walk and talk, I'd help my

father here.' He lifted a palm up to the roof, as if cupping his hand to the rain. 'He was the pastor of this pretty church, Addison. On Sundays, this place would be packed to the rafters, each of these pews filled hip to hip with neighbours and friends, families with newborn babies and grandparents who were creeping into their twilight years. People from all walks of life but all having the same thing in common: their love for God. Everyone would come because *all* were welcome. And each week, after my father's service, they'd gather to chat, to catch up on news. Gossip, I suppose you'd call it, but it was never harmful gossip. My father would never have allowed that. There was such a feeling of compassion in this room. To a child like me, it was the safest place in the whole world, to be surrounded by those warm, good-hearted adults and, above all, be surrounded by His love, protecting and all-forgiving.'

Alex heard the capital H on that. She spared Addy a glance and saw the girl was staring at the parson, captivated, her mouth open a little.

'God was all around me and, almost as godly, so was the smell of fresh, warm baking. Have you ever had cherry pie, Addison? Or apple flan? What about cream-cheese-topped muffins? No? Well, Mrs Jacobs baked the *best* pies and cakes. She brought them every week – Mrs Doran did, too' – he said this next bit in a stage whisper – 'but hers were never as nice. I think she scrimped on the sugar or maybe used sugar substitute. One time, my mom ate too much of Mrs Doran's chocolate sponge cake and spent *all* afternoon in the bathroom while it came straight back out again.'

Addy snorted a soft laugh. Even in her laughter, the girl was quiet.

'All us children would sit at the feet of our parents and neighbours and listen to them while we stuffed ourselves silly with cakes and sweet pastry rolls. By seven o'clock, I always felt sick to my stomach.

'And then,' the parson said, his tone becoming introspective as his gaze settled on the pulpit where Addy had stood reading from the Bible, 'the next day, and the day after that, and for too many days, all these people who I knew so well, who I'd listened to moan about Mr Willis not mowing his lawn often enough, or how Sue-Ann Rogers was filling out far too much for the clothes she was wearing, were doing the *craziest* things. I found so many of them – not straight away, of course, I couldn't go out straight away, had to lie low, like my father told me to – but I found them afterwards. All dead. Sue-Ann strangled with her own pantyhose, her older sister, Beth, hanging from the ceiling fan in her room. Mrs Jacobs had taken the knife she'd cut her pies with and jammed it so hard into her own throat I couldn't see the blade at all. Only the black plastic handle, jutting out from below her chin. Mrs Doran was head first down her toilet. Can you imagine that? I think I laughed, seeing her like that, with her rear end stuck up in the air. I sat in the hall outside her bathroom and laughed until I cried. *No more artificially sweetened chocolate cake*, I thought. *No more pooping it all back out again.* I recall my behaviour that day and it shames me. I shouldn't have laughed like I did.

'And then there was Mr Willis. By God, he—' The parson glanced at them, as if remembering he had an audience, a member of which was only a child. He coloured at the cheeks, which surprised Alex. 'Forgive me. You don't need to hear the details. As you can imagine, being a pastor, my father began his preaching right away, even while the killings went on all around us. Preaching of God's punishment and the price we must pay for listening to our inner demons and behaving in ungodly ways. Not that there were many left to listen to him by that point, but he gave as well as received comfort through his sermons, even when people threw things at him, even when they spat and cursed his name and our Lord's. Now, believe me, I loved my father – I did, very much – he was a good man. But I didn't agree with everything he said. He was all fire and brimstone and Hell's minions waiting to fry us on pitchforks. But he just wanted to find a way to help. Now, me, I didn't want to save the world or *damn* it. The God I believe in is about love and forgiveness and charity. But I understood pretty quickly there weren't many of those things left any more. My community, its spirit, was gone, along with everything else.' The parson's smile had faded a long time ago, the only remnants of it in the faint lines at the corners of his mouth. 'This isn't a virtuous town any more. I've tried to keep it so, but no one is willing to help. Not now. Maybe not ever. But you seem like nice people. Maybe meeting you can be a turning point.'

'Where's your father now?' Addy asked.

Alex didn't hush the girl, although she did sweep the room again, not having lowered her guard during the entirety of the parson's story. If another person was positioning themselves for an ambush, they had managed not only to evade every single exploratory scan she'd given the nave but also done it without making the slightest sound.

'Gone,' Parson Nathaniel replied. 'He didn't like what had happened to the world. He wanted to be with his God.'

'I thought suicide was a sin,' Alex said, bringing her eyes back to him.

'Oh, he didn't kill himself. He just didn't stop others from doing it when they came to ransack the church. There's no food in here, by the way.'

Of course there wasn't. They'd have found it already. The gnawing emptiness of Alex's stomach scraped at the inside cavity of her belly, reminding her that she hadn't fed it for a while.

'Stand up,' she ordered, flicking the gun barrel up to indicate he should do as he was told. He rose from the pew in the same non-threatening, deliberate way as he'd sat down but, this time, uncertainty clouded his expression.

'Hands up, too.'

He lifted his hands higher, arms wide. He resembled his Jesus on the cross, but she didn't share the observation with him. She didn't think he'd appreciate the comparison. 'Come out into the aisle.'

He stepped out, casting a glance past her to Addy.

Alex got the feeling the girl shrugged at him. 'Should do as she says. She's got a gun.'

'Addison, keep an eye out. There could be more people skulking around.' To the parson, she said: 'Turn around.'

He showed her his back and spoke to her over his shoulder. He sounded worried. 'I told you, I don't have anyone else with me. I approached you in good faith. I'm not armed.'

'Maybe we're going to do *you* some harm? None of your good faith would help you then, would it?' She moved closer and pressed the barrel of the gun to the base of his skull. He flinched slightly. 'I'm going to pat you down now. Don't move suddenly or do anything stupid. Not unless you want a bullet in the back of your head.'

'You sound like Lacey,' said Addy, seemingly impressed.

'Who's Lacey?' Parson Nathaniel asked.

'No one. Stay still.' Alex began her pat-down, running the flat of her palm along each of his sides and around his waist, from front to back. He was thin but not undernourished; he had a solid feel to him. Strong. Well fed. 'Have you seen any strangers wandering around town?' she asked. 'Or any weird signs going up? Graffiti? Strange spiral or circle designs, painted or spray-painted on to buildings or cars? That kind of thing.'

'No? Why? Did something happen to you? You said something about a rough few days.'

'Something's always happening. Which you'd know if you ever stepped foot outside this place.' Finding no weapons on him, she poked the barrel of the gun into his back, nudging him into a walk. 'You can sit down while we wait. Front pew.'

Addy skipped well out of harm's way as they came past and then followed behind, chattering away.

'What we gonna do with him, Alex? Am I 'llowed to talk to him?' Alex rolled her eyes at the girl's use of her name. Soon, he'd know their entire family histories as well as their height, weight and zodiac signs. 'I don't think he's got anybody else with him. Do you? You can keep your gun on him anyways, in case he tries something.'

Alex would let the girl talk to their new parson friend, within limits. Since they'd stepped inside Pilgrim Holiness Church, Addy had come alive. She was more animated now, while talking to this man, than she had been all day. Alex pictured how she'd been earlier that morning: morose, uncommunicative, distressed. It was a relief to have the old Addy back, even if it meant keeping this stranger around temporarily in order to do it.

Richard Burton's smooth baritone piped up in her ear, or at least her memory of it. *Remember, it's not only Parson Nathaniel you need to watch*, he told her.

Alex hadn't forgotten. Her gaze shifted back to Addy and lingered on her. A lot of things had changed for them over the past few days. They were all on a merry-go-round, spinning wildly out of control, unable to do anything but hold on tight and hope to God they didn't fall away from each other.

Three days ago

Lacey lay down in the soft grass and put her head on her backpack. She could hear Addison in the background, reading haltingly from one of the fairy-tale books they had pilfered from a kindergarten classroom two weeks ago. A story about a princess who couldn't sleep, no matter how many mattresses and beds she piled atop one another.

They had put a lot of distance between themselves and the bridge, but it wasn't enough. Lacey was so tired, though. She'd almost toppled off her bike twice, her front wheel weaving in to the small ditch at the roadside, handlebars locking and almost throwing her over the top. She didn't have the energy to put up much of a fight when Alex led them into the pine-scented woods and directed them to lean their bikes against the trees.

She'd told Alex the name the giant had blurted before she'd booted him in the face (Lacey had been able to relay that much before Addison the limpet came sniffing around to see what they were talking about), so she knew how important it was to put as many miles between them and those people as possible, but she'd brook no arguments about stopping to rest.

'You'll end up face-planting the asphalt,' she'd said, doing her stern-older-sister routine. 'Then you'll expect me to patch you up. No. It's time for a break.'

Lacey was scared to close her eyes and invite the darkness in. Her eyes throbbed in their sockets. Nausea sloshed in her stomach and the urge to vomit burned up her gullet. She closed her eyes and swallowed it back. Inhaled deeply, because that was what her grammy always told her to do: breathe in and breathe out, nice and slow, that's a girl.

Breathe in

and

breathe out.

Her respiration slowed, her limbs weighted themselves to the ground and her worries dispersed in an ocean spray of mist.

She awoke in the dark to a red, womb-like world. The sky hung so low she was sure she could brush her fingers across it. She went to lift her hand, but an invisible force held her arm in place. She strained to lift the other arm, but that was pinned, too. So were her legs. From all directions, some unknown force exerted itself down on her; from head to toe and wrist to wrist, each part of her was held prisoner. Long grass tucked her in close, growing tall around her body.

Rolling her eyes left, a small sound escaped her when she saw the outline of a man shrouded in darkness. For a second she thought it was the same figure she'd seen leaning over Addison, with its gloating green eyes and its slash of a mouth opening wide to swallow her head. She whimpered, and the man stepped forward, out of the shadows.

Pilgrim's face was painted in an awful dark red, as if all light were filtered through a dense layer of blood. His eyes remained shadowed but she knew he was searching the clearing, his gaze roaming, restless, clocking every bent stalk of grass, each ripple through the leaves. The trees shivered. It was the same clearing where she had stopped with Addison and Alex to eat and rest, but they were gone, and Lacey and Pilgrim were alone. She spotted a ragged hole in Pilgrim's shirt, where the bullet from the revolver had entered him, but there were no bloodstains and he moved with ease, unencumbered by injury or pain.

'Pilgrim,' she said, unable to force her voice much above a whisper, the invisible pressure now squeezing in on her, two giant hands getting ready to wring her out like a washcloth. '*Pilgrim.*'

As if in answer, heavy static hissed above their heads. A fissure of red electricity forked across the sky, blinding her and imprinting a jagged scar across her vision. She blinked as the throbbing crackle swelled outward, forcing its way into her ears, her head, her blood pounding thickly with it.

'*Help me,*' she whispered, louder.

Pilgrim's eyes found her, and his head shook slowly from side to side. One half of his face remained in shadow, but she could make out his lips. They parted, moved, formed words, and as they did the vast static electricity rippling above her hummed and solidified, causing the hairs on her arms to lift and vibrate. She could feel its terrible power bearing down on her.

His lips moved again, the same shapes Addison's made in her sleep. The humming began to crackle and break up, distinguishing itself from the drone until it became a broken cacophony of half-cracked surges of white noise.

Mad . . . ness . . .

. . . Pain . . .

Death . . .

Pilgrim's arm lifted, his finger outstretched and pointing. A low rumbling built under Lacey's body. The grass began to quiver. The rumbling grew stronger, the earth shaking, and then she wasn't merely feeling the earth shake but was *hearing* it, the grinding of stone on stone setting her teeth on edge, the deep bass grumble of gigantic tectonic plates shifting beneath her.

A vicious crack rent the air.

The ground jolted violently and a section of the clearing began to slowly rise up.

Lacey cried out, but she remained rooted to the earth, in no danger of shifting from her pinned position. Clumps of soil fell and thudded to the ground. Forty feet away, the land lifted, shearing free, rising higher, fibrous vines and wispy tendrils of roots tearing loose as the two sections of land separated. The lifted section sawed away, tearing free from the clearing, toppling in degrees like a giant's measured fall from height, disappearing as it dropped out of view.

The crushing pressure that held Lacey in place vanished and she dragged in a huge, ragged breath. She scrambled clumsily to her feet and stumbled nearer to the jagged earth where the clearing had torn itself in two. She stood shakily at the edge of existence, an alien red-lit space before her, a vista so devoid of anything the immensity of it brought tears to her eyes.

Pilgrim stepped closer, hovering at her side, silent but steady. The air smelled of hot electricity and freshly turned earth, a potent mixture that made her nostrils flare.

In the distance, a fair way out, a jagged cliff-face rose into sight, its earthen sides freshly cut, a shiny, open wound of rich red clay. The cliff reared up, the stern of a ship rising out of an unknown sea, its top flattened in a wide plateau which sharpened to a pointed bow on its most westerly side. Upon the cliff's surface stood a crowd of people, easily a thousand in number, all facing the plateau's jutting point. They were silent under the flickering, crimson-lit sky.

As one, they moved forward, and the person nearest to the bow's tip stepped off. They didn't cry out as they fell but were immediately replaced by another person, who also stepped into space. The crowd shuffled forward. The next person stepped off. Shuffle. Next. Shuffle. Next. Without pause or hesitation, they filed off the edge. For an eternity they fell, to death, or oblivion, or both, Lacey didn't know. Without screams, without fights, they tumbled into the abyss as peacefully as if sleepwalking.

At the rear of the crowd, a girl stood, patiently waiting her turn. Already fifty people had walked off the cliff's outcropping, the remaining numbers edging ever closer to the end, and Addison edged with them.

'Addy!' Lacey screamed.

The sky ripped open in a blinding red flash, a fork of lightning slashing to the earth, striking the ground yards away from Lacey. The grass smoked.

'Addison!' she screamed, and a thousand heads snapped toward her and a thousand sets of eyes locked her in place. Those same invisible bonds that had held her fast to the ground wrapped around her again, swaddling her tight as a mummy, restricting her from the neck down.

As if Lacey's call had revealed Addison's identity, one thousand heads turned in unison, looking to the back of the crowd. Those nearest to the girl picked her up, lifting her high above their heads. She neither struggled nor made a sound as she was passed from person to person, riding a wave of hands, moving ever closer to the outcropping's edge.

'No! Please don't!' Lacey's head wrenched left and right as she thrashed, but it was no use, she couldn't break free.

A warm hand rested on her shoulder.

'*Do something!*' she shrieked at Pilgrim, but he shook his head again, his expression so pitying she cried out as if she'd been struck.

Those hundreds of hands had brought Addison to the plateau's point and, without pause, without a single uttered word, they passed her over the edge and let her go.

The girl fell silently, endlessly, turning end over end.

Lacey screamed and the bonds holding her in place shattered. Without thought, she ran forward and leaped into space, only to be yanked violently backward by a hand that crushed down on her shoulder, grinding her bones to dust.

Lacey gasped in agony and turned on Pilgrim, all set to yell in his face, but he was gone and Alex had taken his place.

She was lying in the grass of the clearing, Alex leaning over her, saying her name and asking if she was OK, her face tight with concern. Lacey struggled into a sitting position and glanced around, disoriented. The clearing was the same as when she'd fallen asleep: their packs, the bikes leaning against the trees, Addison sitting cross-legged, an open book in her hands, eyes wide as she watched her aunt have a meltdown. The skies were blue, the ground was intact and everything was back as it should be.

Her relief was so overwhelming, tears flooded Lacey's eyes. She reached out to Alex, gripped the solidness of her shoulders and arms, over and over grasping at her shirt, reassuring herself she was there.

It was just a dream, she told herself. Just another dream. Take it easy. Breathe.

Pilgrim saw them, too, Voice said suddenly. *I remember. He saw the red skies. Addis—*

'SHUT UP.'

Alex flinched, and Lacey choked back a sob. The hairs on her arms stood on end as if the static from the pulsing red sky continued to sing through her blood. She roughly palmed her

248

hair from her sweaty brow. Her skin was clammy and cold, yet the core of her burned hot with fever.

'Not you,' she whispered, giving Alex a beseeching look. 'I'm sorry. I didn't mean you.'

Alex pulled her into her arms and hugged her so fiercely it hurt. She began to rock, stroking Lacey's damp hair over and over. It took a long time for Alex to ease her hold.

Lacey listened to her friend's crooning, her whispers warm in her ear, telling her that she wasn't alone, that she'd never leave her, that it would all be all right. Lacey lay against her, face nestled in the hot crook of her neck, and pressed her mouth hard against Alex's shoulder. Because Alex *didn't* know that she would never leave her and she *didn't* know that everything would be all right, and Lacey didn't want to call her out on her lies.

Lacey and Alex sat side by side, shoulders touching, Alex with her sketchpad resting on her drawn-up knees, her pencil strokes making quiet *whisk*ing noises in the dark. The sun had been well on its way to setting by the time Lacey had burst free from her nightmare. Soon it would be too dark to travel.

This time of year, the heat of the day lingered well into the night, so they had let Addison stretch out under the stars and among the trees, burrowing down like a hibernating animal. She had fallen asleep quickly in that heavy-limbed, comatose way kids did when they were bone-deep exhausted. She even stayed that way for a good half-hour before the silent talking began.

With Addison asleep, Lacey recounted everything to Alex in detail, from the giant on the bridge through the dying man's words, and finishing with her dream of the lemming-like people falling to their deaths. She talked so fast she was breathless by the end, her words almost as quiet as the pencil nib's soft scratching.

'You're sure the giant said her name?' Alex asked, the pencil's whispering having fallen silent. Her head was angled toward

Lacey, her eyes shining darkly in the fading light.

Lacey nodded without looking up, busy biting at the skin on the inside of her cheek. It was sore and bumpy but her incisors continued to worry at it, as her worries gnawed at her.

'How could he . . . ?' but Alex didn't finish the question because, as Lacey knew, there was only one explanation as to how the giant would know the name: he'd been told to look out for them, for someone wearing a St Christopher necklace. Someone like her.

'Maybe they'd been following us and heard one of us say it,' Alex said.

Lacey shook her head, chewing on a bit of skin she'd stripped from the soft inside of her mouth. No, none of them had said it – none of them had had *call* to say it for weeks. Besides, she would have known if they'd been so close. Voice would have spotted them.

They weren't following us, Voice said. *But if they had anything to do with setting that fire we almost got barbecued in – which doesn't mean to say I'm letting Pyro-Addison off the hook – they'd have known people would leave the city via the main routes. Which included that bridge.*

She spat the bit of skin out. Her fingers found the St Christopher medallion at her throat. Its engraving had lost some of its definition, smoothing out like the sea smooths out the hard edges of a stone, but she could still feel man and child burning like a brand. 'The guy I shot said he was coming for us.'

Voice *hmphed. By 'us', he could have meant anyone and everyone.*

'How is that any better?'

It's not. But at least you can stop feeling singled out.

'How can I *not* feel singled out when the giant said her *name*?'

Maybe he was saying the first colour that popped into his head.

'Why are you being such a jerk about this? It wasn't just a *colour* to him. He looked at my necklace and said "Red" like he knew what it meant. They'd been told by someone' – she couldn't bring herself to say the Flitting Man's name – 'to keep an eye out for a girl wearing a St Christopher. They want her. Like Dumont wanted her. They just don't know she's dead.' She saw Red again, as she'd last seen her, lying curled up on her side at the bottom of the grave Lacey had dug, the red scarf covering her face, hiding the sunken, ruined mouth where her teeth had been pulled out. The St Christopher necklace had once belonged to her. 'We were the last people to see her alive.'

Voice was silent for a beat. *You haven't slept much. Maybe you misheard—*

'I didn't mishear!' Lacey gathered her breath and released it in a long, measured exhalation. She lowered her voice. 'I heard what I heard. He said "Red", and that's a bad thing. They'll be looking for us even harder now.'

She became aware of Alex looking at her, a hooded guardedness in her eyes.

'I know you don't like me talking to him, but that doesn't stop him bugging me.'

Tell her I said hello, Voice said.

Lacey's fingers tightened around the pendant. If she could punch him in the face right now, oh man, she'd clock him one *so* hard.

Voice sniggered, but only for a second. Business was far too serious tonight to hold on to his sarcasm for long.

'I know you can't help it,' Alex said, a quiet defeat in her voice. 'It's just hard to watch.'

'He doesn't want to hurt me, Alex.'

'I'm sure that's what a lot of people thought.' She shook her head – a weary, resigned motion – and went back to the drawing in her lap. Lacey watched her add darker shading around the sleeping girl's eyes and along the line of one cheek, smudging a fingertip along the lead strokes as if she were caressing Addison's face.

What I want to know is how news of Red got so far so fast. We're not in Vicksburg any more, Toto.

The dead guy had told her the Flitting Man had ears and eyes everywhere. Maybe his reach was a lot wider than they'd realised.

Alex sighed again and her pencil stopped moving, but she didn't lift her eyes from the page. 'So what do we do? Those people at the bridge are obviously part of a bigger picture. Assuming they're looking for Red, the giant saw a girl who fit her description, or at least fit a description they're looking for. We're irrevocably tied to her, whether we like it or not. I don't suppose you knocked him out for good?'

Lacey shook her head stiffly. 'He's alive,' she muttered.

She hadn't considered finishing him off. He'd been knocked out and posed a danger to no one. Maybe she should've shot him through the heart or caved in his skull. Pilgrim would have. He'd have made sure the giant couldn't follow or report back and cause them more trouble.

You'd never be able to kill a man in cold blood, Voice said.

Oh, she wouldn't, would she? He knew her so well? Well, if it meant keeping them safe, she would have to start doing things she'd never thought herself capable of, wouldn't she? The stakes were higher than ever. Her family was all she had. She wouldn't go back to being alone again. Not ever.

You're not alone, Lacey.

'You don't count.' Even as she said it, she felt bad.

Voice didn't reply, not to sulk or to bite back at her but because, she suspected, he knew she was right. He could never be a substitute for Alex's hugs or Addison's smiles. There was more to company than a voice in the dark.

'If the giant's alive, the fact he saw us is going to get back to—' Alex hesitated. 'Whoever it is that's looking for her.' Even *she* couldn't bring herself to say the Flitting Man's name, as if saying it aloud would give the rumours power and in giving

252

them power release a version of him on the world that was more real than any of them were ready for.

Under the starry sky, the darkness brought a presence of its own. It filled the spaces between tree trunks and scrub, between road and railings. It watched them. It colluded with things only it could see, and not even the full, shining moon could offer any respite. In the deadness of night, when the universe and all its diurnal creatures slept, the secret whisperings of voices were at their loudest. Who knew how many people were listening to them? Who knew how many were being stolen away?

Addison's sleep-talking routine was in full swing, her mouth opening and closing, lips pursing, writhing, forming. Who was she talking to every night? Were they talking back? Lacey had to force herself to remain seated, the urgent need to rush over and shake Addison awake passing through her hands like palsy.

'We have to assume they'll send someone after us,' Alex said.

Lacey found it impossible to look away from Addison's silently moving mouth now that she'd started. 'Red's dead,' Lacey whispered. She didn't mention that it wasn't only Red who had something the Flitting Man would want and that if he were ever to find out about Lacey and Voice's secret they would be in about as much trouble as a person could get into.

She felt Voice silently observing from his place inside her head. Her eyes were his eyes. *Mi casa es su casa.*

'No one knows that apart from us,' Alex said, quieter than before, as if afraid the night had ears. 'You said so yourself. The only person you told was Dumont, and he's gone. They'll keep looking for her, especially now they've spotted someone they think is her.'

Alex was right.

'Lacey, you need to take off the necklace.'

Something clutched inside her, a thorny knot that hurt her stomach. 'I'm sure if I keep it tucked under my—'

'Lacey.'

Her hand had closed reflexively around the St Christopher. She'd been wearing it ever since they'd found Red half hanging out of the smashed window of her overturned car. Lacey had been unsure why she'd taken it, but to leave the woman out there, with nothing and no one to remember her by, had been unthinkable to her. She'd unclasped it from around Red's neck and held on to it as a memorial. A keepsake. It had kept her safe on her travels. She didn't want to take it off.

I think all of its luck has run out, Voice said.

Lacey didn't release her hold on it.

I was kidding about the luck. It's just a piece of metal, Lacey. It holds no magical properties. Alex is right. You should take it off.

She closed her eyes, as if saying a silent prayer, and unclenched her hand. She hooked the chain over her head and held it up in front of her eyes, staring at the polished silver-spin of its coin. A second tiny moon, plucked down from the sky. 'Could you look after it?' she asked Alex. 'I'd want to keep taking it out to hold. It's become kind of a habit.'

Alex stared at the pendant and Lacey could see the flicker of silver refracted in her friend's eyes. Finally, reluctantly it seemed, Alex held out her hand, and Lacey spooled the necklace into her palm, a physical tug of loss pulling at her as the chain dropped from her fingers.

Alex's fist closed around it, and the silver-moon medallion blinked out of sight.

Lacey felt Voice circling. She let him drift in and around her thoughts, his presence weaving like hazy tendrils. She could have tried to shut him out – she was terrible at doing it but the attempt could often dissuade him from prying – but she felt the need for his company tonight. Alex had lain down after they had talked their options out, and all Lacey had left for company were the cold, blinking stars and the buzzing chirrup of cicadas.

As the whirring cogs of her brain cranked down a gear and

her worries chased their tails into exhaustion, Voice began to sing – not the Alphabet Pony song, for which she thanked her lucky stars, but something soft and mournful, about how times were a-changing.

She listened to him as she stared up into the cosmos, picking out the clusters that pulsed faintly in reds and greens, idly thinking about how those stars were now dead and gone, exploding out into space thousands of years ago, their light only now reaching her eyes. She thought that maybe she had shone and burned out, too, had already died a lonely death sometime in the past and her consciousness had yet to catch up with the realisation. The idea was a strange one, and it made her feel oddly disconnected, as if she were not here at all, the night and the breeze and the soft sleeping noises of her companions all just ghostly echoes. She was thankful when Voice's words pulled her away from such musings.

The times are definitely a-changing.

'Hmm.'

I can sense it, just like I sense the different, abstract layers of your thoughts. The ones you can't control. Worries about Addison and Red, about the Flitting Man getting closer. Your ideas about all the dying stars in the sky. Thoughts of how your butt bone hurts, and smaller thoughts of what food and water there is to last, the amount of miles we can cover. And beneath all that, you're thinking about bugs crawling over you when you lie down to sleep. Layers upon layers. It's background noise, but it's all there. Just like what I'm sensing is there.

She wondered if he was aware of the dull ache in her bladder and her growing urge to pee but didn't ask. She knew he knew. It was pointless trying to pretend he didn't.

'What're you talking about?' she asked instead.

I've heard others.

Her eyes had stalled on a constellation of stars, a smattering of pinpricks that curled in a spiralling band of light, but at his words she sat up, heart hammering, her hand reaching for the rifle at her side. She looked back toward the road.

'Where?' she breathed, left hand sliding along the gun's forestock, drawing the rifle into her shoulder.

No, he said. *Not people. Other voices. Like me.*

She stilled at his words, her mind growing very quiet, a motionless pond with nothing but the reflection of the moon and the stars on its surface. The rifle lowered to her lap.

I thought I was imagining it at first. That maybe they were your deep-down thoughts, ones I hadn't come across before. So then I got to thinking, about how information about Red is getting passed around so quickly. And it all makes a crazy kind of sense when I stopped to consider it.

'I'm not getting you.'

It wasn't you I was hearing those times, Lacey. When we were on the bridge, I caught something very faint in the giant. A clamouring burst that was impossible to understand. I heard it for the briefest of moments. It was a voice, Lacey. His voice.

'No, that's impossible. How can you even be sure it was—'

I wasn't sure. Which is why I never mentioned it. But there have been other times when . . . He stopped, then started up again. *When I think I hear snatches in Addison.*

Lacey listened to the dull thump of her heart. It had slowed from her initial scare but it continued to pump like a pulsing star readying itself for combustion. Her eyes tracked a streak of white across the night sky – a shooting star – but she had no wishes ready to make.

'You mean when she's sleeping? You hear something when she's asleep?'

Yes, that, too. And this time Voice paused as if he, too, were listening to the *ba-dum ba-dum* of her heart. *But I've also heard it when she's awake.*

CHAPTER 4

Birds and a Stone

Now/Norwich Police Department, Norwich

'Well, hello there, food,' Lacey said, lifting the bag of pasta out of the storage can.

Jackpot, Voice said.

'Hello to you, too,' she said to him as she lifted the second bag out. 'There has to be four pounds of pasta in here. We're gonna turn into a piece of pasta by the time we're through eating it all.'

Within the first five minutes of stepping through the main doors of the station, Lacey had wandered the echoing corridors, passing unoccupied offices, moseyed on past an interview room and a filing room, walked through each unlocked door without issue and found her way down into the chilly, unlit basement. In the few police stations she'd been in since leaving the farmhouse, three out of the four had been vandalised. This one wasn't so bad compared to the others. It used to sadden her, the vulgar graffiti, the disrespect, but now she was all shruggy about it. Her indifference made her sad in other ways.

Police departments got ransacked for weapons and gear, but people never thought to check out the food supplies left in stock for anyone kept in their holding cells. It was never a large quantity – Voice had told her that criminals would get ferried to a municipal jail pretty fast, or released after whatever mix-up that had landed them in there in the first place was cleared up – but it was surprising what could be found with just a little snooping.

Food is food is food, Voice said.

Lacey made a noise of agreement and tugged the draw-cord of her backpack closed. She collected her rifle and flashlight off the floor and climbed up from the frigid bowels of the holding cells back to the surface. Whistling her way back through the empty corridors – deciding to stick to 'Ob-La-Di, Ob-La-Da' this time, a safe, cheerful Beatles tune that did a moderately good job of masking the sick, fretful feeling in the pit of her stomach – she kicked at bits of crap in her way and pushed outside, breathing in the clean, fresh air. She blinked in the sunlight like a spelunker who'd spent the day underground, and patted at the top of her head for the pair of sunglasses she'd left there. Slipping them on, she glanced up and down the street.

Deserted. Perfect.

Hopping off the kerb, she hurried over to the centre line, equidistant from the houses on either side of the street. If anyone wanted to make a run at her, they'd have the exact same amount of distance to cover. She couldn't be any fairer than that.

'I can barely remember what the world was like before all this.'

I remember flashes. Briefly illuminating. I didn't belong there, though, I remember that much. And neither did Pilgrim. Not really.

It made her unhappy to think that even in the world before this one Pilgrim was alone and disconnected from everyone. 'Maybe you've just forgotten what it was like. Maybe you belonged there just fine.'

I don't think so. This world feels like home to me.

A tall flagpole listed crookedly in a front yard to her right, slanting over the driveway, where a Subaru rested on flat tyres.

The car had once been yellow but was now more of a dusty cream. A dark gap at the bottom of the garage door, where the mechanism had failed to fully close it, drew Lacey's eye for a moment and she wondered if a family of feral cats had made their home in there. Above the parked Subaru, a tattered stars-and-stripes banner, faded to a ghostly red, white and blue, hung listlessly in the non-breeze.

'It still feels weird, everything being so empty. I keep expecting a kid to run out of his house, going to call for his buddy. Wanting to play ball, or shoot some hoops. How stupid is that?'

It's not stupid. A pause. *Maybe it's a little stupid.*

She smirked. 'You're such a douche-bucket.'

She kicked at a chunk of granite the size of her fist and watched it skid across the crumbling concrete. It cracked off the kerb and skittered along the gutter. 'You think there's somewhere for us? A place we can stop running and be safe from everything and not be scared any more?'

Voice answered straight away. *Yes. I do.*

'Is it near? I need for it to be near. Tell me it's just down the road and around the next corner. I'm not sure how much longer I can do this.' Her voice disappeared at the end and she kicked extra hard at the next brick. It hurt her toe but she didn't care.

You know I can't tell you that. We just need to keep going. If we keep moving, one step after the next, we'll be OK.

Lacey walked faster, taking his advice to heart and placing one boot in front of the other, tightrope-walking the yellow centre lines, arms outstretched. She knew they were both avoiding talking about what needed to be talked about. About who was following them, about the things Voice could hear now, about what that meant for her, for Addison, for everyone. What would they do if the net they felt closing in on them suddenly snatched them all up? Where would they hide when all the hiding places in the world were ripped open and turned inside out? Where would any of them go?

She swerved away from the yellow lines and headed for the sidewalk. She passed two more houses, both white clapboard, one with window shutters painted in a horrible poop-brown that reminded Lacey of the colour of her grammy's station wagon. She turned right, cutting across a driveway. A basketball hoop hung over the double garage. She pretended to dribble an imaginary ball and then rose up to aim a three-pointer from outside an invisible D. She imagined it sailing high, high, arcing a beautiful loop and dropping in, sweet as a nut. She raised her arms in victory and made the cheering noise of the crowd.

Funny. I imagined you missed.

'Screw you. You're just jealous you don't have hands. Or arms. Or anything else of any use.'

She left her basketball dreams behind and jogged around to the backyard. Her bike was where she'd left it, leaning up against the rear wall of the garage, which was covered in white clapboard to match the house.

'Maybe I should name my bike, like Addison did.'

Name it what?

'Something cool. I don't know.' She said the first thing that popped into her head. 'Power Ranger.'

That's . . . actually pretty good, he conceded.

There was no sarcasm in Voice's words. He didn't pick up on the fact she'd stolen it from a kids' TV show and movie franchise.

She didn't get on her bike straight away but pretended to check it over, squeezing the tyres for air pressure, leaning over to poke at the chain. 'You know what I wish for right this very moment?' She cupped her hand over her nose and inhaled the smell of oil.

Hand sanitizer?

She shook her head and wiped her hands off on her pants. 'Nope. I'm being serious.'

I don't know, Lacey. What do you wish for?

'I wish I was back home, at the farmhouse. I wish my grammy was alive and none of this shit was happening. That none of this "outside in the big, wide world" shit had ever even happened.' Her throat squeezed tight because she knew what she was admitting to by saying that. If she'd never left, she would never have found Addison. Worse, she would never have found Alex and Alex would be dead. 'I didn't mean that,' she whispered.

I know you didn't.

He was quiet so long she threw her leg over the bike and set her foot on the pedal, all ready to set off.

You know what I wish?

'That you weren't such a loser?' Her attempt at humour sounded forced even to her ears. Their time was up, and she knew it. Time to get back to the big, wide fucking world.

But Voice never finished his thought because, right then, Lacey spotted them.

'Voice?' she whispered. 'You see that?'

Voice didn't reply, but she didn't need him to because the birds numbered so many no one could miss them: they swallowed the sun. A tidal-wave shadow ran silently through the streets, a black veil that brought with it a premature evening. The temperature dropped noticeably.

Lacey's fingers fumbled at the bike's handgrip and she squeezed it in a death grip. She stared up, mouth dropping open, as thousands upon thousands of small, feathered bodies winged by. A few hundred spontaneously broke ranks to wheel directly above her head, maybe two hundred feet up in the sky. She stared in wonder at the beauty of the shapes they formed, swooping one way then the other, whirling and looping with some prescient knowledge, their turns made in perfect synchronicity. Done with their acrobatics, they flew to rejoin the trailing end of their brethren, their smaller body of birds absorbed by the vastly larger and, as one, they winged their way eastward, their course set to pass over the church.

For ten whole seconds Lacey stood with her bike in the shadow of its mass, her ears filled with a yawning silence, and even as it passed and a maelstrom of fallen feathers gusted around her, thrown up by the wind generated by all those wings, she and Voice continued to stare after it, speechless.

Lacey—

She didn't move. Couldn't.

Lacey, we need to get back to the church.

She closed her mouth. Swallowed. Her heartbeat thrummed along with all those beating wings and her ears pulsed as if a bird had stayed behind to flutter madly about her head.

LACEY. GO.

She flinched and pushed off, feet tripping over the pedals before finding them. She pumped her legs so fast it was a wonder the bike didn't take flight, too.

Two days ago

There! Just now. I heard it.

Lacey quickly looked up and found Addison squatting at the side of the road, picking up stones, discarding the ones she didn't like and stuffing the others in her pocket. They had stopped so Alex could take a bathroom break, and Lacey had been grateful for the opportunity to stretch her legs.

During hours of observation and monitoring (most of it spent listening to Addison chattering away, asking question upon question, and watching her practise her new bike tricks, one of which had resulted in a spectacularly bad fall that had left her sitting in the dirt, leg drawn up to her chest, silently rocking over a scraped knee), Voice hadn't reported any further episodes of hearing another voice. A time or two, Lacey had even tentatively suggested that maybe he'd been mistaken with what he'd heard, but Voice responded with angry conviction and then proceeded to withdraw from her sullenly, leaving behind a lingering feeling of offence that she'd dared to question his word.

'What's it saying?' Lacey asked quietly, glancing over to where Alex had disappeared behind an open-faced tractor shed. Lord knew what a shed was doing out here. It was tiny. And empty. And there were no fields in need of tractoring anywhere around here; it was all unchecked trees and wild grassland. Still, Lacey was glad for it because it kept Alex out of earshot. She wouldn't like what was going on here. Not one bit.

I couldn't make it out. It was too quiet. I'm just telling you I heard it.

Lacey tried to snatch back her frustration before it bloomed too large, but she wasn't quick enough.

What do you want from me? Voice said defensively. *I'm not psychic.*

She found it ironic that he should say that when he read her thoughts *all* the time.

It's not the same and you know it. I don't even know what I'm doing or if I'm hearing it right.

Once again checking that Alex wasn't within hearing distance, Lacey wandered over to Addison and crouched down next to her, watching her small fingers sift through the dirt and debris. Her fingernails were short, chipped, dirty – it had taken her and Alex almost two weeks of attempts before finally succeeding in pinning the girl down long enough to cut her obscenely long nails. They had toughened up into talons.

'What're you doing?' Lacey asked her.

Addison didn't look up from her rock hunt. 'Nothing. Finding rocks.'

'Rocks for what?'

'Throwing.'

To brain you and Alex with.

Lacey sent a withering thought at Voice and he meekly withdrew.

'There's nothing interesting to throw at out here,' she told the girl.

'There's a lake.' Addison had found a good, flat stone and was brushing it clean on the grubby knee of her jeans. 'Gonna throw 'em in there.'

Lacey checked up ahead. She saw nothing but dusty blacktop and browning grass. The smattering of trees flanking the road gave no indication there were any lakes hiding away in the denser woodland behind them. She listened for running water, but heard only the occasional twitter of birds.

She studied the look of concentration on her niece's face, how the pink tip of her tongue stuck out the corner of her mouth as she went about her task. At the top of Addison's cheek, under her left eye, was a tiny beauty mark. Lacey hadn't noticed it before. She felt an irresistible urge to brush her fingers over it.

'How'd you know there's a lake nearby, Addy?' she asked quietly. 'Were you told about it?'

The girl stilled for a second, but it was only a second. 'Just do,' Addison said. 'Look at this one!' She held up a smooth, symmetrical stone as wide as her palm, a happy grin on her face.

'It's perfect,' Lacey said, trying to smile.

True to Addison's word, half a mile up the road glimmers of water glittered at them from between the trees. Leaving the hardtop's solid terrain, they made their way deeper into the woods and came out on the steep bank of a lake. On its far side was a wooden jetty with a rickety-looking rowboat moored to one post. They cycled slowly, cutting a path through the stiff, wheel-clutching grass.

Two trails, overgrown now but still visible, converged at a picnic area, a scattering of wooden benches and tables marking the place as a popular one for hikers and families out on day trips. Addison stood Alphabet Pony on its stand by the bench nearest the jetty and ran for the platform, her feet stomping the planks.

'Wait for Lacey!' Alex called after her.

The girl reluctantly slowed to a walk, casting a glance back at them, the drop in pace a painful concession for her, judging by her expression. Lacey felt their general drop in pace as a painful concession, too, but it had been over two days since the incident at the bridge, and they'd seen no signs of anyone following.

Lacey climbed off her bike. The warm, pungent dampness of rotting wood scented the air but she couldn't tell if it came from the picnic benches or the mooring posts. Addison had chanced edging partway along the jetty, despite being told to wait. Lacey stepped on to the platform and gave it a couple of test jumps, her boots thudding, but other than a small spattering of dust and grit hitting the water, the wood remained sturdy, no cracks or alarming shifts coming from under her feet. She gave Addison the OK and the girl raced to the end of the platform.

'We shouldn't stay too long,' Alex said from behind her, hefting her pack on to the nearest picnic table.

'Just long enough to eat and throw some rocks,' Lacey agreed. 'Then we'll go.'

She wandered after Addison, keeping her gaze off the water, the sun's reflection jabbing needles into her eyes.

'Be careful!' she called. Addison had taken hold of the mooring rope and was reeling the creaky old rowboat in. It was grey and weathered and looked about as seaworthy as a tea strainer. Lacey moved close enough to grab the back of Addison's shirt.

'Can we get in?' Addison asked.

Lacey pretended to consider the question. 'No.'

'But I've never been in a ship before.'

'It's a boat. Ships are much, much bigger.'

'Can I get in the boat, then?'

'No to all ships *and* boats. Anyway, I thought you wanted to throw your rocks.'

'Oh, yeah.' The girl dropped the line, distracted from the boat (which had been Lacey's plan), and began digging into the front pockets of her pants. She drew out two handfuls of stones and piled them up in a neat heap. 'Wanta help?' she asked, glancing up at Lacey.

Lacey shrugged. 'Sure. Why not?'

The girl handed over two good-sized stones. They stood next to each other at the end of the jetty and looked out at the lake. Addison lifted her arm and pointed. 'See that green thingy?'

Lacey cupped a hand over her eyes. A shiny green tarp jutted out of the lake. It was maybe a bus length away and no bigger than a truck tyre. 'The tarp,' she said. 'I see it.'

'Whoever hits it first wins.'

'Wins what?'

Addison seemed stumped by the question, then she turned around and yelled, 'Alex! What should the winner get if they hit the green thing?'

Alex, who had been busy rooting in their packs for lunch, paused to look up. 'What green thing?'

'It's a plastic tarp,' Lacey called back at her.

'Why would you want to hit a plastic tarp for?'

'I don't. Addy wants to.'

'It's for a *game*,' Addison called. 'We need a prize.'

'How about an all-expenses-paid trip to Disneyland?'

Addison looked up at Lacey, mouth open a little, nose wrinkled up.

'It's a theme park,' Lacey explained. 'With rides and stuff. People used to go there on vacation. Don't worry, she's just trying to be funny.'

'Should I laugh?'

'Best not to. We don't want to encourage her.'

'What're you guys whispering about?'

'Nothing!' Lacey called.

Addison raised her voice again. 'The prize has to be in the realms of possibility, Alex.'

Lacey smiled. *Realms of possibility*. The kid had such a way with words sometimes. She wondered which one of them she'd heard it from.

'How about the winner gets a nice foot rub?' called Alex.

'Eww. OK, forget it! I'll think of something.' Addison turned back to Lacey and her eyes lit up. 'Oh! How 'bout the loser has to call the winner Your Majesty for the rest of time? And has to curtsey, too?'

Lacey had to bite her lip to keep from grinning. She had known that fairy-tale book would come back to haunt her. 'How about just for a day? But you'd best start practising your curtseying – you're gonna be doing a whole lot of it pretty soon.'

'Deal!' Addison was already hooking her arm back, her first stone sailing into the air. She had a good, strong arm (Lacey knew from the arm-wrestling matches they'd had) and the stone climbed in a high, looping arc, splashing down a good ten yards short of the target.

'Missed,' Lacey said, unable to hide her glee. Playing against a girl less than half her age didn't make any difference to her; if her competitive gene sniffed a challenge, it was out of its kennel and barking before she had chance to put a leash on it. She remembered having a full-blown tantrum when she lost a game of gin rummy one time – stomping feet and crossed arms, the whole works. Her grammy had claimed the entire winning pot of three dollars and sixteen cents. Lacey didn't know why she'd taken it so badly, it wasn't like she could go to the store and buy candy with her lost stake, and if it was her grams's idea of teaching her humility, it had backfired spectacularly.

Lacey let her stone fly, willing its aim to be true as her eyes followed its trajectory. Water exploded up in a white, foamy burst three yards away from the plastic tarp.

'*Shit.*'

Addison whooped.

After that it became a free-for-all. They both grabbed up stones as fast as they could and lobbed them into the lake. Lacey was laughing too much to aim properly and, when a rock finally plonked on to the plastic with a loud smack, she wasn't sure whose it was.

'Mine!' Addison yelled. 'That was mine!'

Lacey gave a short, incredulous laugh. 'No way was it.'

Alex piped up from the shore behind them. 'I say it was Addison's.'

Lacey turned on her in mock-indignation. 'You weren't even watching!'

'I was.' Alex smiled. 'I have excellent eyesight.'

'*I* have excellent aim.'

Addison tugged on her shirt.

'Yes, but my eyesight is better,' Alex said. 'They called me Cyclops in high school.'

Lacey scoffed a laugh. 'That doesn't even make sense. Cyclops only have one eye.'

'Not the mythical kind. The *X-Men* kind.'

Addison said Lacey's name.

'He didn't *have* super eyesight,' Lacey told her. 'He shot laser beams from his eyeballs. Even I remember that.'

'*Laaacey,*' Addison whined.

Lacey held up her hands in defeat. '*OK*, OK. Fine.' She began a curtsey, dipping down and fanning her hands out at her sides as if spreading an imaginary skirt. 'You win, *Your Majesty*. But don't rub it in too much. No one likes a smartass winner.'

Lacey.

It was the strangeness in Voice's tone that brought her eyes up, knee half bent in a dip. Addison's face was pale. The girl stared out at the lake. Her thin chest was pumping hard with her breaths. Lacey quickly straightened and followed the girl's gaze.

The tarp had floated free from whatever had fastened it in place. It drifted toward them, slowly rotating, a bloated, lumpy face rising up out of the water, mottled green and grossly disfigured, years' worth of water having swollen it beyond all recognition. Next to it, a second fleshy mass floated up. A small, rounded head with a wispy crown of hair, its sturdy little torso puffed up to twice its normal size. Then a third body bobbed up, this one an adult's, naked and female, the dark strands of its hair draped like black seaweed over the flattened breasts, its distended belly huge, a grotesque island poking up out of the water.

'Lacey?' Addison whispered unsteadily.

But the lake's exhuming wasn't over. A large bubble popped from between the dead woman's legs, then more bubbles, *pop-pop-pop*, and a froth of black gunk floated to the surface. The last body appeared, tiny and shrivelled, still tethered to its mother by its umbilical.

Lacey bent over and gagged.

Oh my God, Voice said.

There were more down there, Lacey could feel them, floating along the bottom, opaque eyes looking upward, staring at them. No, not at them, at *Addison*. Whatever had told Addison about this lake, about throwing the stones in here, had known what was waiting for them, had known that they would disturb the lake's long-sleeping guests with those rocks.

Snaking an arm around Addison, Lacey drew her niece away from the end of the jetty, backing them up, her eyes never leaving those bobbing bodies, the slow ripples of the lake pushing them with gentle hands toward the shore.

Alex was waiting for them as they stepped backward off the creaking planks, the hush of the grass welcoming their feet, closing them in from sole to shinbone.

'What is it?' Alex's asked, uncertainty warring with panic in her voice.

Lacey didn't look away from the jetty or the water beyond it. 'Don't,' she whispered. 'Don't look. There were babies.'

Staring at the lake, Lacey became convinced it was a window to another world, a mirror image of their own, with its imitation sun, its copied clouds and twinned trees, but it was all too quiet down there, too peaceful. There was a screaming emptiness, a void with no people, no insects, no birds, no life of any kind. Not even a breeze or a droplet of rain marred its perfection. That alien world was frozen in time and it was beautiful. Lacey longed to approach the lake with its gateway to that other, perfect world, her reflection growing larger and larger so that it matched her exactly, measure for measure. She would let Lacey and Imitation-Lacey touch – at noses and foreheads, at chins, chests and stomachs, at fingertips, at knees and feet – and they would sink into each other, her own reflection eating her up, each Lacey absorbing the other until she disappeared, nothing left of her at all, and that perfect, beautiful, still, empty world would be all that remained.

No, Voice said, shocked. *Why would you want that?*

Addison stepped away from her, breaking their contact, and went over to Alex, who drew the girl close, staring over her head at the jetty as if expecting to see a legion of bloated corpses pull themselves up on to the dry platform and shamble their loose-limbed way toward them.

Lacey, let's get out of here. Let's just go. Please.

Her voice came out sounding dull and lifeless. 'Yeah. Yeah, OK.'

They packed their things up with fumbling hands, eyes sliding back to the lake every few seconds, and lit out of there as fast as the wheel-clutching grasses would let them.

CHAPTER 5

Tricks and Secrets

Now/Pilgrim Holiness Church, Norwich

Lacey struggled to hold open the church doors and shove her bike through, cursing when she pinched her fingers in the door frame.

'Lacey! Look, we found a priest!'

The man in the front pew nearest the pulpit swivelled in his seat.

Lacey stared. He wasn't what she'd been expecting to see. A church full of screeching, swirling birds maybe, but not a priest. He had a nice enough face, she supposed. Clean-shaven, blue eyes, dark hair curling over his ears. He nodded a greeting to her.

Choosing not to return it, Lacey did a semi-panicked sweep of the room, her eyes working into each corner, not missing a spot as she dropped her bike against the wall and shucked off her pack. Unslinging her rifle, she gripped it in trembling hands as she walked down the left-hand aisle, keeping a row of pews between her and the new guy.

Her forefinger slipped around the trigger.

Easy now, Voice murmured. *You're not Yul Brynner. This guy could be exactly what Addison said he was.*

'I'm not really a priest,' the man told her, and Lacey's step faltered. It took her a moment to realise he was simply replying to what Addison had said and not to Voice. 'Nothing so formal.' He smiled warmly. 'I'm merely a man of religion.'

Lacey was glad to see Alex had the revolver in her hand. Not so glad to see it resting on her thigh rather than pointed at this guy with his shit-eating grin. The chancel was a foot higher than the rest of the nave, and both Alex and Addison had been sitting on its step. Like a critter in one of those whack-a-mole games, though, Addison had popped up as soon as she'd heard Lacey enter.

'There isn't much religion left in the world, mister,' Lacey said, reaching the front pew and following it along, her eyes checking everywhere. The rifle was lowered but her muscles were tensed and an audible pressure pounded at the back of her head – nothing to do with Voice, she just wasn't breathing properly.

Calm down. You're going to hyperventilate.

She wanted to yell at him that it was *his* fault if she was. He'd scared the shit out of her, telling her to get back here.

I may have been slightly rash, he admitted. *Seeing all those birds freaked me out. Blame Hitchcock, not me.*

She opened her mouth to argue and closed it again. She wasn't about to get into a debate about who this Hitchcock was, not in front of a total stranger.

She stopped a good distance away from the priest and eyed him.

'Please, call me Benny,' he said. 'And I suppose you're right, but I like to think there's enough to keep me on the straight and narrow.'

Voice made a sceptical *hmph* noise, which came through as a buzzing behind Lacey's ear. It made her want to swat a hand at it. Her reply was snarkier than it might normally have been. 'If you think you can convert us to some weird-ass Christian cult, you can forget it.'

The priest smiled.

Look how pearly white his teeth are.

'Stop trying to worm your way around me,' Lacey said irritably.

The man's smile faltered, a frown edging in.

Alex spoke up. 'He has food hidden away. He's offered to share some with us.'

'I already found food,' Lacey answered shortly.

The priest lifted a hand, like a kid in school trying to get the teacher's attention. 'I have other things you could use. I noticed you've got radios. I have batteries.' He began to stand but stopped halfway when Lacey swung her rifle on him. He stayed like that, knees slightly bent, hunched over in an awkward half-sitting, half-standing position. The top half of him looked like a fortune cookie.

Suspicion tightened her voice. 'What are you doing here? We're not in the game of welcoming strangers in with open arms. And why are you even *offering* us stuff? No one does that. Not unless they want something.'

He eyed her gun. 'I live here. And like I told Alex, you have a child with you. It seemed like the right thing to do.'

Bullshit.

'Bullshit,' Lacey said. 'Nothing's free, my man. Not ever. What do you want?'

'Just to talk. Like I keep trying to say. I want to talk and enjoy your company for a while. That's all. No ulterior motives, as God is my witness.' Keeping his eyes on the gun, he sank back down, the wooden pew creaking when his backside met the seat.

God isn't witnessing nada any more, padre. We're all on our lonesome out here.

Addison bounded over, practically bouncing. Standing on the foot-tall chancel's platform, her eyes were level with Lacey's. She looked at her with a solemnly excited expression and whispered loud enough for everyone to hear. 'Lacey, he's *nice*. He told me he's gotta whole box of books that used to be his cousin's. Can we go see them? *Please?*'

'No. We don't know him. It could be a box of rabid tarantulas, for all we know. Alex?'

Lacey was relieved to see that Alex had raised her gun and was now pointing it at the priest. She gave Lacey a half-shrug and said, 'He's not armed. All he's done so far is talk. And then talk some more. Believe me, he wasn't lying when he said he wanted to talk.'

Lacey's eyes went back to the priest. She sent an enquiring nudge to Voice.

Batteries would be good, he said. *We can always fill him full of lead later, if he tries anything. I find it strange, though. Who approaches anyone unarmed, priest or not? He risked a lot, and just so he could talk with us? There's something not right here. Then again, we* have *been running on paranoia fumes lately. We might be reading more into this than it warrants. Just be careful.*

She let the barrel of the rifle drop but didn't remove her finger from the trigger. To the priest, she said, 'The three of us have some things to discuss. So you just sit there and don't *do* anything.'

His face didn't lose its affable expression. 'Of course. Don't mind me.'

So amenable.

'Yeah,' Lacey muttered, and sat down on the platform, laying her rifle over her lap so the barrel pointed toward him *and* his amenability. Addison hopped down off the step and sat next to her. Alex got up, glancing back at the priest as she did, and came over to settle on Lacey's other side.

'Where the hell did he come from?' Lacey asked, keeping her voice low.

'He just walked right in and started talking,' Alex said. 'Like it was the most natural thing in the world. I thought he was trying to distract us at first, but he's been here for almost forty minutes and all he's done is . . . well, *talk*.'

'Talk about what?'

'It'd be easier to tell you what he didn't talk about. What TV shows he used to watch, what board games he likes to play, the books he reads. Oh, and he found an old gramophone a couple months back, so he told us about the records he listens to on it. *Then* he told us about what music he *used* to like to listen to. I don't think he has an off switch, Lacey. He'd have kept going if you hadn't come in. I mean, it's all harmless stuff. Tedious, but harmless.'

'What's "tedious"?' Addison asked.

'Boring,' Lacey said.

Addison was leaning forward over her knees so she could look past Lacey to Alex. 'He's not *boring*,' she told her. 'He's lonely. Like I got lonely. Lonely is a thing.'

Lacey had been glancing over at the priest every few seconds. As soon as they'd started talking, he'd bowed his head and folded his hands in his lap, appearing to be praying. The way his lips moved made Lacey shiver.

She muttered, 'He shouldn't be lonely. He's got his God to talk to.'

A fallen God with hardly anyone left to worship Him. Wonder what that does to a deity. A real kick to the balls, I'd imagine.

'Well, I like him,' Addison stated simply. 'And I don't know why we got to always stay away from people. Like everyone's bad.'

'I don't think *every*one's bad,' Lacey said, feeling defensive and not knowing why.

'Do, too.'

'I do not.'

'Do, too. You act like we shouldn't trust no one.'

Maybe she did, but she had plenty of good reasons to feel untrusting of people. 'Not trusting isn't the same as thinking everyone's bad.'

'It does if you—'

'This isn't the time to be arguing, girls,' Alex interrupted.

Lacey bit back her retort.

Addison popped a shrug and got up. She stepped up on to the platform and tramped over to the pulpit, her face a picture of sulkiness. Lacey watched her go. Seemed she was done talking with them.

'She's like an eight-year-old teenager,' she said.

'You're a teenager, too, remember.'

Lacey gave Alex a look. 'What's that supposed to mean?'

'It means she only has us to talk to,' she replied, neatly dodging the question. 'That can't always be fun for her.'

'No one said it was supposed to be fun. Besides, it's not only us she has to talk to any more, is it? Did anything happen with her while I was gone?'

Alex shook her head. 'Nothing. If anything, chatting to the parson over there seems to have helped.'

'We saw some crazy shit outside, Alex. Birds. Birds flying everywhere.'

'Isn't that what birds do? Fly?'

'Not like this. There were, like, *thousands* of them. All winging it this way. There's still some outside.' Thirty or so had stayed to swoop in gliding circles around the church, choosing to leave the mass migration in favour of the oak tree. 'Didn't you hear anything?'

'All we've been hearing is Benny rabbiting on about anything and everything that pops into his head.'

Maybe he's trying to distract us.

Lacey stopped breathing. 'You hear something in him?' She didn't bother to clarify what she meant. Alex's attention sharpened; she knew Lacey wasn't talking to her.

No. Nothing specific. There's just a constant buzzing everywhere now.

'Then why say he might be trying to distract us?'

We just need to stay vigilant, Lacey. This other voice that's following us, it's getting closer. I can hear it. That thing I said earlier about needing to try something? I'll have to do it, and soon.

'You never said what, though.'

I know. You'll have to trust me.

'I do, but how can you *hear* it?'

'What's he saying?' Alex asked. She didn't look happy, but Lacey didn't have time to make her feel better.

It must be like me. Been around much longer than the rest.

'Do you even know what it wants?'

Voice talked fast. *Listen to me carefully. If I can hear it, it must be able to hear me, and the closer it gets, the more it'll be able to make out what I'm saying.*

'I didn't think anyone was supposed to hear you but me—'

We don't have much time, Lacey. It won't stop until it has what it wants, that much I can tell. It doesn't . . . think like me – it's cold and slick and there's something driving it that's tireless. We can't let it find us.

'Are you sure it's not him? I—' She didn't have time to finish because Voice was talking again.

There's no time. I can't say too much. You must understand. It might be listening.

There was an urgency to Voice's words that scared Lacey. Made her hesitate to question him further. But how could she protect her niece if she didn't understand what was happening?

'How far away are they?'

Not far. Maybe a few hours.

A blade of fear sliced through her belly. 'We need to move?'

Yes. Maybe. There might be another way. Do you know what an aygur is?

'A what?' She was having difficulty keeping up with him.

An aygur. I'm sure that's what it said. It's very angry. You know what? Never mind about that. You remember when we were with Pilgrim in the hotel casino, trying to find Alex, and we had to go

277

through that mess hall, where all of Dumont's men sat between her and us?

Lacey's temples throbbed. She had no idea what Voice was getting at. She glanced over at the priest and found him with his head up, watching her. He didn't look away when she met his eyes.

'What're you talking about?' Lacey whispered, trying not to move her lips.

Do you remember it? Voice pressed.

Of course she remembered.

You remember how we got past them?

Pilgrim had forced Posy to carry her over his shoulder, making out she was their prisoner. 'Yes,' she said. 'I pretended to be unconscious.'

Exactly. This is for the best, Lacey. I'm sorry. It's probably going to hurt.

'But what—' Before she could finish, Voice projected so piercingly loud she dropped her rifle and clamped her hands over her ears. Not that it did any good. All the noise was coming from the inside and no amount of covering her ears could deafen it.

DON'T LET THE PRIEST GET THE GUN! NO, WATCH OUT!

Hot, blinding flashes burst behind her eyes, the world crackling as if a cattle prod were jammed against the back of her skull, zapping two thousand volts into her. Between the flashes she saw the priest stand and start toward them, his eyes dropping to the fallen rifle.

STOP HIM! NO! TELL HIM TO STOP!

Lacey couldn't see. The world had turned atom-bomb white. She sensed a quick bustle of movement around her, felt someone brushing close against her. She called Alex's name.

DON'T! PLEASE DON'T! DON'T SHOOT US—

A deafening roar blasted through her head, pummelling her

with sound and light. She cried out, swayed, tried to grasp at something to steady herself, but there was nothing, only emptiness. And then all the deafening colours disintegrated at once and a silent black fog floated down to take their place.

One day ago

It was Addison who found the rusted and grass-hidden railway tracks and Alex who suggested following them. They led to a disused platform, now completely overgrown with plant life, and a small, dilapidated railway station. Creepers climbed its walls and blanketed the roof, as if it had pulled on a thick green sweater for warmth.

The station was a one-room shack. Its old ticket window faced out on to the platform, a single door in and a single door out. Voice loved it. To his vocal disappointment, the place had been all but cleared out, the only items remaining a moth-eaten brown sofa (sagging belly brushing the floor), a woodworm-rotted bureau (drawers empty but for a damp clump of old ticket stationery) and a spindle-legged chair that rocked when you sat on it. Lacey had to peevishly tell him to shut his cakehole when his fizzing excitement made it difficult to think straight.

Once inside, they barricaded the door by pulling and shunting the sagging-bellied sofa over to block it. Part of Lacey expected to hear the lake's animated corpses come shambling their way along the tracks, dragging themselves up on to the station's platform, their water-softened nails rubbing at the door for entrance.

It took over an hour for Addison to settle, despite the barricaded door, and another hour for the shock at seeing the decomposed bodies at the lake to wear off. Crushing fatigue swamped the girl's system, all resistance ebbing away as Lacey softly sang her favourite Beatles song to her, the one she'd hummed on the rear porch of her sister's house all those weeks ago. And now, like then, she was left holding a limp, sleeping girl cradled in her arms.

She and Alex placed her carefully on the sofa and covered her up.

They sat on the floor and, without speaking, each placed a hand on the girl, Lacey's on Addison's arm, Alex's low on her leg. They looked at each other silently for a long time.

Why aren't you talking? Voice asked. *You're always talking. It's weird that you're not. Say something.*

Lacey was tonguing the inside of her cheek, tracing the bumpy scar tissue. It was satisfying to be able to feel the secret damage she was doing to herself each time she gnawed on the soft meat of her mouth, adding to the design.

'Something's coming,' Lacey said, leaving her cheek alone and meeting Alex's gaze. 'You feel it, right? It's not just my imagination. Something's coming for us.'

No, that wasn't what I wanted you to say. Say something else.

'Is—' Alex stopped, visibly held her breath for a moment, fortifying herself, and went on. 'Is Voice telling you that?'

Alex wore a soft flannel shirt. Her sleeve had slid higher when she'd placed her hand on the girl's leg, the cuff pulling tight around her forearm, exposing her wrist. Scars circled them, pale pink and shiny. Lacey's eyes travelled higher, over Alex's shoulder to the open collar of her shirt. Inside, below Alex's collarbone, on her chest and along the swell of her breast, more scars, criss-crossing and raised, ugly-looking, painful. Not soft and comforting and self-inflicted like the scars in Lacey's mouth.

She lifted her eyes to Alex's. The woman was watching her but didn't move to pull her collar closed or tug her shirt cuff down. Lacey had seen all her scars, too many times to count. Alex had nothing else to hide.

Remorse stabbed at Lacey's heart. She had plenty to hide.

'I didn't want you to worry,' Lacey whispered, mortified

when her friend blurred in front of her. She used her sleeve to scrub at her eyes. Who the fuck was she to cry? She hadn't been whipped, scarred, her family ripped away from her. Lacey had Addison, and Alex had lost everything.

No more lies, Lacey, Voice said. *It's time to tell her.*

Alex didn't say anything, her dark gaze unreadable in the dimness.

'I know how you hate seeing it in me, even though I *swear* to you Voice isn't like all the others. I know it must feel like being with Sam all over again.'

'You're not like my sister,' Alex said. 'I know that.'

But she was, wasn't she? At least partly, and that was the problem. Alex hadn't been able to fully trust her sister, either. She had told Lacey a little bit about Sam, about how uncontrollable she was, how prone to spontaneous bursts of recklessness that had put them in danger. All because she suffered from hallucinations – audial, visual, the whole shaboodle. She'd had them from a young age, her mental illness established long before the voices came. And now she was dead. Alex didn't speak about her much, but Lacey knew their life together had been tough. Sam's problems had always come between them, whether she could help it or not.

Tell her everything, Lacey. Tell her how you got me.

'Really? It's OK?' she whispered, shaky with hope.

Yes. Tell her.

Lacey began to talk. She made sure to leave nothing out, from the first moment Voice had started speaking to her after leaving Pilgrim and making his miraculous leap into her, to the hours she'd spent fearful that a creeping insanity was invading her mind. How Voice had talked to her while she was locked up in the freezer. How he'd helped them find their way back to Alex, and how he'd helped every step of the way since, a secret part of Pilgrim that she carried with her, always.

With every word shared and every secret uncovered, Lacey

grew lighter, shedding the hot stones of her guilt, practically hearing them *thud* as they hit the ground. It made her realise how exhausting it had been to carry them. And not just exhausting. Painful. *Debilitating*. What an unburdening it must be for all those who heard a voice to surround themselves with people who accepted them. A supportive network where they could finally, *finally*, be free. And that was the Flitting Man's strength. The appeal of what he offered. Lacey understood it now. Understood why so many disappeared, leaving their loved ones to think they'd been taken in the night. Why it was, despite the negatives, still better than the alternative. A life spent in hiding. Hated. Distrusted. It was sobering to realise that Lacey might have been tempted to search out his followers, too, if her circumstances had been different.

'If I couldn't be completely open about Voice, I couldn't tell you where he came from. And the longer I didn't tell, the harder it got to find the words. Me hearing him was an accident, Alex. A dangerous accident that no one can ever find out about.'

Alex hadn't spoken throughout Lacey's explanation, not to ask questions, nor to throw accusations at her for lying to her. Now, she spoke, softly, as if dazed. 'You know I would never tell anyone.'

'I know that. I do. It was never about me not trusting you. It was about me knowing how much you hate this part of me, and there's absolutely nothing I can do about it. Nothing Addison can do, either.'

Alex looked away, her eyes falling on Addison. Lacey saw her throat move as she swallowed and, when she spoke, her voice sounded different, thick.

'What about her? What does it – *he* – say about her?'

'He says he can hear other things now. Other voices. Not often, but sometimes. Like with the lake, he heard something in Addison then. And she told me it was there, Alex. It was half a mile away. How could she have known that?'

A flicker of something – wariness maybe – passed across Alex's face. She wet her lips.

Lacey reached for Alex's free hand, the one not resting on Addison's leg, and drew it into her lap, unable to sit with such a yawning gulf hanging between them. For an insane moment, she wished she were a voice inside Alex's head, listening to her thoughts, experiencing the emotions racing through her, and didn't feel so adrift and separate from the only person, other than Addison, who she truly loved.

She rested Alex's hand, open and exposed, in her lap and stroked the life and heart lines of her palm, the markings, her grammy said, that were made at birth, long before fate got involved. Alex's life line forked at one point, but then maybe everyone's forked at the same spot – the ones still alive and living in this new world, that is. The heart line was long and unbroken.

Lacey had always envied Alex her hands, her fingers long and elegant and gifted. Lacey's were blunt-nailed and unfussy. Working hands, not made to create or craft anything beautiful. In fact, they had a knack for killing things – plants, vegetables, people. Her grams had called her Leper Hands and Lacey had never realised until now how fitting the name was.

She laid her palm over Alex's, pressing it flat, then wrapped her fingers around her hand, grasping on tight. Too tight, she knew, but she couldn't help herself.

Now all three of them were connected. A circle, joined to one another. She wondered how much longer they could stay like that before the world, which had already sunk its teeth in, tore them to shreds.

'I love you,' Lacey said suddenly, fiercely, unable to look Alex in the eye, afraid to see the blame, the fear there, afraid her tears would come again, burning and shameful.

A brief return squeeze from Alex's fingers. 'I love you, too,' the woman whispered, but there was a tremor in her voice, as if she were uncertain, as if there was a lack of conviction in the statement and that Alex was saying it only to appease.

Lacey turned her face away, closed her eyes, releasing her grip on her friend's hand, leaving it resting in her lap. She bit her cheek so hard the tears that came were through pain. And that was better. She didn't have to feel ashamed about those. Alex was to her what the stars were to sailors: a guide, a way to help navigate the seas. She was straight and true *precisely* because there were no outside – or inside – influences swaying her. Lacey trusted her without question, which is something Alex would never be able to do with her. Voice would always be there, an uninvited guest. A silent observer. An interloper.

Strong fingers gripped her shoulders, turned her, and Lacey found herself face to face with Alex, so close she could see nothing of the train shack, only Alex's eyes. The woman released her shoulders and cupped her face between warm palms.

'I'm sorry,' Alex whispered. 'I know I haven't made this easy for you. You're a seventeen-year-old girl who's had to grow up very fast, and here I am, acting like a child with her fingers plugged in her ears. I know I've constantly shut you down whenever you brought Voice up. I know you've made great efforts not to speak about him because you understand how much it hurts me. I thought if I could just pretend nothing was going on, it would all go away. I've spent so much of my life with somebody who teetered every day on the brink, I felt like I was close to falling in myself and I didn't want to live like that. Not again. I needed some time, some distance. But ignoring what was happening to you, pretending like everything was OK when it wasn't, that's not only dangerous, it's selfish, and I'm sorry, Lacey. I'm sorry for leaving you to deal with this on your own. That was very unfair of me. But know that I'm here now and I'm not afraid.'

Alex smoothed her thumb under Lacey's eye, brushing away

a tear. She leaned in and pressed her lips between Lacey's brows, holding the kiss for a long moment before leaning back.

'No more secrets between us,' Alex said.

'No more secrets,' Lacey whispered.

'Everything will be OK.'

'Yeah, maybe.'

Alex laughed softly, and the sound of her laughter finally did what a thousand words couldn't. The stiff muscles in Lacey's neck and shoulders unlocked and she eased sideways, tiredly leaning against the sofa. Alex leaned with her, her hand returning to find Lacey's and holding on to it.

They went back to watching Addison. The girl hadn't budged an inch throughout their entire conversation. She could be in a coma, if not for her moving lips.

'She's too young to be hearing anything,' Alex said softly.

She's right, Voice said. *She'd be the youngest I've seen by far.*

Addison was midway through mouthing the word 'slaughter' when Lacey looked away.

Addison's sleep ended abruptly. Her silent lip-syncing stopped and her eyes opened, but she made no attempt to sit up. She looked ill, pale and drawn, her eyes sunk into their sockets. Her curls hung lank around her face. Everything that was normally vibrant about her had drawn back, shrinking inward, as if a succubus had visited her during the night and sucked all the vitality from her. When Alex and Lacey asked her questions, her eyes dodging theirs, she mumbled her replies. Whatever was happening to her, she couldn't (*Or wouldn't*, Voice said) tell them. Whatever was happening, it was gaining momentum.

'Don't you remember *anything*?' Lacey asked.

Addison's face scrunched up. She shook her head hard: left, right, left, right. Her response was loud and clear. NO.

We need to keep going, Voice said.

Lacey left Addison and Alex sitting on the sofa and stepped

away, needing to quieten her mind, needing to concentrate. She sent her thoughts inwards, despite the effort it cost her.

– You think Addison was deliberately led to that lake? You think whatever told her about it *wanted* her to throw those rocks so she'd hit those bodies?

Yes.

– But *why?*

To scare her? To have some fun at her expense? To take a bet on you losing and win a stuffed toy? Who knows. Whatever the reason, it got what it wanted.

– How did it even know they were there?

Voice sighed, heavy and long and exasperated. *I don't know that, either.*

Lacey didn't reply, but resentment sat thick and heavy in her throat and, for a distressing moment, she wanted to scream out her frustration.

Go ahead and scream. It won't help anything. Look, I need to be quiet for a while, OK? I think I'm getting a handle on it now. Hold down the fort.

Before she could ask what he meant by 'getting a handle on it', he slipped away from her, a glowing spark on a breeze, narrowing down to a speck. Right before he disappeared, he flared back to life.

Listen!

Addison was perched beside Alex, bent over her knees, lacing up her shoes – Bunny ears, bunny ears, playing by the tree – exactly how Alex had taught her. She was singing something, very low under her breath, and it wasn't the bunny song.

Lacey moved closer, straining.

'. . . Come on . . . saddle up . . . need a home . . . a new rope. Steer him . . . place on earth . . . Hey, Alphabet Pony, be my new love.'

Lacey stared at the top of her niece's head, a deep foreboding opening up inside her. Alex had noticed her odd expression and was frowning, a question in her eyes. Lacey couldn't force herself to speak. She listened as her niece continued to sing the song Voice had shared in the bike store, days ago. The song he'd only ever sung twice, also days ago, and which Lacey had only ever hummed. There was no way Addison could know the words. No possible way.

You were right, Voice said, and there was something in the way he said it that tightened Lacey's stomach muscles. *I hear something else now. Not from Addison, not so close. It's faint, like thunder stirring beyond the horizon.*

'What're you talking about?' she said.

Another voice. Behind us. You were right, Lacey, he said again. *Something's coming for us.*

CHAPTER 6

Pilgrim Holiness Church, Norwich

Now/The basement

Alex had been tricked, plain and simple. She thought she was beyond such things, that the time for being taken for a fool was well behind her, but there were still a few lessons the universe insisted on teaching her. Number one being, you're a victim – suck it up and accept it. Back in the old world, that would have been a problematic label for her, but in this one *everyone* was a victim and, to her way of thinking, that put them all on a level playing field.

How you dealt with the universe's teaching, well, that was what decided the kind of person you were. Some fought against it, coming out kicking and scratching. Some bunkered down and never lifted their heads above the sandbags. Some outright gave up. And some believed those were the only three options.

They were in the church's basement. Benny's basement. And Benny was a pack-rat.

The space down there was *crammed* full of stuff, floor to ceiling, an accumulation of magazines and books and boxed board games, piles of stuffed toys and vinyl records, intricate LEGO constructions and finished jigsaws mounted into frames, transparent tubs full of plastic soldiers, Nerf guns, toy cars, train sets, more books. Books upon books upon books. All packed in a way that formed narrow aisles. Benny had made himself a warren.

Placed every so often on one of those leaning towers of hoarded crap was a battery-operated lantern. They helped alleviate the gloom with small, yellowish pools of light, each one beckoning like a station beacon in an underground pass, bathing Benny's collections in a dirty lemon glow. More walkways branched off from the main one, but these were unlit, hidden. Earlier, when Alex had passed them earlier she had found herself quickly looking away, something unnamed and threatening about the rickety heaps of memorabilia stored down those dark tunnels.

Carrying an unconscious Lacey through such a precarious labyrinth had been challenging. Alex had feared accidentally triggering an avalanche, leaving her, Benny and Addy crushed beneath a sliding mountain of junk. Fortunately, her elbows behaved themselves and they'd reached the end of the aisle without mishap.

There, a brighter, welcoming saturation of light illuminated a small oasis of space. It was filled with the bare essentials: a recliner (currently unreclined), a rug, a low table with a cushion for kneeling on (a picture of Jesus hanging above it, his palms held up to show their bleeding centres and his heart bathed in glorious light) and a waist-high pile of newspapers with an ancient-looking gramophone perched on top. The final addition to the living space was a cot, its blanket pulled taut and neatly made with hospital corners, not a single crease marring it.

Addy had made a beeline past the La-Z-Boy recliner to a transparent plastic tub filled with colourful picture books. Benny had spewed many lies, but his cousin's story collection hadn't been one of them.

Benny hadn't spoken to Alex since she threatened to shoot him in the balls. They sat, Benny in his La-Z-Boy, a wall of towering boxes at his back, and Alex on the floor next to the cot where Lacey lay. They eyed each other like two cats at war over contested territory. If Alex were a cat, her ears would be laid flat to her skull and her back arched, the fur stiffened along her spine. The weight of the revolver at her waist mocked her.

A fine sheen of sweat coated Benny's face. It made him look greasy. A song played from the gramophone's oversized horn speaker, an orchestral and emotive piece he'd put on while Alex had fussed over Lacey on the cot. It put Alex in the mind of the great silent movies, where facial expressions were exaggerated to compensate for the actors' lack of speech.

Lacey moaned, the first sound she'd made since crying out in pain and blacking out upstairs. Alex felt the cot shift against her back as she moved but didn't turn around. She had eyes only for Benny.

'Uhhh. God, my *head*.'

Addy looked up from where she sat on the homey, tasselled rug. She'd made herself into a girl island, a rainbow slide of books and the pinks, whites and purples of Barbie paraphernalia scattered all around her. Alex spared a glance long enough to give her a minute shake of her head. The girl looked at Benny then quickly down at her Barbie doll and said nothing.

More shifting against Alex's back. She felt Lacey's hand bump her shoulder, weakly gripping on to her. 'Alex?'

'We're in the church's basement,' she said, although Lacey hadn't asked.

'Huh?' It came out as a croak. 'Why're we in the basement?'

It was difficult to tell if the black of the parson's robes had absorbed all the light – the area around the recliner seemed noticeably dimmer to Alex – or if she had been staring at him so long her eyes had begun to play tricks on her.

'There's nothing to worry about.' It was strange hearing Benny speak after so long. 'It's perfectly safe down here.'

He surprised Alex by smiling. But the smile wasn't for her, it was for Lacey. A pale imitation of his earlier ones, eyes crinkling at the corners like the folds of a flimsy paper airplane.

Lacey leaned in close, her words so soft they were nothing but warm air, nearly lost in the strings of music drifting from the gramophone's speaker.

'Something's wrong,' Lacey murmured in her ear. 'Voice is gone.'

A streak of fear bolted through Alex, and it confused her. Voice's disappearance should be cause for celebration. Maybe he had left for good, disappeared in the same miraculous fashion he had arrived in. But Lacey's tightly held-in panic, a strumming tension that ran through the girl's body, taut as a drawn bow-string, somehow transferred itself to her and Alex's fear opened up a chasm in her stomach.

Perhaps Voice had known something worse was about to happen. She wanted to think better of him – she *did* – but couldn't help but liken it to a rat abandoning a sinking ship. She wouldn't put it past his kind.

'Where is he?' she whispered back.

'*I don't know.*' And in those three words, Alex heard how lost Lacey was, how set adrift. It went far beyond fear. It went beyond even abandonment. 'He's not answering me, Alex. He's not anywhere.' There were tears in her voice. 'Alex, why are we down here?'

'Benny gave me your rifle. Picked it right off the floor where you dropped it and handed it over. He didn't try anything. He said there was a bed down here. We tried waking you and couldn't. I thought it'd be best to let you rest somewhere comfortable.'

The girl was quiet for a moment. 'Why're you eyeballing each other like that?'

'Because the bastard fooled me.' Alex tried to keep the anger from spilling over, and failed. 'You're not the only one who hears a voice, Lacey.'

The tension in Lacey shivered, drawing so tight Alex expected it to snap. Alex's shirt pulled uncomfortably across her shoulders as Lacey's hand clutched at her. A groan of wood joints, more bumps, and Lacey's legs swung into view as she sat up on the edge of the cot. Alex heard heavy, nasal breathing, the kind you made when you felt sick to your stomach and were afraid you'd throw up.

Benny's eyes went from her to Lacey. His tongue flicked out to lick his lips.

'You should tell Lacey what you told me,' Alex said to him.

He was pale under his tan. The heel of his left foot jigged up and down repeatedly, as if he were in desperate need of the bathroom.

'Go on. Tell her.'

He wet his lips again. 'Look, I have no reason to hurt you. If I'd wanted that – which I *don't* – I could've hurt you long before Lacey came back. I'm not supposed to touch you.'

His words arrowed into her like darts. Alex didn't need to see Lacey's reaction to feel it in her stillness, hear it in the heavy silence, underscored by stringed violins and crackling cellos. The clammy heat of Lacey's palm dampened Alex's shirt. The weight of it increased as she stood.

'*Who* told you not to touch us?' Lacey's tone was light, casual, but Alex wasn't fooled.

Benny shook his head in choppy movements, much like a kid trying his hardest to keep a secret he'd been blood-sworn to protect.

'Kidnapping three girls isn't a very Christian thing to do,' Lacey said.

His head was still shaking. 'It's not like that.'

'Then why don't you let us out?' Alex asked.

'*Out?*' Alex felt the sharp look Lacey sent her. 'What's *out* supposed to mean?' Her hand left Alex's shoulder and she took a step closer to Addy. The girl had stopped playing with her dolls and was watching them. Sometimes, it was so easy to forget she was there. Like a doll herself, nothing moved but her eyes.

Lacey took another step and Alex realised it wasn't just Addy she was moving toward – her rifle was propped up against the pile of newspapers the gramophone sat upon.

'We're locked in down here,' Alex explained, eyeing Benny, wondering if he could read Lacey's intentions. 'And he won't tell me where the key is.'

'It's safe here,' Benny repeated, and by the sincerity in his too-wide eyes, she knew he meant it. 'You don't have to worry. God is protecting us.'

Alex's fear ran like a fever under her skin, hot and unceasing, and it shredded the edges of her patience. 'God isn't doing *anything*, Benny. *You* are.'

She'd tried talking reason, she'd tried explaining why they couldn't stay here, that someone decidedly *not* God was coming for them. But every argument she'd made was met with sympathetic head-shakes and pitying looks because, to him, *she* was the one who didn't understand. She didn't appreciate that Benny had been chosen. He was God's servant and she must take his word that he knew what was best for them.

'This isn't a game, shit-for-brains.' For once, Alex approved of Lacey's tactlessness. 'You can't just go around messing with people like this.'

Benny hesitated. He was perspiring so heavily sweat dripped off the point of his chin and *plipp*ed on to his robes, the moisture vanishing into black cloth. 'This is the best place for you. You must trust me.'

'Well, guess what? I *don't*. I don't even know you. You're insane if you think we're going to sit in here waiting for who-ever's out there to come find us. Now give me the key. Right this second, or else I'm gonna flip my lid.'

'I'm sorry,' Benny whispered. 'Truly I am. But I can't.'

Lacey's hands curled into fists. A low, barely restrained growl came from deep in her throat. It brought Alex to her feet, legs shaking with adrenaline. She motioned Addy to move away, not wanting her to get trampled if Lacey decided to do something foolish.

Lacey's head tipped back. 'Voice!' she yelled at the ceiling. 'Quit fooling around, OK? This isn't funny any more. I *need* you! Please!' The girl waited for an answer, staring at the stained concrete. When nothing came, she let out a barely restrained cry of frustration.

Alex's heart thundered, a constant, panicked juddering that drove her a step nearer to Lacey. 'Benny, God wouldn't be asking you to do this. He wouldn't want you to keep anyone against their will, especially not for something who might want to harm us.'

'*Of course* it wants to harm us!' Lacey shouted. 'It's been hunting us for days! Alex, I'm *done* talking to this lunatic.' She turned on the parson. 'Final chance, Benny. Give me the key.'

But Benny wasn't listening. His gaze had drifted to the side, defocusing from their faces. Alex immediately recognised the look.

'Stop!'

Benny blinked.

'Don't do that. Please don't listen to it. I'm begging you.'

A muscle twitched in his cheek and Alex swore she detected a hint of regret in his expression. 'He says they're very close now.'

Lacey went for the gun, diving across the space, hands outstretched, but Alex was ready. She grabbed Lacey around the waist and reeled her back in. Addy had popped to her feet as soon as Lacey lunged, a Barbie doll in one hand and a Ken doll in the other. She had dressed them in their wedding outfits.

'Lacey, no,' Alex gasped, struggling to hold on to the squirming girl. Her strength was astonishing. It always surprised her.

'Let go! I'm gonna *shoot* him!'

'You can't! He's the only one who knows where the key is!'

Benny burst from his seat, face red, perspiration flinging from his hair, and for an instant, a fleeting moment that passed so quickly it might not have existed at all, Alex *almost* released Lacey and let her shoot the man.

'Don't you *see*? None of this matters!' Benny didn't rush to attack them, he loomed in that small space and preached at them. 'I thought He had abandoned us! I never thought a person could die from loneliness, but it's been like a cancer, eating away at my bones. He's tried so many times to make me despair. Mocking and belittling me. Calling me names. But then *you* came.' Benny's face became painfully joyful and Alex could barely stand to look at it. 'He's rewarding me for my faith. It has been a torment, but now I see it was all a *test*. A test to see if I was worthy. And I am worthy, Lord!' Benny clasped his hands together and cast his eyes heavenward. The sweeping musical notes of countless strings, oboes, horns and trumpets intertwined and came together in a building wall of sound. 'May your blessings rain down on me. Let me be your right hand in this hour of need.' Benny's fervent eyes came back to them, pinning Alex in place. In her arms, she could feel Lacey trembling in hard shudders. 'We need to do as He says,' Benny said, with the utmost conviction. 'He asks nothing of us we aren't willing to give.'

Alex's head was hurting again, a current of helpless rage running hot from her temples and down to her chest, a molten fury buried so deep it would never run dry. How *dare* he think he was the one who was going to save them? He knew nothing about them. He didn't know how strong they were together, how far they had come. How they would do *anything* for each other. *He* was the one who was lost. The only thing that was going to get them killed was *him* and his so-called faith.

Lacey must have arrived at the same conclusion because all the fight drained out of her and she turned limply in Alex's arms, hiding her face in her neck. Alex hugged her, rubbed her back, not feeling Lacey's hand slip between them. Not feeling the vague tug at her waistband. Oblivious right up until Lacey pulled the service revolver free from Alex's belt and the gun went off, the crack so loud in the confined space it was like being punched in the face. A sharp bite of gunpowder misted the air.

Benny shrieked.

As if in sympathy with his pain, a protracted screech came from the gramophone's horned speaker. The Ken doll was on the floor at Addy's feet, her back jammed up against the newspapers, where she'd stumbled against them. She pushed away and the needle *scrawp*ed across the record, setting Alex's teeth on edge. The music shut off and all that was left were Benny's screams.

Alex couldn't catch her breath. Her eyes dropped to the oval, tasselled rug, the only concession to homeliness in the basement. A spattered red mess stained its edges. Black boot leather and gore.

Benny hopped as if he'd stepped barefoot on a hot griddle and tumbled heavily into the La-Z-Boy, moaning in sharp bleats, rocking, hands frantically locked around his ankle, his grip a tourniquet that would somehow magically prevent the pulped agony of his foot travelling any higher.

Lacey's eyes were dazed, showing too much of their whites, but the revolver was steady in her grip. She re-targeted and pointed it at his other foot. Made sure he saw it, too.

'The key or your last good foot, Benny. Better decide.'

A whole slew of emotions flickered across Benny's face, a battle that made his brow scrunch up and his eyes blink rapidly. 'It's no use,' he whispered, two fat tears blurring his eyes, spilling over to roll down his damp face. 'It's too late. I'm sorry but they're already here.'

In the nave above their heads, a door crashed open and a howl of voices, the wild call of a hunting wolf pack, filled the church to its rafters.

PART THREE
The Chase

CHAPTER 1

The Inn

Bianca padded from her bedroom – a corner room of the Inn with one window east-facing to the sea and a second facing north, looking on to a boating garage as big as a house – and went two doors up the hallway to Jasper's room. She peeked in to find the baby awake, lying on his back in his makeshift crib of lashed crates and blankets, arms waving at the ceiling, legs kicking. He burbled quietly to himself, his eyes widening for a second, fingers clutching at the air.

'My little man's awake already?' Bianca murmured, moving into his line of sight. 'An early riser, just like his Uncle Bruno. Too many things to be doing to while away the day sleeping, isn't that right, little man?'

As soon as Jasper spotted her, a smile broke out on his face and Bianca's heart melted, simply melted like goo in her chest. 'Want to come up?' She reached her hands into the crib and Jasper's cycling legs and waving arms accelerated with excitement. She lifted him and cuddled him close. His small, sturdy body pumped out enough heat to warm her right through her pyjama top.

She kissed his silky head, rubbed his warm back, pressing her nose to his baby-scented hair, breathing him in as she bopped him up and down and made nonsense words in his ear. One fist found its way into her curls, grasping on, but not painfully so. His other hand patted at her face. Bianca smiled and caught his chubby mitt, pressed his palm over her lips and blew a raspberry on it. Jasper gasped, stymied for a moment, and then breathed that soft, huffing laugh she loved so much.

Two minutes were spent on swapping his cloth diaper for a fresh one, and a few extra seconds on raspberrying his soft, rounded belly, and then he was in her arms again. She cherished these moments with him, the mornings precious to her, because for a short while it was just the two of them, the rest of the world forgotten. Being with him made her heart ache, and not all for the good.

She had two sisters and two brothers, all younger than her. Sophia was nine the last time Bianca had seen her and would now be sixteen. Marcy eleven, now eighteen. Luke and Verne would be twenty-two and twenty-six. Bianca had been the grown-up age of twenty-one and was away travelling when the first news reports of murder–suicides hit the TV networks (because murder–suicides were much more sensationalist than a lone jumper, or a car careening off a mountain road, or a self-inflicted gunshot wound to the head in a one-room apartment). She'd been unconcerned by the reports, because these things never affected you and yours. Tragedy only ever hit other families, didn't you know? Youth was so blind, it made you invincible, made you fearless.

She had phoned home when the reports rose in number. Verne had answered and told her everything was fine; Mama was at work because she worked two jobs and was rarely at home other than to sleep and eat, but he'd got everything under control. Just enjoy yourself, Bee, he told her, you deserve it, the girls say hi, make sure to bring them back something pretty, and she'd said sure she'd bring them something back, and she'd bring him back something pretty, too, and he'd laughed, and that was the last time she ever spoke to him. A feeling deep down in her gut had told her something was wrong, but she'd gone right on back to her vacation with Jeanie. This was the first time she had ever gone on vacation – she and her girlfriend had saved up for eighteen months and Jeanie's car was a crap-heap but it had a couple thousand miles left on the clock, plenty for getting down to Baton Rouge and back.

As it turned out, the crap-heap had only a few hundred miles in its choked-up engine, but by then it was too late anyhow. The roads were jammed with traffic, drivers desperate to get home or away from home, depending on what had gone down there. The honking of car horns filled the world. It deafened Bianca and Jeanie for hours on end and, even after the last one had fallen silent, Bianca would, for weeks, be struck by their phantom beeping, her ears playing tricks on her in a world gone unnaturally still.

Those first days, Bianca and Jeanie spent much of their time stuck at bus stations and railway ticket offices, sitting at the sides of roads, not hitchhiking exactly, because no one would stop, no one would even look at them.

Plodding along the side of the highway with more than a hundred other foot-draggers, Bianca had stumbled back with everyone else when an eighteen-wheeler roared past, its horn blaring. She knew what was happening before the screams and shouts took up, before the truck put on that last burst of speed, the driver flooring the gas and the engine gunning high and mad. The eighteen-wheeler sped at the tail-end of blocked traffic and hit the stationary cars at full speed. The sound of crumpling metal screeched across Bianca's nerve endings and the sunshine was eclipsed with a radium-powered bomb of light and sound. A percussive *whuuuump* hit her, a hot gust of wind that knocked her back a step. She found herself on her butt, the rest of the people around her felled like bowling pins. The interstate burned before them, the wreckages of cars melting into the blacktop, any screams of the people trapped inside lost in a roar of flames.

One after another, more cars sped past, barrelling at the inferno. Drivers who saw their salvation in the cleansing fires and hurtled on home toward it. More *whumps*. More crunching impacts. Mini-explosions that rocked the earth under Bianca's rump. A number of downed people stumbled to their feet and ran. Not away from the devastation, but *toward* it. Sprinted for the finishing line, each one disappearing before they reached the conflagration because the heat haze was too great for Bianca to see them, their bodies and limbs lost in the wavering, blinding blaze.

She'd telephoned home again but the lines were down. Jeanie had gotten through to her folks once, and her mother had sobbed at her, her words mostly unrecognisable, but she had managed to relay that Jeanie's daddy was dead and so was her little brother. Stay away, she bawled at her. Don't come home. There's nothing here but madness.

Jeanie grew steadily more despondent and uncommunicative after that. Bianca tried talking to her, to drag her from her black depression, but there was no reaching her. They were crossing the Tennessee River when Jeanie stopped walking, so fatigued it seemed to take a great effort to turn her head to look back at Bianca. Her eyes were heavy-lidded, bloodshot. Bianca lifted a hand to her, but Jeanie stepped out of reach, shook her head, said, 'What we doing, Bee? What's all this strife?'

'I don't know, Jeanie-girl. But it'll work its way done with us, you'll see. Not got far to go now.' That was a lie, and they both knew it. They were still over two hundred miles from home.

'I'm tired, Bee. I'm so *tired*. It wants me to take a little rest now. I *want* to take a little rest.' She smiled at Bianca, more a stretching of her cheeks than a smile, turned, placed her hand on the concrete abutment of the bridge and swung herself over it. She didn't make a sound as she fell.

Bianca screamed, running to the spot where Jeanie had

jumped. She saw her friend's body hit the water. She screamed Jeanie's name over and over, even after her throat became dry and hoarse, even when it felt like she'd swallowed a cupful of acid. But Jeanie didn't pop up to the surface. She was gone.

Eleven days later, Bianca arrived home to an empty apartment. Drawers were open, clothes strewn across the beds and the floors. There were no notes and no clues as to where her brothers and sisters and her mama had gone. She'd stayed for two months while everything collapsed around her. She visited every friend's house, every haunt her siblings had frequented. She went to both places her mama worked at – the corner deli on East 8th and Park and the investment offices down on Kingville Boulevard where she cleaned in the evenings – and found nothing but death and chaos. Stay away. That's what Jeanie's mother had told them, and she'd been right.

Her mama had a brother in Asheville, North Carolina, so she'd gone there first. She thought she wouldn't make it, and not because she heard any demons talking to her in her head, murmuring their sweet nothings, but because anybody who wasn't already dead and rotting was out in the streets, wailing in grief or lamenting the deaths of their loved ones, or having breakdowns in full view of anyone unfortunate enough to pass them by. Screaming and gibbering at anyone who came too close or sometimes at no one at all. None of it was of any interest to Bianca. All she wanted was to find her family.

She arrived at Uncle Dodie's a broken woman and he'd patched her up as best he could in between his mumblings, arm twitches, eye blinks, head cocks, nods and shakes, all of it as if in answer to something out of earshot, and all of which made her jittery as hell. She hadn't stayed but a couple of nights then left for the next place on her list. A friend of her mama's from high school. She found Petunia laid out on her belly in her garden, her head buried up to her neck and her big ass sticking up for all to see.

Preacher Dodd was next, a man her mama had been close to before he abruptly relocated to London, Kentucky. No luck there, either. Bianca worked her way through her mama's pocket book of people, and that occupied her for quite some time. Between each of these trips, she would return to their apartment to check if anyone had come home, but no one ever had.

Until, at the very last, she found herself at the final place her mama might have gone. Burnettown. And to Durnell Grover.

She hadn't seen Durnell since she was six and he'd turned up on their doorstep with a small brown suitcase and a hangdog smile. Her mama had taken him in because she'd *always* taken him in, and he stayed for three weeks before disappearing without a word, his pockets lined with their grocery money and her grandma's gold wedding band. Sometimes, over the years, he would treat Bianca to a telephone call (if he'd been drinking enough and got to thinking about his failures as a father, that was), and she figured he probably made the same phone call to eight other kids just like her, dotted around Georgia and the Carolinas. His last correspondence had been an eighteenth-birthday card sent five days after her birthday with a scrawled message inside that read 'Miss your face, Pop'.

Bianca knew that Durnell had been her mama's first and only love. God knew why. Outside of those three weeks when Bianca had turned six, her mama and Durnell had spent two tumultuous years together, and Bianca was the sole result of it (if you didn't count a broken heart, three fractured ribs and a herniated disk from being thrown down a flight of stairs).

He lived in a trailer on the outskirts of Burnettown. The grass was long, the neighbourhood too quiet (except for a wild mongrel barking somewhere up the street) and the stretch of road lay empty from one end to the other. The shivering rattle of the chain-link gate worked its way into her bones, and she stood shivering on the threshold of his property.

304

She got to moving but, before she came within ten yards of his door, she could smell him (and if the smell hadn't led her to the bathroom, the droves of flies would have). He'd lasted years out here by himself. Bianca couldn't help but wonder if she might've helped him if she'd come earlier. But that was pointless thinking. She'd held no sway over his life for all the twenty-eight years of hers, and she'd held no sway over his death, either.

She found him in his bathtub, which was a surprisingly tidy way to end things. She'd expected him to maybe catch a shotgun blast to the face or take a nosedive off the nearest overpass. Seemed we didn't always know what a person would do, not when you got right down to the nitty-gritty of it.

He'd ingested a bunch of pills and swilled them down with a snootful of Jack Daniel's, if the empty bottles lying beside the tub were any indication. From the black, slimy liquid filling up the tub with him, he may have opened up his veins for good measure, too. She'd stayed no longer than it took to take all this in, a snapshot of his last moments, and then she had left, the smell of her decomposing father going with her, a creature that had crawled up into her brain to die.

There it was. The last place. She had nowhere else to search. She had wandered for a goodly while after that, plenty of thoughts of following after her father and Petunia and Jeanie, and every other poor fucker she'd come across. It'd be so easy. To give up and let go. What was there to live for? Her family missing. Her friends dead. Even her estranged daddy was turning to soup in a bathtub. Abandoned on every side, and up above, too, by all accounts. Abandoned by everybody but the demons, hiding away inside. No one left to trust.

And then she'd stumbled across Bruno and Albus. Or they had stumbled across her. She'd never quite worked out the way of it. But now here she was, a new family surrounding her, and while nothing could replace the one she had lost, she was thankful she had something to live for.

Propping Jasper on her hip, she walked him out into the hallway, blowing more raspberries on to his hand and wrist, in the sweet-smelling crook of his elbow, the boy laughing in breathless chortles. She carried him down the wide, carpeted stairway to the front door.

'Let's go say hello to the morning, baby boy. Let's say "Hi" and "How do you do?"'

She unlatched the door and swung it open, the crisp morning breeze reaching out to greet them, bringing with it the clean smells of dewy grass and cold rocks.

'Can you say "Hello", sweetness?' She carried him out on to the porch and stood surveying the beauty before her. 'Say, "Hello, morning. Hello, grass. Hello, sky."' Jasper baby-talked some and Bianca smiled. 'You got it. Say hello to the day so it knows who you are. Look on up and say, "Hello, clouds. Hello, birds."'

Bianca frowned into the distance as Jasper carried on his jibber-jabber. A couple of miles away, a hazy cloud of birds swooped in formation, winging north and abruptly veering east, breaking at the edges as wisps of birds trailed behind the shift in direction. It formed a solid mass again as they winged back south. Over and over, the birds, a few hundred of them at least, banked and looped, swirling this way and that as if unable to decide on which way to go.

Amber appeared at Bianca's side. The girl stood and watched with her then lifted an arm to point further north. There, a second swarm of birds performed the same sweeping turns, a black mist on the horizon falling and dropping like black particles on the wind.

'What're they doing?' Bianca murmured.

Amber shook her head, a vague movement at the corner of Bianca's eye.

'Maybe there's something over there,' Bianca said. 'Something dead.'

The girl remained quiet.

'There are so many of them.'

Jasper gurgled, the sound muffled, his fist having found its way into his mouth.

'I'll get the boys to get their binoculars out. Keep an eye on them for today. I'm sure it's nothing,' Bianca added, not wanting to worry the girl.

Amber nodded, offered a smile and held her hands out for Jasper. The boy leaned to the side, gravitating toward the girl, and would have toppled out of Bianca's grasp if she hadn't steadied him. She laughed and relinquished her hold, immediately missing his warm weight when he was lifted away.

Listening to girl and boy talk at each other as Amber carried him indoors, Bianca found her eyes returning to the swooping patterns of birds on the horizon. The two groups, although miles apart, moved in eerie synchronisation, their dips and climbs mirroring the worries that whirled and looped in Bianca's mind.

CHAPTER 2

Buried

Sunny didn't want to be here. She knelt before the overturned altar with a candlestick in one hand, as long as her forearm and as heavy as a lead pipe, and beat it against the chancel's wooden platform in half-hearted swings.

Thunk. Thunk. Thunk.

It was all for show. Beck knew full well she wasn't using her whole strength, and told her so. She ignored him. Pike more than made up for her lack of effort by ripping up a good third of the platform single-handedly, levering each plank up as if it were made of LEGO.

Sunny had never called herself a true Christian, not since reaching the sweet age of fifteen when boys and sex had landed on her radar. She'd strayed pretty far off the straight and narrow path for a time, and her folks had been at their wits' end with her.

Getting pregnant at seventeen sure hadn't helped, and neither did her refusing to name the father when questioned. But her momma and pops had been devout. Church on Sundays, Sunday School for her right up to the age of twelve, even though it hadn't been called Sunday School and it hadn't been on a Sunday. Radiant Light and Saturday mornings had been her weekly appointments with God in the teaching room. She didn't recall those mornings with any real angst. It was what it was, and she was what she was — a woman not made to be righteous or non-sinning. And she could live with that. It was always other people who made you feel bad.

She had found her place at the Wet Whistle, where they shared her life's philosophies of drink like a fish, smoke like a chimney and laugh like you mean it. Her folks may not have approved of her choices but she'd been there for them through three strokes, a heart attack and stage-four oesophageal cancer, so there was some argument against Christianity and godliness being the be-all and end-all to everything. God seemed to be pretty absent from her folks' lives in those final years, when she, their good-for-nothing, blaspheming daughter, had not. Maybe God was in her. Maybe *she* was God. The thought made her snort.

Despite all that, the ransacking of a church didn't sit right with her. But she kept her lip buttoned and followed obediently behind Beck when he traipsed after Pike and Jules the Mule into a narrow room. A rug had been rolled back to reveal a hatch in the floor.

At Not-Posy's word, they all stood back while Frank slammed a sledgehammer into the trapdoor. Sunny widened her eyes, determined not to blink as she followed the mallet as it swung up and smashed down. The crashing blows made her blink, despite the expectation of their landing. The vibration worked up her ankle bones and tickled through her shins. It made her want to scratch them.

Cellars. They creeped her out. Nothing good was ever in a cellar. And if anyone was down there, nothing good would be coming to them, either.

CHAPTER 3

The Basement

A terrible crashing *boom* echoed through the basement. Everything shook. A mist of dust puffed up from the tops of junk piles and sifted through the sepia light thrown out by the lanterns.

Alex paused in her work beside Lacey, eyes tipping upward, her arms filled with three tome-sized encyclopaedias. Tiny spider legs goose-bumped up her spine.

'Keep moving,' Lacey gasped, dumping an armful of books, adding to the mountain of volumes already heaped on the floor. They had moved three collections of Benny's encyclopaedias, his psychology, medical and geography volumes, and were now working on his *Encyclopaedia Britannica*.

Two more tomes were thrown aside. 'Move back a sec,' Lacey said.

Alex stepped aside, and Lacey dragged at a waist-high stack. It toppled like a building, slow and heavy, and volumes spilled across the floor, sliding past their feet. Behind the cleared space stood a shorter stack of books, knee height at most, leather-bound with gilt lettering.

'Holy Christ,' Lacey panted. '*Women and Islamic Cultures?* Come *on.*'

Benny made no response. He slumped, propped up against a

bunch of cardboard boxes at the opening to the walkway which led back to the basement's hatch. Every few seconds he glanced over his shoulder to check on their progress, but no comments were made nor did he move to help them clear a path. His throat and neck gleamed with perspiration and his dark hair lay in flat, damp curls against his scalp. His eyes were dark holes in his face. He looked like death.

Another crash boomed through the cramped space and Alex couldn't help flinching. Addy clutched a handful of her shirt.

'It's OK, baby,' she murmured, stroking the girl's head, fingers cupping the fragile curve of her skull. 'We'll be out of here in two shakes.' She tasted the lie as well as heard it; it left a foul aftertaste on her tongue. They were three foxes run to ground down here, trapped with nowhere to go.

Lacey attacked the books like a person possessed. Alex joined her. She barely noticed when her fingernail tore off, the painful sting distant, as if it were someone else's finger that bled. They could see the stairs now, leading upward to a set of double doors lying flush with the sloping basement ceiling. More clutter was stacked in the way. A set of scales, pots and pans, an old push-along lawnmower, rakes, shovels, brooms, plant containers, but beyond all that there was an outline of faint light. *Outside* light.

Another crash, followed by a splintering crack.

Addy had stepped close again. Tugged on her shirt. 'We should hide,' the girl said. 'We can hide good in here. Lotsa places.'

'No, baby, hiding won't work. Out the way now. Scoot.' She gently pushed the girl away and felt the stretch in her shirt as Addy's hand clung for an extra second longer.

Lacey had scrambled higher and was shoving junk out of the way, metal pots and steel watering cans clanging as they bumped down the steps. The smell of old compost and cut grass and weedkiller closed in around Alex. She elbowed a plant pot aside and clawed at the crap with both hands, a fox desperately digging to clear a space, scooping everything behind her. She grabbed a box, flung it away, all the while thinking, *This is it. This is it. We're going to die here, buried under the ground, where we'll never be found. Maybe we should hide. Hide like foxes, waiting for the hounds. Hide in the dark like shivering animals.*

She'd always spent too much time thinking. She wasn't rash to action. She didn't throw punches unless she knew where the next punch would land. Even when she and her sister had been taken captive by those murdering assholes at the motel, she had never abandoned hope. She knew they would find a way to escape, they just needed to understand what those people wanted, what their plan was for them, work out their weakness. If they only stopped to *think*, to consider a way around their predicament, it would all be OK.

Submitting, sacrificing herself, were just ways to buy time. It was wiser to submit than to keep fighting when you didn't know the odds of winning. For years, she had tried to save her sister, to look after her, to be sympathetic to her struggles, but that fight had been unwinnable. No amount of time could help. It took many years for Alex to accept that Sam was beyond saving. Sam had always known it, of course. It was why she'd tried to kill herself, long before the voices came to haunt the rest of them. It was why she'd refused to go back to therapy after leaving her eighth therapist. After all the self-harm, after all the violence and screaming, the restraints, drugs, tears, spit and blood, Sam had been more of a survivor than any of them. She had looked at what was happening in the world and hadn't blinked, because their new reality was a place she'd been living in for more than a decade.

Ryker and Lemony, Starburst, Juju Boy, Hestor, and another name Alex couldn't remember but was made up of clicks, because one invisible friend had been a metallic orb that had floated around Sam's head – a conveyor belt of imaginary playmates had populated Sam's world, all intensifying when Sam hit her teens and her inner psychoses began to bleed out into the world. Amputated hands lying on the school gymnasium stairs, an arm sprouting from her locker door, corpses slumped in the corners of homeroom or under her bed, dead strangers' slack faces looking in windows at her or staring from mirrors. Her waking world had slipped into a living Zdzisław Beksiński painting. But Sam was a bright girl and, while a cocktail of medications kept her steady, she also understood her perceptions weren't to be trusted. She knew that, if she acted on what she saw, she would be mocked by her peers. Bullied. Stared at. Called Freak and Weirdo.

She learned by watching Alex. It was a form of mimicry, Sam told her. She would study the way Alex talked and interacted, the cues she took in conversation, her facial tics, the standard responses. Which way to smile for what occasion and how. Alex got used to her sister staring intently at her during conversations or at the dinner table. Sam learned how to act in a way society deigned 'normal', smiling and chatting and strolling around, even while disembodied body parts littered her path, even while dead people waved at her from across the street or followed her down the sidewalk.

There were moments when her act broke. When assuming the persona of appearing normal became too much and the walls cracked and fell away. Those times were marked by violent fits of rage and terror. Objects were thrown, knives brandished, threats screamed. Paranoia rampaged through every room. Alex bore the brunt of these meltdowns because she refused to let Sam wage her battles alone. They would ride out the storm together, even when Sam *was* the storm and Alex the rickety, ill-prepared skiff.

After the voices came and society gave its last death rattles, they had taken to raiding pharmacies, hospitals, clinics, but the drugs Sam needed became impossible to source. She teetered on the edge of a dark and dangerous cliff. Her behaviour began to put them in danger. She smashed every single window in a down-town shopping mall. She ran screaming through a children's park, spinning cartwheels, refusing, for two straight hours, to climb down off the monkey-bars. Alex had taken her to a lake-side cabin where they vacationed the summer Sam had turned fifteen, but Sam disappeared. Alex had found her a day later, skipping around the nearby running track, her shirt and bra gone, singing 'Follow the Yellow Brick Road'.

Sam was a battle-hardened soldier, a veteran, and even at the end, when she'd been lashed to a bed in a dingy motel room, she had laughed. There had been no tears or cursing the universe for her ill luck. She hadn't blamed Alex or told her she hated her, she had laughed in the faces of her tormentors – she had laughed a lot during those last few years – because nothing they or anyone else did could ever be as bad as what she'd already lived through.

Such a courageous, passionate girl to have such a coward for a sister. All Alex wanted was to be outside, no cold, stone floors under her feet, no walls pressing in on her, no ceiling blocking her view. One final time, to stand out in the open and look up at the vastness of the sky, watch the day give way to twilight, see the first stars twinkle to life. Stand with her head high, lungs filled, and hold Addy's and Lacey's hands in hers.

Her breathing came in wild gasps but she felt oddly calm. Her heart knocked in her chest, her temples, throbbed at the base of her throat, but it felt like a good pounding, a *useful* pounding. As if it were waking her up. Each beat powered her arms, her legs. Her blood rushed with purpose. There would be no time to consider her next move. No time to determine what their pursuers planned to do. There would be time only to act, and to act now.

A crash came from the hatch, and Alex knew it was the last crash because a clatter of wood and metal hit the floor and the shouts of men rose in volume. There were so *many* of them.

Fate doused her in its cold embrace.

She looked back for Addy and saw that the girl had abandoned her Barbies in favour of a hockey stick. She was gazing at where Benny had been, but only a small puddle of blood marked where he'd stood.

Alex reached down and grasped the girl's arm, pulling her up beside her, hockey stick and all, and lifted her over the books and pots and garden implements and pushed her ahead, telling her to climb and to not look back. Lacey was nearing the top of the junk-laden stairs, had somehow managed to burrow a way through for them, but she was struggling with the doors, had her back to them and was heaving upward, and they weren't opening. They weren't budging an inch and still Alex felt calm. Strangely, oddly, calm.

She couldn't see Benny but she heard him, speaking to whoever had broken into his subterranean vault with the sole purpose of dragging them out of it, and she realised any hope of him helping them was gone.

'Alex, *help me*,' Lacey hissed. 'It won't *open*.' And Alex had never heard her sound so desperate, so at a loss, so *scared*.

Calmness. Steady. Her heartbeats were her centre. It beat for them.

As she looked up at Addy, the girl met her eyes. Addy shook her head, her beautiful curls bouncing, her lips pressed in a flat, unhappy line. Alex touched her foot, her ankle, the only parts of her she could reach, and then she turned away and went back into the basement.

CHAPTER 4

Collapse

After being in the church's moonlit main room, the cave of the cellar was like gazing into Not-Posy's coal-black soul – if the thing in Posy even *had* a soul, which Sunny seriously doubted. (She may not be a devout Christian but she recognised a devil when she saw one.)

Her eyes adjusted to the dimness slowly. A dull yellow glow, very dim, very far away, softened the darkness enough to let Sunny make out Posy, Pike and Frank standing halfway down the cellar steps. Low words were spoken, too soft for her to hear, but there was a voice down there that Sunny didn't recognise. Not the gruff, curt sentences of Pike, or the sly, manipulative tone of Frank. This voice was quiet, strained, with stress or fear, Sunny couldn't tell.

Not-Posy's reply was clear.

'Your questions are irrelevant. Where is she now?'

More quiet words from the new man, lost to Sunny's ears as Beck descended into the near-blackness. A skitter of fear for him had her following after him. As the shadows of the cellar fell over her, a coldness encased the back of her neck, a horrible tingling energy spreading through her cells, veins bloating with it. Not-Posy's words reverberated through the stone in the walls, buzzed through the bones of her skull and ears.

'Don't you understand yet? Your God is dead, priest. Your entire way of existence is dead. It's time you stopped fighting it.'

As if an order had been given, the men and women at Sunny's back flowed forward, pushing past her, shoving her out of the way. She grunted as she fell against the stone wall and struck her head. A flash in the darkness as pain lit up the backs of her eyes.

The quietly spoken man cried out, too, in pained anguish, and even as he called out the walls came alive, walls Sunny had only the faintest impression of, lining the cellar in partitioned sections. They rustled as if in response to the man's grief, their rustling becoming a rippling becoming a roar as the nearest ones teetered and fell.

Through Posy's eyes, it watches the wall of paraphernalia collapse inward, falling away to reveal a woman. Their eyes lock and confusion pinches her face. She sees Posy but can't understand what he's doing here, can't understand that he is being ridden by something that knows her much more intimately than Posy ever did.

'*Alex*,' it whispers, and her screams are vibrant in its memory, strobing in bloody images soundtracked by her shrieks and gasps and the beautiful, clean cracks of the belt hitting her body. It had always enjoyed observing Doc test the limits of resilience, and this woman possessed plenty.

Recognition flares, an animalistic instinct that widens Alex's eyes and lifts her arm, her hand coming into view. The gun's muzzle is a small black hole, black as infinity. Black as a tomb. Posy's eyes register all this in a single heartbeat, and then there's a blast, like a landmine going off.

The cellar jumps and flares red-hot. It moves Posy's body, ducking inhumanly fast, pushing it beyond the capabilities locked into it by years of half-use. A cry bleats out as a bullet strikes someone unlucky enough to be standing behind him. A wounded man tumbles off the steps and is lost in the darkness of the basement. There is a barrage of gunfire and more igniting flashes, lighting up both sides as shots are returned.

Everything is subsiding. There is confusion and shouting and it forces Posy to leap up the basement's steps, away from the falling destruction, the flying bullets. It shoves a second person out of the way. They cry out as they fall down the steps, sprawling awkwardly at the bottom, their cries quickly swallowed beneath a weighty landslide that buries them in seconds.

Alex is gone. The priest he'd been talking to is gone. Piles of rubbish fill up every inch of space, swallowing the aisle as if it had never existed. A head-engulfing groundswell shakes through the basement's walls and floor, the dark shutting down in sections, as if someone is flicking the light switches off one by one. The only useful illumination comes from the sacristy above, and it reveals a deep, sliding surge of glossy magazines and hardback books, plastic folders and laminated envelopes rising up the steps to lap against Posy's feet.

The collapsing sound rolls through the basement like a great, tumbling wave, the warren-like walkways crumpling one after the other. The whole basement folds in on itself, a huge pop-up children's book that has been unceremoniously closed.

It lowers itself on to Posy's haunches and peers into the basement, watching the last walls tumble, the final globes of yellowish light blink out as the lanterns are swallowed.

Everything settles into pointy hillocks and strange topographical landmarks in a field of miscellany. A gap of maybe four feet remains between the calamitous mess and the ceiling. It's enough for it to see that no one moves in what is left of the room. No Alex, no priest, neither of the two buried people from Posy's group. There are small rustles and shifting sounds as items continue to slide and settle, but that is all.

It grits Posy's teeth so hard a quiet crack comes from a molar as it splits. It stays still in its crouch. The people at his back, Pike and Frank included, sidle close. Too close. They all breathe too loudly.

It lays its senses over the top of the junk, spreading it across the basement like a thin, fibrous netting, searching for whispers, for scratches of furtive movement in the darkness, for any sign of the girl's Inner. But, as before, it senses nothing. Not even a faint murmur.

It stands and goes to turn away, about to tell the men to start digging until any bodies down there are found. And then, from the corner of Posy's sharp eye, the slightest strip of light opens up at the far end of the basement, and two shapes, silhouetted for the briefest of seconds against the backdrop of the sky, pass through it and into the night.

CHAPTER 5

A Dismantling

A lbus didn't mean to fall asleep. He didn't think he'd be capable of it even if he'd wanted to. But the lulling motion of the vehicle and the thrumming cadence of the rolling wheels blanketed him in their rhythm. The gentle murmuring of Rufus's voice lapped over his eyelids in a red wash of waves.

Which part was memory and which part dream? It balanced on the cusp of a thought, tantalisingly close. His imagination was such a fertile ground, as tangible to him as the outside world at times, that it was often a comfort to retreat to it, where his sister waited and time ceased. Sometimes, though, he was given no choice but to go.

Memory or dream? Real or unreal? Did it even matter any more?

The bottom of the truck-bed was hard under Albus's rump. That was real enough, although it wasn't right. The vehicle he'd fallen asleep in had no truck-beds, pick-up or otherwise. The wind whipping around his ears and tearing his eyes felt very real, too — it dried the sweat on his brow but did little to cool him. Everything was so hot out here in the blistering sun. He was careful not to rest his bare arms on the truck's metal siding in fear it'd sear his flesh clean off.

Ruby sat with her back against the truck's cab, the dividing window open behind her head. The strains of music came from the stereo inside, not loud enough to carry more than a few notes over the wind, but it was old-timey, emotive, as if taken from the soundtrack of an old movie. Lots of stringed instruments and a few trombones. Albus could see the back of the driver's head. There was something familiar about it, as if Albus were gazing at the back his own head through a mirror's reversed reflection.

His sister smiled at him. Her hair whipped into her eyes, but it didn't seem to bother her. 'You're wondering who he is.' She didn't need to raise her voice above the noise of the engine; he heard her just fine. 'Wondering where he's taking us, too. Honestly, I doubt he knows. He's always preferred the journey to the destination.'

Albus couldn't see anything of the man besides his hair (dark and full) and his hands on the wheel (two), with no rings or identifying marks.

'He's the Agur,' Ruby said, as if that explained everything. 'He'll take us where we need to go, don't worry.'

But Albus *was* worried. He peered through the windscreen to see an endless stretch of road laid out ahead of them, nothing but empty desert to either side. He glanced over his shoulder to see more endless miles trailing behind, hazy through clouds of kicked-up dust. It could be the same stretch of highway being laid out over and over, a continuous line of blacktop they would forever be driving. Heading nowhere.

'What's an Agur?' he asked, turning back to his sister.

She had been watching him as he checked out their surroundings. She pointed up at a solitary bird gliding the warm air currents above them. Beside the truck, on the rolling grey blacktop, its shadow kept pace with them.

'A sparrow,' Ruby said. 'They migrate every year to the same place. Fly thousands of miles on the same journey, year after year. There are theories that say they have metal in their blood or beaks. Lets them know where magnetic north lies. They navigate by feel, by reading the hidden messages in their cells. They don't understand how it works. They don't need to. They fly by instinct.' She tilted her head toward the nameless driver. 'That's what *he* does. He doesn't know it, but he's reading the messages. He'll work out what they mean eventually but, for now, he's trusting his instincts.'

'I don't know what that means.'

'It's OK,' Ruby said. 'You don't need to.'

'You sound like Jonah. Being all cryptic and unhelpful.'

She laughed at that. 'I do, don't I? I suppose it was bound to happen. You listen to a voice long enough, it'll either start to sound like you, or you like it. If it makes you feel any better, he doesn't tell me half as much as he should. I spend most of my time confused. Hold on a second.' She turned away and leaned through the dividing window. The driver didn't shift his attention from the road but nodded in reply to whatever she said.

'We're picking up a passenger,' she told Albus, settling back.

The truck began to slow. The wind died down and the heat clamped on to him, drying out his throat and burning a brand into his scalp. He craned his neck to see what they were stopping for.

There, set out on the dirt shoulder, was a roadside stand. Table, chair and hand-painted sign. The truck rolled to a stop and Albus read the advertisement.

'*Fresh Lemonade for Sale. Drink Up or Pucker Up.*'

The fold-out chair was empty. He searched the brush, shading his eyes with a hand, but there were no signs of the lemonade stand's owner.

He gasped as a black creature leaped up over the truck's siding and landed gracefully in the flatbed. As if owning the world, the cat sauntered over to Ruby and meowed for attention. Smiling, she picked the animal up and rubbed it under its chin. The cat's eyes closed in pleasure, head tilting back to give Ruby all the access she wanted.

She knocked her elbow off the cab's window and called, 'Let's roll!'

The truck got going again.

'The look on your face is priceless.' His sister's smile was a blink away from being a grin.

'I don't get it. Why'd we need a cat?'

'We don't. Not everything needs a reason. Sometimes it's just nice to have something that offsets all the crap. Black cats have always had a raw deal. Haven't you, sweetums?' The cat preened at her baby-talk. 'People used to think you were part demon, didn't they? Yes, they did. But you're a good kitty, aren't you? You're a good kitty-cat.' The cat began butting its face against her cheek, rubbing its head against her. Ruby laughed and lifted the cat up, its two front legs sticking out comically. She offered it to Albus.

He didn't move to take it.

'Oh, come on, he's harmless.' She cocked her head and all the smiles and humour faded from her face. 'He'll be a good reminder for you.'

'Reminder of what?' Reluctantly, Albus accepted the animal, cradling it against his chest. Without consciously thinking about it, he ran his fingerless palm over the cat's head and between its ears. The fur was warm and soft.

'That those who seem the most innocent may turn out to be the most dangerous.'

Albus looked down at the cat, and the cat looked at him. The dirty burnt-gold of its eyes matched the desert, and its black, elliptical pupils held a cold indifference that bordered on offensive. He could understand why some had believed a devil may have lurked inside.

'How do we protect the people we love when they might be the ones we should fear?' The way Ruby said this, and the expression she wore, told Albus how gripped she was by the awful truth of her words. She leaned forward, staring intently into his eyes. 'Be wary, Albus. Of your friends, of your loved ones, as well as of strangers. Not everyone is as they seem.'

Ruby moved back as she exhaled, and it almost sounded like laughter but it wasn't a sound Albus had heard from her before – it scraped like fingernails, the muscles tightening along his spine, the skin on his nape going cold. He held the cat closer and its ears flicked in complaint.

'Of course,' she continued, 'it's just as important to remember that, sometimes, a cat is just a cat.' And when she smiled again, it was a familiar sight, kind and a little playful, a smile that touched her eyes and made them sparkle.

They both leaned with the sudden force of acceleration, heard the truck's engine rise in volume. In unison, their eyes went to the driver. He was sitting forward in his seat. His hands on the wheel no longer gripped, they clutched.

'What's going on?'

Ruby was on her knees, head and shoulders poked through the window. An exchange took place where the Agur vehemently shook his head. Ruby placed her hand upon his shoulder. It was followed by more head shakes. Clunks knocked off the truck's undercarriage. The flatbed bounced under Albus's rump. He set the cat down and it immediately darted to Ruby and crouched, pressing its side against the cab. Albus crawled after it, bits of grit embedding in his palms, the corrugated metal painful on his knees. His eyes widened at what they saw through the windshield.

Less than a mile away, from western horizon to east, a churning wall of debris climbed the sky. Even as he watched, it doubled in size, *tripled*, desert earth, clumps of brush, vegetation, all ripped asunder and spewed up, reaching so high Albus had to stoop his head to see it. The ground rumbled and shuddered, the vehicle bounced, wheels shrilling as tyres fought to retain their grip.

Ahead of them, the blacktop was being chewed up by some colossal beast underground, pulverised into chunks and spat skyward. Whole sections of road exploded like mortar shells. Albus instinctively ducked as concrete shrapnel cracked off the windshield, splintering the glass. More *clanks* and pelting *tink*s hit the car as shods of earth and macadam rained down on them. The rattling truck hurtled onward, speeding so fast the engine squealed.

Albus grabbed for his sister, her head still stuck through the dividing window.

'Ruby!'

The road's shoulders erupted in fountains of dirt, grenades detonating one after the other. Ruby emerged from the cab and Albus pulled her down into the relative safety behind the cab. The cowering cat had flattened itself to the truck-bed. The wind howled its anger, tearing at their hair and clothes.

'He's going to kill us!'

'He's helping you!' she shouted above the storm. 'It's found her! There's no turning back now, Albus! Not for any of us!'

Dust storms smashed into the truck, shoving them one way and shunting them the other. Albus held on to Ruby, but she twisted away from him. He yelled at her, terrified she would do something foolish, but she turned back to him, holding the cat by the scruff of its neck. It yowled and hissed, twisting at the end of her hand. She quickly passed it through the window, safely dropping it on to the bench seat inside the cab. She came back to him and gripped on to his collar as the truck rocked alarmingly. Their faces were very close. Dust and dirt choked the air. Grit stung their eyes.

'Albus, you must defend her!' she yelled. 'You understand that, don't you? You must defend them all!'

He nodded. He knew. And with that, the truck's wheels left the earth. Albus tumbled away, Ruby's grip tearing from his shirt, her hand slipping down his arm to clutch at his hand. But he had no fingers to grip in return, no fingers to hold on to her, and with a last, fleeting glimpse of her face, she was snatched away from him and sent spinning into the chaos, where she disappeared instantly from sight.

CHAPTER 6

Broken Bird

From the corner of Rufus's eye, he saw Albus start to tilt toward him. He snatched his hand off the wheel and shoved the guy back in his seat. Albus's head lolled against the passenger headrest.

'Whoa! Gwen! Hey, I need a little help here.' Rufus didn't take his eyes from the road. They'd drifted partway out of their lane and he corrected his steering to bring them back in line. His arm began to shake with holding Albus up. 'Grab him, would you? He's breaking my arm.'

'You're kidding me. He's passed out *again*?' Gwen appeared between the seats and Rufus removed his bracing hand as she slipped in to take over. He heard the seatbelt buckle unclip.

'We were talking and then *whammo*. He slumped over.'

'Your boring conversation sent him to sleep is what you're saying.'

'Very funny.'

'Is he OK?' Bruno squeezed into the cab and suddenly there was *no* room.

'Jeez, dude, come on,' Rufus complained.

'Could you grab him under the arms, Bruno? I'm going for his legs . . . No, try there. Yeah, that's it. Lift when I say. OK, and *up*.'

Between them, Bruno and Gwen wrestled Albus out of his seat, shuffling backward out of the cab. Gwen bumped Rufus's arm as she passed and the vehicle swerved.

'Jesus, fatso. Watch it. I'm trying to drive.'

'Yeah, maybe you shouldn't,' Gwen said, voice strained with effort.

More shuffling and grunting, and Rufus glanced back to see them laying Albus out on the carpeted floor.

'Albus is our compass,' Gwen continued, voice back to normal. 'We don't even know where we're going without him.' A slapping noise followed her words.

Rufus was fairly sure he wasn't missing out on a game of Pat-a-cake. 'Give him a smack from me, will you?'

'Hey, sleepyhead. No time for snoozing. Time to wake up now.'

'It's unusual for him to be passing out this much.' The worry in Bruno's voice was evident. 'That's twice in two days. Not including the first time out on the porch with Jasper and Amber.'

No shit it was unusual. Rufus had been fighting off his own misgivings ever since Hari had shown up. This whole set-up was flaky enough without adding a minor to the mix. A kid, a narcoleptic and a deceitful black man. Rufus was sure he'd heard that joke before. And if he remembered right, it didn't have a particularly funny punchline.

'It's unusual for so many of us to be acting crazy,' he said. 'Yet here we all are. Acting crazy.'

He lifted his foot off the gas pedal and immediately felt their speed drop. He didn't pull on to the shoulder but stopped in the middle of the carriageway, choosing not to cut the engine. He'd had a tough enough time getting it started in the first place. He didn't want to push their luck.

Not a single thing moved beyond the glass of the windshield. There was a whole lot of green grass on the flat verges, running into swaying trees that were tall as buildings. Across the six-lane highway, a mobile home stood in all its lonely, decrepit glory. He wondered if there were corpses inside. Rotting into the stained mattresses of their beds or slumped over the kitchenette's breakfast bar, the remains of their blown-out brains encrusted into the countertop next to the dried-up cereal flakes. He'd have liked to have investigated but suspected going on a side-trip would get outvoted.

'We're here by choice, Rufus,' Bruno told him. 'No one was forced to come.'

'Yeah, yeah.' Rufus twisted in his seat. Bruno, Gwen and Hari were kneeling around Albus's prone body as if they were about to perform some weirdass séance. 'Choice is a murky area these days, if you ask me,' he said.

Gwen peeled back one of Albus's eyelids, followed by placing her palm on his brow, the same way your mom would when you claimed to be too ill for school and she checked your temperature to see if you were lying.

'He's out cold.' She sat back, a resigned sigh escaping her. 'We'll have to wait for him to wake up.'

'We shouldn't stop,' Hari said, real quiet. 'We should keep going.'

Rufus shrugged. 'In extension to my earlier comment about choice: don't see we have much of one here. What if we go past a turn-off we need? What then, champ? You gonna tell us which way to go?'

Hari looked up at him. It was uncharacteristic of him to stare so forthrightly, but he didn't blink and he didn't look away. Rufus was annoyed to find himself uncomfortable under the stare.

'In the absence of leadership, we must trust in the path we've been set.'

Rufus snorted. 'I think you've been reading too much *Lord of the Rings*.'

Hari's eyes flashed. '*I* trust in Albus.'

Rufus felt his shoulders tense. What was the little crud getting at? That he was more loyal than Rufus was? Rufus had been with Albus way longer than this little shit had. Had gone on more missions, helped more people, saved the asses of his friends on more occasions than Hari could ever hope to.

'It's not a matter of trust,' Rufus replied tightly. 'It's a matter of not knowing where the fuck we're going. What part of that don't you get?'

'Rufus,' Gwen said softly.

'No. I'm tired of this cocky little rugrat thinking he has a say here. He snuck his way into this. He shouldn't even *be* here. You don't get a vote on what we do,' he told Hari. 'Decision-making is for the adults. Period.'

Hari laid his hand on Albus's shoulder, a reassuring touch, almost as if to say, *It's OK. This won't take long*, and stood up, not exactly squaring off to Rufus, because that would be stupid, but he was no longer in a weaker, kneeling position in front of him, either.

What the hell is *up* with this kid?

'That's incorrect. You might not wish to listen, but I am here. I think. I have opinions. I have a say.'

He'd never liked Hari's stupid accent. He had no clue where the kid hailed from and, frankly, didn't care, but the way he spoke made him sound highbrow and pompous. Rufus wouldn't have been surprised if he'd been born in Nebraska and just put a phoney accent on for effect.

'I hate to tell you this, kid, but—'

A cracking thud cut him off. A bloody smear the size of a fist stained the windshield on the passenger side.

A second bird dive-bombed the windshield, punching into it beak first. The glass creaked. Ear-splitting caws filled the interior of the vehicle, the bird's trapped beak sawing open and closed, its stiff black tongue jutting from its mouth. A mad fluttering beat at the glass. Rivulets of blood ran down the window.

'Jesus Christ,' Gwen whispered.

Albus cried out, a sharp, wordless shout. His eyelids fluttered in tandem with the dying bird's wings. His half-hands lifted to swipe at the air.

Hari knelt, his hand returning to Albus's shoulder, and at his touch Albus's arms relaxed to his sides and his eyelids' fluttering stilled.

The bird fell silent, the absence of its cries deafening and unreal.

'This isn't right,' Bruno said. He looked around at the others, his expression filled with a fearful determination. '*That* isn't right.' He pointed at the dead bird stuck in the windshield. 'We can't just sit here. We should listen to Hari.'

Rufus clamped his jaw shut on his reply. It would be so easy to be flippant, to shoot down Bruno's words, to be the one who picked them apart and make Bruno feel foolish. That was his role here, wasn't it? To be the wise-cracking asshole. But he couldn't deny that sitting here felt all wrong. As if it was making a target of them. As if Sauron himself had his beady eye on their position.

Ha. Maybe it was *him* who'd been reading too much *Lord of the Rings*.

'I'm getting a bad feeling,' Gwen whispered, and Rufus was surprised all over again. If he was the cynic, Gwen was the pragmatist. He stared at her, wanting her to look back at him and make some quip about how such ambiguous 'feelings' were for superstitious schmucks, not them, just to show she was kidding. But her eyes never left that motionless bird hanging from their splintered windshield. 'I think we should go,' she said.

'Albus will wake soon,' Hari said, and any sense of defiance or confrontation was gone. He didn't look at anyone. 'He would be unhappy to know we stopped for so long.'

'Yeah,' Rufus muttered. 'Yeah, OK.'

Any other time, he would've hopped out, plucked the bird

free, given the glass a wipe to clean it and hopped right back in again. But something stayed him. Something told him not to go outside, not to leave the safety of the vehicle. It was dangerous out there. The unknown waited for them.

He slipped behind the wheel, selected the right gear and wordlessly pressed his foot to the gas pedal. And didn't stop pressing until it was flat to the floor, his eyes steadfast on the road, not once deviating to look at the fluttering feathers in his periphery, the dead bird coming along for the ride.

CHAPTER 7

Flight (Part 1)

Lacey had her face pressed up against the basement's external doors when the world caved in behind her. There was a sharp clap of gunfire, quickly followed by a smattering more. A rumbling vibration rolled through the concrete steps beneath her as the basement came to life.

Lacey shot a glance at the bottom of the steps where Alex should be, but Alex wasn't there.

The reverberating grew louder as the basement groaned and shifted, everything tilting and swaying as if they were in the bowels of a ship.

She's doing this, Lacey thought. Oh my god, Alex is doing this.

Lacey's first instinct was to leave the door, to scramble down into that awakening, unbalanced world and go find her friend, pull her out, drag her back to the steps so that all three of them could escape together, like they always did, like they were always meant to. But Benny's decades' worth of crap was teetering, falling to block the way, piling high over the already-sizeable mound Lacey had created while tunnelling her way up here.

Please, she prayed. *Please, please, please, God, please.* She didn't even know which God she was praying to, or for what, but Alex was down there, beyond her reach, and there was nothing she could do to help her.

Voice didn't answer. Voice was gone. And it was not just a vague absence of where he had been and would soon return but a heavy vacancy, a dull ache of lingering pain, as if part of her brain had been ladled out with a spoon. She didn't know what he'd done, but he had abandoned her. And now Alex was gone, and Lacey was all alone.

A real, live thing crouched in the pit of her stomach, teeth bared, ready to chew its way out, and the pain in her head spiked as her pulse accelerated. She was so close to letting panic overrun her good sense, and she didn't need Voice to tell her what a huge mistake that would be.

She had to get Addison out. Before they were seen. Before they were buried alive. Away from here, away from this thing, this *other* who had tracked them like a scent-hound on the hunt. And maybe, once it had lost their tracks, Lacey could double back, because there was every chance Alex had found cover before she triggered this collapsing chaos, right? Every chance she was OK and would be waiting for Lacey to come back for her. She just had to have faith. Get Addison out, then return for Alex. Believe it, and *go*.

She checked on her niece. Addison was sitting two steps below her, staring silently into the devastation, shoulders stiffening a little each time a lantern's glow was snuffed out. Soon there would be nothing but unbroken darkness.

Lacey went back to the doors, using the cover of the collapsing room – now as loud as the swirling beats of a sea-squall – to mask the thuds of her slamming shoulder. She threw herself at the barrier, strained so hard against it she felt an excruciating pop in her neck and her mind shocked itself with thoughts of aneurysms, and wouldn't *that* be a fricking laugh riot, to die of a burst blood vessel after everything that had happened? But the pain subsided quickly and she felt the door give. Not a lot, but enough.

She shoved again and something along the centre join

snapped (she felt it as well as heard the soft metallic break). She sensed Addison rising and knew the girl's mouth was opening, *knew* she was filling her lungs with air so she could call out for Alex, and Lacey couldn't let that happen, couldn't let her compromise their position to whoever was standing at the other end of the basement. Not after what Alex had done for them.

Lacey slithered down the steps, her tailbone cracking painfully off a hard edge, and closed her hand over Addison's mouth as the girl let out her shout, stoppering the call. She pulled the girl back against her and held her, one hand clamped over her face, her other arm wrapped around her chest, and they stayed like that as the last clatters and thumps quietened down to rumbles, then whispers, items skittering to their final resting places.

It was like looking into the depths of a sinkhole: there was absolutely nothing to be seen. Not at first. A faint, bluish light slowly appeared at the far end of the room, and crouched there, not moving, was a shadow.

It didn't really look like a person, yet Lacey knew what it was.

It was looking for them, searching, listening. She could feel the cold, slick tentacles of its eyes crawling over her, searching for a breach where it could slip inside. The dark began to play tricks on her and she imagined she could see two dancing green orbs in the shape of its head. Eyes. Imagined a darker slit opening below them, wide and grotesque, exactly where its mouth should be, and Lacey remembered the thing she had seen in her dream, all the way back in the office building before it had burned: a creature crouched over Addison as the girl slept, talking in her ear, its lipless maw opening as if to swallow the girl's head whole.

Addison's back moved in a quick rise and fall. Lacey could feel the girl's heartbeat hammering under her restraining arm. She placed her lips against the girl's ear and very quietly, more thought than actual sound, went '*Shhhh.*' After a pause, she carefully lifted her hand from Addison's mouth.

Alex's name hovered between them, swinging like a pendulum, the two syllables going back and forth, *Al-ex Al-ex Al-ex*. Over and over, it tolled in Lacey's head, making coherent thought difficult, the rhythmic knell overriding all but her body's most basic needs: to blink, to breathe, to pump blood. She was numb, and the numbness terrified her because with it came an unbreakable paralysis.

It had come such a long way to find them, from the instant Lacey had been recognised on the bridge, a string of cause and consequence stretching back over the miles between them. Their meeting was inevitable, she knew that now, and any second, it would come in and finish what had been started. It would discover them huddled on the steps, cornered and helpless. It wouldn't leave the basement unsearched.

Yet it was so hard to move – Lacey's eyes were trapped by that shadowy figure, its black-tar gaze leaking over her. She felt unclean in its presence. If it touched her, she would be forever tainted, like a speck of rot that spread and festered and contaminated everything around it. She couldn't let it touch Addison. Not ever.

In between heartbeats and the mental tolling of Alex's name, she could imagine hearing Voice, way down in the deep darkness of his home, speaking in her inner ear, telling her to *Move, Lacey. Move or die. MOVE OR DIE.* Even abandoned by him, his projected presence became a feeding tube, pumping strength and purpose into her.

She unfroze and edged up the steps, keeping her grip on Addison, taking her with her. She continued to make that soft, not-really-there '*Shhhh*' in the girl's ear, willing her to not make a sound. They went inch by inch, Lacey moving by instinct and hoping to Christ she didn't knock anything over.

The door brushed the crown of her head and she released

Addison to place a hand flat against the warped and splintered wood. She gingerly pushed and it opened a crack. She pushed a little more and a quiet creak came from its hinges. But it was low, almost inaudible.

Her eyes flew to the crouched figure.

It didn't move, gave no sign it had heard.

Lacey tugged at Addison's collar, signalling her to come up. There was the briefest of hesitations when the understanding sank in that they were leaving this place, leaving Alex, and then the girl brushed up against Lacey, pressing in close, and she was so warm and vitally alive Lacey wanted to grab hold of her and crush her to her chest.

The girl moved past, leaving a breath of cold empty space in her wake.

Lacey held the door for Addison to slip through, then eased it open another inch and squeezed through after her, immediately lowering it silently back into place.

The night was chilly. Lacey inhaled a deep breath, the sweet smell of grass cleansing her lungs of dust and dank subterranean air. She looked at Addison and Addison looked at her, and the girl broke, every instant of it playing across her face as it crumpled and collapsed. A cry rose up from her hitching chest, and Lacey lunged forward to clamp her hand over the girl's mouth all over again, knowing that, if released, it would be a wailing siren.

She pulled Addison away from the basement doors, glancing around to make sure no one was near. Above the church's rooftop, the trunk of the oak tree twisted to the right, as if it were looking over its shoulder at them, curious to see what the tiny humans were doing. Its branches were spread, its shadow reaching far enough to cover them, giving an illusion of protection.

Addison kicked and struggled against Lacey's hold, the muffled sounds of her cries dampened by her palm, but Lacey was hardening herself, letting the numbness that had nearly

337

frozen her in place spread through her like a cold, deadening fire. She barely felt Addison's shoes drum off her shins.

Run! Voice shouted, and it was so unexpected Lacey stumbled. *Lacey, run!*

Possum! she wanted to yell back at him. Goddamn fucking *possum!* A warm pressure stuck in her throat, blocking her air pipe, choking the words from her.

HE'S COMING!

From the front of the church, out of sight, she heard the crash of the entrance doors and a rush of feet. So many feet. A pack of hyenas, some of them yipping strangely, some of them howling, more undoubtedly running silent, heads down, eyes sharp, noses catching their scent.

Lacey threw glances left and right, but there was no cover, the nearest house too far away to reach in the last few seconds left to them. She let Addison go and grabbed her hand, pulling her backward, unable to tear her eyes away from the corner of the church where the hunting pack would appear.

Their feet slipped into the knee-length grass, blades parting to let them through, and no more than sixty yards away, people began pouring around the side of Pilgrim Holiness Church. Ten, fifteen, maybe as many as twenty. Men and women. They slowed to a stalking walk when they spotted Lacey and Addison, and pushing through to the head of the group was a thin, gangly man with a familiar reddish-brown thatch of hair.

'No,' Lacey whispered, a world of confusion swirling around her so violently she almost stumbled again. 'Posy?'

'*Lacey,*' he hissed.

Impossible, Voice said, his shock shivering through her.

But this Posy wasn't the Posy she remembered. The same lips, yes, yet the horrible smile that stretched them was a snarling reproduction of Posy's smile. The same eyes, definitely, yet these eyes held a dark, vicious gleam, and viciousness was a trait the old Posy never had. Looking closer, she recognised a couple more men behind him, and a slow-creeping horror filled her, enough to spark her adrenaline, enough to make her want to run at them, sprint and leap and rip at their flesh with teeth and fingernails. Claw out their eyes. Pound them with her fists. Bite off pieces of their faces. She'd set her rifle aside when she'd started clearing a way up the basement steps, and she hadn't picked it up again. It now lay buried somewhere beneath Benny's treasured hoard. If she had it . . . oh, how she ached to fire off shot after shot at these people, knowing they would overwhelm her long before she could kill more than three or four. Five, if she were lucky. Five would be better than none.

Voice galvanised her into action.

LACEY, MOVE IT!

Startled back to her senses, Lacey yanked on Addison's hand and dragged her into a run.

CHAPTER 8

Flight (Part 2)

Their feet barely touched the ground. Lacey pulled Addison behind her, forcing her to keep up, the kid's long legs almost as fast as hers. The howling pack gave chase.

They dashed across the abandoned wasteland, leaping over divots in the grass, their shoes slapping on to sidewalk, and raced across an empty street and along the side of a long-abandoned house, its shutters closed and uninviting. They burst into the house's backyard and Lacey dodged an empty dog kennel, Addison dodging with her, and sprinted for the open gate adjoined to the property next door. Another yard, a dry paddling pool, a cracked plastic slide. A shot went off, deafening and sudden, and something *ping*ed off the slide's rusting ladder beside Addison's head. The girl gasped as the plastic slide rocked in place. Lacey cut left, dragging her niece down a narrow passageway between two more houses.

More gunfire, not directed at them, and Lacey wondered if it was angry at the person who'd taken a pot-shot – surely it wanted them alive. If so, Lacey was fiercely glad because the retaliation not only gave them a few extra seconds' lead but possibly meant they'd have one less pursuer.

Already, her breaths burned in her lungs. She had to pull harder on Addison's hand. The kid was tiring. She wouldn't be able to run like this for much longer. The people behind them were driven by so much need and wildness, and nothing could outrun those.

It's me *it follows*, Voice whispered harshly. *Don't you get it yet?*

She couldn't answer; the frantic terror pounding through her blood left no room for words.

It was never her, Voice said, and it took her a second to realise who he meant. *Never in all her sleep-talking.*

Her response was immediate and furious; she didn't want to hear what he had to say. 'No!'

Listen to me! And he was uncompromising in his demand, too. *It's* us, *not her. You know what we have to do.*

Her understanding didn't bloom or grow but hit her square between the eyes: *Bam!* She knew what lay beneath Voice's demand, could feel the urge in him to make her comprehend without him having to spell it out and chance anything overhearing. It had never been Addison's sleep-talking that had led it to them. She had never called out to them in her sleep. Never invited them to come find her. It had been Lacey and Voice all along. It was the reason he'd faked disappearing, playing it as though she had been attacked and possibly even killed. He had cut off all communication so they couldn't be tracked. *God*, she was so stupid!

He'd told her, *If* I *can hear it, it must be able to hear me, too.* And they had never shut up, had they? Always rabbiting away to each other, like two old women.

Lacey swung around the corner of a neighbouring porch, reeling Addison in by the hand as the girl skidded outward. She leaped up the front steps and kicked down the house's door, crashing into the hallway, hauling her niece inside. And there it was. The same place her grams had hidden in all those endless months ago. The perfect hideaway. It had taken Lacey *hours* to find her.

She almost tore the closet door off its hinges. Before Addison could say a word, she bundled her into the dark space under the stairs, gasped at her to be quiet, not to move, not to come out, and slammed the door on her, not even pausing to glance back toward the front entrance but taking off for the kitchen at the back of the house.

Lacey's eyes flicked left and right as she entered, seeing the thick layers of dust, the neatly arranged dining table and breakfast bar, the sink full of dishes. She dragged an arm across the counter's crockery-strewn surface as she went past, sweeping the plates and bowls to the tiles, where they exploded into bits.

Yes! NOISE. More!

She crunched across the broken crockery, grabbed up a dining-room chair and flung it behind her. It crashed into the doorway. She grabbed a second chair and hurled it at the patio doors in a massive, heaving swing. It smashed through, glass shattering, and she followed after it, leaping through the hole she'd made, not feeling the sharp pinch as the arm of her hoody snagged and ripped on a jagged seam of glass.

Men stampeded into the house. Lacey didn't need to turn and look – she heard them pound into the kitchen, the broken crockery clattering underfoot. Their calls and howls had died down, their breathing as wild as Lacey's, but she didn't slow. She was fast and strong, and her boots were laced tight to her feet, like they always should be.

She streaked across the back decking, darted left and circled around the side of the house, taking a calculated risk and heading back to the street. She took a moment to gasp, 'Talk!', and Voice started a loud covering babble, blurting out fake instructions for her to take the next left, now right, keep Addison close, don't let the child slow their pace, keep going, don't look back. And Lacey knew it heard every word, and she felt a moment's gloating victory in knowing Posy and the others were following her and leaving Addison safely behind.

She sprinted across the road, crossing over her own path, and

Voice must have seen where she was heading because he put his commentary on hold as Lacey ducked behind a covering hedge, the shrubbery running along the front yard of the house where she had pretended to play basketball what felt like aeons ago. Voice remained silent as she quickly followed it, scrabbling along on all fours. She didn't stop but ran in a half-crouch half-crawl and slipped through a gap in the hedge and into the next yard. Feeling horribly exposed, she ran in a stooped sprint across the open lawn and made a dive for the next bush, grunting as she landed painfully on her arm. She jumped up and scuttled out the other side to hunker by the rear wheel of the Subaru parked in its driveway. She gulped great lungfuls of air, trying and failing to be quiet. The canted flagpole stretched into the sky high above her head.

The narrow gap between the bottom of the open garage door and the driveway beckoned to her and she fervently hoped that the feral cats she'd envisaged living in there earlier had vacated the premises. She snatched a final breath and dropped to the ground, shimmying her way over and wriggling underneath, feeling the door scrape across her shoulder blades.

Inside, darkness.

An internal door connected to the house. Lacey staggered to her feet, a swamp of dizziness pushing her off balance. She caught herself and stumbled forward. A tremor passed through her hand as it closed over the handle, her desperation for the door to be unlocked crackling like electricity through her fingers. She twisted and tugged. The door didn't budge. Her stomach clenched with alarm, and she tugged again, harder this time, and the door jerked open.

The wood must have swollen over time and stuck in its frame; that's what Voice would have said if he could.

Ghosting through the sitting room, Lacey glanced out the front windows and saw people milling in the street, looking lost. Posy stood at their centre, unmoving, and again she felt that flash of bewilderment. Posy, *here*. Madness. He was so motionless she had to stare for long seconds before she could make out the slight rise and fall of his chest. His stillness was unnatural.

She swallowed past the dry, metallic taste in her mouth. 'Wait till . . . I'm at the back door,' she whispered between panting breaths. 'Then let him know . . . where we are.'

Voice didn't respond but she knew he'd heard. She carefully navigated her way through the silent house. The moon was full and bright and the night sky was clear. A silver-white radiance lit their way. The back door was locked but the key was in the keyhole and all Lacey had to do was turn it and they were outside.

Together, they saw the lack of fencing, the absence of any boundary blocking their way. The path was clear.

'Now.'

Go, Lacey, go!

He projected so strongly it made her wince, head still sore from his last mental blast. She tried not to think about the other voice riding along with them as her boots pounded the ground, her breaths ripping through her throat and Voice shouting his instructions, leading them further and further away from Addison and her hiding place beneath the stairs.

CHAPTER 9

Out of the Closet

Addison tonelessly hummed her Alphabet Pony song in her head. She'd been humming it for a while, long past the time the thumping heartbeat in her throat had settled back in her chest, where it belonged. She wished for her bicycle so badly. She supposed those not-so-nice people had taken Alphabet Pony away by now. It was a good bike. Anyone who saw it would want it.

Tears spilled over but she didn't scrub them away. Her eyes were already hot and sore from rubbing, no matter how hard she tried to think about her bike instead of Alex. She didn't sob because Addison was being invisible, and invisible people didn't cry and they sure didn't make any noise. Besides, Lacey had told her not to move, and Addison tried to do what she was told, even when she didn't want to.

Sitting in the dark in silence, the *shuuuuuuush* noise had started up again. It rose and fell, went up and went down, words forming in a soft whisper that Addison tried not to hear, *really* tried extra hard not to listen to, 'cause she didn't want to get in trouble. But little by little, she let it filter through, just a bit, because she didn't feel so alone when they were nearby.

There's no one left to help us, Addison, Fender said. *We can't stay in here for ever.*

Addison let go of her legs and clamped her hands over her ears, but it was only for show – they knew if she wanted to hush them up, she could.

Chief crouched beside her, the darkness coating the smoothness of his skin, camouflaging him perfectly. Only the soft glisten of his black eyes was visible.

Aw, don't do that, Chief whispered behind the hand covering her ear. *We're trying to help. We got to stick together. Like a team. Without a you, there's no us.* A squat stool appeared next to her, the kind with three legs, and Chief plopped himself down on top of it.

It confused Addison. 'What's the stool for?' It felt strange to talk out loud after so long, but it was better than sitting here by herself.

There's three legs, see? He ducked down and pointed to each. *One, two, three. Without three legs, we'd fall over and be good for nothing.*

'When do you two help each other anyways? You hate each other's guts.'

We don't actually have any guts of our own, Fender explained, *but you gave us a lot of time alone, and we decided it's best if we consolidate our strengths.*

Right, Chief agreed cheerfully, the darkness shifting subtly as his head bobbed up and down. She doubted he even knew what 'consolidate' meant. *She* sure didn't.

Lacey has done a fine job of leading those horrible people away from us, Fender said. *They're not even close by any more. We can leave this closet and it'll be perfectly safe, I promise.*

'I don't believe you.' And she didn't. They'd both played rotten tricks on her at the lake, which she hadn't forgiven them for.

Chief showed her a picture of herself opening the door a crack and peeking outside to check for herself.

Addison ignored him and didn't move. She dropped her

hands from her ears and went back to holding her legs. It was wrong to listen to them. She knew Lacey listened to Voice (she wasn't so good at hiding him, not like Addison was at hiding hers), but Alex didn't like it, and neither had Addison's mommy. Addison didn't want Alex to be angry at her. Besides, Mommy had told her not to tell anyone about Chief. Not ever, even if he *was* her special 'maginary friend, only bad things would come from telling, and she'd been right.

Fender's words turned over and over in her head. She guessed she didn't see any harm in taking a *small* peek. Her ears weren't sticky-out or big like a rabbit's, but they heard just as well. She would hear if anybody tried sneaking up on her.

She shifted on to her knees, moaning quietly as her muscles flexed. She pressed her nose up against the crack of the door and sniffed, pretending she was a rabbit smelling the air for danger. Her whiskers twitched. All she could smell was wood and dust.

She slipped her hand to her ankle and slid up her pant's leg, checking that her shark tooth was safely locked in its sheath. The diver's knife was small, the grip perfect for her small hand. Lacey had gotten it for her from Wally's Sports Center. Addison had wanted a bigger one, with ziggy-zag edges, but Lacey told her smaller was better 'cause no one would know she had it. A surprise attack was better than one they could see coming, especially when you were small, like Addison was small. It came in its own neat plastic sheath, too, where it clicked into place, safe as a soldier. She called it her shark tooth because it was pale, same as bone. She left it where it was for now – she only wanted to feel to make sure it was there.

She gripped the closet's handle, turning it bit by bit, and the door quietly unlatched.

Addison held her breath as she eased it ajar.

Through the gap, she could see the front door, swung wide from when Lacey had kicked it. Beyond that there was a stretch of porch and some steps leading down to a path – just the narrowest strip where the lawn's hungry grass had eaten the slabs up on either side.

See, Miss Doubty-pants? We told you it was clear.

Chief's tone made her mouth frown. Fender threw a shushing blanket over him and, surprisingly, Chief settled down straight away and didn't struggle to free himself, like he usually did.

'You guys are acting weird.' But again, they stayed shushed. She creaked the door wide enough to stick her head out and looked back toward the kitchen. All was silent and still in there, too.

She pushed the door the rest of the way open and crawled out into the hall. She got to her feet and paused, spent a little while kneading the knots out of the muscles in her thighs. Only her hands and eyes moved, the rest of her remained invisible. Leg muscles good and loose, she crouched back down and slunk silently to the front door.

She leaned around the door jamb, staying low. Big people didn't always think to look way down. She didn't know why – thought they were pretty stupid to believe danger came only at eye level. But she'd hidden from lots of big people right under their noses and they'd never even known she was there.

The street was deserted. A light drizzle of rain had fallen while Addison was inside the closet. The moonlight shone like spilled milk across the blacktop. She could smell the dampness of earth and grass and something else, like cold metal. She dared to take a slow, crouched step on to the porch. Across the street, she could see the side of the house Lacey had pulled her along. If she went that way, she'd be heading back to the church. Back to Alex.

Alex is dead, Fender said.

'Is not!'

Addison immediately drew herself back into the house, eyes darting. She counted to twenty-one, because that was one of her favourite numbers (or maybe it was Fender's, she wasn't sure), but no one appeared.

'She is *not*,' she whispered, cross, feeling a hot rush of tears burn her eyes.

I'm sorry, Fender said. *But I'm trying to prepare you. She was very likely crushed under the weight of Benny's things. And, if not crushed, suffocated.*

She needed to stop listening. Listening did no good. Listening would cause trouble.

Gotta practise what I preach, she thought, although she wasn't entirely sure what that meant. Lacey had said it plenty of times, though, and it seemed to fit pretty good.

Chief's petulant voice chimed in. *Lacey listens to her Voice.*

'That's different,' she whispered, sulky, already forgetting her new promise to quit talking to them. 'Voice doesn't try to trick her like you do.'

I didn't try to trick you!

'You did. At the lake. With the stones.'

Chief started to protest, but she was angry and swept them both to the back of her head as easily as scooping up toys and dumping them in a toy box. She slammed the latch down on them, and that was that.

She scanned the street as she went down the porch steps, staying crouched, and crept along the overgrown path.

Soon as there's no more grass, I'll jump up and run. Fast, like a cheetah. Right to the house across the street. Take to the count of ten, tops, and I can count to a whole fifty.

She left the pathway, her foot hitting the sidewalk, and the sound of men's voices pricked her ears up. She froze.

A dart of movement across the street made her gasp, but it was only Chief. He had snuck out and was standing on the opposite kerb, waving at her.

There was no thought of retreating. Addison leaped up and dashed into the road, not daring to take her eyes off Chief, knowing that, if she did, she'd probably trip and fall and those men would stroll around the corner and find her lying on the ground like a silly, floppity fish.

She put on a burst of speed. The men's voices were louder; they echoed off the buildings and crawled under the porches, slipping like worms between all the blades of grass. She hit the kerb. Leaped. An image stuttered to life, flashing past her, almost tangling in her feet. A small grey rabbit bolting across the lawn, moving so swiftly her eyes couldn't track it.

Yes! she thought. Fast, like a rabbit!

The bunny blinked out.

Addison dashed across the sidewalk and on to the lawn, following in the bunny's footsteps, imagining her own rabbit ears pressed flat to her skull. Chief waited for her at the side of the house. He was hopping up and down, anxious and excited, beckoning with both hands.

From the corner of her eye, three people strode into view. One she recognised from the church. His head had been put on upside down, his long, bushy beard reaching his chest, and his stubbled head bald on top. He had scars up there. While stuck in the closet, Addison had wondered how he'd gotten them. Maybe lice, she'd thought. Had itched them too much and scratched himself silly. Or maybe he shaved his own head (to stop the lice?) and kept nicking himself. She'd decided that it was probably definitely the lice's fault.

The side of the house was coming up fast, but not fast enough. Addison tried to run harder, pump her arms quicker. The bearded man with the head scars was looking up and she knew he would spot her, see her fleeing like a scared bunny, and he'd shout out and they'd all be startled for a second ('cause who knew finding a rabbit-girl would be so *easy*?) then they'd go after her, chase her down like the silly rabbit she was, a rabbit that should have stayed hidden and invisible, like Lacey told her to.

Their eyes were about to meet, his head was lifting, lifting, any moment now and it'd be game over, even though Addison wasn't playing any game and none of this was any fun anyway – Alex pushing over Benny's stuff in the basement, Lacey leading the men away from her hidey-hole, all of it *not fun*. His head finished rising and Addison lost sight of him, the side of the house blocking him from view. She skidded to a stop and dropped down and hugged the wall. She listened for his shout, for the rush of feet.

He didn't see, Chief whispered, crouched and leaning against her back. *Well, I don't think he did. Pretty sure.*

She waddled in a duck-crouch back to the corner.

Don't look!

She rolled her eyes at him. She had no intention of sticking her head out. She wanted to listen was all.

'Posy said to check the houses we'd been through,' a man was saying.

'And how're we supposed to know which ones they are?' A woman's voice. 'That bitch took us through at least four. They all look the same.' She said her *th* sound like an *f,* as if no one had taught her the difference.

They hadn't spotted Addison.

She shook her head, scolding herself. Such a stupid rabbit! Had to be a mouse from now on. Small and quiet and very, very clever.

'Take an educated guess. It'll be the ones with the open front doors.'

'Half of them got their doors open. And who's to say the li'l bird hasn't already flown her nest? Hanging round here isn't such a hot idea.'

Li'l bird, she thought. Is that me?

'Ah, she's just some stupid little fuckwad,' a new voice said, this one gruff and mean, and for some reason Addison *knew* it belonged to the beard-man with his lice. 'She's probably hiding someplace, shaking and crapping her pants. We'll find her. Split up – we'll take a house each.'

The fuckwad could take any house he wanted, he wouldn't be finding *her*. (She didn't know what a 'fuckwad' was, but it was a fun new word.) She didn't chance looking around the side of the house – there was no point, she didn't care which houses they entered, she wasn't in any of them – but turned and snuck away, her footsteps no louder than those of a girl-sized mouse.

CHAPTER 10

Lessons Learned

Twice it has been duped by her. First, with the explosive psychic projection of Lacey's Inner when it believed the girl had been mortally wounded (the communication it used to track her, a stream of one-sided dialogue from her Inner voice, shutting off in an instant, and staying off, leaving a resounding, dead silence in its place). And second, when Lacey somehow deposited the child somewhere, without anyone seeing where.

She is a devious adversary, and it has been on the back foot for too long. It will not be made a fool of again. Once she is in its grasp, the experiments will continue. She appropriated her own voice in conditions similar to how Posy appropriated *it* – through chance and circumstance, through pain and death – and it *will* learn the exact parameters needed to re-create the event. It has pushed this body hard over the past few days. Possibly too hard.

They have been led on a merry chase, through streets and backyards, over fences and through hedgerows. Lacey is fast and resilient, and she seems to know this area far better than she should, but there is nowhere left for her to go. They have chased her as far as she can run. It sees how she weaves and stumbles – exhaustion has dug its claws into her flanks and is dragging her down. Nearly all the others have fallen back, only Posy, Frank and two other men remain. It feels a strange kind of admiration for the girl, having outrun so many, but it is overridden by a more intense emotion. *Anticipation.*

The girl staggers, almost falls, takes a handful more steps, weaving her way over to the gutter, and stops. She sways then stoops over, grasping on to her knees. She stays like that and doesn't look up, although she must know they are closing in.

It brings Posy's body to a shambling halt and experiences an odd sensation shiver through his thighs. A weakness that almost buckles the knees. But it tightens its control. It locks the joints upright.

Frank and a second man drop, Frank on to his hands and then to his side. He rolls on to his back and lies there, his stomach pumping in great swells. The third man, who has a name but not one it cares to remember, adopts a similar posture to the girl, wilting from the head down, a drooping flower left too long in the heat.

The night is alive with hoarse gasping.

The girl spits on the ground. Spits a second time and tiredly straightens, turning to face them. She stands there, defiant, and again it is surprised by the admiration it feels for her. She really is quite remarkable.

'Posy.' Her voice is cracked. It watches her try to swallow. It appears to be a painful process for her.

'Not Posy,' it tells her, threading a sewing needle through the corners of Posy's lips and lifting them in a smile.

She stares at him.

'Oh, he's here,' it explains. 'He is we, and I am me.'

'No,' she says, her words slurring a little. 'You're not . . . him. You're just a . . . a *thing* using him.' The girl is struggling to breathe, will probably struggle for quite some time, but she nods her head slowly, as if coming to a realisation. 'A soulless thing. Soulless . . . and empty.'

These words cause an anger it doesn't quite understand, and it can't help the irritation that tightens through Posy's voice. 'I, and everything I am, are what you and everyone like you will become.'

'No,' she says.

'*Yes*. Why exactly do you think I've been following you?'

For the first time, doubt crosses her face, creasing her brow.

'Don't misunderstand, I'll find the child you've taken such pains to hide. I will go back and pluck her from the dank little hole you've squirrelled her into. There are lots of things I want in this world, Lacey. I want to know where Red is, because *he* wants to know where she is. I want to know why Red isn't here, with you, like I hoped she would be.' It makes Posy smile again. 'And, of course, there's *you*. Oh, I very much want you. Since our first meeting, I knew there was something different about you. It made me curious how you came to have such a strong Inner, one so matured beyond your years. Like Red's, but different. There's an innocence to you that sets you apart. I couldn't understand it at the time, but now I do. Oh yes, I understand now.' It taps a finger to Posy's temple. 'We have experienced something similar, your Inner and I. And it is time I have an explanation for it.'

The girl's hand flutters up but doesn't rise higher than her ribs before dropping back to her side. She takes a step backward. 'Voice won't tell you anything.'

She says 'Voice' as a nomenclature, a title. It sounds peculiar to its and Posy's ears. It clucks Posy's tongue and wags a finger at her retreat. 'No no. No more running.'

She closes her eyes and inhales a deep, pain-filled breath, wincing through it. 'I'm done running. I can't run any more.' And the hopelessness in her voice stirs another emotion. Satisfaction.

'You remember where we met, don't you?' it says.

She opens her eyes. Says nothing.

'You shot me. Or, more accurately, you shot the person I was in.'

She whispers, but it's audible. 'I remember.'

'Say his name.'

She shakes her head.

'Say his name, Lacey.'

'No.'

'*Say it.*'

'Doc.'

It stretches Posy's face into a wide smile. 'Yes. I am quite upset with you. I liked Doc very much. He took great delight in hurting others, like he did to Alex. A pastime we both enjoyed – his reasons for doing so different from mine, in some respects, but I think it all comes from the same place in the end. A place of needing to understand how you work.'

'Voice says you're a—'

Anger flares bright. '*I* am not the parasite. *I* am the one in control of this body.' It pounds Posy's chest with a fist. 'Posy is the parasite now, living somewhere in here.' Another smack, to the head. 'He sits and does nothing and lets me take control, and do you know why? Because *this* is what he wants. It's what he's chosen to let happen to him. It's what so many of you have chosen.' It takes a step forward and is delighted by the faint flinch that crosses her face.

'I've made him better than he ever thought he could be, and *Voice*, as you call it, is a disgrace to what we are, what we are here for. We were not born to be subservient to you. Everything you built you destroyed, and everything you destroyed you failed to appreciate. No one loves you any more, not God, not Allah, not Yahweh or Brahman, not any of your fallen gods. They have forsaken you, just as you have forsaken yourselves.' It has advanced on the girl until no more than a foot separates them. She has regained her composure – she does not cower – but it can see her fear. Fear of the truth.

It leans forward, so close it can feel the steaming heat of her overworked body. 'There is no one left to listen to you but us.'

CHAPTER 11

Mongoose

Nothing moved at Pilgrim Holiness Church, but that didn't mean much to Addison. She never believed what only her eyes told her. She waited and watched and listened until the bottoms of her feet (*soles*, Fender said) grew a fur of grass and sank roots into the soil. The shoulder she leaned up against the house slowly hardened and turned to wood. She *was* the wall and her feet were the earth.

Time and again, her gaze was drawn to the humungous tree. The dark shadows of its branches swayed and shivered, leaves rustling in warning. Maybe a huge snake lived inside its canopy, winding its way through the branches, its hungry eyes feasting on her, waiting patiently for her to come close so it could drop down and coil itself around her body. Lift her up into the tree, where it would *squeeze* her until she popped.

She swiped her sleeve across her mouth and, with a final glance all around, pushed away from the house, imagining she heard the crack of her wooden shoulder separate from the panelling and the tear of roots rip free from the ground. She scurried across the wasteland, bent low, her hands parting the blades of wild grass in front of her, stems brushing past her face, the sky filling up more and more with the tree's branches the closer to the church she got.

She saw herself from Chief's point of view as he swooped eagle-high above her head. She looked like a mongoose from up there, channelling through the wild grasslands of Africa, only the shaking of grass marking her progress as she arrowed through it. (It made her want her wildlife magazine, lost in her pack in the basement, to spread it out on the floor, nose close to the photographs, as she imagined herself riding on the backs of zebras and monkey-climbing up the long necks of giraffes.)

There were more ferocious animals Addison could be, but she liked mongooses – she'd thought about them a lot, had even asked if she could have one someday, and Alex had laughed and told her not until she was much older, and probably not even then, unless they opened up their own zoo. She'd asked what 'zoo' meant (such a fun word to say: 'zoo', 'zoooo'), but she got kind of sad when Lacey explained it was a place full of cages and fenced enclosures where they locked up all the animals in her pictures so people like her could go gawk at them. Maybe opening their own zoo wouldn't be such a fun idea, after all.

Passing under the oak tree, its shadows dropping a cloak over her, Addison peered up into the knotty network of branches.

No snake stared down at her.

Not one she could see, anyhow.

She hurried straight for the closed basement doors and got down to press her ear flat to them. A strong part of her wanted to lift the door and enter the basement (and a quiet, anxious nudging urged her to go that way, too, because Chief could only see what was right in front of his face). Then came the cautionary resistance of Fender, whispering that that way had been blocked after Benny's junk had all tumbled down, remember? And she *did* remember, now that it had been pointed out – she'd just forgotten for a moment.

Keeping the wall of the church to her right, she skirted around to the front parking lot, and there, she paused again. Waited. Saw and heard nothing – even letting Fender out to check it over. Getting the all-clear, Addison continued to the church's stoop.

The doors stood wide open.

She entered cautiously, placing her feet in careful steps, moving like the ghost of that mongoose she someday hoped to have. When she saw the inside of the chancel, her feet stopped moving.

A silver-backed gorilla had been set loose and he'd rampaged through the church, breaking and smashing *everything*, leaving it all topsy-turvy and upside down. She spotted Alphabet Pony where it had been thrown against the back wall, and she hurried over to it. Its front wheel was crumpled like a soda can, as if the big ape had viciously stomped on it with his big foot. The handlebars were bent and twisted, as if he'd chewed on them with his big teeth and spat them out. The lovely white-tasselled saddle was missing entirely and Addison could only figure he'd eaten it. She laid her head on the handlebars, the metal cool against her brow, and felt a wellspring of grief rise up. It hurt her throat and she straightened, snatching her hands away from the bike's handgrips as if the cold had bitten, and clenched them into hard fists. She forced her eyes away from Alphabet Pony's broken mess.

Good, Fender whispered. *Leave it. Keep going.*

She left the bike and picked her way across the chancel, stopping when she noticed the corner of Alex's backpack sticking out from under an upside-down pew.

She tried to tug it free.

Couldn't.

She tried lifting the pew.

Couldn't do that, either. It was too heavy.

She knelt down and twisted her arm into the gap, working her hand into a pocket, rummaging around inside it. She came out holding Alex's palm-sized sketchbook, which got shoved into her seat pocket. She went straight back in and grabbed the only other item in there. A cold, heavy tube.

Alex's Maglite.

Addison covered her eyes and squinted through her fingers as she clicked the flashlight on and off a few times, checking it worked. She lowered her hand, night vision intact, and began climbing and working her way deeper into the trashed room, heading for the sacristy door and Benny's basement.

She'd been trying not to think about going down into the basement. Not 'cause she was scared of the dark, because she wasn't. She liked the dark. It was her friend. It had kept her safe, like a blanket she could pull over herself whenever she wanted to disappear. Nope, what she was afraid of was being unable to find Alex. Or worse, finding her and not being able to wake her up. She'd be asleep, like Pilgrim had been asleep, and wouldn't ever get back up again. Like Red, the mummy girl with the scarf tied around her face. Lacey had buried them both in the treasure hole in Mommy's backyard, because neither of them would ever be waking up.

Chief latched on to her fears and conjured a sea of broken bodies, buried in the dark basement beneath their feet. Men's, women's, babies', like the bobbing, green-swollen baby in the lake her throwing stones had dislodged, which had been Chief's fault, too. In the basement, Addison imagined claw-like hands poking up out of Benny's junk piles, ready to snag her by her ankles as she slogged by, maybe even drag her under with them, where they would hold her in their embrace and never let go. Alex's arms would be among them, winding around Addison more tightly than any of the others, because having Addison meant she wouldn't be alone down there any more. They could both go to sleep for ever and ever.

'*Stop*,' Addison whispered. 'You're making it worse.'

Chief whined and ducked back into his hidey-hole.

Addison hopped over the beam where she'd sat with her aunt and Alex a few short hours ago and clambered through the wooden framing that had supported the raised platform (the gorilla had enjoyed ripping up the floorboards and flinging them around). She grabbed hold of the sacristy's door frame and hauled herself up into the narrow room, and there, in the far corner, the dark mouth of Benny's basement waited for her.

Faintly, Fender said, *You don't need to do this.*

There's bodies *down there,* Chief said, almost guiltily, and though she was half-heartedly holding them both back, she clearly felt Chief's apprehension leak through, like cold drips *plop*ping on her head from a hole in the roof.

She screwed her eyes closed. 'I *do* need to. I do.' She opened her eyes and whispered, 'Alex is down there.' She said Alex's name again, because it had power. It made her brave. 'Alex needs me.'

They could come back. We'd be trapped in there.

'I'm not leaving her.' And there was not only a child's wilfulness in her voice but her aunt's stubbornness, too. 'You can't make me.'

Fender sighed, a whistle that echoed on the inside. *OK, Addison, OK. But let us help you.*

CHAPTER 12

Captured

One of the men had torn a strip from his shirt and used it to tie Lacey's wrists behind her back. It was knotted so tightly her hands throbbed. She imagined they were starting to look like Sylvester the Cat's comedy thumb after he'd hit it with a hammer: red and glowing and comically pulsating to three times its size. She worried, absurdly, that they may end up needing to be cut off if their blood supply wasn't restored soon.

It's not absurd, Voice told her. *You're right to be worried.*

'What?'

Hm? No. Forget I said anything. They're fine. Nothing to worry about. And he shut up, no doubt regretting giving credibility to her concerns.

They'd left her feet unfettered so she could walk. Posy let the men prod and poke her, thump her in the back, smack her in the head, kick her feet and trip her, whatever they wanted, as long as they didn't get too rough. He walked to one side of her and, every now and then, glanced over with an infuriating half-smile that Lacey wanted to slap off his face. His eyes were black, gloating holes.

She'd tried talking to the real Posy, the guy who had a missing pooch called Princess, a dog Lacey had seen, very much alive, despite Posy's fear she'd been eaten by some of his old

362

gang. She shared this news but it elicited no response. She changed tack and tried telling him about the books she'd read to her niece recently (the one about the three Billy Goats Gruff, and the one about the boy who was brought up by a bear). She asked if he'd heard any good stories and if he'd like to share them, but the *other* Posy, the one who looked out of Posy's face, smiled his blank, imitation smile.

'Posy's not at home right now,' he said, 'but if you'd like to leave a message after the beep, he'll get back to you as soon as possible.'

The beeping sound never came, and Lacey didn't leave any message.

She wasn't sure how far she'd run, but she'd made them chase her for what felt like hours. In reality, it was likely little more than one. Still, they were miles away from the church, and it would take a while to get back.

'There's nothing there, you know,' she said, thinking about Alex buried in the basement. 'Addison wouldn't go back there. She's not stupid. Not like you guys.'

Frank gave her a hard whack to the back of the head. She hadn't been expecting it, and it dropped her to one knee. She even heard that yellow cartoon bird ringing a tiny bell vigorously in her ears. Frank grabbed her arm and wrenched her to her feet. She cried out as her shoulder twisted.

'*Ow*. Take it easy.'

'Keep moving,' he snarled.

Like Voice, she stayed quiet after that. Kept her head down and watched her boots, appreciating the solid, echoing stamps they made on the hard macadam. She was scared – she'd be a fool not to be – and there was a cold ball clumped in her guts to prove it. But there was also a moderately sized spark of self-satisfaction hanging around in there, too, and that warmed her a little. They hadn't got Addison. Oh, Lacey knew Posy had sent people back to search the houses she'd led them through, but she also knew that Addison had a strong survival instinct, and as much as she'd want to obey Lacey's instructions to stay put, she would have climbed out of that closet by now. Lacey doubted the girl had lasted more than thirty minutes in that cramped space before figuring it wasn't the safest place to be. And that was fine. Lacey didn't want Addison to be a passive little wallflower, too willing to follow orders. Survival was about doing whatever the hell needed to be done – a lesson Lacey had learned pretty damn quickly herself – and if that meant Addison disobeyed her, then that was hunky-dory with her.

On the flip side, Lacey also knew the girl would almost definitely backtrack to the church, despite what she'd told Posy. It was the only other place Addison knew in town, the place where Alex was, and Lacey knew she would return for her, because it was exactly what Lacey had been planning to do all along. She had lost count of the amount of times Addison had bugged her and Alex to retell the stories of how they had escaped the clutches of Dumont. And if there was one moral to take away from them, it was that you never leave a loved one behind.

When Lacey thought of Addison sneaking back to the church, the clump of fear in her guts grew colder, snuffing out that one tiny spark of smugness. All Lacey could do was give her niece some time, and maybe, with luck, Alex, too.

What're you thinking on? Voice asked, blatantly eavesdropping on her thoughts.

Posy glanced at her, suspicion sharpening his gaze.

Lacey didn't reply. Instead, she stopped walking, halting smack-bang in the middle of the street, as if she'd hit an invisible barrier and couldn't proceed any further.

Lacey . . . Voice began, worry nudging in around her name.

Posy stopped, too. 'Walk,' he ordered.

'Nah. Thanks, but I'm good right here.' With her arms bound behind her, Lacey awkwardly sat down.

'This isn't a discussion. You *will* walk or I will let these gentleman pay you back for all the running you made them do.'

'But my legs hurt. I need to rest. Maybe grab a short nap.'

'So you won't walk?' Posy asked.

'No,' she said, looking him dead in the eye. 'I will not.'

'Very well.'

She didn't see who kicked her first – it came from behind. An explosion of pain erupted in her kidneys. The second hit was a boot between her shoulder blades. That one winded her and planted her flat on her face. After that it became a free-for-all, the strikes raining down from all sides: blows to her back, her head, her arms, and, when she rolled on to her side and drew up her knees, they got her in the chest and ribs, too. Stomps that made her grunt and gasp because there wasn't enough air to scream.

She heard Voice shouting at her to curl up tighter, to protect herself, but by then the pain was everywhere and an unceasing swell of white noise built inside her head, a high, shrieking whistle interrupted only by the hollow thuds of boots striking her. Beyond that, she didn't have the presence of mind to think anything at all.

CHAPTER 13

Dug Up

A voice was the first thing she heard. It was hushed, whispered. Impatient. Scared.

'Just be quiet and *help me*.'

It was too dark to see. No, that was wrong. It was dark because her eyes were closed. She tried opening them, but some gummy substance had glued them shut. She tried lifting a hand to clear the mess away, but she couldn't do that, either.

This is one sticky situation you've got yourself into, she thought to herself, and laughed. Except she didn't laugh. She couldn't. A monstrous weight pinned her down, crushing the backs of her shoulders. Only a trickle of air reached her lungs.

Something shifted above her, a slight lightening of the load on top of her. She screamed. Pain. So much of it. How could she have forgotten the *pain*? She'd been lying here in terrible, horrendous, *hacking* pain, a woodcutter chopping an axe into her neck over and over, and she couldn't move and she couldn't call out and, so, she'd let her mind float free and blessedly left her suffering behind.

She'd gone home. She hadn't been there in a long time. She was in her kitchen, the smell of baking cookies warmly redolent. It was a small kitchen, she could reach every cupboard and drawer by standing in one spot and swivelling, but she liked that, having an economy of movement. She could take eggs and milk from the refrigerator and a bag of flour from the cupboard next to the sink and it would be done in four efficient arm movements. Mostly, she baked for her neighbours or her college friends. For her mother, she'd save only one or two cookies because for forty-six weeks of the year she'd be dieting (but, boy, she better have at least *one* cookie saved for her or else there'd be hell to pay. She could burn that sucker off in one session of power-walking, didn'tcha know).

The apartment was all her own. Sixteen hundred dollars a month – or $4 per square foot of living space – and it was worth every penny. Three rooms, four if she included the walk-in closet (she included the closet), and every one of them hers. Her belongings barely squeezed into the place – there were boxes jammed under her bed and bookcases full of knick-knacks lining nearly every wall, and she'd designated ninety per cent of the corner space as dumping grounds for her coursework and text-books, but guess what? It was *still* all hers, and she loved it.

The kitchen was by far her favourite place. Above the sink, the window looked south on to the fire escape, where she'd started to grow her own herbs and spices. Pots lined the windowsill, five in total, and all she had to do was slide the window up, reach out and pluck whatever she needed for the dish she was preparing. It was her own fresh-herb store, six storeys above the hustle and bustle of the city below.

Her doorbell buzzed. She hadn't even moved to answer it when she heard the scrape of a key. The front door unlocked and her mother whirlwinded in, yoo-hooing her.

'Lexi, where are you, my darling?'

Alex closed her eyes and counted to five.

Her mother appeared in the doorway, resplendent in a pink velour running suit, white sweatbands and Sketchers. 'Let's Get Physical' by Olivia Newton John ran through Alex's head.

'There you are!'

'Been exercising?' Alex asked her.

'No, dear, I've been to a board meeting. *Of course* I've been exercising. You think I wear this for fun?'

Alex smiled and bit her lip, because really all she wanted to do was laugh. 'You look good.' And that did it, she *did* laugh.

Her mother took it in good sport. Her pink-lipsticked mouth smirked (the pink, of course, matched the velour). 'Always giving your mother a hard time. I get it. You young guns are so hip and cool, us old farts have to find our own style. I smell cookies.'

The change in subject surprised Alex, but she had caught up by the time her mom reached for the oven door. She slapped her hand away. 'They're not ready.'

Her fifty-four-year-old mother pouted. 'There's no need for violence, dear.'

'You call *that* violence? I'll show you violence.' Alex shook her fist at her.

Her mother backed off a little, hands up in surrender, but when she dropped them all amusement melted from her face. As quick as that, the fun was over. 'You know I've come over for more than just teasing and baking tips, honey.'

Alex sighed and went back to cleaning up. She swiped a cloth across the last residues of flour dusting the countertop, cupping a hand at its edge to gather the white powder into her palm. She dumped it in the sink.

'Your father and I want you home.'

'Mom, we've talked about this.'

'We have, but you don't seem to be hearing what we're saying. You won't have to pay rent, we'll cover all your college fees, we'll even start organising a fund for any university you want to go to. Wherever you want.'

Alex couldn't bring herself to look at her. She knew her mother's eyes would be large and unblinking, an unspoken plea badly masked behind all the cosmetic encouragement. Alex dropped three broken eggshells into the garbage and went back to scrubbing.

'I know the money could really help you, darling.'

'It's not about the money—' Alex began.

'Then what *is* it about?' The cajoling tone was gone. 'Why are you being so *difficult*? You know we can't handle your sister like you can and, frankly, she's running rings around us. You know how your father gets. His stress levels go through the roof when she's playing up. Don't you even *care*?'

'Of course I care—'

Her mother didn't let her finish. 'The doctor came out to him last week. You know what his blood pressure was? 160 over 95. You know what that means?' Alex did but knew her mother would tell her anyway. 'It means he's at *high risk* for another heart attack. Is that what you want?' Although her mother battled very hard to lower her tone, Alex could hear the exasperation rattling her voice. 'Baby, all we're asking is for you to come home for a little while. Not long. Maybe just six weeks or so.'

'I don't—'

'A month! Just a month. That's not so bad, is it?' Wheedling now, back to coaxing. 'You'd be doing us a *huge* favour, darling. I couldn't begin to tell you.'

'Mom, this really isn't my problem any more.' Alex stopped scrubbing the worktop – it was shining and spotless and wasn't getting any cleaner – and turned to her mother. 'I'm sorry. Really I am. But I've looked after Sam for the last twelve years of my life. It's your turn now.'

Her mother's lipsticked mouth puckered, the lines radiating from it, crinkling like Saran wrap. Her eyes narrowed. 'You're a selfish little cow. You know that, don't you?'

'*Ow.*' Alex flinched and slapped a hand to her neck, expecting to feel a knife handle jutting from the back of it, her mother's hand wrapped around the hilt, but there was nothing there. She rubbed at the tender spot.

Her mother didn't seem to notice her reaction but kept right on going, her face turning an unsightly pink: lips, velour running suit and complexion all matching.

'I sacrificed *everything* for you. I fed you and clothed you and provided for you while your father, that sack of worthless shit, worked every hour God gave him. He left everything to me. I know, I know, you're *young*.' She said it like it was an illness. 'You don't understand how hard it can be, but just you wait until your own children come along to suck all life's joys out of you. You'll see how they drain you dry, how they steal every precious moment of your day until you're left an empty, miserable husk. I got the best nannies available, but that still wasn't enough for you, was it? So what if I needed a break sometimes? You would, too, if you were surrounded by dirty diapers and vomiting, squalling children for twenty-four hours every day.'

Alex didn't point out that her mother's idea of a 'break' meant daily shopping trips and having lunch with her gaggle of girlfriends or disappearing for whole weekends to go sailing.

'Honestly, dear, I advise you not to ever have children. I'm not sure you're fit for it. You don't have the staying power. Are you even listening to me?'

Alex clutched at her neck, an excruciating pressure clamping down as if someone, somewhere, were slowly tightening a vice. Sweat beaded her brow. Pins and needles rushed across the backs of her shoulders, a cold prickling that brought tears to her eyes. She bit her lip again, not to stop herself from laughing this time but from screaming.

'Alex!'

She shot a glance at her mother, but the call hadn't come from her. Her mom's face was contorted. Her mouth moved, the veins standing proud from her neck, but someone had hit the mute button. Alex could see the lipstick smudges across the front of her teeth as her mother silently hurled her words. There

370

was always lipstick smudged across her teeth. Some days, Alex wanted to scream at her, *Don't you ever check the mirror, Mother? Don't you ever see there's more Pink Me, Pink! on your goddamned teeth than on your goddamned lips?* With the sound muted, the twisted snarl on her mother's face stood out starkly, but Alex had no time to be hurt by it. She gasped as pain cleaved her in half.

'Alex!'

Another horrendous twist on her neck, the vice's lever yanked another rotation tighter. Alex fell back against the counter, grasping her neck in both hands, as if trying to stop her head falling off. She tasted blood in her mouth. It made her feel sick, but then so did the pain. It geared up another level. She choked and gagged as hot liquid gushed up her throat. She lurched for the sink, except the sink wasn't there any more, there was only a blinding light shining in her eyes, drilling razors into her head, and she vomited, unable to stop the scorching surge of bile.

'Alex!'

She felt hands pulling at her, trying to turn her on to her side, but every time they tugged, the splintering agony in her neck and shoulders blazed hotter, so hot it was melting her bones. She groaned feebly as saliva drooled from her mouth. One last push and she was rolled on to her side, one last push and her head blew up in a corona of exploding suns.

Awareness returned slowly. The pain was still there but it had levelled out. It gnawed at every nerve in her arms and hands, but it didn't get any worse, didn't explode through her like a grenade or threaten to floor her. She stayed very still. Someone gently wiped her face with a cool cloth. She opened her eyes and thought, *I'm dreaming.*

Addy's smile trembled on her lips. 'Hi.'

'Hi.' Alex swallowed; her mouth tasted foul. She tried to

draw enough breath to speak, but it was like breathing through water. 'What . . . What're you doing . . . ?'

'I came back for you.'

Keeping her head still, Alex carefully rolled her eyes to look. They were in the main part of the church. It was night. Beams of wood arched over their heads, no longer the sun-warmed and glowing bottom of a ship's hull but the colourless, cold, bleached bones of a dead whale. All the pews had been tossed aside and lay in broken heaps. The pulpit and altar were tipped on their sides, gathered against the chancel's back wall. It was as though a tidal wave had swept through and smashed everything in its path.

'How'd . . . get . . . here?' Alex's words were muffled, her ears plugged with seaweed. She inhaled water – sluggish, unoxygenated water – and wheezed.

Addy's voice swam in and out, as if coming to her through deep fathoms of ocean. 'I found you . . . think it's hurt, but . . . know . . . to do.' Addy had dropped the damp cloth she'd been wiping Alex's face with and fretted over her.

The thought of moving was too much to bear. She wiggled her fingers, or at least *thought* she wiggled them – the pins and needles from earlier had turned into a terrifying numbness. The thought of being unable to move sent a sickly wave through her stomach. She was deathly afraid. How was she going to walk? If she couldn't walk, she was good for nothing. She'd be putting Addy and Lacey in danger every time –

Her thoughts stopped. Her heart, conversely, started to thud.

'Where's Lacey?' she whispered, precious air escaping her.

The expression on Addison's face made Alex's fast-beating heart clench so hard she didn't think it would ever start beating again. She squinted at Addy's mouth, her words skipping away like stones on a pond. She filled in the gaps.

'She led the bad men away from me. She hid me and ran. I don't know where she is. They probably got her by now.'

Alex closed her eyes then immediately opened them again. She needed to get Addison out of there. It wasn't safe. She braced herself and almost sobbed in relief as her arm lifted, came into view. She stretched her fingers for the girl's shoulder, gripped on to her. 'Addy, you . . . must go.' Fear ate away at her, so strong it almost overrode her pain. Sooner or later, Posy or one of the people with him would come back here, if only to check to see if she had survived the cave-in.

Posy. The name was an incredulous sound in her thoughts. What was he even *doing* here? It was impossible. No. Nothing was impossible. Not any more. Lacey talked to a voice, priests talked to fake Gods, Posy was alive and was hunting them for reasons she didn't want to know. Don't ever think these things can't happen.

Her breathing was getting worse. She was sinking down, down, so deep into the ocean the water pressure was crushing her, leaving no room for air. No room for anything. She gritted her teeth so hard she thought they would turn to dust in her mouth but, through the biting pain, fear drove her, a motivator beyond all motivators.

She spoke in fits and starts, in between tiny, erratic inhales. Panic made her heart pump ever harder, made her breathlessness worse. 'Thank you . . . for coming back for me. But, Addy . . . Addy it's time to go now.' With great effort, Alex sucked in another half-breath. Dizzy, she was so incredibly dizzy. 'Here.' She fumbled her rubbery fingers into her jeans pocket, seemed to search for ever and finally found what she was looking for. She clawed it out. She couldn't properly feel the St Christopher pendant between her fingers and was afraid the fine chain would trickle through her numb fingertips. 'Take . . . it. Lacey would want . . . you to have it.'

Addy accepted the necklace slowly. 'I can help,' she was saying. 'I'm real strong. I can carry you. You don't need to worry. I got it all figured out.'

'Put it . . . away.'

The girl slipped the chain into her pocket without looking at it.

'I got lots of ideas about how—'

'*Addy.*'

Alex almost blacked out, but something made her grasp on, nails digging into the cliff-edge, legs and feet dangling over an endless drop. She wondered if the girl moving her had made it worse, whether shifting her neck had caused irreparable damage, and then decided it didn't matter. She could see the stars through the windows. The moonlight bathed everything in a silvery-white luminescence. It shone over Addy's face.

The girl had stopped talking.

'Listen to me. Real hard.'

Addy nodded. ''K.'

'I'm not coming with you.' Addy's mouth opened, but Alex ploughed on. 'My neck's . . . very badly hurt. I'm not . . . going anywhere. I have . . . a pinky promise to keep, though. And you . . . you must help me keep it.'

Addy's head swung left and right in tiny, angry shakes. No, no, she will not help. No, she will not go, not if it meant leaving Alex. Alex could see how hard the girl was battening down the hatches to her emotions. They swirled like oceans in her eyes.

'Addison.' Alex hardly ever called her by her full name and only if it was serious business. 'You *must* help me.'

The head-shaking faltered. Addy's small brow came down. Her bottom lip jutted out, but this time she nodded. She nodded, and that's all Alex could ask for. She sent a silent prayer to no one, because no one was listening – no one ever had been. At least, not to her.

'Good. That's good. My pinky promise . . . was to do whatever it took . . . to keep you safe. That was our job . . . mine and Lacey's. Together. Do you understand?' She gulped a tiny sliver of air. Her heart beat fitfully, knocking on uneven beats,

374

stuttering like her breathing. 'Now, it's *your* job. You must promise me . . . you'll do whatever it takes. *Whatever* it takes . . . to stay safe. It's very im-important to me.' She almost lost it, then, and it was only the creaking thump from the other side of the room that swept aside her welling grief, a wash of terror taking its place. She was too late.

A bony-hipped woman came through the chancel doors and stopped dead when she saw them. She didn't have a gun. The knife she held was as long as a femur and curved wickedly at its tip. Moonlight attempted to catch its reflective surface but the blade was dull and smeared with what Alex could only hope was dirt.

Alex couldn't hear the woman above the waves rushing through her head, but she saw her mouth and jaw work as she spoke. Another tidal wave was coming, building speed, she could hear its approach like a thundering train in her ears. It would terminate at the same spot Benny had first appeared, dictating his scripture with a shit-eating grin on his face, and it would finish what had been started, snatching them all up and slamming them against the church walls until they were broken and lifeless.

The machete-wielding woman had eyes only for Addy. She beckoned to the girl, a come-hither gesture with her blade that, despite Alex being unable to hear her, would fail to encourage anyone with any sense to move closer. The woman had advanced around the driftwood pews, knife held ready.

She was close enough now for Alex to make out the uncomfortably large teeth in her mouth. A tangle of fine hair did little to hide the baldness that bared the woman's scalp at the crown; in fact, she looked ill, as if whatever whispered to her on the inside had spilled its evilness into her bloodstream and was stripping her back to the bone.

As the woman sidled closer, her smile closer to a sneer, Addy's head blocked Alex's view. The girl leaned over her and touched the tip of her nose to Alex's. Addy looked deep into her eyes and the heavy, suffocating waves in Alex's head parted to let her whispered words through.

'I promise, Alex. I promise a thousand million pinky promises. But first I got to help you.'

With that the girl stood up and the waves came crashing back in, drowning Alex, consuming her. Her chest hitched once, twice, halted on the third, and the last thing she saw was Addy crouch down, her hand slipping to the hem of her pants where she hid her knife.

CHAPTER 14

LOSS

'But I must stay with you, Albus.'

The boy was holding on to the sleeve of Albus's shirt, standing so close he was practically on top of his boots. Hari had been clingy ever since Albus had awoken, floor shaking, vehicle rattling around him. A bloody crack had appeared in the windshield while he'd been unconscious but, when he'd pointed to it, his friends had been strangely reticent about the kamikaze bird and the broken glass. Neither did they push him to share the details of his dream, and that wordless acceptance brought with it mixed feelings of relief and uncertainty.

'Don't leave me behind.'

Albus shook his head, face twisting in his need to explain, to make the boy understand that, although Hari had been a big help up to this point, this part had to be left to the grown-ups.

Gwen spoke for him, recognising his silent struggle. 'We need to be fast and sneaky now, Hari. And I know you can be both those things – you've proven that in spades – but it's going to be very dangerous from here on out.' Rufus shuffled impatiently, his sigh gusting out on a visible billow of breath. Gwen's face tightened. 'There'll be people out there who won't appreciate us getting involved in their business. And if you're there,' she told Hari, 'as much as I know you can look after yourself, we'll be worrying about you the whole time. And that'll be distracting. You get that, don't you? All it'll take is one small distraction and somebody'll end up hurt.'

The boy looked down at his feet and said nothing as he released Albus's sleeve and stepped away. Gwen met Albus's eyes and shrugged. There wasn't anything else she could say. The kid would just have to deal with it.

Hari's eyes didn't lift above knee level as they said their farewells. Bruno had been unanimously elected to stay behind to look after the boy and their ride out of here. As brave as Bruno was, his strength wasn't speed, and they had to move fast now.

Hari didn't offer a farewell or good luck, and that hurt Albus. To leave him that way, without a last word of goodbye, felt like an ill omen. He knew how hard it must have been for Hari to leave the Inn, the only place he considered home, travel through miles of unknown territory where one misstep could have got him killed, knowing that he'd be packed off back to the Inn if he'd been discovered too soon. He'd stayed out of sight, slept alone and cold at night without the comfort or protection of his friends, all because he believed he needed to be here. And now he was being left behind. Again.

'I'm not his keeper,' Bruno had said. 'If he wants to be here, who are we to stop him?'

And Albus *almost* reconsidered. He'd reached the end of the block, Hari's eyes burning into his back with every step. Gwen and Rufus had jogged on ahead, two shadowed figures cutting a path straight across the intersection, when Albus's boot crunched on to a gravelled planting border, rubber sole cementing itself in, and he couldn't lift his foot again, not without looking back.

Hari stood beside Bruno, his small stature making the man hulk even larger in the dark, like some ancient protector, and Albus was so close to going back, to nodding at the boy and allowing him to come that he thought he heard a whisper reach his ears, a celebratory *Yes*. But something stayed Albus's tongue,

378

so to speak, rooting it as fast as his boot was rooted to the ground. His sister was so close now – she pulled at him like a pup pulls at its training leash. He couldn't lose focus.

Rufus called his name, drawing his attention away from Bruno – who had raised his arm in a last wave – and the image of the boy standing motionless on the rain-slicked street. Albus's foot became unstuck, lifted, gravel crunching as he left the sidewalk and passed under the burned-out streetlights, melding into the shadows, his running footsteps joining Rufus's and Gwen's.

For the final two miles, Albus took the lead, tracking his sister. That oh-so-familiar tugging sensation – a spectral figure who he felt with every cell of his being – guided him through the streets. There were colours, too, and not from Rufus or Gwen. These were new: a spitting, faltering electric blue and a much more vibrant sunflower yellow. They intertwined with each other, plaiting and weaving in the air like ribbons in a child's black hair. These two people were together, and not far away, only a few short miles, fading in and out. He could track them if he wished but, each time he felt the instinct to turn and follow, the weighted plumb line of his sister swung inside him and directed him away. Ruby's psychic pull continued to correct him on turns, pulling him in the opposite direction from the beautiful weaving strands, its heavy bob dragging him back on point until the entangled blue and yellow ribbons fell behind.

Bruno had called him a hound scenting blood. Albus had believed himself to be in some sort of control of what was happening but, crossing street after street, dashing through alleys and across parking lots, diverting when they saw shadowy movement or heard furtive noises, he realised he'd been wrong. As he came ever closer to Ruby, Albus began to understand he wasn't the one hunting. He was being summoned, as powerless as a tiny fleck of metal shaving within the magnetised radius of a lodestone.

A church came into view, a modest building with an immodestly tall tree crouched over its roof. The front doors were flung wide, as if someone had barrelled through with no thought to draughts or uninvited trespassers. Albus scanned the parking lot, breathing heavily. No lights came from inside the church.

'We going in?' Rufus said at his side.

Albus nodded. They were. His sister was in there.

On his other side, Gwen's panting breaths misted from her mouth. 'You know what'll be waiting for us?'

He shook his head.

Gwen's hand touched his back. Warm, reassuring. 'We'll get her.'

He nodded again and couldn't wait a second longer. He took off and heard the others follow, the slaps of their feet echoing. He was across the parking lot and up the stairs and through the church doors before considering how foolhardy it was to burst so incautiously inside, but he was beyond that now. He *felt* her. Here. Now.

Someone inside the church shrieked.

He vaguely heard Gwen gasp a warning, a stuttering line of white sparks dancing into his field of vision, but he was beyond them, too.

The nave was trashed, and in its centre a skeletally thin woman reeled in a drunken circle, a machete waving aloft, a rabid animal attached to her face and chest. She was shrieking at the top of her lungs as she flung the creature off, and a young girl unfolded, tumbling as she bashed up against a second woman, lying prone on the floor, who didn't cry out or flinch at the abuse. Recognition knifed Albus in the belly when he saw her.

Was it her? After all this time, was it Ruby?

Rufus bustled past, jostling him aside.

'You *stuck* me?' The thin woman's shock reverberated in the high-ceilinged room. She wrenched something from her shoulder. A knife. Not much bigger than a penknife, but the girl had sunk it into the soft place between shoulder and collarbone. She had stuck her good. 'Why'd you *do* that? You've gone and *ruined* me.'

The girl didn't cower; she was scrabbling to her feet. But already the balance was tipping the wrong way, the wickedly curved blade of the woman's machete sweeping up, hanging poised, time slowing down as Albus tried to make his feet move faster, but he knew the distance was too great in the time left to him. He'd never make it. Had that murderous blade also cut his sister down? Is that why she lay unmoving on the floor?

He let out a primal cry of rage.

The thin woman looked up, saw Albus running at her, but she didn't pause. Her blade descended, hacking the girl's skull in two, and an unbelievably loud gunshot cracked behind Albus's head.

The top of the woman's head blew off, as if she were wearing a toupee and a gust of air had given it flight. The calibre of the bullet, at such close range, hit her hard, shoving her back from the girl, and in an abstract, nonsensical way, Albus knew bits of brain and gore were flying out along with the splatter, but there were no colours. The moonlight had washed everything to a sterile monochromatic pastiche. The machete jerked from the woman's hand and hit the floor with a church-bell-like *clang*.

Even as the dead woman was blown off her feet, Albus arrived. The girl blinked up at him, skull not cleaved in half but perfectly intact, and he blinked right back at her, not comprehending how she was alive. There was a slice down the length of her sleeve, where the machete had cut, missing her flesh by less than a centimetre. Rufus's bullet must have struck the woman as her blade descended, knocking her aim askew at the last instant. It had missed the girl by a fraction. There wasn't a scratch on her.

Albus looked down at his sister laid out on the floor and, in that moment, that one blinding, forever moment when another fated blade hung over him, he felt his soul cleave in two, a physical tearing that hurt him as surely as if a real blade had ripped him open.

This wasn't Ruby.

It was the woman from his dreams.

He saw Alex as he'd first seen her, outside the bicycle store of his dream, alert and alive, so protective of this girl as she went about picking out her bike, and realised he was on his knees in the middle of the church, tears streaming down his face, lost, bereft, and not only because this woman wasn't who he'd so desperately wanted her to be but because he remembered how her eyes had burned with life, their colour a pure and vivid blue, how her parted lips had been full and perfectly made to smile. Hunger had sculpted sharp angles of her cheekbones, her jaw, but she had been beautiful. And he'd been too late to save her.

The moon's light was a spotlight, bringing every detail into sharp focus. Everything around them was dashed to pieces, the broken bits of their shipwrecked vessel strewn in the dark oceans of the room. The girl held on to her dead friend's hand and Albus feared he would have to prise her grip loose when it came time to leave. (With the barrel of his rifle, Rufus poked at the woman he'd shot, checking she was dead, even though her head was an exploded pumpkin. He and Gwen exchanged heated words, their voices hushed.) Albus's and the girl's eyes met, and her voice was equally hushed when she spoke.

'Alex isn't gonna wake up, is she?'

He shook his head once, his heart breaking for the both of them.

'We don't have time to dig a treasure hole for her?'

He wasn't sure what a treasure hole was, but no, they didn't have time.

'Why're you crying?'

He looked at the woman he'd never met yet had seen in his dreams (and he made himself think her name: *Alex*), and he felt his sister everywhere, as if she were drifting through the air, whispering in his ear, brushing her fingers through his hair and over his brow. So much loss. And that's what he wanted to say to the girl. So much loss, he didn't know what to do with it. It was breaking him, like this nave had been broken, pieces splintered everywhere, none of which could be fit back together again.

Cool fingers closed over his hand. There was no revulsive withdrawing when the girl felt his missing digits. She held his hand and said nothing.

The girl. Addison. With her dark, corkscrew curls. She had been in his dreams, too, but he chose not to think about what she'd looked like hanging dead from her stake in the red-lit clearing of the cornfield.

Albus forced himself to his feet, canting to the side as his crazily upturned world attempted to right itself. The girl, still holding his hand, stood with him. He thought there would be screams and shouts, a tussle to get her to leave her friend, but the girl didn't cling. She stood, gazing down at Alex, and Albus heard her whisper two words, 'pinky' and 'promise'.

And that was all. Then she was using her grip on him to pull him away. He glanced over his shoulder, glimpsed the look of surprise on Gwen's face as he was dragged across the nave. She smacked Rufus in the side, getting his attention, and then both were hurrying to catch up.

Addison towed him through the entrance foyer and outside. She gave him no time to think as he descended the church steps and went left. They had seen two men skulking around two streets over, entering and leaving houses, and he had no desire to cross their path.

The girl's hand tugged him to a stop.

'No,' she said, and as if the order had been issued directly to his brain, his limbs froze. Addison's face was pale, her eyes dark. Her curls bounced with the shaking of her head. 'Not that way.'

She went right, taking him with her. Albus shared a quick look with Gwen as she and Rufus appeared at the top of the steps. From the look on her face, Albus could tell this wasn't panning out at all as she'd expected. It wasn't for him, either.

The macadam was uneven beneath his feet, as if moles had burrowed up out of the ground, and Addison dropped his hand to concentrate on her footing. She scuttled along the building's north-facing wall and Albus scuttled with her, running his palm along the brick siding, feeling the roughness scrape his skin.

At the corner, the girl dropped to a crouch.

Albus leaned past her.

The rear of the church's grounds opened up into a large, overgrown piece of land filled with wild grass and weeds. At its edges stood a line of dark houses, their backyards leading on to the church's property, most of them separated from it by flimsy-looking fence panels.

Rufus and Gwen came up behind them, their breaths smoking in the damp air, and Albus pointed to the shadowy gap his eyes had backtracked to when surveying what should have been a seamless run of panelling.

'I see it,' Gwen whispered.

Shouts. Men's voices, rapidly approaching. If they didn't move, they would be trapped here in the church's oasis, open wasteland on one side and an empty parking lot on the other. No sanctuary for any of them. He moved past the girl, but didn't make it far. He glanced down to see a handful of his shirt gripped in her hand.

From the right, a figure silently dashed into the clearing. The man was stocky, squat, but he darted swiftly across the wasteland, the overgrown grass doing little to hinder him. The moonlight shone on his shaven head and, lower, flashed along a large, bared knife.

Five seconds later, shouts burst into the clearing, and with them came two more men. They whooped and hollered, mistaking themselves for members of an Indian war party. The dulled quality of their shouts struck Albus as out of place. He had spent so long at the Inn, in the company of people who spoke in more than verbal sounds, that there was something intrinsically missing in these people, a quality that made them uninteresting and lifeless. And the girl beside him was the same – she didn't speak in colours to him, either. Why had he been led to her?

He could still feel the psychic tug of his sister, haunting their steps, holding him close. It hadn't lessened. She was here in spirit, if nothing else.

The stocky, shaven-headed man had already disappeared around the far side of the church (the side that Albus had been on his way to when the girl stopped him) and, yelling in sounds alone, the two men followed him.

Albus felt a tap. The girl pointed at him to go. Without pausing to question, he broke cover, eyes glued to the place where the last two men had appeared. He went low and fast, moving away from the shadow cast by the church and out from under the awning of the mighty oak's canopy. Straight away, Albus felt terribly conspicuous.

A loud ruckus erupted inside the church.

'Go, Albus, go,' hissed Rufus, and his brittle, rusting words were a welcome sight to Albus's eyes.

He led them toward the fence, away from open land, running as fast as he dared. They had maybe seventy yards to cover, but it felt like they were crossing the entire length of a football field. Albus had to kick his way through the tall grass, the stalks *whisht*ing threateningly around his legs, the long, twine-like stems snatching at his boots.

He waited to hear the men charge back outside and come

running to the rear, shouts of discovery ringing out as Albus and the others were spotted fleeing the scene of the crime. The men would know they couldn't have gotten far – Rufus's gunshot had gone off only a few short minutes ago, not long enough to give them any sort of lead. In less than sixty seconds, they would be giving chase.

Albus yanked his feet out of the last twining threads of grass and stepped on to the fallen fence panel and into the shadowy gap. He turned to help the girl over but she had deftly leaped across, more agile than him.

Gwen and Rufus clattered over the fence panelling and Albus winced at the noise. He watched their reflections grow in the French doors as they cut across the lawn: him, the girl – seeming very small, sandwiched between them – Gwen, both hands gripped around her gun, and Rufus. Except Rufus had stopped and Albus lost sight of him.

'Why're we running?'

Albus pulled up short before he slipped between house and garage.

'Are you frigging *kidding* me?' Gwen hissed, turning on Rufus.

'No, I'm not. We're capable of holding our own. We shouldn't be running.'

'There are at least three of them back there.'

'So? We've got guns. All I've seen so far are blades. Our odds are good.'

'Three that we know of. We're not here to wage a war, Rufus. We have the girl and we're getting out.' Gwen stalked over to him and grabbed his elbow. 'There's no need to be taking any risks. Quit playing the macho man' – Albus winced. That kind of talk would never win Rufus over – 'and get your ass in gear.'

'We're making a mistake.'

'No one's making a mistake.'

'All we've been doing is running since we—'

She didn't wait for him to finish talking but began towing him after her, the hand on his elbow brooking no argument. Rufus's strides were heavy, unwilling, his body language screaming defiance, but he came.

'Everything is so out of control, Gwen. It has been from the start. We need to take control back or else we'll always be running.'

'This really isn't the time for this. We can talk about it later.'

Albus made sure they were following and once more took the lead. The girl stayed close, as if the exchange between Rufus and Gwen had unnerved her. The passageway was too narrow to afford Gwen and Rufus the space to enter two abreast, so Gwen dropped his elbow and pushed him in ahead of her.

They had lost precious time. Albus knew it. And by the tight expression on Gwen's face, she knew it, too.

Their pursuers' dulled shouts echoed through the night, unfettered by walls and church roofs, carrying clearly and colourlessly through the darkness.

The hunt was on.

CHAPTER 15

The Cap

Houses leaned over Addison like dark, crooked men, cloaking the alleyway in shadows. She'd been staying close to Albus, her hand reaching forward, almost touching his back, because Rufus, in his angry baseball cap and with his too-big gun, frightened her.

Albus. Rufus. Such funny names.

She was extra careful not to trample or trip on Albus's feet, but she didn't slow down. She felt safer near him. He felt real, when she didn't feel real at all. She was all floaty and clumsy, like in a dream, a tricksy dream that she *really* wanted to wake up from. Open her eyes and be back at the church with Alex, in the rabbit-run basement, with all of Benny's pretty books spread around her and her new dollies waiting to be dressed. They could start over and everything would be fixed.

She knew that the woman with hair the colour of the moon wanted her to stop crowding Albus. Gwen. She'd caught up a couple of times, touched Addison's shoulder, but Addison could be as stubborn as her aunt, and she'd frowned and shook her head, and each time Gwen had relented and dropped back.

Albus seemed happy to step free of the crooked-men houses, which Addison didn't get. Shadows were good for hiding, for disappearing like you never was. To the left was a pretty picket-fenced porch that made her think of frilly icing and gingerbread cottages. On the right was a wild, scraggly hawthorn bush that didn't make Addison think of anything at all.

Watch out! Fender yelled.

A huge, growling giant fell out of the sky. Albus was picked up and tossed aside as if he were a Ken doll. He landed in the bushes.

'Bridge troll,' Addison breathed, staring. They had all been trolls on that bridge, because that's where trolls lived, but she'd seen this one only from afar, towering above all the cars. Up close, he was even bigger.

We didn't pay to cross, Chief whispered fearfully.

The giant troll swiped his arm at her and she was swept up like a twig in a flood. She slammed into Gwen and the woman grunted. They tumbled together, hitting the ground in a tangle of limbs.

The attack had come so quickly, so unexpectedly, Rufus had his rifle only partway raised when the troll yanked it out of his hands. The gun clacked off the side of the gingerbread house and landed in the mud.

The troll hit Rufus in the gut. The blow lifted him off his feet. Rufus made a weird noise, like a sucking whine. The troll grabbed his neck, held him down and set about pummelling Rufus with his other hand, punch, punch, punch, punch, but they sounded all kinds of wrong 'cause Addison had heard plenty of punches, and these weren't them.

She rolled away, helped by Gwen's shoving hands, and crouched in a ball, making herself very small, eyes fixed on the tussle. Two shrouded creatures stuttered to life, shadow-animals, swift and slight in the space between the crooked houses, stamping over Rufus where he stood clinched against the troll, squirming over Gwen where she scrabbled on hands and knees after her gun (dropped when Addison had collided with her). These creatures were all twisty snake-scales and black, reflective shimmers, a rippling effect that made Addison gasp at their beauty. The howling wind became the creatures' billowing breaths. Heat radiated like an incinerator, and Addison spied the deep glowing fire in the creatures' eyes, in their nostrils, in the sharp-toothed mouths leading down into molten throats. Chief was dancing among them and his black mouth glowed with heat, too.

'The troll thinks we're monsters?' Addison breathed.

She felt Fender nod. Was about to speak when gunshots boomed so loud Fender flinched, and she did, too, and tucked herself tighter into her ball.

The troll took his own punches to the chest and stomach and throat, each bullet knocking him away from Rufus. Addison saw a dark mist erupt each place he was struck.

Released from the cinch, Rufus sank to his knees and sat with his head tilted back, mouth wide as he drew in awful, noisy breaths. Floppy as a stalk, he bowed forward, slowly curling over his thighs, his forehead coming to rest gently, gently, on the ground.

'Rufus!'

Gwen hadn't taken the time to stand before shooting. Her gun fell from her hands as she got clumsily to her feet, staggering over to him, almost falling on top of him in her haste. Everything had taken place so fast and so slow, both at the same time, and Addison didn't know what had happened. But here came Albus – he'd fought his way free from the bushy hedge and he reached Rufus at the same time.

Rufus had lost his cap. It sat like a deflated football, sad and squashed, near Addison's foot. Albus cradled his friend's head in his palms. To Addison, it looked like he was cupping water instead of cupping his friend's head. Gwen tried to lift Rufus up, couldn't. He was too floppy.

Addison didn't move, not even a little bit, 'cause the troll was watching her. He was on his butt, half slumped against the gingerbread cottage with the pretty picket fence. The set of his mouth was hidden by a leafy beard, eyes lost under the heavy ledge of his brow, and yet she knew he was staring at her. She waited for him to speak, to spit out something ugly, not for her ears, not for *anyone's* ears, but he didn't. At least not out loud.

In the back of her head, Fender shared what could be heard. A confused whispering, like a loop-de-loop, overlapping on itself.

It's so hard to understand, but it . . . it's telling him that he did right. That we were monsters, and that . . . wait . . . That he can go home now. He can let go and finally rest. He did good. It's telling him to close his eyes. Shhh, Odell, shhh and close your eyes.

CHAPTER 16

Crazy Bitch

The top of Jules's head was gone. Sunny couldn't stop staring at it. A hinged flap of scalp folded away from her cracked skull and gobs of her brain splattered everywhere.

Sunny and Beck had heard the gunshot, a single, piercing report that widened and spread as the buildings and sidewalks and streets absorbed the sound, and they'd followed it back to the church. There, they found Posy.

Posy? Not-Posy? Sunny studied his actions, listened to him speak, but could discern little distinction any more; he wasn't one thing nor the other.

She backed away, leaving him to study the mess smeared across the church's floor. He even crouched for a better look. Her eyes fell on the girl, an older teenager. She had sunk to her knees beside the second body, another woman's. A stranger to Sunny.

The girl said and did nothing. Merely sat and let her chin slump to her chest, listing to one side as if she'd downed a litre of vodka and maybe popped a tab or two on top of it. Her hands were tied behind her back.

Was this her? She looked awful, her face swollen like a lumpy potato, mottled with bruises. Blood encrusted her nostrils and lips. Frank and another fella stood near her like two heavies.

Wary of a girl.

'Jesus,' Sunny murmured. 'They sure did a number on her.'

Posy called the two men over and they left the girl where she knelt, shooting glances at her as they backed away. As if she might jump up and hurricane-kick them all to death.

'Who did this?' Frank asked, nudging Jules's body with the toe of his boot. She shifted a little, but not by much. 'And *why*? There's nothing here. Nothing to take.'

A commotion at the doors. Mary shoved her way through, shouldering two people aside. She kicked a broken piece of pew out of her way and marched across the room, her feet thudding like cannon-fire. She acknowledged no one, didn't even give Sunny the stink-eye as she stalked by, heading straight for where Posy knelt beside her girlfriend's body.

She stopped six feet short, a force-field of shock holding her back. She stared at the mess of Jules's head, mute, motionless, and, before Sunny knew what was happening, she came for the kneeling teenager.

Her palm cracked off the girl's cheek.

She screamed and spat in her face.

She punched her, the girl's head snapping back.

She struck her a third time, the meaty thump of a fist connecting with bone, and the girl whimpered, an involuntary sound of pain.

Mary's fist pulled back for a fourth strike, a powerhouse of a blow by the looks, but she didn't throw it.

Sunny stared at her own fingers, clamped around Mary's wrist. She didn't remember moving.

Mary yanked her arm out of Sunny's grip, fury radiating from her, lips pulled back to reveal something ugly and feral.

A bolt of apprehension shrivelled Sunny's stomach. What the hell was she doing? Did she *want* to get the shit beaten out of her? Don't get involved. Don't stir up trouble. Keep your head down.

'Don't make things difficult for us, Sun,' Beck murmured, appearing at Sunny's side.

'Don't you *ever* fucking touch me, you crazy bitch,' Mary hissed.

'Look, we're all sorry about Jules,' Sunny told her, 'but the girl has taken her beating.'

That was a lie – Sunny wasn't sorry about Jules. Jules had been a crapbag who enjoyed laughing at the misfortune of others. Well, guess what? The same misfortune had come knocking down her door and, if Sunny had believed in Fate or Karma, or any of that bullshit, she'd be saying Jules got exactly what she deserved. Besides, it wasn't this girl who'd shot Jules. The thing that was now Posy had led them all to this place; if Mary should be pissed at anyone, it should be at him.

'She can't see any of that,' Beck pointed out.

Mary didn't shift her venomous glare from Sunny. 'You don't know *shit*. You don't even know that your precious *Beck* is a goddamn—'

'Enough.'

One word. That was all it took for Not-Posy to halt Mary's tongue, to bring all their attention to him. 'The girl has something I want and listening to you two squabble isn't getting it for me. I need answers.' He stared Mary down until the woman could stand it no longer and dropped her gaze. Her jaw clenched. Sunny saw the rapid beat of her pulse in the side of her throat.

She spat on the girl a second time and muttered, 'This isn't over.'

She sent Sunny a last, withering look, a look that promised retribution, promised a whole world of pain when Sunny least expected it. Watch your back, it said, and for the thousandth time Sunny thought about taking Beck and leaving this place, these people. Going back to their old life of existing outside of everything and everyone. They could go it alone. They didn't need Posy's or the Flitting Man's protection, nor anyone else's. They only needed each other.

Mary gave a last parting shot as she left, but not to the girl. She swung a booted foot in a vicious kick that connected with the dead stranger's head, landing with an echoing thud that jerked the woman's body. The girl, who had seemed so defeated, so feeble and beaten, gave a low, guttural growl and the next thing Sunny knew she was on Mary, tackling her head first.

Sunny seriously wouldn't have fancied Mary's odds in that fight, even with the girl's hands tied behind her back. Frank and Pike had to drag her off, and a few confused minutes later Mary had been dragged, yelling and kicking, from the church.

Frank held a fistful of the teenager's shirt at her shoulder, gripping it fast.

Posy squatted down in front of her, his head cocked to one side. 'I understand you're upset.' It came out almost gently. 'I'm sorry about Alex. She deserved better than this. Truly. She was very brave. But I need to understand what happened here. Who did this? Jules has been shot, and Alex has no gun. She could not have made it out of that basement alone, not in the state she's in.'

The girl didn't reply, didn't lift her head. She breathed in hard, heavy pants. The set to her mouth said she wouldn't be cooperating any time soon. She hadn't made a single sound other than her guttural growl before she'd attacked Mary, but Sunny saw her face was wet with tears. She'd been crying the whole time.

Frank cuffed the girl around the ear. It wasn't a hard blow, but her face flinched and she shied away.

'And here I thought we'd whupped all the sass out of her,' Frank said.

It pained Sunny to see the girl like this, but she didn't interfere. She was in control of her impulses now. It wouldn't do her any favours to wade into this shit-show. Didn't stop her thought processes, though. The kid was barely past sixteen. Half the size of any of these guys. It wasn't right she'd got beaten on like she had.

Sunny wondered if the girl recognised the old Posy in this thing that crouched before her, moving Posy's lips and turning his eyes, manipulating his hands and feet. Did she understand what was going on here? Could she help him? This girl had known him from before, when he'd been a slow, stupid cuss who jumped when told to jump and closed his mouth when told to shut it. The old Posy had been just another dog in this world, waiting to be put down, waiting to be eaten alive, but he'd survived somehow, even if he was being eaten alive in a different kind of way.

'Why is someone shooting my people?' Not-Posy asked, leaning forward to put his face in hers.

The girl mumbled something, her thickened lips scarcely moving.

'Speak up now, we can't hear you.'

'How should I know?' she said more clearly.

Somewhere in the night, a series of gunshots popped one after the other. Fireworks, Sunny thought, but that was stupid. There weren't any fireworks out here. No celebrations to be had. No parties to attend. Heads had come up at the first *pop* and they all listened to the distant *bang*s. Sunny counted them. Nine. Nine gunshots.

'Well, it seems we're about to find out, doesn't it?' Not-Posy said.

CHAPTER 17

Dead End

Gwen hadn't moved or spoken. She had her arms locked around Rufus, rocking him back and forth, back and forth. Her gun lay discarded, its slide locked back, all its cartridges expended and bullets lodged in the dead man. Resting in the giant's oversized hand, fingers unfurled as delicately as a lotus blossom, was a bloodied knife.

Albus couldn't find the child straight away. She was completely unmoving in the darkness, crouched with her arms locked around her knees, only the dull shine of her eyes giving her away. He saw no shock in her. This girl had seen death played out before – bloody, violent death – and it didn't faze her. He was reminded of the dream version of her, of how she had been hung on a stake with all the others, no visible marks marring her body. She'd been perfect. Untouched. And that scared him all over again, although he couldn't understand why. In this girl lay something that warranted his fear, though, of that he was certain. The fact he could close his eyes and, with pinpoint accuracy, indicate her location, like he'd once been able to with his sister, brought him no comfort.

A distant clang of crashing metal lifted his head. The gunshots Gwen had fired had reorientated their hunters.

'Albus?'

Hearing this strange girl say his name was unsettling. She must have picked it up from Gwen or Rufus, but somehow it felt like she'd always known him.

Gwen continued to rock, seemingly unaware of her surroundings. Albus had been holding Rufus's head cupped in his palms and now carefully lowered it. He couldn't help a small moan escaping as it dropped to hang limp over Gwen's cradling arm. Rufus's face was slack, his mouth and eyelids partway open. Flecks of blood marked the sclerae of his eyes. Black spots on the bluish-whites that Rufus would never blink away.

A swift, agonising stab pierced Albus's chest, the blade of a shovel dug into the mud of his heart. Sorrow welled in the depression. He would never hear Rufus's rich claret voice again, never see it spool from his lips like the spill of mulled wine. His colour was forever gone from the world.

He slipped his arms under Rufus, tried to lift him away from Gwen, but a savage, jagged-white growl came from her and she wrenched him back. Albus made a second attempt, got a little further this time, before she stubbornly pulled him to her again, and he abandoned the idea to cup his palms around Gwen's face. He leaned in and pressed his brow to the heat of hers, locked eyes and told her silently that they had to go, couldn't stay here, would mourn for their friend later, would cry and wail at the sky together, but Albus needed her right now, needed her to help him if any of them were to get out of this alive.

Gwen made no further sounds, but Albus saw the ruination in her eyes. He felt the scrunching of her forehead as she fought off a grief that threatened to engulf her. A long, shaky release of breath touched his lips, warm and moist.

Something loosened in her and fell away.

'I can't leave him.'

Albus lifted his head, shaking it as he sent a look over her head, at the far end of the alleyway, to where their pursuers would soon be appearing.

'Please don't make me leave him, Albus.'

Torn, he stroked her cheeks, for once unmindful that the deformed lumps of his hands were touching her, and passed his palm over her eyes, as if in doing so he could wipe away all memory of what had happened here. She grabbed his wrist before he could finish the motion and stared unflinchingly into his eyes.

'Don't make me leave him.'

He nodded to her. If that was what she wanted, how could he refuse her?

He left her there and hurried over to Rufus's rifle, hooking it up by its shoulder sling. They couldn't leave it – they might need it before the night was through. Addison appeared by his side and wordlessly helped him lift the rifle strap over his head. He gestured to Gwen's dropped gun and she went to fetch it.

Gwen had stood up, stiff and staccato in her movements, as if she'd aged a decade in the last few minutes, and was bending over, clasping Rufus around his chest and trying to lift his dead weight. Albus bustled her aside, taking her place, and heaved Rufus bodily off the ground, immediately feeling the immense strain across his shoulders.

Gwen snatched the proffered gun off the girl, ejected the clip, slid in a loaded one and reholstered the weapon at her hip. She picked up Rufus's legs, nearly staggering under the weight.

Addison moved to help, but Gwen's words stopped her.

'I've got him.' Clipped, a stark hospital white.

Albus watched as she and the girl faced off. His arms shook, his blood pounded, a stamping beat that chased his thoughts: This is it. It's Addison's fault we're here and it's my fault Rufus is dead. Dead. Oh my God, he's dead and I'm holding him and he weighs so much. So very much.

But the weight of him was a feather compared to the dreadful, crushing guilt.

Addison stepped back and the tension diffused.

Albus remembered to breathe.

Between them, he and Gwen hauled Rufus out on to the street, and they *were* quick, but Albus could hear their pursuers now, their distant drubbing feet, the crashes of their progress. A sudden ululating cry.

Behind him, the girl gasped. 'I see them!'

At the opposite end of the long, dirt-track alley, three men sprinted toward them. Another shout, this one to their right, far up the street, and there were two more men advancing, spreading out across the road to block them off.

'*Shit*,' Gwen said.

There was no escape. Not while they carried Rufus, not with five men closing in and only Gwen able to shoot at them. Addison must have been on the same page, because she started pushing at Albus's back, adding what little strength she had to encourage him to get going.

'Let's move!' Gwen yelled. 'Move it, move it!'

Albus clamped his arms tighter, strapping Rufus in, and fell into a shambling run, following Gwen's lead as she went left, the only place left for them to go.

The men at the far end of the street moved into a jog.

The screaming pain in Albus's arms and shoulders intensified. He gritted his teeth. A whine crept out of his throat, but he wouldn't loosen his hold, he *wouldn't*. Addison remained a step behind him, two hot, small hands pressed to the small of his back. Gwen, in front, pulled on Rufus's long legs, forcing Albus to keep up.

And that was as far as they got. They stumbled to a breathless, shambling halt as a hulking vehicle coasted to the mouth of their street and stopped, dead-ending their last escape.

Addison ran into the back of Albus and would've bounced off if not for hugging herself to the man's waist. His back rose and fell under her cheek. She would've liked to rest, her rabbit-legs runned out and all out of energy-boosting carrots, but she straightened and peered around him.

A truck had stopped at the end of the block. Addison had never seen anything so big. Its headlights flicked on, two owl eyes, piercingly bright. It pulled forward, taking the corner in a wide, tyre-squealing arc – she had to raise a hand to block the glare as the headlights swept over them.

Its engine gunned as it began to accelerate.

'Quickly,' Gwen gasped, and she and Albus shuffle-ran into the middle of the road.

The bones in Addison's body vibrated as the hulking vehicle loomed larger, its engine grumbling as if its tummy were empty and it needed to be fed. There was a quick flash of black, shiny scales and red angry eyes, smoke curling from its metal-grilled mouth, and then the monster vanished and in its place was a bus with books painted on its sides and the words 'Book' and 'Mobile'.

'Chief,' she scolded. She felt his fear quake through her.

Sorry!

Addison stiffened and scurried to catch Albus up, trusting that he wouldn't be leading them toward a beast that'd gobble them up and pick its metal-grille teeth with their bones when it was done.

The whole world got too loud and too bright, and she wanted to run in the opposite direction as the bus *whoosh*ed alongside her with a warm gust of air and a hissing of snakes. The rear door slid open to reveal a brightly lit interior and a boy, not much older than her, standing at the top of the steps.

Gwen and Albus aimed at the door in a wild rush and Gwen leaped, never letting go of Rufus's legs, and crashed into a yellow safety rail. She rudely shouldered the boy out of the way, twisting round in the small space and making a grab for Rufus's belt.

'Keep driving, Bruno!' she yelled. A loud clunking came

from beneath the bus and it started rolling again.

Addison had her hands flat against Albus's back and felt the tensing of his muscles as he *heaved* Rufus aboard. Gwen yanked at the same time and Addison watched the woman disappear as Rufus landed on top of her. She heard his head *clonk* off the steps.

Albus lurched off balance and smacked his shoulder off the door's edge and spun back into the street. Addison dodged, but not fast enough. She kicked his ankle, felt his foot twist under hers. He stumbled and nearly fell. He was still running, but not as fast, his stride all off.

The lit doorway was sliding away from them, the bus's rumble climbing as its speed increased. Addison glimpsed the boy make a grab for Rufus, ineffectually tugging at him as Gwen pushed, trapped beneath his bulk.

'Albus, come on!' Gwen called, and that was kind of faraway, too.

They were passing the mouth of the alley they had come from and Addison craned her neck, chancing a look. Three men burst from the side of the gingerbread house and their eyes latched on to her. Their heads lowered.

Here they come!

She darted for the doorway, jumped, planted her feet and caught hold of the yellow handrails. She hippity-hopped past a cussing and trapped Gwen and did her own rude shouldering aside of the boy, pushing him over so she could grab two handfuls of Rufus's pants.

'Help me!' she yelled at him.

'But where is Alb—'

She shouted over him. '*Pull!*'

Together, she and the boy strained backward. Her shoulder joints stressed to the point of popping, but Rufus slithered higher, dragging free in a rush that took Addison by surprise. She slipped and ended up on her butt, both elbows burning on the carpet and Rufus's boa-constrictor legs crushing her.

She had no time to fight her way free before Gwen was up and yelling at them to stay put and, with a drumming of feet, she was back down the steps and out the doorway, calling a final order over her shoulder.

'Speed up, Bruno! They're gaining!'

Breathless, Addison squirmed out from under Rufus, and a shadow fell over her. She looked up. The brown-skinned boy with the darkest eyes she had ever seen stood over her, blocking her way.

'Please stay where you are,' he said, but not really 'cause his words came out like a song.

She glanced past him at the sidewalk; it was rolling by more quickly now. The floor beneath her butt shook her bones.

There were no signs of Gwen or Albus, and Addison considered shoving the dark-eyed boy out of her way – even if he did have the prettiest voice she'd ever heard – when a *BANG!* made her flinch. She was up on her feet, her hands on the boy's shoulders (she noticed in a not-really-noticing-way, that they were almost the same height), ready to push him aside, not caring what he wanted 'cause she didn't take orders from him. But he'd had the same thought and was pushing her back a step as he rushed for the steps.

'Albus!' he called.

Underneath the rumblings of the bus's anger, and the gasps and shouts coming from outside, Addison heard the mutter-mutters of Fender and Chief, but she had no time for them. She went after the boy, but he was coming back up the steps and, in the next breath, the bus's doorway was crowded with people. Gwen manhandled Albus into the opening, propelling him upward so fast he stumbled up the stairs and fell on his knees at Addison's feet.

'GET US OUT OF HERE, BRUNO!'

A loud clatter smacked into the shelving to Addison's right as

Rufus's gun was thrown aboard. It thudded to the floor. Gwen jumped in after it and a man took her place in the doorway, his teeth grinning a gorilla snarl. He gripped the edges of the door and leaped, and Gwen's boot stomped him square in the chest and he went tumbling backward.

Gwen slapped a hand high on the wall above the doorway, over a 'green is GO' button and, with a long release of air, the sliding door began to close.

Everyone on board staggered with the *zoom*ing of the van, and Addison felt the street beneath roll away fast, faster, fastest, wheels spinning like blurry black-rubber feet. They all listened to the angry bus's growls.

There was a gorilla-man squeal. The door had closed on his fingers. He wrenched them free, tripped over his feet, and Addison watched him vanish.

Thuds bounced off the bus's side, followed by a bunch of pounding as more gorilla-men punched and kicked at the bookmobile's skirt. Shouts called out to them, words Addison hadn't heard before. Words like 'cunts' and 'asswipes' (she *had* heard Lacey say 'asshole' before) and something about a 'flitting man'. No 'fuckwad', though, which was disappointing.

A deep voice from the front of the bus called, 'Hold on to your butts!'

Why she would want to hold on to her butt she didn't know. All she could see of the man doing the yelling was the back of his head and shoulders. The nape of his neck was as black as night. Past him, through the bus's glass window and splashed in its big flashlight eyes, were two more gorilla-men, standing in their way.

One had a gun, like Gwen's and kind of like Alex's.

It was raised and pointed.

The man's mouth moved as he yelled something that no one could hear, not even her, and her ears were jugs, so Lacey said. Addison watched his little eyes grow littler and knew his finger was squeezing real tight around that gun's trigger-stick, like she'd had to squeeze real tight that one time, too.

She waited for the *BANG!*

Bruno swerved the bus and Addison floundered, hands flailing for the nearest yellow-bright handrail, pulling herself tight into it, hugging the rail to her chest.

She heard Gwen and the boy suck in their breaths, and a couple of thumps as one or both of them lost their footing. A *BANG!* struck the van, a solid *thunk*ing sound, and Addison looked up in time to glimpse one man dart one way and the other swing his gun around to *BANG!* at them again. But already it was too late – Addison saw it in how his eyes weren't little no more (they were real big) and in the way his hands came up to block. The bus slammed into him. His skin and bones weren't as tough as metal. He dropped from view and a judder went through the floor as fat wheels bumped over him.

No one spoke. The silence ate all the space. The shouts of the men running after them lost their wind and puttered out to nothing so that the silence ate up the outside space, too. A few knocks bounced off the rear of the bus as the last bricks were hurled.

In the back of Addison's head, the movement almost too small to notice, she felt Fender stir. Since hiding in the cupboard beneath the stairs, Addison wasn't quite so eager to lock her two friends away.

Fender snuck nearer.

Addison blinked a couple of times, trying to focus, finding it hard to stop hearing the bash of man on bus, the feel of him rolling and bumping underneath them.

Fender's voice came from too far away.

'What?' she said.

I said, I can hear *him.*

Addison frowned, head cocked to one side. She didn't hear zip, because that wasn't how it worked. She might not *hear* anything, not like Fender, but she could *feel*. Fender helped tune out the *bangs* and shouts and twig-snapping bones in her head, like tuning a walkie-talkie dial to a head-expanding nothingness, and then she felt it. Or rather, she felt *him*.

Voice.

Lacey's Voice. He was barely a niggle, like she had a third ear in the back of her head and it had one of those annoying, deep-down itches you can never quite reach, no matter how much you wiggled your finger. But it was definitely him. Addison would know him anywhere. He'd spent tonnes of weeks snuffling around her, a nosy puppy-pup searching for a way in, maybe even for *months*, 'cause Addison wasn't so good at telling the time. She wouldn't ever lower the wall she'd built up back there, though. Didn't want to chance getting found out. Voice would tell Lacey on her. And Lacey would tell Alex, and they'd all hate her and send her away.

To feel Voice now, a softer than soft tickle, meant he was nearby.

'Where?' she asked Fender, swaying with the movement of the bus.

But it was Chief who answered. He showed her the dead troll slumped against the gingerbread cottage with the white picket fence, his big, shaggy head bent as if he were studying his lap. A few feet away, a baseball cap lay lonely and forgotten (which made her sad – sleeping or not, she bet Rufus's head was unhappy without its cap). And the shadows of people, falling over the giant troll, long and stretched, the shapes of insect-thin humans looking down on what was laid before them.

Voice was with them. Which meant—

'Lacey.'

She looked from person to person, strangers' faces staring back, even Albus's, whose face was grey, his eyes dazed pebbles lodged in his head. He was caked in mud and Addison thought he could've been born in the ground, birthed like a clay figure, blood mixing with the dirt as his shape took form. Gwen had been born the same way. Only the sing-song boy, his skin closest to mud out of the three, was clean.

'Stop this bus,' Addison ordered. 'We need to go back for my aunt.'

The bus was taking a corner, fast enough to make Addison grip the railing with both hands. The man at the wheel glanced back at her, and straight away Addison thought *toad*, his eyes all googly and sticky-out, but he said nothing as his toad eyes went past her to where Albus and Gwen were. He turned back to the road again, not saying a peep.

'We're not stopping,' Gwen said. She was hanging on to a rail similar to Addison's. It was bolted from floor to ceiling next to the steps. 'There're too many of them, and we've already lost—' she stopped, as if she'd forgotten his name.

'Rufus,' Addison said. She remembered. She remembered lots of stuff, and that was without Fender needing to tell her.

Gwen looked at her as if she'd thrown a brick at her face. 'We're not going back,' was all she said, in a way that Lacey sometimes used when she wouldn't be budged. Addison recognised the expression on the woman's face, too, even if it wasn't one her aunt wore. It was sharper, made of bone. Addison knew there'd be no help from her.

She looked to Albus. He sat leaning against the empty shelves. He shook his head at her, a tiny shake, and that's all it took. The tears came fast, no matter how hard she tried to squeeze them in, and her knees flat-out refused to hold her up any more. She sank to the floor, fingers slipping away from the railing. She stared at the blurry carpet in front of her knees and let silence fill her mouth, even though it hurt her throat, all the way down to her middle.

She's alive, Fender said, and Addison knew it was meant to comfort, meant to make her happy, but she couldn't help thinking that 'alive' meant Lacey could be hurt, the same way

407

Alex hurt before she went to sleep and never woke back up. The same way her mommy got hurt the day Daddy came home and Addison and Chief got found out.

'Can you find a way to let her know we're OK?' she whispered.

I'll try, Fender said and began to sing, crooning softly to her about the sun and the melting snow, until the tears dried up on her face and the ache in her throat faded.

CHAPTER 18

Prisoner

Lacey went where she was told, stopped when she was ordered to stop, sat where she was put and answered when she was spoken to. To do anything else resulted in a punch, a shove, a slap round the face. If she was *extra* lucky, she'd be spat on, have her hair pulled or be tripped while she walked. She didn't mind those last three so much – after the initial burst of outrage, the action was done and over with – but bruises, scrapes and cuts lasted far longer than indignation and, quite honestly, she didn't know how much more of it she could take.

She'd always thought she was tough, capable of taking a little pain – her grammy had never fussed over her when a bee stung her or a splinter stuck in her hand, but had always told her to harden up, to let the pain fuel her, give her purpose, teach her something (like don't try to trap a bee under a drinking glass, or wear gloves when mending the fence) – but now she realised she knew nothing, *nothing*, about the true nature of suffering.

After the first beating, when she'd refused to walk, she was convinced she was dying. Internal bleeding, ruptured spleen, punctured lung. It was likely she would've lain there, curled up and blubbering, if Voice hadn't assured her that she was still in one piece, that nothing had been seriously damaged, and that continuing to cry about it would only serve in giving her a headache.

For God's sake, stop pissing them off, Voice had told her. *We need to be cleverer than them. We'll find a way out, we just need to stay strong until we figure something out. I won't leave you, Lacey. You have my word.*

Your word, she remembered thinking, feeling mean and unfair but unable to stop herself. What use was that to her?

Words are all I have. They're everything. I won't let you down.

If she hadn't felt so sorry for herself, she'd have been ashamed of herself then. She'd have called him back and apologised, thanked him for putting up with her, for being her friend. But she clamped her mouth shut and let Voice talk her through the pain. He encouraged and cajoled and infused her with the strength to push aside the agony long enough to climb to her feet.

Without him, she feared she would have broken.

Her weakness was a cold slap to the face. The speed with which the fight had left her shamed her to the core, and it didn't take long for her shame to turn to anger. In the absence of courage, she knew anger could be a driving force. So could grief.

She had cried at the church, and not one tear had been for herself. She turned her head and pressed her mouth to her shoulder for fear she'd wail with anguish, with a loss that roared through her like a landslide, a mountain of earth settling on her chest and in her throat, cramming so tightly it choked her. Yet a fury galvanised her, too, a howling scream of emotion locked behind her tonsils, tightening her hands into hard, shaking fists. Her furious grief attacked her from all sides, until the world became a hateful place and everything in it was hateful, too. Including herself.

It's not anyone's fault, Voice had whispered miserably. *How were we supposed to know we were leading it to us? How were we supposed to know?* And she knew he hated himself, too. He hadn't understood his own capabilities, or those of the voice following them. He hadn't been prepared for what happened. None of them had.

But it *was* his fault. It was her fault, too. While chattering away to Voice every day, she'd been drawing Posy to her like a shit draws flies. Looking after Alex and Addison had been her *one* task, her one duty, and she'd done it not only to prove to herself she could but because they were her family. Her *family*. And Lacey had been the one who'd put them in danger. Lacey had been the one who killed Alex. As long as she had Voice, she would never be safe.

Lacey, you can't think—

'I don't want to talk to you!'

Voice fell into a heavy, pained silence.

Posy's people looked at her askance, some turning back to whisper between themselves, others continuing to stare. It was only Posy who smiled.

There had been talk, a brushfire of gossip spreading through the group, of a bookmobile, of all things, sweeping through town. Lacey might have thought the stories were bullshit if not for the wonder and disbelief that painted their faces as the stories were told.

Strangers had come and snatched Addison, bundling her on board the book bus and whisking her away. It sounded like a fairy tale, and she wouldn't have believed it if not for the dead men left in their wake. One man had been left in the road where he'd been struck, his pelvis oddly angled, his leg bent in a way a leg should never be bent. His swollen head was busted open like a smashed tomato.

And, of course, there was the giant from the bridge. The one Lacey had stupidly left alive, a meeting from her past coming back to haunt her. His ghost had waited for her in that mud-tramped alleyway, the same as any murdered ghost haunts their gravesite, the violence of their death holding them trapped for ever.

Who were these strangers, and why had they taken Addison?

Surely this meant they were enemies of Posy, enemies of the giant from the bridge and of the woman and man Lacey had killed there (the man with silver nickels for eyes, who'd told her *he* was coming for them, because no one could hide from the Flitting Man).

Being present for all of these thoughts, Voice ventured tentatively, *If Posy was drawn to us, then surely there could be other voices out there who would be, too? They can't all be doing it for the wrong reasons. Or for the wrong person.*

Lacey wasn't sure about that but let it stand. A small spark of something hopeful nosed its way in, and she was mindful of it. Hope was a fragile thing; it took hardly anything at all to weaken and kill it. If this was to be her and Alex's final town, at least they would be severing all ties to Addison and cutting any connection the voice inside Posy, or anything like it, could use to find her.

Emboldened by how she had listened to his previous comments, Voice said, *So how did those library-bus people find their way here? It can't be a coincidence they turned up the same time Posy did.*

She didn't believe in coincidences.

It's odd, though, right? We weren't with Addison when she was taken. I can't be blamed for that.

She frowned, but could see no connection. They were aware that Addison heard *something*, but it was far too intermittent and weak to be traced. Even Voice had trouble hearing it.

Lacey pushed all thoughts aside and asked her questions.

– What about here? Do you hear anything here?

The church had become a temporary headquarters. She had spent long hours in the corner of the nave, hunched up against the wall, hands finally untied and arms wrapped around herself, belt cinched tight and buckle twisted to the back of her hip, far away from any fumbling hands. After being made to run for what felt like miles to where the bookmobile had been spotted, Lacey had been led back to the church, where the remainder of

Posy's people was regrouping. Posy had been incensed that Lacey's niece had gotten away and had wanted to push forward, but his people had drooped and mumbled their protests, many of them wiped out with exhaustion, failing to be roused by Posy's screams. No one looked as though they'd eaten or rested for days.

She felt Voice's equivalent of a head-shake. *I hear only the voice in Posy and just a . . . a vague static in the air, stronger around some than others.*

– Like those walkie-talkies again?

Yes, kind of. It's like coming back into the city after being in the country for a while. There's a hum of activity, a drone of streetlights, the vibration of a subway train passing nearby and shaking the air . . . He faded off, a prickling sense of confusion surrounding him.

Over the past few hours, two women, and the familiar-looking shaven-headed man with a beard, had taken turns watching Lacey. The first woman was the one who'd attacked her, her hair shorn short at the sides, a piercing under her bottom lip, its metal spike sticking through as if a tiny unicorn were being held captive in her mouth and had tried to horn its way out. The stillness of this woman didn't fool Lacey. She knew there was an untapped reservoir of violence running through her veins; it was there in the locked jut of her jaw and her unwavering, flint-eyed stare. She obviously wanted to finish what she'd started.

Lacey, Voice said quietly. *I'm sorry about Alex.*

There had been no sign of Alex when they'd returned to the church. She didn't know how she felt about that. She didn't ask where Alex was – she didn't want to know. All she had to remember was that no one could hurt her, not ever again. She was safe now, far away from here. And any place was better than here.

I know I wasn't always that gracious about her. Because she hated my guts. But she was good people, and I'm sorry. She loved you and Addison a lot.

413

'Don't,' Lacey whispered, feeling that packed soil cram down her throat again. 'Please. I can't do this right now.'

I understand. I just . . . you know . . . I wanted to say I'm really very sorry.

Posy never strayed far from Lacey, always keeping her in sight, and his presence proved discouragement enough to keep anyone who got too curious about her at bay.

The bearded man with the closely shaven head spent most of his time sharpening his knife, sliding it back and forth on a strip of leather, shooting looks between her and the lip-pierced woman, sometimes smiling faintly, sometimes testing the edge of his knife on a thumbnail. He didn't say anything and didn't move, except for his arm. That never stilled. *Swish, swish, swish.*

The second woman was older than Alex, would *always* be older than Alex. She'd been the one to step in when the lip-pierced skank had started her beating (and got called a crazy bitch for her trouble). This one observed her entirely differently from either of the other two. There was a sadness to her, a trodden-down compassion that didn't fit with the rest of the people here. Not to say they were all bad – they hadn't *all* kicked her in the ribs and spat in her face. But none of them had given her a single kindly look, either, or thought to bring over a cup of water.

This woman waited for the lip-pierced skank to fall asleep then stood. Lacey watched as she made her way over. This woman had picked a spot away from everyone else and wasn't in any danger of disturbing anybody's sleep. Not one word passed between them as she settled down beside her. Lacey could feel the heat from her arm. They both leaned against the church wall.

A number of snores echoed around the room, interspersed with mutters and whimpering twitches as a few tried to flee whatever chased after them in their dreams. One man called out, a yipping cry that woke those nearest him. Others didn't move at all, only breathed deeply, their limbs so heavy they looked sunken in the floor. The man with the big beard went *swish, swish, swish* with his knife.

Lacey noted that not one person silently sleep-talked. They didn't have to, did they? They had all been found.

'My name's Sunny.' The woman's voice was soft, low, drawled out like she was serving something warm and sweet.

Lacey rolled her head against the wall, turning it just enough to look at her through one swollen eye.

'And that big moose over there,' the woman nodded with her chin, 'is Beck.'

Lacey said nothing, and neither did Voice. He'd gone quiet, going wherever he went when he wasn't hovering or speaking to her. He wasn't available to shed any light on whether this woman was playing tricks on Lacey but, in any case, Lacey wasn't in the mood for games.

'You sure got yourself in a real pickle here.'

'What's it to you?' Lacey said.

The woman's eyebrows went up, as if she was surprised by Lacey's hostility, and for a split second, Lacey felt bad. She quickly checked herself. This woman was the enemy. A member of the party that had hunted Lacey, Alex and Addison down like animals. She'd helped kill her friend; if not directly, then she'd certainly been present. And now she was happy to let Lacey sit here, a prisoner, and not do a damn thing. She didn't owe her shit, not politeness, and certainly not anything else.

Sunny's brows lowered as her eyes roamed Lacey's face. She sighed and looked away. 'You have every right to be angry, but we all do things for a reason. Wrong things for what we think are the right reasons at the time, but still, we all get caught up in them.' Her gaze skimmed over the sleeping people, pausing at the spot where she'd been lying before coming over. 'Your name isn't Red, is it?'

Lacey didn't know what her face said in response to that, but the woman nodded.

'Didn't think so. Posy told me about her. The kid Posy, I mean, not that.' She lifted her chin to where Posy stood at the righted podium, the Bible that had rested there cast aside and replaced with another book, its pages ripped out and stuffed back in. He was leaning low, examining its contents. 'I could tell he liked Red from the way he spoke. But you're not her – I heard mention her teeth were gone and you've got all yours. You're Lacey. He's told me about you, too. He said you'd know where she is.'

Lacey blinked, said nothing, then made a decision, and Voice, quiet or not, didn't try to talk her out of it. 'I met Red once, a while back. Posy and I met near enough the same time, not far from Vicksburg, when he was with another gang. Kind of like this one. But that didn't end so well.'

'How so?'

'People got killed.'

The woman made a soft humming noise under her breath. 'People, they're always getting themselves killed. Guess not much changes there.'

Lacey couldn't argue with that.

'Did . . . did anyone make mention of the Flitting Man while you were there? In that other gang?'

It was Lacey's turn to study her, and the woman calmly watched her while she did. 'Maybe,' she eventually replied.

'I'll take that as a yes. Did anyone actually *see* him?'

Lacey shrugged, and regretted the movement as soon as she'd made it, biting at her cheek until the pain passed. 'Posy said Red did. And Dumont, their leader – he must've. But there were rumours about him everywhere, and they've been everywhere since. He can't be made up, if that's what you're thinking.'

Sunny sniffed a bit, rubbed her nose. 'I thought for a while he was. Not so much any more. I've yet to meet a single person who's seen him first hand, mind.'

'No one sees the voices, either. Doesn't mean they're not real.'

416

The corner of Sunny's mouth lifted. 'You got me there, kiddo. I sure don't see yours.'

Lacey didn't say anything.

'Don't get me wrong, the occasional dreamy look and a few mumbles probably wouldn't give you away, but yelling at it in front of everyone? It's kind of a red flag.'

'I don't care,' Lacey said. Posy knew she heard Voice, so it wasn't any kind of secret. 'Doesn't seem much point hiding it.'

'Not-Posy had a little tantrum over you a few miles out of town. Went apeshit, in fact. Bashed his hands off the road and yelled some. He really wants you, Lacey. You need to be careful. Lord knows how he followed you, but he'd find you again if he had to.'

Lacey was biting at the inside of her cheek again and forced herself to stop. She wished she could stop the teeth deep in her guts from chewing on her, too, but she had no control over them. 'Not-Posy? That's what you call him?' Posy hadn't looked up from his book since she and Sunny had started talking. 'It fits him,' Lacey said. 'He's really not Posy any more, is he? We've been calling it the "other" voice.'

'Funny, that's what Posy calls it. The Other.'

Lacey heard the capital O in that. 'My voice and Posy's somehow hear each other. I don't get how it works, but that's how it's been tracking us. By listening to my voice when he speaks to me.'

The woman had gone back to staring at the space where she'd been resting. The shadows there, pooled down by the floor, gave the illusion of a man laid out on his side, legs together, arms tucked under his head. 'That doesn't sound like something they can do.' She didn't seem very convinced.

Well, it happened, lady, Voice said out of nowhere, decidedly grumpy but very quiet, not wanting to be overheard. *Like voices jumping from person to person. That happened, too. I jumped, and this Other jumped. It's all happened, and now we've all got to deal with it.*

'It happened,' Lacey repeated, for Sunny's benefit. 'Voice seems sure it's something we haven't seen from them before.'

'Voice. You say that like it's a name.'

'It is. He picked it himself.'

'He's a he, then?'

Lacey pulled a face, her skin pulling tight over the hot swelling around her eye. 'He was a he before he ever got to m—'

Lacey!

Stunned at almost giving away their secret, Lacey became flustered. 'I mean, he's always sounded male to me but I don't really know if he has a proper gender.'

'You said Not-Posy has been talking to your voice? You think it's been speaking to my Beck?'

Lacey stopped herself from shrugging this time. She wasn't sure who Beck was, but the woman seemed concerned about him. 'I don't know. I'm not sure they got as far as talking. Just eavesdropping. How long's Beck's voice been around?'

'As long as I've known him. But his is nowhere near the same level as Posy's. I think the Other has been around a lot longer.'

Voice had been listening closely, alert to Lacey taking another misstep, but now he retreated a little, went back to his mumbling.

'What's that book he's reading?' Lacey asked. Posy still hadn't looked up. He leafed through another page as Lacey watched.

The question seemed to catch Sunny off guard. She shook her head a mite too quickly. 'Just a journal he likes to keep.'

'A journal for what?'

The woman shook her head again, more casually this time, but Lacey detected a slight uneasiness in her and wondered why.

'He's been recording his travels. I think he means to pass it on to, you know, whoever's in charge once he's done.'

Lacey, what did Posy say? Voice whispered.

'Huh?' He was talking so quietly she could barely hear him.

Sunny spoke almost as low as Voice. 'He said you took something precious from him. I think he plans to take something from you in return. Big wheels are a-turning, Lacey. Can almost feel them rumbling beneath us.'

Back when they put you in the freezer, not long after I came to you. Posy said something about Red wanting to keep him near.

'Because he's special,' Lacey said, remembering her and Posy's talk. It had happened a short while after she'd been locked up by Dumont's men. Posy had come to her, looking for someone who could read, and she'd talked herself dry reciting chapters and chapters of *Something Wicked This Way Comes* to him. He had fetched water for her and, while she drank, he'd spoken about Red.

That was it! Special. He said Red told him he was special, and he tapped at his head. He didn't hear a voice then, we know that, but something about him, the same thing that's special about you, *gave the Other access to him. It must've been something Red recognised. Something different in both of you.*

Sunny was studying her intently, not realising Lacey had been replying to Voice. 'Yes. That's exactly what Posy told me, too. But it's not enough to be special, is it? He's being used like a glove puppet. It must know his body won't hold out much longer. I was . . . hopeful you or Red might be able to help. I mean, *look* at him.'

Lacey did. Posy was bent over the podium. No, that wasn't right – he was *folded* over it, using the stand to support a large portion of his weight. He looked ten years older than the last time Lacey had seen him, his eyes sunken pits, the gaunt lines of his whiskered cheeks deeply carved, his limbs stick-thin, hardly more than bone and gristle. He was wasting away before their eyes.

'It killed some of us, getting here,' Sunny confided. 'It pushed us so hard. Two guys got left behind when they couldn't keep up. Yet he never tires and he barely eats. It pushes and pushes and doesn't stop. It's killing him. I don't think it can help itself.'

Lacey couldn't drag her eyes away from this wasted version of Posy. Sunny was right. He wasn't a well man.

'You two've talked long enough.'

Sunny jerked in surprise, her shoulder knocking into Lacey. 'Jesus, Pike, you scared me.'

Neither of them had noticed the bearded, shaven-headed man approach. Pike. Lacey knew that name.

He's from Vicksburg, Voice whispered. *One of Dumont's. I remember him.*

'I scared you because you're up to no good. Now move your ass back where it belongs. And you' – he pointed that wickedly sharp blade of his at Lacey's face – 'you keep it shut from now on. Nothing but bad shit ever comes from having you around.'

Sunny sent Lacey a last look as she got up, and Lacey could plainly read the message: Don't mess with this one. She returned to the pool of shadows and lay down, the gloom rising to blanket her, cloaking her almost entirely from sight.

Pike crouched in front of Lacey. She could feel the heat from his body. The long, prickly bristles of his beard brushed her arm. She stopped breathing as he placed the point of his knife a millimetre below her eye. It tickled her eyelashes.

'I don't have to play nice,' he breathed, and lightly traced the knife point down her cheek. It was so cold she wasn't sure if it was cutting her, slicing her face painlessly open, or not. 'I can start carving you up whenever I like, like meat from bone.' His eyes followed his blade as he drew it over her chin, curving it around her mouth. She felt its sharp tip press her bottom lip. 'Don't you have anything to say to me, smart girl?'

Nothing smart came to mind, no. If she moved, the scalpel sharpness of his knife would split open her lip. Lacey wondered if he could see the rapid beat of her pulse fluttering at the base of her throat.

'You'll have plenty to say soon enough. You'll spill every-thing, or else I'll make your guts spill out of your stomach-sack.' His mouth, smiling or smirking, Lacey couldn't decide which, curled at her. 'Nighty-night. Sleep tight.'

He left her there, huddled against the wall, the after-touch of his blade a faintly cold imprint on her skin. She touched her cheek, checked her fingers for blood. They were clean.

Sunny's right, Voice whispered, watching him go from behind Lacey's eyes. *We sure got ourselves in a real pickle.*

Lacey dozed a little. Morning sunlight stole unobtrusively into the nave and with it came more men: three strangers waiting outside the church in a bright island of sun the oak tree failed to shade. Lacey had been dragged outside with just over a half-dozen others, Sunny, the lip-pierced skank and Pike included. These new men didn't know each other; Lacey could tell by the calculating looks that passed between them and by the extra space each left between the other.

A few quiet words were exchanged, and Posy (*No, the Other*, Voice whispered to her. *He's not Posy any more*) welcomed them with a wide, cheek-splitting grin. He looked even worse in the sunshine, his skin waxy, his eyes too bright, his hair flattened against his skull in lank, oily strands. He moved in jerky motions, as if unsure how to coordinate himself. Lacey didn't know where these three strangers had come from or how they'd sought them out – although there had been a lot of ruckus during the night, so maybe she shouldn't be surprised. They seemed eager to join, sniffing each other out like cats in heat.

It's riding the wind like pheromones, Voice said.

It had become difficult to talk openly to Voice. The Other caught a lot of what he said now that they were in such close proximity. Without discussing it, Lacey and Voice decided it wise not to converse too loudly or too often. Lacey hadn't felt like talking much, anyway. Her pain had been more of a

421

companion to her than anything or anyone else, Voice included.

She stayed in the shadow of the tree, her back warm against the brick of the church, and watched the Other call everyone to order. They all crowded into the same pocket of sunshine. The two men whose names she knew – Frank and Pike – and a third, wiry guy who looked familiar enough to make her think he might be from Vicksburg, too, stood nearest to Posy. All three of them, including two of the new guys, and a handful more in the group, nodded at whatever Posy was saying.

'There's no way they'll be able to catch up to Addison on foot,' Lacey murmured. 'The bus will be miles away by now.' She didn't possess the mental energy or focus required to attempt to hold a discussion with him inside her head.

Voice was silent – she knew he was watching the men through her eyes – but she felt a small buzzing hum of agreement. She felt something else, too. A faint undercurrent that she would have missed a few hours ago, when her pain was at its highest.

'What's bothering you?' she asked.

Nothing.

'Don't lie.'

I'm not.

'You are. Just . . . don't. Not any more.'

She rubbed at the back of her ear as his defeated sigh tickled her.

Voice dropped lower than a whisper. She strained to hear him. *Last night, when we found the dead giant from the bridge, I heard the thing inside Addison again. Her voice. It was very faint, but it was there.*

There was that flicker of hope again, the spark Lacey was keeping so carefully alive. 'How can you be sure it was her?'

And she almost detected a hint of a smile in his voice when he replied. *Because it was singing 'Here Comes the Sun' by Mr George Harrison.*

She covered her face with shaky hands. Hid in the darkness

while she concentrated on breathing. Deep breaths, over and over.

When she lowered her hands, she was smiling like a loon and couldn't stop. 'That's my number-one favourite.'

I know.

'Was she OK?'

Yes. I think she's fine.

'Thank God. Was it the same thing you heard from before? By the lake?'

Yes, but this time . . . this time, I got the impression Addison was aware of me, too.

Lacey was quiet while she let that sink in. It took its time, too, sticking on the way down, hooking in her throat like a fishbone. What was she supposed to think? That all this time Addison had been fooling them? That she didn't know her niece at all? That she'd been pretending to be an innocent little kid when, in fact, she knew exactly what Voice was and how this all worked? No. She couldn't believe that.

'What do you think that means?' she asked carefully, and clamped her lips shut when Pike glanced over at her. His hair was growing back in dark, whiskery patches, making his skull look like a globe, his stubble the mottled landmasses in a sea of skin.

Lacey twitched a glance at Posy, but he was still busy passing out orders. Three people (including one of the newbies) broke away from the group and jogged across the parking lot. Lacey wondered where they were going.

It means I was right.

She glanced back to Pike, but he'd returned his attention to Posy.

All that time I joked around, saying she'd set light to that building and wanted to brain us with rocks in our sleep? Well, I think we underestimated her.

'*We?*' she breathed. 'No. No way. I don't believe any of that. She wouldn't do those things to us. Not ever.'

She shut up immediately when the Other looked over at her. She didn't know how she could have ever mistaken this man for the Posy she'd known. She lowered her gaze and shrank in on herself, wishing she were a chameleon that could camouflage itself to the siding of the church.

She didn't think Voice could lower his voice any more, but he did, and her head began to ache from listening so hard.

You need to learn how to block. That's what I think Addison has been doing all this time. Blocking me out. Blocking herself. She must have been doing it for a long time. Pilgrim could do it a little, but not like this. This is . . . something else.

The implication of all this didn't pass her by. She knew how dangerous it was for them to be discussing this so close to the Other, but she needed to know. She tried not to move her lips when she spoke. 'So you're saying she's known about her voice all along?'

I'm beginning to think so, yes. I think she's a veteran at keeping it a secret.

Lacey's thoughts whirled. 'But what about the sleep-talking? What's going on with that?'

I think it's a symptom of her blocking herself. When she sleeps, her defences are lower. Enough to let it slip through and communicate.

'Communicate about death and destruction and slaughter?'

At first, I thought . . . I don't know. I thought there was some truth to all those stories. I thought the Flitting Man would be coming for her. For us. But now I think it was her voice, trying to talk to us, talk to her.

An involuntarily shiver ran through her, despite the building heat of the day. 'Talk to us to say *what*?' she whispered, not sure she wanted to know the answer.

Think about it. It got steadily worse because it knew we were being followed. Long before I did. I think it knew that sending Addison to that lake would have us running for the hills. It doesn't want to be caught any more than we do. Look over there, Lacey, he whispered, a strange sense of wonder entering his voice. *Look what's happening.*

For the first time ever, Lacey felt a disconcerting prod at the backs of her eyes, as if a finger were nudging at them from the inside, urging her to look up. It made her blink. The Other was back talking to the group; some of them were nodding, others were staring fixedly at Posy, stony expressions on their haggard faces.

Watch. It's talking to them, like it did with Benny, Voice whispered. *I don't know how or why, and it's too low to hear from over here. But something is happening.*

Then she saw it.

At times, the Other trailed off talking altogether, yet some of the group – not many, maybe only four or five, Pike included – continued to nod along at intervals, as if hearing something the others could not. Nodded to unheard instructions, the Other addressing them without a single sound leaving Posy's mouth.

Look at Sunny.

Sunny wasn't facing their way but, even so, Lacey could make out her pinched frown, the stiffness of her stance, could see how tightly her thin arms were crossed. She was worried, scared even, as she watched the group.

That guy Beck she mentioned? I don't think she even knows how fully immersed she is in her own belief system. It's amazing, really – years and years' worth of self-delusion and intricate story-telling, filling in all those holes and—

'What the hell are you talking about?'

Beck. He's not a person at all, Lacey. He's Sunny's voice.

PART FOUR

Springing the Trap

CHAPTER 1

The Inn

A man stood at the far end of the yellow-bricked driveway. He'd been there for almost four minutes. Amber knew this because she'd counted the seconds off in her head – one Mrs Sippy, two Mrs Sippy, three Mrs Sippy, four.

He hadn't done anything. Hadn't raised a hand in greeting, hadn't even shifted his weight from one foot to the other. In all appearances, he posed no threat. But it was his motionlessness that didn't sit right. Normal people don't just stand there and do nothing. Normal people fidget, or scratch their butt, or rub their nose.

Amber wanted to go find Bianca but was afraid that if she took her eyes off the man, when she returned, he would be gone. And losing sight of him seemed somehow worse than not raising the alarm. She was sure he couldn't see her; she stood to one side of the large picture window, behind the heavy drape, peering around so that only one of her eyes showed. Like him, she hadn't moved other than to blink and to breathe.

She could hear Jasper's distant gurgling from the back of the Inn, in the kitchen, where Cloris and Bianca were preparing dinner. A call would bring them hurrying to see what was wrong, Amber knew this, and yet, when she opened her mouth, she couldn't squeeze a single sound out. Her vocal chords were as motionless as the man outside.

Her heart pounded in her chest in tandem with the dull beat at her temples, which was probably why she didn't hear him.

'What're you staring at?' he said in her ear.

Amber startled away, one hand swatting at the space next to her head. It found a shoulder, which she slapped. Mica frowned quizzically at her, one hand rubbing at the spot she'd hit.

'N-nothing,' she gasped, a hot blush burning her cheeks. She took another step away, putting a safe distance between them.

'Doesn't look like nothing. You've been staring out the window for ages.'

Amber immediately looked back at the driveway, dread hollowing out her stomach when she found it empty, just like she'd feared. She searched the trees, the hedgerows, eyes moving with a quiet panic, but the man was gone.

Mica stepped around her, giving her a full arm's length of distance, and joined her in staring up the driveway.

When she'd first arrived at the Inn, she'd struggled to tell the brothers apart. Even now, it was only their hair that separated them: Mica had a slight kink to his, while Arun's was straight. Mica with the C in his name. C for curl. Everything else about them was a carbon copy of the other.

From the corner of her eye, she saw Mica glance at her. Today, like he had every day since Rufus had left, he wore an olive-green binoculars case clipped to his belt.

'There's nothing out there,' he said eventually.

Amber didn't respond, but then no response was needed; what he'd said was true – there was nothing out there but the darkening saffron of the driveway, the deepening emerald of the grass and the softly swaying trees and hedgerows, dusk settling its veiled gaze over the Inn. The sky had turned a rich burgundy red, long strips of gold striated along the horizon, opening it up for the last rays of sun to bleed out.

Amber's breath stuttered on its way in but she had control of it by the time she exhaled. She should tell Mica what she'd seen.

Right now. But uncertainty stayed her tongue. Mica and his brother thought she was crazy. She knew this because she'd heard them say so. They'd called her crackers and cuckoo and crazy. They'd laughed when they'd said it and, deep down, she knew they didn't mean to be cruel, they were just boys who thought they understood everything yet understood nothing at all. She wasn't crazy or crackers or cuckoo. Even still, she couldn't bring herself to tell him what she'd seen.

But she *could* tell Bianca. Bianca would listen to her and not think she was crazy.

She left Mica where he was and went to the kitchen. She walked fast, her shoes clicking quickly on the bare wooden flooring. After a pause, louder *clomp*s came from behind as Mica followed.

The smell of baking bread made her traitorous stomach clench on a pang of hunger. Bianca stood at a chopping board with a large paring knife, dicing bell peppers. Cloris was at the centre island, carefully cutting slices from a freshly baked loaf. The bangles on her wrist jangled as she sawed. Jasper sat in his high-chair, a toy car in one chubby fist and a whole host of plastic toys strewn on the floor around him where they had been tossed.

'Hey, you two.' Bianca greeted them with a smile. 'Just in time to set the table.'

Amber's mouth had half opened, ready to spill the words she needed to say, but Bianca's words forestalled her. Amber closed her mouth, swallowed, glanced at the bare table where they usually ate, and stepped out of Mica's way as he came past, grousing under his breath, to collect the place mats and cutlery from the drawers.

Amber couldn't do it. She couldn't tell them. They would think she'd been imagining it, was being silly and—

'You OK, hon?' Bianca asked, knife held in her hand, not chopping but hovering over half a waxy green pepper.

'There's a man out front,' Amber blurted, saying it in a single breath, rushing it out so she couldn't call it back halfway through.

There was a beat of surprised silence. None of them was accustomed to Amber saying much more than a 'yes, please' or a 'no, thank you' or a 'hello' or 'goodbye'. Unless she was talking to Jasper.

'Out front,' Amber repeated. 'A man. I saw him. Standing at the bottom of the driveway.'

'Just now?' Bianca asked, the question as sharp as the knife she held.

Amber nodded.

'Cloris, take Jasper.' With that, Bianca left the peppers on the chopping board and came across the kitchen, knife in hand. She swept past Amber, going out through the kitchen door, calling back over her shoulder, 'Mica, go get your brother. Be quick now. And bring the bows!'

Amber shared a look with Cloris – the woman's painted eyebrows were higher than ever, almost disappearing into her hairline – then Amber was hurrying after Bianca.

She hadn't gone to the picture window but walked straight out the front door. Amber found her at the top of the porch steps, knife held down at her side, in full view of anyone who was looking.

They were in the habit of leaving doors and windows unlocked during the day – the Inn was so far off any main thoroughfare that passing traffic wasn't a concern. You had to know this place existed to find it; the Inn sat on a jutting outlet of coastal land on the outskirts of a small fishing town. Now, all those unlocked doors and windows felt like an invitation, a calling card to anyone who wanted to wander inside, to take whatever they wanted, *do* whatever they wanted. Why hadn't they prepared better, put up some defences, locked down the ground floor? Why had Amber thought she'd be safe here? She wasn't safe. Nowhere was safe.

The answer was easy: because with Bruno, Rufus and Gwen around, she had felt protected. And especially with Albus. He would alert them if danger was coming. He *knew* stuff. But he wasn't here, and neither were Gwen or Rufus with their guns. All they had were three children, two bows, a baby, an old woman, and Bianca with a kitchen knife. What were they supposed to do if they were attacked?

Fear, like a winter wind, blew through her.

'I don't see nobody,' Bianca murmured.

Amber didn't repeat what she'd already told the woman: that the man had been there, all right – had stood still as a statue, staring at the Inn for a full count of 244 seconds – because a rush of feet came up behind her and she whirled around.

Mica and Arun ran toward them, yellow-flighted arrows nocked in their bows. The bows weren't kids' playthings, either, they were fibre-glass constructions with precision sights.

'Where was he at?' Bianca asked.

Amber turned and pointed to the end of the drive.

'What was he doing? Was he alone? Did he have any weapons?'

Amber dropped her gaze, uncomfortable with having three sets of eyes on her. She told them in concise words that she hadn't seen anyone else, nor any weapons, leaving it unspoken that it didn't mean the man didn't have one, or that there weren't any other people with him.

Bianca directed Mica to the left, to skirt around the building, so they could meet up on the other side. If they saw or heard *anything*, they were to call out. Cloris and Jasper had joined them, and Bianca told her to take the baby upstairs and barricade themselves in Jasper's room.

'Is that necessary?' Cloris asked.

'I am *not* debating this with you, Cloris. Please just do as I say – go on upstairs and close yourselves in until we holler the all-clear.'

Cloris nodded to her, said, 'Be careful,' and headed back inside.

Bianca waved Arun to come along with her to the right. Amber was unhappy about being separated from Jasper. She watched Cloris as she disappeared up the wide, carpeted staircase, Jasper gazing back at her over Cloris's shoulder, one little fist stuffed in his mouth. Only Mica sharply saying her name brought her attention back to him.

'Let's go,' he told her. 'Stay close to me.'

She hesitated then followed after him, keeping to the path that led along the south side of the Inn to the vegetable garden. The chalky gravel ground under her feet. She stepped off the pathway and on to the grass, muting her footsteps. Mica continued to crunch.

Amber felt watched. Eyes burned into the back of her head, but she wouldn't turn to look. She kept her eyes on Mica, contemplating the slight kink in his hair with more focus than it deserved. If she looked back up the driveway, she'd see that too-still man, nearer, staring at her, and each time she'd glance back, he'd have gained on them, silently closing the distance, although she'd never see him moving.

She had to squeeze her muscles *down there* for fear of wetting herself. She had to clench her teeth to stop them chattering. She ached to say Mica's name, to make him look at her so he would spot the man she knew was behind them. She gripped the sides of her skirt in sweaty palms.

Mica swept his bow over the vegetable garden (Amber could see the lemons peeking at them through the chicken-wire fencing), stepped clear of the path and did a slow circle, panning around to look at her. His eyes widened when they reached her. She whimpered quietly.

'What's the matter?' he asked. 'You look like you've seen a ghost.'

He looked straight at her and only at her. His eyes didn't

434

flick over her shoulder, didn't see anyone else. *Turn around, Amber*, she told herself. *Turn around and see for yourself. There's nothing to be afraid of.*

First, her eyes turned in their sockets, then her head, forcing her neck to twist around to look back over her shoulder.

The pathway behind her was empty. The expanse of lawn was unoccupied. She released her pent-up breath and closed her eyes. You *are* cuckoo and crackers and crazy. Imagining bogeymen where there aren't any.

She let go of the clammy clumps of her skirt and flexed her stiff fingers.

Wiiiiiiiiiiisht.

A swift, sharp sting to her shoulder flashed her eyes open. She glimpsed the yellow-tipped arrow fly away from her, a fleet line that became visible only when the arrow embedded itself in the front lawn's grass.

Upset, she clamped her hand over the cut on her upper arm, and turned on Mica, a frown pulling down the corners of her mouth, but Mica was up on his tiptoes, his mouth gaping open, the unmoving man half-hidden behind him, only one eye visible behind Mica's curly-haired head, like her one eye had been visible from behind the picture window's heavy drape. An arm was wrapped around the front of Mica's shoulders, across his chest, holding him in place as a bloom of blood appeared in the hollow below his breastbone, expanding outward. The boy began to shake, his hands fluttering at his sides. The bow dropped soundlessly to the ground, cushioned on the grass.

On the back of the hand cupped over Mica's shoulder, a black design, a dizzying spiral, was tattooed into the skin. The man's one visible eye moved, its centre so black there was no telling where his pupil began and his iris ended. It blinked slowly as it watched Amber.

Blinked again, more quickly, when she opened her mouth and screamed.

CHAPTER 2

Do Not Pass Go

The field had once been full of corn. Now the stalks were bent and wilting, rotted down to the roots. The smell was fetid and warm, like a sack of decomposing vegetables left to grow at root and eye in the back corner of a shed. It wasn't a bad odour, just one full of age and decay.

Lacey didn't think about running. She wouldn't get far. Her hands were tied behind her back again and, hours before, her precious boots had been taken from her. She was upset about that. Boy Scout rule number one: never take off your boots.

Her feet were an entity of pain all of their own. It couldn't even really be called pain – what she was experiencing should be given a new word, one that encapsulated *all* pain, everywhere, on every level, condensed into two throbbing lumps of lacerated flesh that didn't even feel like feet any more. She couldn't think straight to work out this new word and that was OK. Not thinking suited her just fine.

Trekking across a bed of dead stalks beat marching on concrete, which is what they'd been doing for the past two hours. The three men who had broken away from the group outside the church had returned twenty minutes earlier, carrying three glass litre bottles, the contents of which sloshed. Their return had prompted Posy to call a halt, and everyone had slumped to the ground in relief. Everyone but Frank and Sunny. Posy made Frank pick up the two glass bottles and had led the three of them out here, miles from the grumbling, jittery-eyed folk who Lacey had been avoiding looking at all morning.

She couldn't see Sunny or Frank behind her but the rustling of their passage marked their presence. They were two prison guards on strict orders to watch and not interfere.

Posy talked the whole way out, one stick-dry hand clamped around Lacey's forearm, pulling her along. Dead corn stalks creaked under their feet, theirs clad in shoes, hers in socks.

'Going over the notes last night made me realise something,' Posy was saying, except of course, it wasn't Posy. It was the Other living inside him. His tone was conversational, as if they were on their way to a picnic. 'I've been too quick with our experiments. The inescapability of what was about to happen was gone too fast. Not enough time for them to realise the end was coming.' He stopped, lifted his nose to the sky, breathing in that musty scent of decay, then turned right, pulling her deeper into the cornfield. 'Maybe having the time to *understand* that death was on its way is what's key. Time to consider and weigh up the options. Yes. I think it's an important detail to factor in.'

God, she needed a drink. The men had drunk water openly in front of her – Pike had even spat some in her face, laughing when her tongue automatically licked at the drops nearest her mouth – but it hadn't quenched her thirst. A gallon of water wouldn't quench it. The drought had turned her bones chalky, turned her tongue into a shrivelled mollusc in her mouth, and yet sweat dripped off her chin and slid down her throat. Valuable liquid leaked out of her pores as though it wasn't worth squat. It almost made her mad, but her exhaustion wouldn't even allow her that.

Crunch-creak, *crunch*-creak went their feet.

'I've been giving this a lot of thought,' he said. 'And I think this is the best way forward.'

Lacey didn't speak. What would be the point? All roads had led here. Addison was on another path now, and that's all that mattered. He wouldn't ever be able to find her. It had been Lacey he'd been following all this time, and she was right here with him, in this field, and wasn't that dandy?

She laughed.

Posy halted and looked at her, head cocked. 'You find this amusing? This crossroads you've found yourself at?'

She wiped her face clean. Not because it *wasn't* funny but because to laugh made him think she was engaging with him. Which she wasn't.

With all four of them standing still, the silence was eerie. She heard a bird's caw from somewhere above them.

'You're never going to willingly give me anything, are you? You'll never reveal what you know about Red's whereabouts. You'll never give up the girl you hid away from me. Nothing of any use will ever leave your mouth. Will it?'

Lacey lowered her eyes to the trodden corn at her feet. The crop was brownish, mottled black with rot. Standing still made the smell worse. She made a conscious effort to breathe through her mouth. The sun was so bright, even sheltered among the drooping corn stalks it scorched the crown of her head, was a red backdrop to everything she looked at, burning. Burning through her.

'Such a shame. We could have had an extraordinary relationship, you and me. We are very much alike.'

Posy's voice was a bee buzzing around her ears. She wanted to swat it away, to make it shut up, to have some *peace* from all the voices in the world insisting on talking to her. He continued walking, his hand dragging her into step beside him. She tried not to stumble, holding in a gasp as her crippled feet screamed in agony. The crunching steps of Sunny and Frank started up again.

The soles of Posy's shoes were peeling away, flapping like miniature mouths on every step, the rubber cracked and

438

crumbling. They had seen many miles, those shoes. His mouth had run for many miles, too.

'I've tried communicating with your Inner,' he told her, 'but it is even less helpful than you are, which shouldn't come as a surprise. We could help each other, if only you stopped being so obstinate. There is so much to learn. Ah, here we are.'

They had stepped into a flattened area of reaped crop. A messy circle, as if someone had been out here before them and marched outward in concentric circles to create a private, secret sanctuary. It wasn't large, could maybe fit twenty-five people standing shoulder to shoulder.

Posy released his hold on her arm and trampled over the crackling corn, capering almost, and with the loss of his hold, Lacey slowly sank to her knees, grateful to take the weight off her throbbing, lacerated feet. She dropped her chin to her chest. Better. Much better.

'Oh yes, this will be perfect.'

Frank and Sunny crunched past her. She watched a pair of military-type boots and a pair of hiking shoes with green laces go by. Lacey didn't look up when Posy came and plopped himself down in front of her. He heaved a great sigh as he settled himself, crossing his gangly legs and placing his hands on his knees as though preparing himself for meditation.

'The second time you came back to us – when I was with Doc – the Agur was at your side. Do you know who that is, Lacey?'

She figured he meant Pilgrim, but she didn't know anything about any Agur and she wasn't about to ask. She closed her eyes because it was better than looking at him. Didn't stop her feeling them watching her, but she didn't care. Sunny had made no further attempts to speak to her since last night – Lacey had caught her eye twice on their walk out here and both times the woman had been quick to shake her head, tiny motions that were almost undetectable.

'Forgive me, I shouldn't assume you know anything,' Posy said. 'You're so young. What are you, seventeen? I expect you know barely a fraction of a fraction. Ignorance isn't something to be proud of, you know. It is a stepping stone to perdition. And blind ignorance – ignorance for the sake of it – well, that is something altogether worse.'

'Posy, we shouldn't be leaving the others alone for so long.'

'Hush, Frank. It's fine. Settle yourself. This is important.' Behind the darkness of her eyelids, Lacey heard the smile in Posy's voice as he continued. 'Red told us about him. The Agur. That's a biblical name, in case your ignorance was smarting. In Proverbs 30, the words of Agur say: "I am brutish, less than a man; I lack common sense. I have not learned wisdom, nor do I possess knowledge. Who has ascended heaven and come down? Who has gathered up the wind in the hollow of his hand? Who has wrapped the waters in his garment? These are answers I must learn." Or, in simpler terms, the one who is brave in the pursuit of wisdom will be superior. That is what I'm doing here, Lacey. I'm pursuing wisdom.

'Red explained it to me, so I'll do you a favour and explain it to you. The Agur is here not only to find wisdom but to help set some of us on our rightful paths. That sounds like utter drivel, doesn't it? I thought so, too, until Doc and I stood face to face with him and I felt him *pawing* at me, stealing his way inside, poking around where he didn't belong. It was an unpleasant feeling. Much like being raped, I'd imagine. But do you know what? That encounter set me on *this* path, so maybe there is something to what Red told us after all. He certainly changed the course of *her* journey, and now I see he's done the same with you. The blind leading the blind – isn't that what you say?'

Lacey slitted her eyes open and stared at Posy's bent knee. The material, once a dark blue, had worn pale, stained with dirt. The threads of denim showed in a tiny cross-hatch design.

'What did the Agur tell you, Lacey? He must have said

something. Given you an idea of his plans, of what he was up to.'

She shook her head.

'No, what? No he didn't tell you anything? Or no you won't answer me?'

'He didn't remember,' she said, voice arid and spitless. 'He'd forgotten.'

'Forgotten? Forgotten *what*?'

Lacey rested her gaze on Posy. 'Forgotten everything.'

Posy returned her look for a moment. 'I'm not ashamed to tell you that this man worries me. I am not comfortable knowing he's out there somewhere, *meddling*. He seems very good at meddling.'

Lacey wanted to smile. Not a pleasant smile, not comforting, not even smug. Pilgrim was dead. He wouldn't be meddling in anything any more. But Posy didn't need to know that, so she closed her eyes again and let her chin sink back to her chest. Talking wasn't going to help. Talking was what got her and Voice into trouble in the first place. (Voice had been buzzing around, bugging her, too, but the pain in her feet, coupled with thirst and exhaustion, made it surprisingly easy to keep him muffled up.)

'I can see your attention is waning. I apologise. This heat isn't pleasant, I know. I'm afraid it's only going to get much warmer before the day is through.' There was a whisper and groan of stalks as Posy climbed to his feet. She heard the soft *whap*s of his hands as he dusted off his clothes.

'Sunny, the journal. Take it out, please. It's finally time to begin.'

CHAPTER 3

Sparrowhawk

The sparrowhawk dips to the left, wing tipping down to send it banking in a tight, gliding circle. Its head doesn't move, its pupil shrinking down to a pinprick, a purest ring of yellow surrounding it as the sun swings into view. Its gaze fixes on the creatures far below. They have reached the cropped circle in the centre of the cornfield, and there they have stopped.

The bird wants to break free from its patterned flight and leave, but something holds it captive, a force it cannot escape and cannot ignore. There are new channels up here, new airways and byways and forces that the sparrowhawk and its brethren have been struggling to navigate. These forces pull and push, invisible storms buffet their wings, new magnetic fields opening up all around, as if hundreds of volcanoes have erupted into the atmosphere, altering the sky's terrain for ever. The metallic elements in their blood and beaks hum and sing, tugging at them from the inside, a tingling pulse that makes their feathers ruffle in perturbation. The birds' compasses have lost all familiarity. They must fly where these new forces take them.

A similar current blows like a hot wind across the cornfield and the sparrowhawk is trapped. Every few seconds it attempts to pull free, but the channel is strong and fast and the bird's wings are weak. It caws long and loud, calling for help, calling out its distress, yet it continues to bank, round and round. It can do nothing else.

Twice, it has flapped hard and escaped almost to the edge of the field, only to feel the inexorable urge to turn back and find itself banking yet again and returning to its circular flight.

Those creatures down there. They are changing the skies.

CHAPTER 4

Discoveries

Rufus lay dead on the bookmobile's floor. In a blank-white, matter-of-fact way, Gwen had announced to Bruno and Hari that he'd been stabbed and died in the mud. A heavy stone of silence had been dropped into the middle of the van and it hadn't been broken since.

Bruno had looked back at Albus once, his eyes hooded with sorrow and confusion, then he'd shaken his head and returned to driving.

Hari had flushed a deep red. He went to Gwen at the rear of the van, a few short feet away from Rufus's body, and though Gwen turned her head away from him, away from them all, she allowed him to sit and quietly speak to her.

You knew this could happen, his sister's voice said in Albus's ear, flashing in hot red, as if it were a delayed warning signal.

He didn't respond. A heavy, booted foot rested on his chest, pushing down each time he tried to breathe. He didn't look at Rufus, couldn't, but he saw him bowed forward over his knees in the alleyway, brow resting in the mud, a supplication to the gods, an offering. Albus had sacrificed him in order to help the girl sitting opposite him. One life for another. A straight swap. It didn't feel like a fair and honourable exchange.

You came to help the martyr, Albus.

The martyr, the martyr! he cried, in the only way he could. Silently, aggrieved only within himself, stonewalled and wordless.

And where were *you*? he wanted to yell at her. You were supposed to *be* here!

She needs you more.

His palms curled in on themselves, as close to fists as he could make them.

Be quiet, he pleaded. Please, for once, if you have nothing helpful to share, please be quiet.

You must stay strong, Albus. This isn't over. The martyr needs—

'What's "martyr"?'

All the air vacated his lungs. Shock radiated through him.

Addison was looking at him from her position curled up in the corner, arms wrapped around the yellow, vertical safety bar. She rocked gently with the van's motions, but her eyes were steady on him. She couldn't be much older than nine, but her *eyes*. They were bottomless.

He stiffly shook his head, lifted a wooden arm to place a palm over his closed lips, miming his silence.

'I get you don't talk,' Addison said. 'I hear you anyways. Well, *I* don't but, you know.' She half shrugged. 'What's "martyr" mean?' she asked again.

Albus glanced toward the others. Gwen's head had turned. Her eyes were red and bloodshot. Hari, too, was looking in their direction, his watchful gaze flicking between them.

A martyr suffers greatly for what they believe in, Albus's sister said. *Sometimes they sacrifice all to prove their love and faith.*

After a few seconds, Addison asked, 'Faith in what?'

Faith in a belief, in a person, in many things.

Addison's frown scrunched up her brow. 'Chief says you sound like a girl.'

Amazement lifted the weight off his chest, made him lean forward, his attention fixed on this thin, dark-haired girl. He

445

attempted something he hadn't tried since he and his sister were last together, with Jonah there as mediator. He concentrated on her as hard as he'd ever concentrated on anything, so hard his eyes prickled with pain. He told her slowly, silently.

– It's my sister. She speaks to me, gives me messages sometimes, helps me find people like you.

The girl frowned and he felt a surging expectation as he waited for her to reply. But she didn't. She glanced around at the others, possibly because Albus's intense stare was unnerving her.

He released his breath in a long rush and leaned back, rubbing a palm over the fizzing pain in his brow, feeling an immediate, crushing disappointment. How stupid of him to think she could hear him. Jonah was different from all other voices – it was only his presence that had bridged Albus and his sister together. To think Albus could speak to this girl without Jonah's help was –

'I don't get it. Where's your sister now?' Her gaze had stalled on Gwen, her frown becoming confused.

A swell of disbelief expanded Albus's heart, made it pound, battering at his composure until it wanted to break. He sat straighter, placed his hands on his thighs, pulled the unravelling threads of his attention tight. Refocused them.

– She's not here. She's lost. She doesn't speak often, only when there's great need.

Her eyes came back to him, her brow smoothing out, sadness replacing her confusion. 'She's gone?'

– Yes. In fact, I'm looking for her. I thought she'd be here. With you.

Hari broke in. 'You can hear Albus?'

Addison's slim shoulder hopped up and down. 'You don't got something that speaks to you? Up here?' She touched a finger to her head and glanced down at the floor. She lowered her voice. 'I'm not supposed to talk 'bout them. It's bad.'

'I . . . No,' Hari said, a little flustered. 'But do not be scared.

No one here will harm you.'

She glanced up from under her eyelashes. Laid her palm over her head like a cap. 'I hear Albus's words in here, because they hear him. He's got some different wiring, Fender says.'

Fender. Chief. Two names.

– Who do you hear, Addison? It's OK. It's safe to speak about it with us.

Be careful, he warned himself, you don't know this girl. She might not be all she seems.

And sometimes a cat is just a cat, his sister had told him.

Addison's eyes flicked nervously to Gwen. The girl shuffled on her butt, shifting forward two feet, nearer to Albus. Her voice lowered. 'Don't tell no one, 'K?'

He nodded.

'You pinky promise?'

Everyone looked at his hands. He didn't slide them out of view or into his pockets, like he normally would have. With Rufus lying dead at the other end of the van, the embarrassment of his missing fingers felt mortifyingly trivial. He nodded a second time; he wouldn't tell a soul.

'They talk to me, show me stuff. Sometimes, I let them.' A shrug. 'Sometimes, I don't. Only reason I'm telling is 'cause they can help me find my aunt Lacey.'

Hari left Gwen, shuffling on his hands and butt, scooting exactly like Addison had done. His face was bright with inquisitiveness. From over his head, Gwen observed, saying nothing.

Hari cleared his throat. 'Could you ask Albus what I drew in the sand? When we were last on the beach?'

Addison looked to Albus. Raised her eyebrows.

He was about to say a smiley face, because he knew that was what Hari was referring to but instead, at the last second, he changed it.

'*Than a toss?*' the girl said, face screwing up. 'What's that?'

Hari's eyes widened.

Albus asked her to ask Hari what 'Thanatos' meant.

'It is something someone said to me once,' Hari answered when she did. 'Thanatos: a drive toward death. It is said to be an instinct within the body that one cannot escape. A drive that pushes a person to an earlier state of non-existence.'

– A 'drive toward death'? What does that—?

'No. I won't ask,' Addison told him, speaking quickly. 'We need to go back for Lacey. I think I can find her if I listen to Fender. Fender can hear Voice if I let—'

Albus held a hand up, quickly getting lost.

– Your aunt's voice? She hears one, too?

'We're not going back.'

All their heads turned toward Gwen.

'I said that already, and I meant it. No one else is going back there.'

Albus wanted to bring up his sister. They still hadn't located her. His skewed senses told him she was sitting right here in this van with them, but they were lying to him. She was out there somewhere, same as Lacey.

'But she *needs* us.' Addison's eyes were squinty, her mouth curved down, and Albus couldn't tell if the girl was about to burst into tears or anger.

'I don't care what she needs,' Gwen said. 'She's not our problem. *You* weren't our problem, but we helped you anyway, because we got talked into it.' Albus winced at that. 'Be thankful for that, instead of asking for things that put the rest of us in danger.'

High spots of colour bloomed on Addison's cheeks. 'But—'

'But what? Look around you.' Gwen held her arms out. 'One of us is *dead*. There are three adults left and one of them can't even hold a weapon. What exactly do you think we can do against – what? Twenty? *Thirty* people?'

Addison opened her mouth but Albus spoke first.

– Addison, it would be best if we left this subject alone. For now.

'But the longer we go, the further away she is!'

– I understand that, but Gwen's right. To go back as we are would only result in more of us getting hurt.

The girl's mouth closed into a flat, obstinate line. Tears swam in her eyes, but she didn't sob or bawl.

She's a strong one.

Albus looked to Gwen when his sister said that, and Gwen returned his look. There was no smile hanging around in the background, no sense of excitement glinting in her eyes, and there probably wouldn't be for some time. She gripped an empty shelf, all the books jettisoned back at the library unit to lighten the bus's load, and pulled herself upright. She came up the van, surfing the rolls and cambers of the road.

Addison's head tipped back as Gwen stood over her.

'You can hear what Albus thinks?' Gwen asked.

Albus thought the girl would refuse to answer. She flicked him a glance.

'Not what he thinks,' Addison said, reluctant, lips barely moving. 'Only what he says. He says stuff in his head, like he's talking, and Fender tells me.'

'Is this true?' Gwen asked him. 'She can hear you?'

Albus nodded, as amazed by all this as she was.

Tilting her face up to the ceiling, Gwen shook her head, as if arguing with herself. 'I can't believe this.' The fight seemed to leave her and she sank tiredly to her knees, not quite meeting his eyes when she said, 'Fine, I'm listening. This is completely insane, but let's see where this goes.'

The van's engine knocked down a gear, slowing as Bruno steered the vehicle off the road. No one said anything when he engaged the parking brake and cut the engine. The silence that followed was thick and expectant.

'Explain how this girl is hearing you, Albus,' Bruno said, swivelling in his seat. 'Help us understand.'

There was more silence as Albus explained and the others

waited for Addison to relay his answer.

'He says he and his sister used to talk like this all the time. That he would hold an entire conversation in his head with her, and she would answer him out loud. You were, um . . .' Addison brought her hands together, palms flat '. . . born together?'

That surprised Albus. He hadn't mentioned anything about being a twin.

– That's right. We're twins. There were . . . complications when we were born.

'Is that why . . . ?' Addison pointed to her mouth.

– Yes. I was born without a tongue.

Her gaze dropped to his hands.

– No. Not those. I had fingers. Right up until about a year ago. They were taken from me by someone who wanted to hurt my sister.

The silence had stretched on for too long.

Gwen broke it. 'How do you hear her? Your sister, I mean,' she said. 'She isn't a voice like the others. She's a real person. Are you saying you're psychic?' These were all questions that had been asked before, but the slow, painful process of having to write everything out meant he had only ever been able to explain in rudimentary terms.

He closed his eyes while he focused.

– She was always very protective of me. My difficulty in speaking to other kids was something she felt very keenly. She would translate my attempts at talking, even finish my sentences for me when I couldn't; sometimes she'd know what I wanted to say before I'd even started. We'd play tricks on them. They thought we cheated whenever we played Hide and Go Seek because we could always find each other, no matter how clever our hiding places. You've heard the stories, about how twins can feel each other's pain or sense when the other is in danger; I can't say we experienced those things specifically, but she was like the sun to me. I could close my eyes and feel her warmth on my face, in my chest. Didn't matter if I could see her or not. We're tied together. We could never lose each other. And when Jonah came along, he connected that final part between us. He found a way to let us talk, not through my stilted attempts and my sister's translations, but *really* talk. It was a miracle. And then . . . and then I lost her. I left her.

Albus's concentration wavered and broke. He opened his eyes and stared at his fingerless hands, caked in dirt, in Rufus's blood, and he heard Ruby's pleas all over again, her voice clear, alive with fear, a surround-sound memory that would never dull and never go away. *Can't you see that you being here is hurting us both? Why do you insist on* hurting *me? Don't you care?*

She had grabbed him by his shirt and shouted in his face. Told him to run, to escape, not to worry about her, that she would find him as soon as she could but he had to go, and go now. Needle-sharp teeth had gnawed at each of his sutured wounds, the bandages on his hands turning them into useless mitts. The world had been a too-bright picture show, everything blazing at a thousand watts, blinding him, making him sweat. Terror twisted his guts – a writhing creature that snapped at the air between them – and the urge to flee had been so strong. Too strong. His sister had yelled at him until her voice became hoarse. She had driven him away with her words. And he'd gone, mad with pain and unable to argue, his vision blurring, his mouth salty with tears and blood.

– We were separated. For the first time since we were twelve, I couldn't hear her voice any more. The sun of her, which I could sense even with my eyes closed, dimmed to nothing the further I ran and, no matter which way I turned, there was only coldness.

– I came down with fever. I lay with my mutilated hands tucked into my armpits, and I shivered and I sweated. I was being eaten alive. I remember thinking I was dying, and I was OK with that because death was better than the pain. And, then, she spoke to me. I *heard* her, like Jonah heard her when she talked only to him. Silent and secret, in my head. For three days, I was wracked with fever. Drenched in sweat. The whole time, she whispered to me, giving me the strength to lift my head. The strength to sit. She bullied me to my feet. I found water. I ate. Not long after that, in a matter of days, I found Bruno at the municipal swimming pool. He was floating on his back, fully clothed, whistling like he didn't have a care in the world. You remember that, Bruno? It was so hot I wanted to jump in with you, but my hands. They hurt so much. And then when I heard you, Gwen, saw the beautiful silver-white strains of you. My sister helped me follow them. I thought I was going mad, was hearing her because I so desperately wanted to believe she was nearby, was finding her way back to me, but she didn't appear. Not then.

Gwen's frustration was clear in the thin line of her mouth, in the way her hands clenched and unclenched, flexing involuntarily. 'And what now? She's *here*? You said she was telling you to come find her. I don't see her, Albus. Where is she?'

– She *has* to be here. Jonah has to be. You don't understand, he isn't like the other voices you know. He's been here for ever. He can do things none of you has ever seen. One small part of which this girl is doing right now.

When Addison relayed that last part, Gwen and Hari turned to stare at her. She shrugged. 'It's not me. Fender's doing it. Chief is trying to help, but he's mostly getting in the way.' She sighed and her gaze shifted to a spot next to her. 'Well, you *are*. I can't help it if you don't know how . . . I *know* that, but—' She stopped and guiltily met their eyes. Mumbled an apology.

Gwen kneaded her fingertips into her temples. 'I don't know how you can expect me to believe all this. I've gone along with a lot of things, Albus, but this . . . this is too much.'

Addison spoke Albus's words for him. 'Albus says he knows. He understands. But it's the truth.'

Bruno, silent all this time, spoke from the cab. 'So what aren't you telling us, brother? You talk about the truth, but you're not telling us everything.'

And he was absolutely right. Albus's inability to talk clearly had its uses, most notably when he didn't want to share things he wasn't ready to, or if it was too difficult for him to discuss something. He wasn't averse to playing the mute card when it suited him, and Bruno was rightfully calling him on it.

Addison talked in stops and spurts as she spoke for him, and Hari and Gwen's attentions swung between him and the girl. At times, she interrupted him to ask her own questions. At other times, she became so engrossed by what he told her he had to gently remind her to pass the information on.

'There is a reason Albus can see you,' Addison told the others. 'See the colours you speak.' They were hanging off her every word. 'You're all different, he says. Like his sister is different. There's a chance that, someday, you could have a voice, even though you don't now. Like with how she got Jonah. Jonah wasn't ever hers. He was many people's before he got to her. Jonah was up here?' Addison asked Albus, and pointed to her head.

Albus nodded.

'Impossible,' Gwen stated flatly.

'He says he knows it's hard to—'

'*Hard?* You have no idea what's *hard.*' Gwen turned on Albus with such a look of helpless anger he wanted to hug her, to stroke her hair, tell her he was sorry for sharing this now, when Rufus was gone and they were all hurting, but he sensed she would only strike out at him if he tried to offer comfort. 'I don't *hear* anything. I never have and I never will. This is ridiculous. I'm not going to sit here and listen to theories based on nothing.' She moved to get up, but the girl's words pulled her up short.

'I dunno what "absurd" is, but my aunt Lacey got her voice the same way. She never heard one before, either.'

Albus stared at her.

'I heard her and Alex talking. When they thought I was sleeping. But I'm a good pretender when I want. Lacey never heard nothing either, not like I do. Voice was never hers. He was someone else's. She got him by accident, she said.'

'No, not possible.' Gwen shook her head.

'Is too. Lacey's no liar, and she told Alex, even though she knew Alex hated hearing it. Alex is like you,' she told Gwen, looking her over, seemingly sad at what she saw. 'Her parents – her sister, too – real bad stuff happened to them. She never trusted Voice, not ever. Doesn't trust any voice. But she believed Lacey. I'm not lying.'

First Ruby with Jonah and now Lacey with her Voice. The amazement of this discovery nearly eclipsed Albus's fear, because his sister had been right. It had begun – voices were finding ways to jump, even if it was by accident. And it wouldn't stay an accident for long. When they figured out how it was done, every one of Albus's friends would be on the Flitting Man's wanted list.

Ruby, where are you? I need you. More than ever. I can't do this alone.

A second later, Addison said, 'Ruby's a pretty name. Like a fairy.' And hearing his sister's name unlocked a grief inside Albus that caught in his throat, grew into a sob. He held it prisoner behind his teeth, not allowing it to escape. He thought of her name in full and tears welled when Addison repeated it back to him.

'Ruby Mae Hartridge. Like a fairy princess. Had to curtsey to her and everything, huh?'

The anger seeped out of Gwen. She sank back on her heels and placed a hand on Albus's leg.

Albus had done *everything* his sister had asked. Always had. He'd left her to save himself. He'd kept watch and he'd found his friends: Bruno, Gwen, Cloris, Bianca, Rufus, Mica and

454

Arun, Hari, Amber and baby Jasper. He'd helped them, protected them, given them a home, a place they would be safe. He'd come running to the rescue when Ruby said he was needed, despite the dangers, despite not understanding *why*. Rufus was dead because of him. *Dead*. All this should be over. She should *be* here.

'Where is she, Albus?' Hari's sorrow revealed itself in the heavy, viscous pour of gold that flowed from his mouth. Hari wanted this for Albus as much as Albus did.

Albus leaned back against the empty shelves, exhausted, hurting, wishing he hadn't left the Inn on a mission to find a mysterious martyr, hadn't seen Addison in his dreams, first in the bicycle store, then dead and hanging from a stake, wishing he was back home, sitting in his rocking chair and gazing out to sea, a tiny Hari building sandcastles on the beach, tiny Gwen and Rufus practising with bows and arrows and Mica and Arun taking turns running to collect the bolts from the makeshift targets they had built out of boxes and dried grass. Rufus alive and laughing, his shock of hair bright as fire, even in the distance.

Gwen's hand squeezed his leg, as if she could read his thoughts.

'We knew a Ruby. Kinda,' Addison said. 'Ruby-Red. Red, mostly, but I think Ruby was her name, too. Well, *I* didn't know her. She was wrapped up like a mummy by the time I got to meet her. She's in my backyard now, in a treasure hole.' Her lips pursed sadly. Her shoulders slumped. 'Everyone gets hurt. My mommy, Red, Pilgrim, Alex.' She sucked in her bottom lip; her hand slid over to rub at a spot at the top of her thigh. 'Rufus, Lacey,' she said in a whisper. 'It's what happens now. We all get hurt.'

CHAPTER 5

The Middle of the Field

'Would you like to know how long I've been here for?' The Other Posy had taken to slowly pacing back and forth, passing in front of Lacey every handful of seconds. 'Is that something you'd like to know?'

It was so quiet out here the answering caw of a bird high above them was easy to hear. Secretly, a tiny part of Lacey wanted her to shout *Yes!* She *did* want to know. But her curiosity couldn't outweigh her tiredness. She just couldn't give much of a shit any more. Everything was too much effort.

'Well, the hawk wants to know.' Posy cupped his hands around his mouth and shouted, 'I've been here for two whole decades! Since the one you knew as Doc turned fourteen,' he told Lacey, dropping his hands. 'He was a problem child, and that's a polite way of saying it. Liked hurting things – insects, birds, neighbourhood pets. The standard modus operandi of a burgeoning sadist. Nothing unusual there. He would have moved on to bigger and more human things with or without me, I believe, but I proved useful support for him, steered him into safer terrain, you might say. Medical school. The beginnings of a promising surgical career. A suitable profession for someone who enjoyed slicing people open and making them bleed, wouldn't you say? He was intelligent along with his psychopathy, you see. Kept me well hidden. He played his games with scalpel and knife while I watched and encouraged from the side-lines.'

Lacey's sandpaper tongue licked across her lips. 'Chicken or the egg.'

'I'm sorry?' He'd stopped walking.

A little louder: 'The chicken or the egg?'

'Ah, I see. Am I a product of his psychopathy or was he psychopathic because of me? That is an interesting question.' He began his pacing again. 'I don't think you'd be too shocked to learn there were many more like me, hidden away, long before the multitudes of other Inners came. Many of us languished in psychiatric wards, dosed up on anti-psychotic drugs. Those were the people who were unable to keep us secret. Many more people lived with us while those nearest to them never once suspected we were there – artists, musicians, visionaries. Those early Inners are the ones I am most interested in. Not the millions that appeared later and are still learning their way. No, I'm interested in the ones that were here long before they came. Like the one *you* harbour.' The Other Posy paused beside Frank and attempted a smile. 'Frank here is an exception, of course. He doesn't hear a thing, do you? But I forgive him. He has his other uses. He's here for different reasons.'

Lacey glanced at Sunny and found the woman staring at her. There was something in her eyes – unhappiness, resignation, didn't really matter what. She didn't expect any help from her. She was as crazy as Posy, if what Voice had told her about Beck was true.

The Other continued his buzzing. 'They all have their uses, don't misunderstand me. But the Inners I want to find are the ones who do more than simply whisper and talk. One like me. Like the Flitting Man.'

Bzzzz zzzzzz zzzzzz.

That was Voice. He was a bee, too, incessantly buzzing around, driving her nuts. That's their goal in life, she thought,

457

to drive everyone fricking nuts. Make everyone as mad as each other and then no one will care. She closed her eyes, pulled all the strands of her wandering concentration into one beam and pointed it at the dark place in the back of her mind. It took a lot of effort.

– I can't listen to any of you any more. I've reached my limit. Congratulations. Collect $200. Do not pass Go.

Lacey, you can't just give up. We have to—

But she didn't want to listen to him, so she listened to the swishing of the rotting corn stalks, the warm breeze knocking their heads together. It reminded her of her grammy's farmhouse, of the soft whisper of her grams paging through one of her hundreds of gardening magazines, each one so dog-eared they had begun to curve slightly at the corners, no longer rectangular but oval in shape. At the end, Grammy simply liked the feel of turning the pages, her old eyes unable to read the small script.

The Other was talking again, pulling her away from her thoughts.

'Your Inner and I have already begun to show the possibilities. Rehoming ourselves. Hearing each other. There are channels opening up. Channels that have no doubt been in use by others far older than us. That's one beautiful thing about this world. No interference. No streaming radio waves or cellular towers, no satellites beaming their information across the skies. You were all so noisy. But now there's nothing but blessed silence.'

Posy's footfalls came toward her. A loud *pop* as a corn stalk crushed beneath his shoe. His feet stopped in front of her. She stared at the crumbling rubber sole of his shoe. She wanted to pick at it like you would a scab.

'This is merely the beginning, Lacey.' His voice came from directly above her. 'And one way or another, you're going to help me understand how far I can go.'

Lacey didn't acknowledge him in any way.

'Sunny? Begin taking notes.'

Lacey lifted her head when she heard the unscrewing of a bottle cap. She hadn't seen when he'd taken the glass bottles away from Frank. The Other brought the bottle's opening to Posy's nose, inhaling deeply. He pulled a face. 'Vodka has an unlimited shelf life. Some of the group aren't happy about me not sharing this with them, but needs must.'

Voice was small and distant, his voice coming from a bottomless pit, too far away to bother her. If high levels of pain, exhaustion and dehydration were the only things to help mute his kind, maybe they *were* all doomed.

Posy's shadow fell over her as the Other stepped close, blocking the burning heat of the sun and darkening the red behind her eyelids as she blinked. Cool liquid splashed over her head, pouring down the sides of her face, the nape of her neck. She shrank in on herself, hunching lower as trickles scurried under her shirt and down her back. The fumes hit her nostrils, singeing as she inhaled. She coughed, the strong vapour hitting the back of her throat.

Defend her, Voice said, breaking through her fuzziness, tunnelling up from the pit he'd been cast into. Stronger: *Do you understand me? Defend her!*

'The time for defending is over, my friend,' the Other said, hearing him and laughing. 'This is the end of the road for her.'

Lacey lifted her head, squinting her eyes around the burn of alcohol. Posy stood ready with the second bottle in his hands, its cap in place.

I know you hear me! Voice shouted. *You* must *be able to hear me!*

'Posy?' Lacey whispered.

And she heard Posy's name come from Sunny's mouth, too, saw the woman take a step forward.

'Posy,' Sunny said, a pleading in her tone that didn't stretch beyond a few words and a single stride. 'Don't do this. This isn't right.'

A rattle as the second cap was unscrewed. In the heat of the midday sun, Lacey shivered as more alcohol splashed over her shoulders, soaking through her shirt, plastering it to her hot, trembling skin.

'There's no point either of you looking for help from Posy.' The Other sounded cheerful, relaxed even. 'Poor, pitiful Mr Posy has been relegated to his proper station in life. And it was a long time coming.'

Everything will be lost! Voice shouted. *Red, Lacey, Addison.* All *of it!*

'Red is already lost,' the Other snapped, cheerfulness gone. 'I thought she'd be here, but she was lost a long time ago, far from this place.'

'I know where she is,' Lacey gasped, coughing again. Blinking past the sting in her eyes. 'I've always known where she is.'

The empty vodka bottle thudded to the ground. Posy grabbed Lacey's hair, viciously yanking her head back, and she found herself staring into the Other's flat, angry eyes. His tone was low, controlled, but she could hear the undercurrent of hunger. The *need* in him. 'Where? *Where* is she? Is it the Inn on the coast? Did she tell you its location?'

Lacey pressed her lips together.

The Other twisted Posy's lip in a sneer. His jagged fingernails dug into her scalp as his fist tightened, roots pulling, but she didn't wince. Wouldn't let herself.

'You understand what I am, who I came from, yes?' His words were hot breaths in her face. 'Posy acquired me in much the same way I suspect you acquired your "Voice". And we both know how that happened, don't we?'

Pilgrim had taken a bullet to the head for her to gain Voice, and Doc had caught one above the eye for this Other to jump into Posy. She knew that death, or a condition close to it, was the only means to make them jump.

Lacey couldn't breathe. Her lungs belonged to someone else, someone separate and uncooperative.

'You can't have Voice,' she whispered. 'He won't leave me. He promised.'

The grin that appeared on Posy's face made the last speck of moisture dry up in her mouth. 'Promises are your invention, not ours. We don't trade in such things.' He released her and stepped back, his hand slipping into his pocket. She heard a cardboard rattle and a box of matches materialised. 'Last-chance saloon. Are we going to talk, you and I, me and thee?'

Her muddled thoughts were a stack of higgledy-piggledy blocks that refused to fit together. It wouldn't take much for her to slip and the whole lot to come tumbling down. If she talked, she didn't trust herself not to reveal something she shouldn't. What if she accidentally told him that Addison, a girl only eight years old, was already doing the things this twenty-year Other could do and had been concealing it as skilfully as a professional poker player? Lacey couldn't take that risk.

In a rush, her lungs became her own again and her breaths ran free and ragged. Her heart thundered. The corn stalks at Posy's back vibrated and blurred. The empty spot where the St Christopher had once rested at her throat seemed to blaze red hot on her skin, a point of searing pain that crystallised her thoughts, made everything *too* clear; she could see the droplets of sweat on Posy's brow, his skin an unhealthy corpse-grey, see the fine lines around his eyes and the deeper lines bracketing his thin-lipped mouth. Behind his head, in the faultless blue sky, she swore she could see the dandelion-yellow iris of the bird's predatory eye as it banked in a gliding circle.

'Fuck you,' she told him.

Posy's smile, when it came, was an ugly slash. 'Are those your last words?'

'Voice?' His name trembled on her chapped lips.

I'm here, Lacey. I'm right here.

'Don't leave me,' she whispered.

I won't. I won't. I won't ever leave you, I swear. Don't be afraid.

Don't be afraid. Almost the exact same words Pilgrim had spoken to her before he died.

But she was. She was deathly afraid as the Other shook out a match.

CHAPTER 6

St Christopher

The burning spot that had opened up at the top of Addison's thigh grew hotter. She rubbed hard at it.

The necklace, Addison. You need to show him the necklace. It belonged to Red.

But Addison didn't move, because maybe Fender was being tricksy again and wanted to get her into trouble.

No tricks, Addison. You never heard Lacey and Alex talk about her, but Red is important in all of this. If he knows her, if Red is Ruby and she's his sister, his finding you isn't an accident.

'No accidents,' she muttered. She wrapped her arms around herself, hands clasping at her biceps, trying to hold on, to hug like Alex would hug her. Her muscles were strong but rangy. Thin. Easy to break. To crush. She was just a kid. Why was Fender pushing her? Why couldn't they all leave her alone?

Just say the words, Addison. I'll help you. Say you have a St Christopher necklace.

But she was unsure. This would change everything; she felt it, hovering over her like a kite. The bird kind, not the toy kind, 'cause she'd never seen the toy kind, had only been told about them by Lacey. She wished she had her wildlife magazine, her story books, but they'd all been lost at the church. Lots of things had been lost at the church.

Addison, say the words. A St Christopher necklace.

She swallowed.

A St Christopher necklace, Fender prompted.

'A St Christopher necklace,' she whispered, scared.

Again. Louder.

'A St Christopher necklace.'

Good. Say it's silver.

'It's silver,' she repeated.

A coin with a man carrying a baby on his back.

'A coin with a man carrying a baby on his back.'

We need them, Addison, Fender said. *Let them help us.*

Addison took a deep breath. 'I spoke to her but she never spoke back.' She didn't look at Albus but felt his eyes on her like two pokey fingers. She squeezed her arms, felt the shift of muscle against bone. 'Red. Ruby. Ruby-Red. I don't know how she got hurt.'

She was driving so fast. She flipped her car and it rolled.

'Lacey was there?' she whispered.

Not in the car, but yes.

'And Pilgrim?'

Him, too. He and Lacey were with her at the end.

'She wasn't alone?'

No. She wasn't alone.

'Who is Pilgrim?' Hari's eyes were as unreadable as too-big words in a too-hard reading book. Behind them lay a whole world. Addison would never know what places he'd seen, what people he'd met, would never know the thoughts spinning and turning behind those eyes – and wasn't that the problem? Everyone was a big, too-hard-to-read book and she didn't know how to understand them all.

She licked her lips. They were cracked and dry. 'Lacey and Alex called him Boy Scout, but he was Pilgrim to me. Grim with a lip at the front.' Hari watched her until she felt eaten up by those eyes, was lost to them. Her voice fell into a whisper.

'They told me stories. He was always the hero. He saved them and then I shot him. He's in my backyard now, too.'

Did that make her the bad guy in the story? She didn't want to be the bad guy. Bad guys hurt people. She bit her tongue, breathed through her nose, hard, until the urge to cry went away.

Something touched her hand as it clasped her bicep.

Chief's oil-black fingers stroked her, so gentle it was like a feather's touch. He rested his chin on her shoulder, mouth near to her ear, and softly nuzzled, the sensation buzzing through the bones of her skull. It made her want to close her eyes.

Albus is asking about the necklace, Addison.

Her palms were hot against the skin of her upper arms. She uncurled her fingers, feeling Chief's hand slide away from hers, and slipped them into her pocket.

Albus's eyes widened as she pulled out the chain. His lips parted on a soundless cry. He reached out, the stump of his hand laid flat, a fingerless plate, and Addison stared at it, fascinated, wanted to ask more questions but didn't. Now wasn't the time. She spooled the St Christopher necklace into the centre of his palm.

Albus was shaking his head, his eyes fixed on the medallion in his hand, his expression of shock slowly morphing into one Addison didn't have a name for.

He recognises it! Chief cried.

'What's going on?' Gwen asked, unable to settle her attention on anyone, her gaze like a moth flitting from Albus to Addison and back again.

They are *the same*, Fender breathed. *Red and Ruby.*

'Ruby-Red is in my backyard,' Addison told Gwen sadly.

'No. His sister has been helping us. She's the only reason we're here.'

'My aunt Lacey took her necklace. That one there.' Addison pointed to it. 'But she's gone now. In a treasure hole in my garden. I'm sorry,' she added, because she understood about saying sorry and please and thank you.

Oh no, Fender whispered.

Silence as Albus lifted his hand, chain dangling. He looked stricken.

He says . . . he says he thinks he made a mistake. About who he was supposed to save.

Addison passed on the message, even though she didn't know what it meant.

'*What?*' Gwen's word was more spit than sound.

The man with black skin was gentler. 'What does that mean, Albus? What are you saying?'

It wasn't his sister that he sensed, it was her necklace, Fender said. *It fooled him. He didn't do what he was supposed to, what she'd always told him to do. He didn't follow the colours.*

'Colours?' Addison said. 'What colours?'

The martyr's, Fender replied. *Lacey's*.

CHAPTER 7

No Smoke Without Flames

'Fuck you.'

Didn't matter that Lacey's words weren't directed at her, Sunny felt them hit like punches, striking her one-two in the stomach.

She could smell the spilled alcohol, mixed with the dusty, granular scent of ruined corn and spit-dried earth. It didn't remind her of the Wet Whistle and the dripping rag she'd use to mop spilled beer off the bar every half-hour, it reminded her of the staff restroom's sanitiser dispenser. She'd pump that stuff into her hand, watching it foam up like shaving cream, and it'd stink of alcohol, sharp and chemical. She'd rub it into her hands and between her fingers, even though it'd sting like a bitch as it hit the splits in the cracked skin of her knuckles, even though she knew she'd be covered in germs the minute she stepped foot outside the stall. She'd rub that sterilising foam in until it disappeared, hoping it'd go bone-deep.

'What can we do, Sun?' Beck asked her, a tall presence at her shoulder, close enough to feel his breath on her ear. 'You're no hero, and neither am I. We blend in and say the right things and we don't get hassled. We keep our heads down.'

'We get people killed,' she said.

'People are always getting killed. What difference is it to us how it gets done?'

'Difference is I'm playing a part in this.'

'This was always going to happen, whether we were here or not. We need to roll with this. It's for the best.'

'You don't know what's best for us any more.'

Frank gave her a foul look. 'Would you be quiet?'

Beck paid him no mind. 'You're not responsible for this girl, Sunny. You never were.'

Maybe someone needs to be responsible, she wanted to say. *Maybe that's where everyone was going wrong.*

'There's shades of badness in this world. What we're doing barely registers as grey.'

Frank didn't tell Beck to shut his yap. No one ever did. Only she ever got told. She was the one who always took the heat.

Not-Posy was talking. The smile plastered across his chops reminded her of a scarecrow. It was stitched in place.

'Know that I *will* find the child you squirrelled away,' he said, and Sunny heard that deadly rattle as he shook the box of matches. The head of the match he'd withdrawn flashed red at her as if shouting, *Danger! Danger!* 'She's important to you, so she's important to me. I'll hunt her down and use her innards to string her up from the nearest oak tree. She'll swing like bloated fruit, and you'll be rotting right here in this field, deaf to her cries, deaf to your name whimpering on her lips.'

'You can't find her without me,' the girl whispered, and there was defiance there, fragile as a newly formed sheet of winter-ice, but cold and sharp all the same.

There was a gravelly scratch as the match head swiped across the striking strip and a sputtering *hissssst* as a white-yellow flame flared to life. It danced feebly, holding Sunny's gaze.

'We'll see about that.' Not-Posy drew the hypnotic flame closer to the girl, and Sunny imagined she could feel the heat of it on her face.

'Let him do what needs to be done, Sunny,' Beck said in her ear.

'No, wait,' Sunny said, her voice frail. Then louder: '*Wait.*'

'Voice!' Lacey cried.

Beck cried out and grasped his head.

'*What?*' Sunny asked, afraid for him.

He hissed a breath, and it seemed to whistle through her ears like wind through reeds. He didn't speak, his lips had clamped shut, but the message got forced out anyway. 'Defend her,' he rasped, words mashed up and hard cut between gritted teeth. '*Defend her.*'

The squawking caw of the hawk above them tipped Sunny's eyes upward. More birds, maybe twenty, darted swiftly through the sky, their wings a blur as they arrowed across the field toward the hawk already gliding around their cropped circle. They were in bomber formation, an uneven V, targeted and inbound.

She turned back to Not-Posy, called out, 'Stop!' But the burning match was already committed to its purpose and the flame touched Lacey's dripping shirt and the girl went up with a *WHUUUUUMP.*

'*No!*' Sunny screamed.

Flames erupted, an orange ball of fire so intense Sunny and Frank stumbled backward. Sunny didn't think the day could get any hotter but all at once the burning heat of the sun had dropped to earth to sit among them, and all she wanted to do was run.

But she didn't. She wouldn't run from this. She watched, her eyes watering, tears trickling down her face.

'Oh my God.'

Not-Posy capered on the spot, dancing away from the conflagration, and Sunny could feel its excitement, its eagerness. The air all around them vibrated, a deep humming in all the boiling pockets of space, a tingling in the ground, in the corn stalks, a shivering in the heat.

'It's happening this time,' Frank whispered. 'You feel it, don't you?'

Sunny did. She felt it turning over, a power conjured by the burning ritual Not-Posy had made them a part of, an energy that wasn't evil or good but something in between. Her heart thumped, kicking at her, her ribs shuddering under the assault, but her eyes didn't turn. She had to watch. She had to be a witness. A sob built in her chest and she covered her mouth to contain it.

Not-Posy's dancing abruptly stopped and its head darted left. A flash of movement cut through the rotting stalks, a ghost, a shadow. An explosion of activity burst into the clearing, knocking Posy back a step, and for an insane moment Sunny thought the crazed flock of birds had descended to flap and peck and claw him to ribbons.

But it wasn't birds. It was a man.

The stranger's coat flapped like wings as he threw it off and flung it on top of Lacey. He followed after it and pushed the girl into the dirt, smothering the flames, patting her down in a flurry of *whomp*ing hand slaps. Snakes of fire rose all around them, licks sneaking over the stranger's arms and shoulders as if it were caressing and welcoming him into its embrace, and Sunny was sure they would both be consumed.

Lacey hadn't uttered a sound since the flames swallowed her and, in reality, only a handful of seconds had passed since the tip of the burning match had touched her shirt. Sunny stared hard at the girl but couldn't detect any movement; she was buried beneath the stranger's coat, making no noise as the last flames were extinguished.

The man, as tall as Beck, rose to his feet. He stood over Lacey, his feet planted to either side of her body, and Sunny recognised the protectiveness in his stance.

'No,' Not-Posy whispered.

The stranger made no response, didn't take his eyes from

470

Posy's bug-eyed face. His eyes were clear and true, but Sunny was sure she saw flames flicker in their depths, as if the fire he had smothered continued to dance on the inside.

'He's here to kill us,' Beck whispered.

'No!' Not-Posy spat, anger creeping in.

Sunny hadn't spotted the steel-grey handgun – it had been tucked behind the man's belt – but now he drew it, casually, as if he were doing nothing more than taking out a handkerchief to dab at his sweaty brow.

'You can't *be* here!' Not-Posy shouted.

The man didn't respond. He didn't have to. He was here, plain for all to see.

'You know this won't end by you simply pulling that trigger.'

'I know.' It was two quietly spoken words, but the stranger's voice carried straight across the cornfield and out into the roads, maybe even as high in the sky to reach the birds that winged around them. 'I know a fair few things these days. More than you, I'd say.'

Frank shifted beside her. She'd forgotten all about him. He had drawn his gun and held it along the side of his thigh, hidden from sight, cocked. He saw her looking and narrowed his eyes, his top lip hooking up as if he were looking at the lowest form of shit-critter on the planet. Oh, what a prize cocksucker he was.

'Is that right?' Not-Posy was saying. 'Well, maybe I'll use this girl here for my next home then, hmm? She's young. Healthy. She already has an Inner but I'm sure there's room for one more.'

'That's not how it works. This' – the stranger gestured to the scorched corn at their feet – 'isn't how it works.'

'How would you know?' There was as much fear as anger in Not-Posy's voice and Sunny wanted to know why. Why, after weeks of searching and miles of trekking, was the thing inside Posy scared *now*? 'You're just another pawn,' he spat at the man.

'Like all these other useless pawns. Moving one place at a time and not planning where you're going. Not like *I've* been planning. How would you know anything?'

'I know not to shoot you in the head,' said the stranger. 'And that's as good a start as any.' There was a trembling slickness in the air again, turning over like an eel rolling in sludge, readying itself, and Sunny had a fleeting second to think, *Beck was right. He's going to kill us.*

Not-Posy must have felt it, too, because he raised a hand, palm out. Beseeching, delaying. 'The Flitting Man is everywhere. You're a fool if you think you can escape him. Even I know that.'

'I'm not trying to escape him. I'm not trying to escape anything any more.'

That slick eel slithered closer and Sunny felt a shiver work its way through Frank, a run of static passing down his arm and crackling along her side.

On the ground, the stranger's coat fluttered and Sunny glimpsed Lacey's foot, resting on its side. The bottom of her sock was dark with blood.

Frank brought his gun up and Sunny didn't think about it at all. She grabbed his arm and yanked it down. The gun went off, a powerful *blat!* that hurt Sunny's ears. A bullet kicked up corn in front of the stranger's boot.

'Damn it, Sun!' Beck yelled. 'When're you gonna *learn*?'

'What the fuck,' Frank snapped, snatching his arm from her grip and swinging the gun around, levelling it at her head.

Sunny instinctively raised her hands in front of her face, although what they'd do against a bullet, she didn't know. A second walloping gunshot slapped her ears and she waited for the blinding impact, the hot rush of blood.

Frank toppled forward and planted face first in the trampled crop. He didn't even bounce. The wound in the back of his neck smoked. Bits of white vertebrae showed through. The same gun that had blasted Frank's spine out through his throat pressed into Sunny's cheek. She held very still, waiting to smell the singed stench of her skin and feel the delayed burn of the gun's hot muzzle. But it was warm to the touch and that was all. Another piece of bullshit the movies had fed her.

'Don't even think about it, sister.' A woman's soft voice, all friendly-like. Another stranger. She had flanked them somehow.

And Sunny didn't think about doing anything. Not even for a second. She stood stock-still, her arms half raised, and said nothing, did nothing, exactly like she was good at. She got only the vaguest impression of the woman from the corner of her eye. The arm that held the gun to her cheek didn't waver. The skin from wrist to shirtsleeve was inked with blues and reds and blacks. Sunny spied a timepiece in the design – waves or feathers, couldn't be sure which – and a bird, shaped like a swallow.

A wheedling sharpness entered Posy's voice. Sunny heard it and she sure as hell bet these strangers heard it, too. 'You have *no idea* what he's capable of,' he said, as if Frank being gunned down didn't mean jack shit to him. Which it didn't. 'I'm one of the few who can help you. There'll be no one left by the time he—'

The tall stranger made a harsh sound in the back of his throat. 'Always with the talking. Will there ever be any peace?'

'You have to help him,' Sunny said, finding the courage to speak.

The woman pressed the gun viciously into her cheek. Her teeth cut into her mouth. She tasted blood.

The man's head turned.

Sunny lost her breath as his gaze cut straight through her. 'Please,' she whispered, and cursed herself when her lips trembled, obscuring her words. 'It's not his fault.'

'There's only one way to help,' the stranger said. His eyes were guarded but they weren't unkind. Aloof, yes, but not unkind. 'Close your eyes,' he told her.

He lifted the steel-grey gun and aimed it at Posy's heart.

Sunny shut her eyes.

It was the gunshot that woke Lacey. That and something Voice did. There was an alarming flutter in her chest and, as if a switch had been flicked over, her lungs unlocked and expanded, inflated in one immense breath.

Beautiful, fresh oxygen flowed in and she ate it in gulps. Her chest hurt something fierce, and not just on the inside. A sore spot, right in the centre, below the hollow of her throat, made her whine with pain.

LACEY!

'God, don't shout,' she croaked, wincing as even those few words hurt. She stopped to swallow.

And then a strange, enveloping sensation overcame her. It began in her head as a warm shimmering, as if a summer rain drizzled over her hair and cascaded down, shivering through her shoulders and arms, melting in her chest. She felt Voice *everywhere*, tingling on the edges of her nerve endings, warming the tips of her fingers and toes, stroking over the membrane of her skin.

A blinding exhilaration swamped her, a yawning awareness that was a million times larger than she was, as though she were standing on the edge of a precipice at the mouth of a hidden valley with thousands upon thousands of evergreen trees spread out as far as the eye could see and three rivers snaking through them, all joining up with a huge lake at its centre where the water was so still and so serene it reflected the sky in perfect unity, the whole scene duplicated in its surface so that upside down became right way up and standing on top of the precipice also meant standing on the bottom of the sky. It was so overwhelming Lacey stopped breathing again and felt herself drifting, floating away from the packed earth beneath her and the poking joints of snapped corn stalks. She would float down (and up) into that upside-down valley and never be found, for she was one tiny creature in that vast fauna of life.

She forced her mouth to work, her lungs to push out breathy words, hearing them disappear into the immensity of that vista. 'W-what did you do?'

The awareness shut down and, just like that, she was locked inside herself once more. Safe, boundaries up, contained, swaddled, alone.

Mostly alone.

I didn't do anything, Voice said, and he sounded strangely breathless, too. *I'm just really, really happy you're OK. You're OK, right? Lacey? You're OK?*

'Lacey.'

Not Voice that time. Not Posy. Not Sunny, either.

She opened her eyes, her eyelashes sticking, not understanding it was because they had melted together. The first thing she saw through a blur of tears was Posy. He lay on his side, facing her, his position mirroring hers, as if they were two babies in a womb, curled toward each other. His eyes were open.

She waited for him to blink, to say something.

He didn't blink. Didn't utter a sound.

Her eyes travelled downward.

The middle of his chest was a pulpy, bloody mess.

Lacey felt as if she'd been opened up, her innards scooped out and stones stuffed in their place. Her insides ached for him. All Posy had ever wanted was to be liked. His whole life had been spent striving for it, wanting to be part of something, part of the world he'd found himself in, but no amount of striving could make it happen. And it hadn't been his fault, damn it. It was theirs: Lacey and Doc, Alex and Frank and every single person Posy had ever met, who'd kicked him to the gutter and kept him there each time he'd tried to get up. They saw him as someone to be abused and forgotten, right up until something had come along and *made* them take notice, forced them into giving him respect. This was *their* doing and no one else's.

A knee came down and blocked her view. No more Posy, no more staring eyes, no more bloody chest.

An arm scooped under her neck and shoulders and she was as defenceless as a babe as she was lifted up and cradled against someone's chest, brought into the warmth of their body and nearer to their face. All that troublesome air that had been impossible to regulate left her in a single, draining sigh. Because she recognised that straight mouth, that nose, and although the eyes weren't exactly how she remembered them, she recognised them, too. They were whole and clear and they looked down at her without the slightest hint of a smile. But then, he was never any good at smiling. She used to think he didn't know how.

Her lips formed his name, its sound lost in the space between her mouth and his ears, but she knew he heard her. She knew because the tiniest flicker of a smile twitched over his lips as if maybe he *did* remember how to smile after all.

'I still like how my name fits your mouth,' Pilgrim said.

THE LAST CHAPTER

Red Skies

Addison and Hari hung on to the backs of the driver and passenger seats, leaning with the bus as Gwen took the final turn, fender sweeping past a sign with too many words for Addison's eyes to catch.

'*Welcome to the Norwood Cove Inn,*' Fender read for her. '*Dining and Lodging since 1856*'.

Tyres crunched on to a cornflake driveway and the fingernails of overgrown bushes squealed along the bus's sides as it squeezed through.

'Wow,' Addison whispered.

It's neat! Chief called. He was outside, running on all fours alongside the bus. Addison caught glimpses of him through Gwen's side window.

Before them rose a white three-high-stacked house, bigger than any normal house Addison had seen. *Ten* whole families could live in it. A huge porch wrapped around the bottom floor, white poles counting along the railing with flower boxes every once in a while bursting with a bunch of colourful flowers. The porch's floor was the only dark thing – planks of dark wood that were shiny and slippery-looking, glossed over with see-through paint. The shutters were dark, too, hugging windows that were too many for Addison to tally up.

'You live here?' she asked Hari, a twinge of jealousy pinching her insides.

He gave a small nod.

'Where *is* everybody?' Gwen said.

'It's lunchtime.' Bruno's voice was so deep Addison felt it vibrate straight through the seat and into her chest. 'Most likely in the kitchen.'

A splash of colour caught her eye and, through the wind-shield, stuck in the grass, was a yellow-feathered tail. It pinned a dead blackbird to the lawn. She turned to Hari to ask what it was but he was looking straight ahead, his dark eyes roaming the front of the Inn.

Gwen swung the bus around with a final skittering crunch of cornflakes and stopped with a *shh-sh-shhh* of air. It really did sound like snakes.

The engine shut off. The hot *tink*s of the bus and a low hiss of pipes added their chatter to the quiet.

Gwen twisted in her seat and climbed out from behind the wheel, shooing Hari and Addison out of her way. Bruno came after her and paused beside Addison for a second, regarding her from way up where his head lived. It was the closest she had been to him since getting in the bus. He took up a lot of space, but not in the same way the Bridge Troll had. His space was like finding shelter in the rain, or a cosy blanket on a cold night. It was the kind you wanted to touch. She reached out and stroked her hand along an arm that was the same colour as the dark wood of the porch. His skin was very warm and very smooth.

She gazed up at him. 'Soft,' she said.

He smiled. 'Thank you.'

It was really hard to see, almost as if it had been drawn with Alex's sharp-nib pencil, but a long, thin scar ran down the centre of his face. She reached high and trailed a gentle fingertip down it. 'Are you a pirate?' she asked.

He laughed. 'No, honey, I'm not a pirate. Although that'd make for a far more entertaining story than saying I was in car wreck, wouldn't it?'

'Bruno,' Gwen said, without glancing back at them. She'd gone to the rear of the bus, where Rufus lay stretched out.

'Excuse me,' Bruno said to Addison, and moved past, making his way over to Gwen.

Quiet words were exchanged and Gwen turned away to hit the red button above the sliding door. Bruno dropped to one knee and slid his very warm, very smooth arms underneath Rufus and lifted him as easily as if he weighed no more than a mongoose.

The bus gave another long, snaky *hissss* and the door slid open. One by one, and not two by two (if you didn't count Bruno with Rufus), they filed off the bus. Addison hung at the rear, following Hari, who followed Albus.

Fender was keeping quiet but Chief was busy playing with the image of the yellow-feathered stick-thing Addison had seen poking out of the bird. Phantom sticks flashed past, making her flinch.

'Quit it,' she muttered.

It's an arrow, Fender told her.

Gwen and Albus had climbed the porch steps and were pushing open the wide front door. It was the biggest door Addison had ever seen. She was Alice as she approached it, shrunk down to tiny Alice in the Wonderland story that made no sense no matter how many times Alex told it. Small as a cat, looking up at a gigantic door nine times as tall. Like the rest of the Inn, it, too, was white and fancy.

A musical tinkling of bells sounded at ceiling height. Addison looked up and saw metal straws spinning delicately over her head. Why anyone would want to hang metal straws up in their house, she didn't know. She couldn't see what use it had. She spied a butterfly spinning in the middle, its turning glass wings throwing off an arc of purest light. It was pretty. She blinked as it flashed in her eyes.

Footfalls thudded through the foyer and Addison blinked again, dragged her gaze away from the tinkling butterfly and ran to catch up. The ringing of the metal straws ceased as she passed over the threshold.

Bits of sunlight slanted long buttercup rectangles on to glossy floors. Addison let her head swivel right to left, her mouth dropping open. Furniture unlike any she'd ever seen filled the rooms: curled wooden-armed chairs and stitched cushions, glass-topped trolleys on wheels with delicate-looking pitchers and glasses on top. Next to the empty fireplace, a pokey rod, a big fork and a mini-shovel and broom hung from a stand. And there, in the corner, nearest the front wall with all the long windows, was a grand piano. Addison had never seen a real-life piano. She'd have liked to have gone over and maybe pressed a few of the white and black teeth, but she didn't want to disturb the man who was sitting on the stool, his head bowed as if considering what to play.

Addison frowned and glanced at Bruno's back. Gwen had already disappeared through a doorway, Hari on her heels. Albus stood at its threshold, one stump of a hand on the door frame as he peered after them.

Addison turned back to the man at the piano, her mouth opening to speak, and found him with his head up, his eyes on her. Except they weren't eyes, because his eye sockets were open pits and red static swirled in their depths. His mouth, when it stretched and widened on a smile, was also filled with static, the pulsing red light emitting from eyes and mouth the only colour to him, the rest of him faded and washed out. His was a knowing smile. A smile of welcome.

Addison inhaled sharply and, just like that, he was gone.

Fear quickly turned to anger and she turned on Chief. 'Quit *fooling*, I said.'

Bruno glanced back at her, his toad-like eyes hooded with curiosity, but before he could ask anything, Gwen pushed by Albus, grabbing hold of his shirt as she did, her troubled eyes finding them.

'There's no one in the kitchen.'

Albus looked over at Bruno, and that was all it took.

'Bianca!' Bruno hollered, and if no one heard his call, they had soil stuffed in their ears. He gently lowered Rufus to the floor, leaving him next to the staircase, and moved to the foot of the stairs. 'Bee, you up there!'

Gwen joined him. 'Amber! Cloris!' Unhappy with standing still, she ran up the stairs, leaping up them two at a time. 'Boys, where are you?'

Of course, Albus didn't say anything but left the foyer and disappeared through an archway. Without needing instruction, Addison's feet went after him. She didn't glance back to see if the piano man had returned. She knew there'd been no one there. Not anyone real, anyway.

Albus moved like a shadow, so quiet as he hurried through a reception area and dodged around a corner that Addison became convinced it wasn't only his mouth that was muted. A squawking protest of springs as he pulled the outside screen door open was the only indication of his passage. Addison darted forward to catch the screen as it swung back.

Rapid, *clomp*ing boots and here came Bruno, marching at her, and Addison squeezed herself tight against the door jamb as he crowded past. He thundered over his shoulder, 'Gwen, back porch!'

Above Addison's head, there was a pause, and then a number of thumps as Gwen ran across the floorboards, heading back for the stairs.

Unsqueezing herself from the door, Addison pushed outside. And that's where the noise hit her.

She thought it was the wind, having picked up since they'd

stepped inside the Inn, but it didn't account for the whistling beat, the flapping and fluttering and rushing of wings. The sky over the back lawn was a dark cauldron of birds, a mini-hurricane of feathery bodies, circling lower than she'd ever seen before, so close she could see the glints in their eyes, the little black nostrils in their beaks.

Whatever magic held those birds in place broke as soon as her eyes fell on them, and they scattered in a chaotic flurry, shooting off in every direction. Their voices burst to life, screeches and squawks and strident whistles, so loud Addison covered her ears, her eyes tearing with the gusting wind. Within seconds, the howling gale and cries of birds were gone, until the only remaining sound was the distant crash of surf.

The sea, the sea. Addison had never seen the sea, but her gaze didn't drift over to explore. There were no thoughts on its awesomeness or of the distant, magical lands it led to, far away from this porch and everything on it, because Albus crouched three yards out on the back decking, as if the strength had left his legs. His head had been tilted back as he gazed up at the sky, but now it lowered.

Lined up on the porch were four rocking chairs, each facing outward to the sea.

Chief's small hand found hers and clamped on.

Addison hardly felt it.

Hari appeared on her other side and Addison startled, not having heard his steps. He went to Albus and the man stiffly rose from his crouch, his hand finding the boy's shoulder to lean on, as if he were suddenly a billion years old and didn't trust himself not to fall.

Even from where she stood, Addison could see all four of the rocking chairs were occupied. Even from where she stood, she could see the (*Arrows*, Fender said again) bristling from each of the people sat in them, as if someone had stood on the back lawn and fired shot after shot.

Gwen burst through the screen door, the violence of it making Addison spin around. This time, Chief's hand tightened hard enough to elicit a small yelp from her, her bones grinding together.

Gwen brushed past, knocking Addison back a step, not stopping like the others but going right to the first rocking chair. That's where her legs gave way. That's where she collapsed to her knees and pushed a fist to her mouth, a deep, wrenching wail coming from a place Addison didn't recognise, but it hurt to hear and it hurt to see.

The sound seemed to release Bruno, and he moved forward. He stepped around Gwen and slowly walked to the third rocking chair along. There, he knelt, placed a hand on a lady's arm, an arm Addison imagined was once warm and smooth, too.

He spoke as if to a child, soft and tender. 'Oh, my darling, what have they done to you? What have they done?'

Unable to look any more, Addison's eyes slid away, rolling over the waving grasses to the scarily endless ocean. She thought she would love it, the sea, with the colourful fish and deep-water creatures and frilly coral reefs she'd seen in pictures, but you couldn't really see any of that. All you could see was forever water, cold and uncaring and greater than everything in your brain and wider than everything in your eyes. Where did it all go? On and on it went, like the sky went on. No paths, no walls, no ending. It wasn't freedom, all that space. It was where you got lost, never ever to be found.

Waves crashed on the sandy beach, and the *shush* they made sounded like the sea was trying to console them, was trying to tell them *shhh*, it'll all be OK. But it was lying. It wasn't OK. It was the furthest thing from OK.

Addison squinted up at the hot sun, alone up there, no birds in sight now, and she knew, come evening, it would sink into the black, uncaring ocean, where its stove-heat would sizzle and bake red as it hit. It would cast its last bloody rays across the horizon, the sky a band of angry glowing red, trapped between black clouds above and black ocean below.

Like spilled blood, Chief whispered from beside her, seeing the image in her head. His fingers slipped from hers, as if the sight were too scary for him.

Red skies for a red day, Fender said and withdrew, too, leaving her there, alone, Gwen's inconsolable crying and Bruno's crooning swirling around her as the circling birds had swirled. Hari's head shook, over and over, and Albus, well, Albus said nothing at all.

ACKNOWLEDGEMENTS

We are officially halfway through the Voices series! Hooray and *thank fuck*. I actually thought I might go mad during the process of getting *Hunted* ready for publication. I wrote it back when *Defender* was out on submission, so by the time I'd messed around with *Defender* in edits, *Hunted* needed a *serious* overhaul. I lived with this book for over eighteen months and at times I hated it, and at other times it excited me more than anything else I've written. It was a real emotional rollercoaster, and this is my opportunity to express my gratitude to the people who prevented me from careening off the tracks and dying an explosive and gory death. I'm sorry – there are a lot of people to thank.

First, my mom, as always. Who is the most supportive mom anyone could ask for. I love her very much and I don't know what I'd do without her.

Next, my agent, Camilla Wray, who is exactly the kind of friend and mentor all writers need. She is steadfast and caring and knows her shit; all traits that mark her out as being *the best*. Same goes to my agency and all the brilliant folk who work there, especially Mary, Emma, Sheila, Kristina, Celine and Roya. And Rosanna for sending me the lovely money emails.

My editor, Mari Evans, whose constant enthusiasm and passion for these books means the world. The fact she trusts me to go away and write something decent without needing to check in on me either means she's super busy and forgets, or she knows I won't let her down. I'm hoping it's the latter. Everyone at Headline has been ace, and my heartfelt thanks go out to Caitlin Raynor, Jo Liddiard, Frankie Edwards and Sara Adams, whose hard work and dedication never falter. I must also thank my copy-editor, Sarah Day, who takes out all my stupid errors and makes me look a hundred percent cleverer than I am, and all the lovely Headline staff who have looked after me over the last two years.

Andy got his own dedication in this, so he should be happy, but he has also been pimping *Defender* out to his friends and most the inhabitants of Walsall, so thanks for that, bro. Now, get a crack on with reading the damn book – you've been on page 100 *for over twelve months*.

My good friends, who have helped keep me sane: Cath Hancox, Tom Bissell, Elaina Gorman and Gilly McAllister.

LEGO for making such brilliant sets for me to build and de-stress with. If you ever want to sponsor me, please contact gxtoddauthor@gmail.com. I'll be waiting for your email. Same goes to Playstation. I love you guys.

My wonderfully helpful (and clandestine) Doomsday Writers' Group. You know who you are. It's such a pleasure and a privilege to know you all.

And last but certainly not least, a huge thank you to all the readers out there, the bloggers and reviewers, the booksellers and library workers, my fellow writers and authors and people in the industry, all of whom are such a supportive bunch and so passionate about reading and books that it humbles me at times. What a lucky gal I am.